SPIRIT OF THE
DANCE

By the Author

Twice Lucky

Spirit of the Dance

Visit us at www.boldstrokesbooks.com

SPIRIT OF THE DANCE

by

Mardi Alexander

2015

Credits
Editor: Ruth Sternglantz
Production Design: Stacia Seaman
Cover Design by Jeanine Henning

Acknowledgments

Writing has opened so many new and exciting experiences for me since releasing *Twice Lucky*, made all the richer and more special because of the love, support, and encouragement of family and the most incredible friends, near and far.

A special thank you to Franci, who talked me into embracing my Australianism; C.d. for her friendship as we travel the adventurous road of "author" together; Tracy for your eye for detail and help with cover concepts; and to my good mate Laurie, who is always ready with sound advice and good cheer at all hours. You are all very special and I am forever grateful.

To all the crew at BSB, to Rad for giving this story the nod and to Sandy, Stacia, and Ruth—this ship cannot sail without you—I have the dream, but you are the amazing craftspeople who help to shape, mold, nip, and tuck, so that this story boat can come to fruition and be allowed to set sail.

A special wave to all the BSB authors I met at Nottingham this year. To travel overseas and to meet all of you was quite simply the best. You are a wonderful, wonderful mob for sure.

To my gorgeous Flamingoes—you are just the best kind of crazy wonderful. Your support, excitement, and steadfastness is more precious than gold. Love you guys to bits.

And finally, to Michelle, who holds me steady in all that I do. Cheers to you, babe. xxx

Chapter One

B loody flies!" Sorla Reardon swatted wildly and shook her head in a vain attempt to remove the sticky, annoying creature from her face. She hadn't missed *them* while she'd been away. Driving through the heat haze rising off the road, the distant eucalypt-lined hills stood sentinel over the town. They shimmered in reproachful welcome as if to say *What took you so long?* She scanned up and down the street from her truck and realized not much had changed in nearly twenty years. The main street of town was still largely the same; even the people looked the same, hardworking, a little tired and worn around the edges. She recognized the local grocery store, the hardware place, and even the local agricultural feed supply and veterinary outlet—the Stock and Station—was still here. Apart from a lick of paint and some new signage, it all but looked like time had passed the town of Stonesend by. For a brief flickering moment, it almost felt like she had never left the country, like she'd never lived overseas, never left this quaint little inland Australian town. The return of the sticky black fly buzzing around her ears reminded her that she was well and truly home.

Sorla took a deep breath and squared her shoulders. She knew coming back after all these years would be a challenge. Beating the odds was something she was used to, but this would be her biggest challenge to date. She had great plans. All that was needed was a lot of hard work and a little bit of luck. Jamming her baseball cap on low, she stepped out of the truck and grimaced at the assault of heat pressing down on her head and shoulders as she quickly crossed the road and made her way over to the Stock and Station. This was the last store on her list for the day. She was amused to hear a bell announce her arrival as she pushed the door open. She stepped inside and quickly closed the door to keep the cool air trapped inside.

The store was divided into various sections, with animal welfare to the left, clothes to the right. A counter at the back of the store had two labelled doorways behind it, pointing to *Feed* and *Saddlery*. A big metal fan stood off to the side, vainly trying to circulate air in the room. Sorla walked up to the empty counter and looked around. She couldn't see anyone. Spying a brass bell, she tapped the metallic top, stealing a chime to ring out, and waited.

A door off to the side opened, and a man in his late sixties bumbled down the short walkway towards the counter. Time had not been kind to him. George Johnson was still a big man but bent with age. His eyes were rheumy, his nose a large red fleshy boulder, contrasting starkly against his skin, which carried a light tan. Sorla had a vague memory of big-time rodeo stories and wild living. Looking around the walls she spied some old faded photographs of him riding broncs and bulls, holding up trophies. Looking back at George, it looked like the years of hard living had finally caught up with him.

"What can I do for you?"

"Hi. My name's Sorla Reardon. I live out on Cherry Hill. I'm looking to do the place up a bit and wondered if I could place an order here for some supplies. I have a list of things I need to get started." Sorla handed him the paper.

Squinting down the list of goods, George nodded and grunted. "Couple of these things we'll have to order in, but the rest we can get for you, no trouble at all. You can either pick 'em up later this afternoon, or we can deliver it out at the end of the week."

Sorla didn't fancy waiting around town for another couple of hours. "Delivery would be great, thanks. The address and phone number are on the paper. If you could just call ahead and let me know what time you'll be there, I can arrange to have someone help unload the truck."

George squinted at the fancy letterhead on the paper and then up into Sorla's face. "You Ged's girl?"

Sorla squared her shoulders. "I am."

"You been away awhile."

"I have."

"Good judge of horseflesh, your old man."

"Yes, sir, he was."

George looked her up and down, grunted, and then looked back down at the list. "Says here you want some clothes." Sorla nodded. "You need to see RJ, next door." George flicked his chin in the direction of the saddlery. With that, George turned on his heel and exited out into the *Feed* doorway, leaving Sorla standing at the counter.

I wonder if RJ's as warm and fuzzy as George is? Talk about overwhelming customer service. Sorla followed the sign and walked through to the adjoining saddlery. The further she went in, the more oppressive the heat became. Off to her left, there was a work station with some saddle stands. A figure in a long-sleeved cotton top and jeans was bent over with their back to her, tapping away on the bottom of an upside-down boot balanced on a shoe last. Sorla cleared her throat. "Excuse me? I'm looking for RJ."

Slowly the figure straightened and turned around. Sorla's eyes opened wide in surprise. Facing her was a gorgeous woman. Her fawn hair was tied up in a bun at the back of her head, with loose tendrils escaping, but only as far as her long neck, where they were captured in damp strands. She took some tacks from her mouth and placed them in her apron pocket. Laying a small tack hammer down on the bench, she strolled over to where Sorla was standing. Aegean-blue eyes met Sorla's.

"I'm RJ. How can I help you?"

"Hi. George said to come in and talk to you about some clothes."

"Ah, yes. Clothes are next door. If you want to head back there, I'll clean up and come in and give you a hand."

"Thanks."

Sorla made her way back in to the main body of the store and wandered over to where the clothes were. There was everything in stock, from gaudy bright-coloured cowboy shirts, through to plain, heavy cotton drill-work wear. Sorla smelt her almost at the same time as she heard her approach. Leather and soap.

"Was there something in particular you were after?" RJ's voice was like smoke on the water, dusted with husky undertones. She had removed the apron and stood before Sorla in a long-sleeved white cotton top whose grandpa collar opened at the neck with three buttons and soft faded jeans that hugged her waist to perfection, the ensemble rounded off with well-worn light tan boots.

Sorla swallowed and gathered her thoughts. "Some jeans, work shirts, boots"—Sorla tipped the brim of her baseball cap—"and a new hat."

RJ smiled crookedly, looking at the cap. "Yep, caps don't help much in weather like this. What say we start with the shirts? Do you know what size you are?"

Together they picked out some shirts and Sorla tried on a couple of pairs of jeans. Sorla carefully eyed off the selection of boots on the shelf, studying the size and height of the heel, dismissing several styles of boots, until she found what she was looking for. Selecting one, she sat down and tried the left one on and walked around in it. "That feels good. I'll take two pairs of them too."

"Don't you want to try the other one on first?"

"Nah. If it fits my left, then it'll fit the right."

"You sure? I'd hate for you to get home, only to discover that it's not right."

"It's good. Really."

"Okay. Now, a hat. Did you have a style in mind?"

Sorla shook her head. She tried a few on, but they looked too big and over the top.

RJ nibbled her bottom lip thoughtfully. "Hang on. I got a new shipment in the other day, some Akubras. Nice felt. Good quality." RJ got a stepladder and pulled some boxes down from the top shelf. She stood and looked at Sorla with narrowed eyes and pursed lips, before selecting and handing over a box. "Try this one."

Sorla lifted out a sand-coloured hat. It had a pinched crown with a broad dipping brim. She put it on and turned to look in the mirror. It was perfect. The light tone of the hat set off her dark short bobbed hair and brown eyes. Sorla pulled off the hat and looked inside. The style name said *Cattleman*. How ironic was that? "It's perfect! How did you know?"

RJ shrugged. "I have to confess, it's one of my favourites. I've got a tan-coloured one. I've tried a few other kinds of hats, but I end up looking like a pimple with an umbrella on top. This hat'll not only do a great job, but it's softer and subtler looking. The lighter colour is good in the heat and…it frames your face and shows off your eyes nicely."

Sorla tilted her head sideways as she listened to RJ. *I do believe she's blushing!* "Well, I have to say, I love it. Thank you."

RJ flashed a perfect set of teeth as she smiled. "A pleasure. Is there anything else you need?"

"No, I think we've covered it nicely for the minute."

"How would you like to pay for this?"

"I left quite a list with George earlier, for things to be delivered at the end of the week. I'll pay for these now, but is it possible to set up an account while I'm here?"

"I can do that. If you'd like to follow me to the counter and I'll wrap these up for you." Sorla paid for her clothes and gave RJ the details for the account. RJ folded the receipt and handed it to Sorla. "So, you're at Cherry Hill?"

"Uh-huh."

"You going to run horses again?"

"Horses and cattle."

RJ nodded. "Be nice to see the old place up and running again. If you need help with anything, feel free to give me a holler. I can point you in the direction of some good workers and tradies who'll do a good job for a fair price."

"Thanks. I appreciate that. Well, I'd better get this stuff on home."

"Here, let me help you."

They each carried a couple of bags out to the waiting truck. Sorla put her sunglasses on. "Phew! The day's not getting any cooler, is it? I'd forgotten how hot it can get here in February."

RJ smiled. "It'll cool off tonight, when the storm comes."

Sorla looked up doubtfully into a clear blue sky. There were no clouds, no wind, and certainly no sign of a change in the weather. She opened the truck door and hopped in. She wound the window down and stuck her head out. "Hey, RJ? What does the R stand for?"

"Riley."

"Well, thanks for all your help today, Riley. I really appreciate it."

"You're welcome."

Waving farewell, Sorla pulled out and pointed her ute to home.

❖

Hearing the front door shut, Claire looked up. "Hi, stranger. How was town?"

"Hey, Claire. Hot, dusty, and over and done with for the minute."

Claire had been Sorla's friend since enlistment at Duntroon, the Royal Military College. They'd signed up and gone through basic army training together, meeting up again several years later overseas when they were selected to join a Special International Task Force, with Claire a senior officer of the nursing corps, and Sorla a logistics squadron officer. Over the years, they had remained the closest of friends.

"Was it that bad?"

"Nah, not really. I managed to get pretty much everything on the list. Some of the gear will have to be ordered in and it'll take a bit longer, but most of it will arrive on Friday. The store in town offered to deliver it out. I've set up an account too, so if we need anything else we can just charge it up and they'll send us the bill at the end of the month."

"Nice."

Sorla waggled her eyebrows up and down with a cheeky grin. "Mm, so was my supply store fashion assistant."

"Come again?"

"When I went in to order the gear from the Stock and Station, they had a clothing section and I had a very lovely assistant help me to select and accessorize my farm attire. Check out the hat!" Sorla put her new hat on and ran her fingertips over the brim in a mock salute. "I was told it framed my face beautifully."

Claire whistled. "As much as I hate to fuel your ego, that hat does look damn nice. Whoever that girl is, she pegged you well."

"How do you know it was a girl?"

Claire grinned at her friend and bumped her playfully with her hip. "Because you're drooling."

Sorla couldn't help but laugh. "How did you get on at the hospital?"

Claire nodded. "Pretty good. I don't know what Colonel Field wrote in the letter of recommendation, but it must have been something pretty nice because when I went in and introduced myself I was treated a bit like the prodigal daughter returning home. They're happy to take me on and even happier for me to pretty much pick the days I want to work."

"I bet they are. It's not every day a top-notch trauma surgical nurse lands in your lap. So have you thought about what you want to do?"

"I've a vague idea, but I want to talk it over with Ed and see what he thinks before I make up my mind. I was thinking maybe three or four days a week in town at the hospital, and the rest of my time here. I could maybe do a clinic one day a week here later too, if all works to plan. And if I'm not doing nursey stuff, I can muck in and do bits around the farm."

"Well, if you're planning on becoming a real country gal, perhaps I'd better take you into town next time and get you kitted out in some decent farm clobber."

"That depends. Would the trip be to inspire a new dimension to my fashion wardrobe, à la country? Or would it be an excuse to chat up your new fashion cutie?"

Sorla wrapped her arm around Claire's shoulder as they chuckled and walked towards the house. She playfully put her free hand over her heart. "You wound me with your cutting barbs, Major Hanson."

Claire laughed with her friend. "Oh, I can assure you, I haven't even *started*, Major Reardon."

As Sorla pushed through the door into the house, they were instantly wrapped in the cool of the interior. Sorla put her bags on the floor. "God, it's nice to be out of the heat. I *love* you, air conditioning."

"How 'bout you dump your bags next door and I'll cobble together some lunch?"

"Sounds lovely. I won't be a minute." Sorla dodged the boxes on the floor in the large sitting room and headed off down the hall. By the time she threw her bags on the bed and returned to the kitchen, Claire had the makings of lunch on the table and was pouring some iced tea into two glasses. She handed a glass to Sorla. "Here, wrap your lips around that."

"Mm, priceless. Thanks. Wow, you've had a busy morning. Looks like the kitchen's all unpacked."

"Pretty much. I figured I'd start with the kitchen first, so that no matter what else we're doing about the place, we can always come in and grab something to eat and drink without having to work out what box everything is in. I know I said it before, but this is a remarkable house. It has the weirdest design I have ever seen, and yet it's perfect."

Sorla nodded. "I know. My great-great-grandfather loved his family, but he also understood the need for everyone to have their own space. So he designed the kitchen and dining-cum-family-entertaining-area to be the central hub, where everyone could come together. Off that, each family had a hall or passageway that led off to their own living space."

Claire clinked her glass against Sorla's. "Novel concept." In companionable silence they finished the sandwiches and stacked the dishes in the sink. "Oh, that reminds me, while you were out, Ed got a message to say the horses won't be coming tomorrow. Something about one of the trucks breaking down and waiting for parts. They hope to be here on Friday."

"Did they say what time? That only gives us a day before the first of the cattle comes in."

"I know. Ed was trying to pin him down, but until the parts arrive, it's a bit of a wait and see."

"Fair enough."

"In the meantime, shall we make a start on those boxes in the lounge room?"

"Lead on, my friend."

❖

"RJ? RJ? Where the hell are you?" George stormed through the doorway and into the store's main floor.

"I'm up here, just putting some things away." High on the ladder, Riley was putting the last of the hatboxes back on the upper shelves. She stepped down off the ladder and wiped her hands on a cloth hanging from her back pocket. "What's up?"

George handed her the list of items Sorla had given him earlier. "Need you to sort this out and order in what's not out the back. You can add the rest to your delivery run on Friday."

She looked down the list. There were only a handful of things they didn't stock, and if she called through the order today, they should be in by early next week. "Do you want me to invoice them with the delivery, or leave it and send an invoice at the end of the month?"

George scratched his chin. "Invoice 'em now and take it with you on Friday. Better to see how good they are for money before they get to thinking to order up too much."

Riley nodded. "Be nice to see Cherry Hill up and working again."

George grunted. "As long as it brings in some business, don't much care what they do out there. Speaking of business, you finished fixing Mickey's saddle yet? He rang this morning and wanted to know if it'd be ready for the weekend."

"It's as good as done. Just needs a quick polish and wipe over. It's the first thing on my list of deliveries to drop off on Friday."

George grunted. "See you do." With that George turned and ambled back to the office.

Riley shook her head, carefully folded the list and placed it in her back pocket, and headed towards the phone on the counter. She dialled Mickey's number and left a reassuring message before heading out the back to make a start on the list of items for Cherry Hill.

❖

"Oh God, shoot me now. I swear, I don't want to see another box that needs unpacking for a good long while." Sorla threw herself down on the couch and tossed her boots up onto the coffee table.

Claire groaned as she mirrored Sorla, resting her head on the back of the couch next to her friend. "I know what you mean. Stick me with a fork. I am *so* done."

There was an appreciative whistle from the doorway. "My, oh my. Just what every hot-blooded man needs, two gorgeous women, powerless, and lying at his feet." Ed stood before them with a huge grin on his face and three bottles of icy-cold beer in his hands.

Sorla rolled her head tiredly in his direction. "The only reason I'm not jumping up to slap you upside your silly head is that I am too tired, and I am *desperately* hoping one of those beers has my name on it."

"It does at that, Fender."

Sorla grinned back at him and reached forward. "In that case, all is forgiven if you hurry up and hand it over, ya big dag."

Ed dutifully gave the girls their beer and stood back taking in the room and the pile of empty flattened boxes in the corner near the door. "Jeez, you two sure moved mountains in here today."

Claire saluted him with her bottle and took a long sip. "Mm, that's awesome, thanks, babe. The only thing we didn't get done was the infirmary. We figured we'd do that in the morning when we can work out what we'll need to order in. The library and entertainment rooms are done, guest suite mostly finished, and the laundry's all sorted."

Ed shook his head and looked at each of them, smiling. "I learned a long time ago that each of you was fantastic, but together, you're a force to be reckoned with."

Claire winked at him. "You better believe it, gorgeous. Now come and throw your manly self here between us and tell us all about what you got up to today."

Ed collapsed on the couch and put his long legs up on the scarred table alongside their booted feet "Fencing, fencing, and more fencing. I want to make sure the front boundary line and yards are right to go, for when we get the deliveries. Speaking of deliveries"—he turned to Sorla—"did Claire tell you about the horses?"

Sorla nodded. "Yeah, that's a bit of a bugger." She frowned. "I s'pose it can't be helped. I was really hoping to have a bit of time to settle them in before the cattle come. I don't fancy working a couple of hundred head on foot."

Ed patted her on the thigh. "Well, we know that at least four of the horses from my brother are good to start work straight up, and we've always got the Jeep and the quad bike as back up. We'll manage."

"I know. You're right. You know me, I hate it when plans go awry."

Claire laughed gently at her friend. "You, my dear, are such a Virgo. Everything has a place and every place has its thing."

Sorla kissed her on the cheek as she rose. "And you wouldn't want me any other way. How about you two finish your beer while I rustle us up some dinner?"

Claire waved at her. "Thanks, hon. Holler if you can't find anything."

Sorla wandered into the kitchen and opened the fridge, retrieving a selection for a quick Thai stir-fry. The kitchen was too hot and she was too tired to make anything too complicated. As she set about preparing the ingredients, she thought ahead to the coming days. There were a few more things still to sort, including organizing her own suite. *Can't live out of a rucksack forever.*

Then there were the stables. They would need to set up a space to store feed, and she and Ed would need to sort through some of the equipment to work out what they had, what worked and what needed replacing or fixing. *Wish you were still here, Da. You'd have loved the excitement of setting everything up. Then again, if you were still here, we wouldn't have to set it up, you'd have it all spick and span. Shame some of the family weren't half as good keeping things going as they were at helping themselves to what was left after you'd gone.* Sorla shook her sadly. She closed her eyes, took a deep breath, and squared her shoulders. *Here's my chance at putting all of what you taught me into practice, Da. I just hope I do a good enough job.*

As she stirred the veggies in the pan, a flash of light caught Sorla's eye from out the kitchen window. Turning the heat on low, she grabbed her glass of wine and stepped outside. Although it was now dark, the heat and humidity weighed heavy in the air, quickly wrapping around her shoulders as she stepped beyond the door. She paused and sipped her wine, felt the chilled liquid coating her throat, languidly making its way downward. Leaning against a porch post, she turned her face to the sky. She closed her eyes and breathed in—the moist air held hints of earth, grass, and a freshness that she had missed all the years she had been away. A kookaburra laughed in a nearby jacaranda tree. She opened her eyes in time to see the sky flash with distant lightning in the east. A gentle breeze had begun to pick up and she could smell the promise of moisture on it.

Sorla smiled wryly and toasted the night sky with her wine glass. Looked like Riley was right after all with the storm. Pushing off from the post, she returned back inside to finish dinner.

CHAPTER TWO

Riley pulled up at Mickey's gate right on seven a.m. The last of the morning mist had burnt off, and the day's heat was beginning to pick up. Climbing out of the truck's cab to open the gate, Riley could feel the beads of moisture beginning to form in her hairline under her hat. *Looks like it's gonna be another warm one.* In no time at all she had the truck through the gate and was heading down the road that led to Mickey's house. A skitter of excitement ran through her as she wondered how Mickey would like his present. She had worked long and hard on this particular design and filled it with as much love as she could muster to honour the man who played an important role in her growing years. For many years, Mickey had been one of the rodeo clowns who ran out in front of bulls to protect riders. It was on the rodeo circuit that Riley first met Mickey and his wife Pearl, spending many a time sleeping in the back of their caravan while George was out all night drinking and playing up with his rodeo mates.

Never a more devoted couple could be found than Mickey and Pearl. When they looked at each other, it was like everyone else in the room simply disappeared. Theirs was a love that most people could only dream of. The only thing missing in their lives was children. For years they tried, but it was not meant to be. It ended up being lucky for Riley, in a sense, as they practically raised her in the early years when George, widowed young, had no idea how to raise a small girl child. On those nights when it rained, or when George stayed out carousing with his rodeo-circuit buddies, Riley could often be found asleep in Mickey and Pearl's van.

A flyer promoting the end-of-year rodeo rustled on her dashboard with the breeze from the open truck window. Reaching out to pick it up and stuff it in the glovebox, the rearing horse and rider logo stared back at her in all its colourful glory. It was a powerful image, which to this day still visited her in her dreams on the odd occasion, especially at this time of year as the big season-ending rodeo drew closer. It was George—his free arm up to balance himself on the back of a bucking bronc, a flash of lightning exploding behind him and the horse. The perfect signature backdrop to mark his last monumental battle, and an iconic award, known far and wide on the rodeo circuit.

As Riley pulled the truck up beside Mickey's front fence, she spied him sitting on an old rocking chair on the front porch in the sun, waiting for her. Pearl had been gone a good few years now, and still the loss of her crept up on her at moments like now, seeing Mickey alone, causing a hitch in her breath and leaving a dull ache in the middle of her chest. Smiling, he turned and waved at Riley.

Riley got out of the truck, walked over, and kissed Mickey's leathery cheek. Mickey patted her on the face. Riley grabbed his hand and held it in hers.

"Hey, kiddo. 'Bout time you called 'round. Haven't seen ya in ages."

Riley lowered her lean frame to sit on the edge of the verandah boards next to Mickey's chair, swinging her feet back and forth over the edge. "Sorry. Things have been pretty busy. How're you doing?"

"I'm still above ground, so I can't complain. How's your week been? What's the news 'bout town?"

Riley smiled at the familiarity of their weekly banter. "Do you remember Ged Reardon, out on Cherry Hill?"

"Nice fella. Good eye for horses, that one. Died too young. Why?"

"Well, you remember he had a daughter?"

"Yeah, lived with her mother mostly, from memory. Only saw her in the holidays. Grew up and went overseas I think. Why?"

"Well, she's back and is looking to fix up the place and run cattle and horses on it again."

Mickey grunted. "Well, I'll be. Be interesting to see how much of her old man she's got in her. Cattle and horses, you say? It's a good piece of land, if you know how to make a go of it." Mickey looked over at the truck. "Looks like you got a lot of deliveries in the back there."

"Uh-huh. Cherry Hill put in a big order. I'm going there after I finish up here, but I wanted to drop off your saddle first, as promised, because I know you'll want to make sure it's right for next month. Hold tight and I'll bring it over." Riley fetched the saddle from the truck and brought it back to the porch, placing it on a stool in front of the old man. He put his glasses on and looked it over. It gleamed in the morning light. The silver highlights she had worked into the cantle's moulded rib at the back of the saddle winked in the sun. Mickey ran a shaky hand reverently over the fine detailed decorative work along the front and rear skirt, with the horn proudly holding court with its finery. Riley had worked mother-of-pearl along with silver in delicate swirls on the horn and matching conchos. It was regal and elegant, but it was on the signature plate at the front of the saddle that Mickey's fingers stilled and came to rest.

It was not Riley's usual signature that she attached to her crafted saddles. Instead, it was a polished silver plate with a lily of the valley flower stem, woven through a horseshoe. He traced the pattern. The flower had been Pearl's favourite. The breath caught in his throat and his eyes misted over. He took his glasses off and wiped his eyes. He fondly patted her hand. "You have a real gift, girl. And that seat looks comfortable enough to sleep in. It's truly beautiful. Thank you."

Riley didn't realize she was holding her breath until she exhaled in relief when Mickey said he liked it. She had spent months secretly working on the designs. Although Pearl had been gone now for five years, she knew that she had to incorporate something of Pearl into the design somehow, so that she would be with Mickey on his big day.

At this year's rodeo, Mickey was being inducted into the association's hall of fame for his services rendered over the years both as a rodeo clown and as an instructor for younger clowns coming through the ranks. The cowboys and girls got all the glory, but everyone in the industry knew that the clowns were the true heroes who kept everyone safe and entertained day and night. This year, in honour and recognition of his award, Mickey would ride in the grand parade leading up to the ceremony. Riley and George had talked Mickey into allowing them to provide him with a special saddle in honour of his big day.

Riley smiled. "Shall we go and see how it looks on Jeri?"

"Damn straight. Lead on, girl."

Riley loaded the saddle and a new blanket onto Mickey's horse Jericho, a deep dark chocolate gelding. Against the horse's deep walnut tones the rich burgundy blanket showed off the magnificent new saddle. Riley had worked the straps so that they were supple and supportive for the aged horse. She had come out months earlier and measured Jeri to get the saddle size and mould just right. Mickey sat in the saddle and walked the horse around the house yard several times before pronouncing it to be perfect.

By the time they finished up and shared a pot of tea, it was getting close to nine. Back in the truck and waving out the window in farewell, she promised she would call in the following week to see if he wanted any adjustments made to the saddle fitting. Riley had said she would be at Cherry Hill by half past nine and knew she'd better get her skates on if she wanted to be there on time.

CHAPTER THREE

I swear there's more dirt on us than there is on the floor!" Claire pushed back sweat-soaked bangs from her forehead, managing to add a smudge of dirt in their place as she straightened and stretched her back. "I was just thinking, if we run out of dirt here on the barn floor, we can just scrape it off the benches, or us for that matter."

Sorla leaned on a broom and grinned back at her. "I'm not sure I knew what I was expecting, but I didn't think it was going to be quite this big a job cleaning up the old stables. What a mess—I can't believe how run-down the place is. Still, if we can get the basics done, like get some of the stalls ready and a place to store the tack and feed, we can work away at the rest as we go."

Ed came in through the big double-opening barn doors. "Yo, Fender?"

Sorla stood up. "Over here. What's up?"

"Your delivery truck's just turned in to the main gate. Should be here in a minute or two."

"Bewdy, thanks." Sorla put the broom aside and went to the wash sink in the corner and washed her hands. She dried them on the legs of her jeans before running her fingers through her hair. She turned to Claire. "Okay?"

Claire wiped dirt off Sorla's chin and nodded. "Okay."

Sorla and Claire walked out into the sunshine to see an old forest-green 1960s Ford F-500 truck with wooden slat sides pull up. Riley stepped out backwards and put her hat on as she shut the truck door. She turned, looked around, and waved in greeting. "Morning, Miss Reardon."

"Please, call me Sorla, and this is my friend, Claire. Claire, I'd like you to meet Riley Johnson."

Riley extended her hand. "Nice to meet you, Claire."

Claire shook Riley's hand. "And a pleasure to meet you too, Riley."

"Where would you like me to unload your order?"

Sorla looked at the truck and then over at the stable doors. "Can you back it up over there? We'll just unload it in the stables for now. We haven't quite got things ready yet, so we might just set the stuff inside and sort it out later, I think."

"No problems."

Riley hopped back into the truck and backed the old Ford deftly in through the open double doors. As Claire and Sorla followed, Claire playfully bumped her with her hip and leaned over to whisper in her ear, "I can see why you were drooling when you came home the other day."

Sorla swatted her arm. "Cut it out. And I was *not* drooling." Claire snorted as they made their way to the back of the parked truck.

Stepping from the truck, Riley joined the girls at the mouth of the barn. "Is there a particular place you want this stuff?"

Sorla looked into the truck bed at the contents. "We might put the fencing gear over here to the left in that empty stall for the minute, the food can just be stacked inside over there to the right, and everything else can go into the workroom off behind the tack room at the far end."

Riley nodded. "How 'bout I winch the pallet of mixed goods off and you can put that where you want while I unload the fencing gear?"

Sorla said, "Sounds like a plan."

"Okay," Riley replied, "just give me a minute to get things set up."

Claire patted Sorla on the back. "I'll go and make some room out back. Back in a jiff."

Sorla only just acknowledged Claire's departure. She watched, captivated, as Riley dropped the back and sides of the truck down, then swung herself effortlessly up into the tray bed to set up the winch and hook up the pallet. Sorla was never one to pass up eye candy when she saw it, and she was cheerfully appreciating Riley's lithe legs as they balanced over the truck's contents. Riley wore a cream long-sleeved heavy cotton drill shirt, neatly tucked into the waist of a well-fitting pair of faded jeans. As Riley hooked up the chain on the winch, Sorla caught a gleam of a silver bracelet fitted snugly around her left wrist, poking out from the sleeve. Looking for more jewellery, the only other piece that she could see was a silver thumb ring on her right hand.

Riley picked up a control box and proceeded to lift the pallet clear of the truck bed. She quickly paused the lift and hopped down off the truck before finishing lowering the pallet off to the left of the truck, onto the dirt floor. Sorla watched as Riley efficiently unhooked the winch chain and returned the arm back to its resting position behind the truck's cabin window, then took her hat off and tossed it into the open window of the cabin to rest on the bench seat. She looked up and nodded at Sorla with a shy smile before heading to the back of the truck. As she pulled a roll of fencing wire to the edge of the truck tray, she bent her knees and slid the load to her shoulder before straightening and carrying the roll over to the stall Sorla had indicated earlier.

Sorla saw how the muscles rippled underneath the shirt and got a hint of the tone of Riley's arms and legs. She quickly turned and felt her chin. She grinned and shook her head. Claire might've been right. She just might be drooling.

"Hey, I found these out the back, thought they might make carrying this lot a bit easier." Claire lowered a wheelbarrow to the ground and unloaded a jump trolley from its tray.

"Good thinking, ninety-nine," Sorla said. She and Claire proceeded to load both the trolley and the barrow and trotted off to the workroom with their first load.

Claire stopped in the doorway. "You want this anywhere in particular?"

"How about against the back wall over there. We can sort it out later." They made a couple more trips back and forth before emptying the pallet. Riley had finished unloading the fencing gear and was stacking the last bale of lucerne hay next to the door.

Claire wandered over to the sink and opened a small bar fridge that was under the sink's bench. "Anyone up for a cold drink? I've got Coke, tea, and water."

Sorla leaned against the tray of the truck and watched as Riley loaded the now empty pallet back onto the truck tray bed. "I'd love a water. Riley?"

"A water would be nice, thanks."

Claire handed drinks all round. She held up a spare water. "I might just run this over to Ed, and see how he's doing. Be back in a minute."

Sorla saluted her with her bottle. "No problems."

As Riley leaned against the truck's side, she sipped the cool water, taking a moment to look around the barn. It had big double doors at its entrance, where the truck currently stood. The barn itself was part stone and part wood. The walls, up to about six feet high, were stone, with wooden frames and cypress boards making up the rest of the building's structure. The big high bloodwood beams looked old, but strong, as they steepled high overhead. There was a balcony running along the southern long wall of the barn roof. Underneath and on the opposite side at floor level were fifteen large horse stalls a side. A doorway led off to the tack room with a paved floor, which in turn led through to the workshop, where she had seen Sorla and Claire head off to unload the goods.

"Thanks for bringing everything out so early," Sorla said, interrupting her admiration of the barn. "I really appreciate it."

Riley smiled and nodded. "My pleasure. If you don't mind me saying, you have a lovely place here."

"Thanks. Would you like a look around?"

Riley pushed off the truck to stand. "Oh no, I don't want to take up any more of your time."

"It's no problem, really. Come on, I'll give you a quick tour while we cool down." Riley hesitated. "Unless you have somewhere else you have to be?"

Riley felt herself blush. "Um, no. You were my last delivery today."

Sorla grabbed Riley's hand. "Well, that settles it, then. You can be my first touring guest. Come on." Sorla gave her the whistle-stop tour of the stables and talked about her family's history.

"Long story short, my great-great-grandfather came out from Ireland and fell in love with this place. He wanted to make a new beginning for his family in a new land. Several generations lived and died here. In the end, the big family numbers dwindled, partly due to the various wars over the decades, and those who were still alive, most of them moved away to the cities and lost the taste for living on the land after a string of lean years with drought and disease going through the breeding herds. Only Grandad stayed, worked hard, and basically rebuilt things. He still ran cattle, but he began to specialize in racehorses. Dad followed in his footsteps. He was a legend. He could spot a horse with potential a mile away, pay pittance for it, and turn it into a champion.

"When Mum and Dad divorced, Mum got me and Dad got the property. Mum was always a city girl—she couldn't stand it here. She hated the country life. My dad, on the other hand, loved it. He used to say that this was where his soul was. That the dirt was in his veins. I got to come here on holidays. Dad and I, we're like two peas in a pod people used to say. I think that's why Mum insisted I go with her when she left him. To take me away from my father was the ultimate revenge. Mum never really wanted me as such, she just wanted him to hurt. To show him how much he hurt her when he dragged her off to live in the middle of Nowheresville."

"Your poor dad."

"Mm. She broke his heart. It was this place that kept him going, that and school holidays. For me too. I couldn't wait to get here. It was like I couldn't really breathe until I came back. When I finished school, I wanted to come here, but Dad wanted me to have a trade and to see the world first. So, like so many of my ancestors, I joined up. Then of course, while we were off gallivanting around the world playing war games, dementia grabbed him, and then the business suffered and downscaled dramatically to what you see today."

Riley shook her head. "It's quite a tale."

"Well, lucky for us, Dad left it all to me in his will, and here we are, trying to make our own adventure out of it. I think Dad'd be proud."

Riley listened intently, asking a few questions from time to time as they went. "So when you say you want to breed horses, do you mean racehorses, like your father?"

Sorla shook her head. "No, I was thinking more of starting off with some stock and cutting horses and see how I go from there. The cattle will be the main business to start with. Which reminds me, can I get your opinion on some of the gear in the tack room while you're here? I want to know what you think might be salvageable and what else I might need to get in."

"I'd be happy to. Lead the way."

They spent a good half hour in the tack room sorting the gear into three piles: good condition, a pile that was declared as needing a little work to bring it up to scratch, and the last section was stuff that needed replacing.

"I can make a list of the things you'll most likely need and can organize to get the middle pile of gear here back up to working order again if you'd like," Riley offered, "or I'm happy to come out and get you up and running and show you how to do it yourself if you'd prefer."

Sorla tilted her head and looked at Riley. "If you showed me how to do it, wouldn't that be doing you out of a job?"

Riley shrugged her shoulders and looked down at her boots as she scuffed her toe on the pavers. "It's not always about the money. Sometimes it's about the enjoyment you get sharing an experience and learning how to do something for yourself that's the important thing." As Riley looked up, her eyes ran smack bang into Sorla's intense deep brown eyes.

Sorla smiled and said, "I know what you mean."

For a brief moment they both stood looking at each other.

Riley heard approaching footsteps, and then Claire popped in, breaking their private moment. "Hey, thought I'd find you two in here. Ed sent me to tell you he thinks the horses are here. A truck's just pulling into the main gate now." As the three women walked out of the barn, Riley heard the commotion long before she saw the truck. Kicking and whinnying noises could be heard above the engine.

Standing at the yard gate was a tall blond-haired man, midthirties, broad shouldered and ruggedly handsome from his hat to his toes. Claire sidled up to him and hooked her arm through his. "Ed, I'd like you meet Riley Johnson. Riley, this gorgeous man is my husband, Ed Thornton."

Ed held his hand out. "How do you do, Ms. Johnson?"

Riley accepted his hand. "Please, it's Riley, or RJ. It's a pleasure to meet you, sir."

Ed gifted Riley with a wink and a big broad grin showing perfect teeth. "And I'm just Ed. Looks like you're just in time to witness the arrival of the first shipment of horses to kick-start Cherry Hill's newest chapter."

Sorla had her hand shading her eyes as the truck began to slow, ready to pull up. "Sounds like someone's not happy."

Riley watched as Ed talked to the driver, while Sorla looked over the clipboard details that the truck driver had handed her. The whole time, a very unhappy horse was doing its utmost to bust down the walls of the truck with explosive kicks against the metal sides. The truck, whose mechanical youth was quite some decades ago, was closed sided, with an open, grated roof. Riley had seen the type of truck before and knew that it could house up to twenty horses packed in en masse or smaller numbers using separation barriers. Sorla and Ed walked alongside the truck with the driver, taking turns talking and gesticulating towards the truck. As the driver passed the head section with the unhappy horse in it, he thumped the side of the truck. Riley jumped slightly and winced.

Squinting, Riley turned to Claire who was shading her face from the sun's glare with a hand. "How many are you expecting?"

"Ed said ten. A couple from his brother's place, Sorla's horse, and five green horses Sorla and Ed picked out last week at the sales."

They watched as the back door opened down to a ramp, and the driver went in, returning minutes later to hand out the first horse to Sorla. She led a chestnut mare out of the truck and into the holding yard. She patted the mare down and unclipped the lead rope from the halter. She turned and passed Ed, who was holding a tall grey gelding. One by one, all bar the last horse, who was still kicking in protest, were led out. The driver refused to let Sorla or Ed into the truck and was inside, trying to get the last horse out. Cursing and swearing could be heard coming from inside. After ten minutes the driver stormed out of the trailer and went to the truck cabin and retrieved a length of plastic pipe. He banged it upside the truck as he returned, only to be answered back with equally angry kicks from inside.

Riley leapt off the fence and trotted over to the truck to stand between the ramp and the driver. "Hi. Looks like you've got an unhappy traveller inside."

The driver rolled his eyes at her. "You don't say." He shook his head. "Damn thing's been givin' me grief right from when it was loaded. Now if you'll just get outta the way, I'm gonna sort this out once and for all and be on my way."

"Do you mind if I have a go?"

"Listen, Pollyanna, this here's a mean horse and only listens to a firm hand. Now I'm not gonna ask you again nicely. Move."

The driver made to push his way past, but Riley held on to his forearm and continued to block his path. "What's your name please, sir?"

"It's Greg."

"Hi, Greg. I'm Riley. I see you work for Springer's Transport. You must be new. I don't think I've seen you around before."

"Yeah, started last month. Now, if you don't mind…" Greg went to push past.

Riley put a hand on his chest and halted him. Her voice was quiet, but firm. "Actually, I do mind. Unless you want me to ring your boss, Hugo, and explain that his new driver is being difficult, it would be in your best interests to back off and give me a few minutes to see if I can't get the horse off nicely. You've had a big morning. How about you take five over there in the shade for a bit?"

While the driver stood red faced and mouth ajar, Riley quietly stepped to the side and closed the ramp shut. She turned to Sorla and Ed. "When I ask, can you let the ramp down, please?" Before they had a chance to open their mouths, Riley had monkeyed up the trailer side and dropped down inside. The horse continued to kick and whinny its protests at the intrusion.

Sorla, recovered from her initial shock, reached up to open the ramp door. "Oh, this is bloody ridiculous, help me open this up."

Ed reached over and covered Sorla's hand with his own much larger one. "How about we give her a minute, like she asked." Sorla opened her mouth to protest but Ed held up his hand. "Let's see how it plays out."

Scowling, Sorla reluctantly agreed. "All right, a couple of minutes." She folded her arms, frowning, and waited near the rear of the truck.

At first, the only sounds were the kicking, snorting, and stamping of the horse. As the minutes began to build and tick by, the kicking slowed to stamping, and finally to snorting only. Sorla looked at her watch. Twenty minutes had passed. And she realized she could hear a voice offering soft murmuring noises. Suddenly, there were no more sounds. After so much noise, the silence hurt almost as much as the deafening kicks echoing off the metal walls.

Ever so quietly, so that Sorla only just heard it, came the request. "You can open the door now, please." She nodded to Ed, who reached up and released the latch. He lowered the ramp slowly and they both stood back. Riley stood in the doorway beside a magnificent dark blue roan mare with a jet-black mane and tail.

The mare stamped once, as if to announce herself, and then calmly allowed Riley to lead her off the truck and into the holding yard to join the other horses. Ed followed, shutting the gate behind them. Riley gently stroked the mare's neck as she unclipped the lead rope. She backed away a few steps before turning and meeting Ed at the gate, who let her out with a big grin on his face.

For a few moments, no one said a word as they leaned on the fence and watched the horses settle in. Finally, Sorla turned to Riley and bumped her with her hip. "Bit of a ballsy move back there."

Riley, looking straight ahead, just shrugged. "Not really."

Sorla turned to look at her incredulously. "What do you mean, *not really*? That mare could have kicked the shit out of you."

Riley stepped off the fence and dusted off her pants. "Nah. She'd just had a crappy morning and needed someone to listen to her."

Sorla stepped off the fence and faced her. "What?"

"She was frightened and frustrated. No one was listening to her. She just needed to vent and for someone to acknowledge her feelings. She vented, I listened, and now she's happy to take her place with the others. See?" Riley raised her arm and pointed to the herd.

A small stain of red blossomed on Riley's sleeve. Claire stepped off the fence and gently grasped Riley's hand, carefully raising the sleeve to look at a bleeding mark midforearm. "Looks like the horse may have had a bit of a nibble, as well as a chat with you."

Riley shrugged her shoulders and tried to disengage her arm. "It's nothing. Just a nip."

Claire looped her arm into the crook of Riley's elbow and began to guide her towards the house. "Well, nip or not, let me look at it and clean it up for you. I don't know much about horses, but when it comes to the human body, I'm your gal."

Riley tried to pull away. Claire held gently but firmly. "Please, it's the least we can do. Besides, while we clean up, the other two layabouts can make us some lunch. Okay?"

Riley realized when she was on the losing end and graciously gave in and allowed Claire to lead her to the house, with Ed and Sorla following in their wake. As the group walked into the main sitting room, Claire steered Riley off to a doorway on the left. "We won't be long." Sorla and Ed headed in the opposite direction towards the kitchen.

CHAPTER FOUR

Claire led Riley down a passageway and into a side wing door. The main room looked like a health clinic or hospital exam room. There was a bed on wheels in the middle with benches against the walls and a couple of trolleys parked to one side. There were doorways off the room, but the doors were shut, so Riley had no idea what lay beyond them.

"If you want to take a seat on the bed over there, I'll just get a couple of things to clean that arm up."

Riley looked around. Although there were still boxes in corners on the floor, it was pretty obvious the room was going to be a clinic of some sort.

Claire was opening and shutting boxes and cupboard doors. "Just bear with me a minute. We haven't finished unpacking in here yet." A bit more rustling around, and Claire triumphantly held aloft a box of non-stick dressings. "Aha! Gotcha." She put several things on a small stainless-steel trolley and wheeled them over to Riley, sitting patiently on the bed. "Okay, let's have a look."

Claire gently rolled up Riley's sleeve past her elbow and turned the arm this way and that in the light. She gently prodded around the edges. "Is your tetanus up to date?"

"Uh-huh."

"No tingling or pain when I do this?" She manipulated Riley's wrist and fingers. Riley shook her head. "Any allergies?"

"No."

"Okay, we'll just get this cleaned up. Might sting a bit." Claire gently wiped the wound and surrounding area clean before patting it dry and having a last look. It was clearly a bite mark, with the telltale semicircle of bruises showing in brilliant reds and purples, with several bloody, oozing breaks in the skin at a couple of points along the wound. "More nasty bruising than anything, but you'll need to keep an eye on those cuts over the next few days. Try to keep them clean and dry so they don't get infected. Did the horse get you anywhere else, apart from your arm?"

Riley shook her head. "No."

Claire finished off by putting a non-stick dressing over the bite site, and a light crepe bandage to secure the dressing. She'd started to roll Riley's sleeve down when she stopped and gestured to another hand-sized bruise on the top side of Riley's arm. "That's a pretty decent bruise too. Looks like you've been in the wars this week."

Riley shrugged and finished rolling down her sleeve and buttoning up the cuff. "Misjudged a feed bag when I was unpacking a load early in the week. Occupational hazard sometimes. Thanks for cleaning me up."

"You're most welcome. Okay, well, we're about done here. I'll just clean this away and then we can check out what banquet the terrible twins have whipped up for us." Riley watched silently as Claire tidied the dressing pack away and wiped down the trolley.

Sorla was just placing a pitcher of iced tea on the table when Claire and Riley walked in. "How'd you go?"

Riley felt her cheeks warm with embarassment. "All good, thank you."

Claire plonked down in the seat. "Just needed a bit of cleaning up. She'll have a nice bruise for a couple of days though, but nothing much to worry about." Claire poured herself a tall glass of the tea. She raised the pitcher at Riley. "You want tea, or would you prefer something else?"

"Tea would be lovely, thank you."

"Tea it is. Sit down and take a load off."

Ed brought over some plates and napkins while Sorla carried over a plate of mixed sandwiches and wraps. "There's chicken, beef, and plain salad. Help yourself, everyone."

Over lunch, Riley watched the playful banter back and forth between the three sitting around the table in the kitchen. Riley didn't know if Sorla was related to them or not, but it was clear they were all very good friends.

Claire folded her napkin and placed it on her now empty plate. "So, Riley, tell us a little about yourself. Are you local?"

Riley traced a glistening bead of dew on the side of her glass. "Depends what you call local, I guess. Local usually means you have to have been here for a couple of generations. We've only really been settled here a bit over fifteen years or so. So, technically, we're not really, but George kind of got a bit of a leg up in the local stakes with his involvement in the town's rodeo."

Ed looked at Riley. "Who's George?"

"George is my father. He owns the Stock and Station store in town."

"I see. And you said your father was into the rodeo? Is that where you learned about horses?"

"Mm. For the first dozen or so years, I pretty much grew up in the back of a horse trailer, while we travelled around from town to town following the rodeo circuit. I've been around horses all my life. When I'm not working at the store, I help out around the district with horse training and stuff."

Ed sat back in his chair smiling. "Well, you certainly worked some pretty impressive magic out there this morning."

Self-conscious, Riley changed the subject to take the attention off her. "What about you guys? What's your story?"

Claire topped up everyone's glass again. "We're all ex-Defence Force. Sorla and I first met at basic training before signing up for a Special International Task Force. I finished my nursing with them, while Sorla went off to join logistics. That's where she met up with Ed. We all ended being shipped off to Iraq. She introduced me to Ed, and we've all been as thick as thieves ever since." Claire took a sip of her tea. "For years, Sorla always talked about coming back to run this place. We ended up falling in love with the dream too, so when our tours all ended at roughly the same time, we signed on, and here we all are, waiting on our first shipment of cattle tomorrow."

Riley noticed Sorla hadn't said a word. "Must be nice to be home."

Sorla gathered up the plates. "It is. It truly is, but there's a lot of work to be done to get this place up and running. I didn't realize how run-down it had become."

Riley picked up the empty glasses and walked them to the sink. "I'm at a loose end today. I'd be only too happy to help out."

Sorla smiled. "That's a really nice offer, but we've taken up a lot of your time already this morning."

"I don't mind, really. I'd be only too happy to help. I'm a dab hand with a broom, or I could help out fixing up some of the stalls if you'd like."

Ed and Claire looked at each other. Claire grinned. "You sure you wouldn't mind? You could help Sorla in the barn, which would free me up to finish unpacking the infirmary. I'm afraid I'm a bit out of my element out there. What do you say, Sor?"

Sorla tilted her head and looked at Claire. Claire smiled innocently back at her. Sorla turned to Riley. "Well, if you're sure you wouldn't mind, we'd love another set of hands. On one condition though—you have to let us pay you for your time."

Riley shook her head. "No, it's not about the money."

"Fair enough. Okay, then how about you stay for dinner?"

Riley took a moment to consider the offer. Normally she wasn't one for company, but she felt extremely comfortable with the trio of friends. "Assuming you're not sick of me by then, that sounds like a fair exchange. Just tell me what you'd like me to do and point me in the direction."

"Well, why don't we head back out and make a start on some of the horse stalls?"

"Horse stalls it is."

They were in a stall whose sides had more boards missing than not. Sorla measured and marked out the lengths of timber needed, while Riley cut them to the length and laid them in position, ready to fix to the wall studs. Sorla stood up and stretched her back. She watched as Riley walked over to get more timber from the stack against the far wall. Sorla couldn't help but notice how Riley's hips gently rolled as she walked back with several lengths resting against one shoulder. Riley had a balanced hourglass figure, with softly flared hips, a trim waist, and wide strong shoulders. As Sorla's eyes travelled up Riley's torso, she noticed a bead of sweat roll down an elegant neck, only to have it disappear down the vee of her shirt and into the mysterious boundary line of cleavage which lay suggestively underneath. Sorla cast her gaze up to see if there were any more droplets readying for a journey south, only to realize she had been caught staring. She dusted some dirt off her hands, cleared her throat, and swallowed with a suddenly very dry mouth. "So, tell me how you came about to being a saddler."

Riley braced the new boards between two sawhorses before straightening while Sorla measured and marked the next length. "When I was about eight or so, I remember George came back to the trailer one night after a bad ride. The cinch strap on the saddle had broken and he fell off his ride. He threw the gear in the truck and stormed off. I looked at it and saw where the stitching had come undone. I remember thinking it looked simple enough to fix, in theory. I went and talked to my Uncle Mickey, who lent me some of his gear and gave me some tips on how to do it." Riley cut the board and waited for Sorla to finish marking the next length. "I started looking after George's gear after that, fixing or replacing whatever was needed. Back then, it saved us some money, which was always a good thing. Travelling around the circuits, I got a lot of time to study the different types of saddles and gear that people used. I borrowed some books from the library and started experimenting. Pretty soon, other people began to ask if I could fix their stuff up, and it sort of grew from there. People started to pay me, and as a bit of money came in, I could afford to buy a few more tools. When the day came to set up the store, I already had enough gear to get started and a clientele list."

Sorla listened, fascinated. "So how old were you when you set up?"

Riley blinked. "A bit over fifteen."

"What? Are you serious?" Sorla's eyebrows nearly went over the top of her head.

Riley kept her head down and finished cutting the last board. "Yep."

"What about school?"

"I didn't go."

Sorla stood up and folded her arms with a grin on her face. "Okay, now you're shitting with me."

Riley moved the sawhorses out of the way. "Nope. Never went."

Sorla felt her grin dissolve. "You're serious, aren't you? You never went to school?"

Riley slowly stood up, frowning. "I'm not stupid." Her voice was quiet and serious. "I know how to read and write. I do all the books, orders, and accounts for the business."

Sorla realized how arrogant her question suddenly sounded. "Oh God, I'm so sorry. I didn't mean to sound so patronizing. I just never imagined, in this day and age, that it would be possible for someone not to get an education. What I mean is, that I thought everyone went to school…Oh hell. I'm making this worse aren't I?"

Riley picked up the drill and screws and brought them over to the first of the cut boards. She knelt with her back to Sorla and shrugged. "It's okay."

Sorla closed her eyes. *I am such a horse's arse.* She crossed the difference and knelt next to Riley, putting a gentle hand on her forearm. "It's not okay. And I'm sorry. I grew up in a different world to you. I'm the stupid one for not being able to appreciate your world better. I don't for one minute think that you're not smart because you didn't go to a school. I don't know you very well, but I know one thing for certain, you're obviously an intelligent, strong, and resilient woman, and one who has been very generous in helping us out today, and here I am insulting you with my stupidity. I'm so very sorry."

Riley sat back on her heels and shook her head. "Don't be, it's okay. It's my fault, I got a bit overdefensive."

Sorla opened her mouth to protest, but was stalled by Riley handing her one end of a board.

"How about, while we hang these, you tell me what inspired you to join the special forces?" Riley bumped her playfully with her hip, a smile on her face.

Sorla was impressed not only at how smoothly Riley had changed the subject, but that she also took the focus off the awkward situation by getting her back on comfortable familiar ground. Sorla smiled inwardly. Riley might not have gone to school, but she was a hell of a lot smarter than *she* was, and she graciously accepted the get-out-of-jail-guilt-free card she'd just been handed. The conversation flowed freely during the time they managed to repair six stalls. There was one left to repair. It had a big hole in the back wall measuring a good two feet square.

Sorla was carrying the sawhorses into the stall when she noticed Riley had crouched down to look intently into the hole. "What are you thinking?"

Still squatting, Riley turned to face Sorla. "I'm thinking this one might need a slightly more radical approach."

Sorla frowned. "What sort of radical are we talking about?"

Riley's lips curved and morphed into a cheeky grin. "I'm thinking some fresh mince, or maybe a tin of tuna radical." She put her fingers to her lips in a shushing sign, then crooked her finger for Sorla to come closer. She pointed into the hole.

Sorla squatted carefully to peer inside. At first, all she could see was the black, gaping hole—then a movement in the right-hand corner caught her eye. A pair of green eyes blinked up at her. As her eyes adjusted, she made out a small tabby cat, nursing two small kittens. Her hand flew to her mouth in surprise. She turned to see Riley looking at her with a beautiful smile. Sorla leaned against Riley's shoulder. "Hello, Miss Pusskins. What beautiful babies you have there. What a wonderful discovery you are." She turned to Riley. "How old do you think they are?"

"Their eyes aren't open yet, so I'd say only a week to ten days old, maybe. Mumma puss looks tiny herself, maybe five or six months old. And a bit on the skinny side too."

"Should we pick them up and bring them inside?"

"How about we go see if there's something in the house she can eat, and we bring the food back out here? If you feed her out here for a couple of days, you'll give her time to get used to you. Then see how you go from there."

Sorla stood up stiffly, limping slightly on her right leg. "Okay. I'll be back in a minute." Ten minutes later Sorla returned with two bowls, one of finely diced beef and one of water. As she squatted she noticed that the mother cat had moved slightly and was now lying on a soft brushed-cotton blanket with a red, green, and black Aztec-looking design on it. Sorla smiled and looked at Riley with an eyebrow raised in question. She was met with a dazzling smile and a shrug. "I remembered I had a scrap of blanket in behind the seat of the truck. I thought her majesty might like it."

Sorla put the food down just outside the hole. The cat's nose twitched and hunger overrode her caution as she slowly crept out of the hole to sniff the meat. Sorla held her breath as she stood stock still, watching as the cat, with one eye on them and another on the food, began to eat. Neither party said a word. Sorla looked up with a big grin, only to see Riley sporting a matching smile which reflected the shared moment of joy perfectly. The cat made short work of the meal before retreating back to her nest. The blind kittens snuggled in close and began to suckle, as the mother cat purred and licked the tops of their heads as they fed.

Sorla said, "I think we just got the seal of approval. How about we leave this stall for another day?"

"Good idea."

"You up to helping finish up the tack room? That might see us through to dinner."

"Too easy. After you."

CHAPTER FIVE

Between them they managed to sort five complete working saddle sets that were of a satisfactory standard and fit to be used, with another four sets needing repairs or parts replacing to get them into full working order. Riley looked at the pile before them. "I can help you with a list of things you might like to get and I've got some spare bits and pieces at work that you're welcome to have. It might save you forking out for brand new kit. I'll drop them off sometime so you can have a look and think about it. No obligation either way." She dusted her hands off and looked at the neatly organized tack room. New hooks were installed, locker bins rehinged and cleaned out, bridles hung up, and new saddle mounts made and attached to the walls.

Sorla pushed a stray lock of hair off her forehead. "I can't believe how much we got through this afternoon. Thank you so much for all your help. This would have taken me days. I don't know that dinner is nearly enough to say thank you." Sorla had a big grin on her face as she looked Riley up and down. "I think I also owe you a new shirt. We might've killed that one."

Riley looked down at her shirt. There were very few patches of the original cream colour left to be seen, hiding behind varying shades of dust grey, grease, and big brown smears from the timber. Riley chuckled softly. "Nah, it's all good. It'll wash out. No point wearing a work shirt if you can't get it dirty."

"What say we call it a day? Don't know about you, but I hear a nice cold drink calling my name, and a shower. You're welcome to borrow some of my clothes if you want to freshen up too, before dinner."

"I'd love a shower. Thanks for the offer of clothes, but I've got a spare set in my truck."

"Really?" She couldn't tell whether Sorla was puzzled or amused. "Do you always carry around a fresh set of clothes?"

"Usually. Sometimes, some of the jobs I do, I can get a bit messy. So if I'm seeing more than one customer in a day, I can change between jobs. Just give me a minute." Riley jogged over to the truck, where she snagged a small kit bag from behind the seat. She held it up, smiling. "Right to go." As she walked back to the house, Riley's eyes took in not only its size, but also the unusual design.

"It's big, isn't it? We're splitting it up so one section can be for us, one for guests, and you've already seen the infirmary." Riley nodded. "And there's an entertaining area, a library, and an office. Ed and Claire have one wing, and I have another. I can finish the tour later, if you'd like."

"Okay, that'd be great, thanks."

"I haven't finished unpacking the guest wing yet, so you can use my bathroom. If you just want to follow me?"

They wandered down a corridor, past several doors, until they reached the end where a door stood open. There was small hat-and-coat area set back off the wall, which in turn led through to a large lounge area. The walls were rendered in cool cream, which offset the bare oak beams bisecting the ceilings and walls. There was an old leather couch with a faded purple woollen rug thrown over the back and a beat-up coffee table next to two old single recliner chairs. Scattered on the floor were several unopened boxes.

Opposite the couch was a large fireplace, surrounded by an ornate oak mantelpiece. There were several photo frames on the mantel's shelf and an open, half-emptied box directly underneath on the floor.

One side of Sorla's mouth quirked up in a half grin. "Haven't quite finished unpacking in here either. But the bathroom's in working order. Hang on and I'll fetch you a clean towel." She disappeared around a corner and came back brandishing two thick forest-green towels. "Bathroom's that way, second door on the left. Help yourself to whatever you need in there."

Riley nodded her thanks. She was pleasantly surprised when she opened the door. Given that the rest of the house hadn't been unpacked, the bathroom was something out of a magazine. There was an ornate wrought-iron linen shelf, complete with colour-coordinated sets of towels and washcloths neatly folded and stacked. A deep oval bath that looked big enough to do laps in took up one wall, with a large window above it, overlooking a small garden outside.

But if the bath impressed Riley, the shower blew her away. It was the largest, most decadent shower she had ever seen. It had clear glass panels on two sides with a stainless-steel grab bar built into a bronze-coloured tile wall. Looking up to the ceiling, she spied a square sheet of stainless steel with holes in it that she surmised must be the showerhead.

Excitement bubbled up inside at the thought of stepping into the world's biggest shower. Quickly setting up her clean clothes and toiletries, she stripped and stepped in, feeling childishly giddy. The large showerhead meant that warm water cascaded down her front, back, and sides. Riley stood with eyes closed, a huge grin plastered on her face, savouring the brief moment before quickly washing her hair and turning off the water. In no time at all she was dry and dressed and headed back out to the lounge room.

Sorla saw her walk in with a huge smile on her face. "Better?"

Riley nodded. "Better than better. I think I'm in love with your shower. That is the most amazing thing I've ever seen."

Sorla nodded and grinned back. "I know. It's just the best isn't it? It was the one decadent thing I promised myself when I got out of the service. After years of crawling in mud, with dirt and sand getting in all sorts of unmentionable places, and having two-minute showers, the one thing I always wanted was a deluxe bathroom."

"Well, deluxe is delightful. Thank you."

"You're most welcome. What would you like to drink? I've got wine, white and red, beer, soda, iced water, tequila, or scotch."

"Just a water for the minute, thanks."

Dropping a couple of ice cubes into a tall glass of water, Sorla finished it off with a slice of lemon on the rim. "One water, madame. Make yourself comfy. I won't be long."

❖

Deciding to follow Riley's lead, Sorla left her hair damp from the shower. With the warmth of the night, it wouldn't take long to dry. She'd decided to keep her hair short after she delisted, having grown used to its coolness and ease of care. For a number of years she had prided herself in her longer locks, past her shoulders, but in basic training she got tired of loose strands escaping the ties and getting in her face. She remembered, on one of her precious days off, going into town and having it cut into a stylish bob, just below her ears. Funny, but she'd grown used to it and never really thought of going back to having long hair. She walked down the hallway, running her fingers through her hair and smiling at the memory.

As Sorla stood on the doorway, she snuck a look at Riley, who was looking at the photos on the mantel. She was wearing a long-sleeved white shirt with pearl-press studs and soft blue stonewashed jeans that hugged her form. Her hair, lightly toweled dry, was still damp and tied back up in a loose bun. Sorla wondered what it would be like left out to gently cascade over her shoulders and to run her fingers through the pale lengths.

Riley, still standing at the fireplace, turned as Sorla entered the room, a shy smile on her face. "Feel better?"

Sorla blinked slowly, sporting a grin. "Oh, yeah. It never ceases to amaze me, the restorative powers of a shower."

Riley chuckled quietly. "I don't doubt the magic of that shower at all." Riley put her glass on the mantelpiece and turned back to face Sorla, crooking her finger at her to approach, while walking towards her at the same time, smiling. "You missed a bit."

Sorla was briefly conscious of her legs not working as she watched Riley walk towards her. Her mouth went dry as her voice closed over, suddenly husky. "Did I?"

"Uh-huh." Riley was biting the side of her lip as she reached up to run her fingernail through the part in Sorla's hair, realigning the stray lock that had crossed the division, gently smoothing its path until it once again sat back on the right side. "There you go. All better." Riley blinked briefly before she cleared her throat and stepped back, running slightly trembling fingers through her own hair. "Sorry. You have such beautiful hair, and that one piece was out of line, and it seemed like the right thing to do."

Sorla couldn't help but notice a pink flush stain Riley's cheeks and throat as she turned her back and reached for her glass and seemed to take a moment to compose herself before turning back to Sorla with a raised empty glass. "I think I might be ready for that wine you offered earlier, if that's okay?"

Sorla laughed nervously. Her knees were shaking. "Yes, I think a wine is definitely on the cards. Can I interest you in that tour while we sip?"

"I'd like that very much."

Sorla poured them each a white wine. "Well, you've seen the stables, what say I show you the library and entertaining area, then we can swing by and see if Claire's finished for the day, and end up in the garden? I was thinking maybe a barbecue for dinner, seeing as the night looks to be so lovely. What do you think?"

"That sounds fine."

"All right then, follow me."

The entertainment room was huge, with a games area, some comfortable couches, a pool table, and table-tennis table. There were two music rooms—one a small soundproof room, with a stand-up piano in it, the other a larger music room with a small grand piano and several guitars on stands in the corner, classical and steel, with a handful of seats scattered around the room. Riley stood on the room's threshold with her eyebrows arched high.

Sorla shrugged with a grin. "I know, it's a bit ostentatious, isn't it? But that's the Irish for you. Music, mischief, love, and laughter, with a few star tantrums and arguments chucked in for good measure. Nothing in half measure." Sorla noticed how Riley's eyes went to the guitars in the corner. "Do you play anything?"

Riley shrugged nonchalantly. "I played a bit of guitar when I was younger, but nothing now for years."

"Why not?"

"I don't have a guitar." Sorla looked at her with questioning eyes. "As kids growing up on the circuit, we would sometimes spend nights in different camps. We didn't have much in terms of entertainment, like television, or going to the movies. So some nights we played games, read stories, or would sit around while some of the bigger kids played guitar. Over the years they taught us littler kids bits and pieces."

"Well, you're welcome to borrow one of these, or come on out and play whenever you like."

"Thanks, that's very generous of you."

"Well, as you can see, there's plenty to go around. You're more than welcome. It's a shame to see them sitting around, not getting used."

"Do you play?"

"I play a little piano, enough to get by, but nothing fancy. Claire's the one with the talent. She can make the piano sing. She is something else. And Ed plays a mean blues harp. The two of them together can make a room sweat."

"Sorla's instrument is her fingers. She plays a mighty fine fiddle." They both turned to see Claire leaning with her arms crossed, watching them from the doorway, smiling.

"Ah, you finished for the day too? I was just showing Riley here around the joint."

Claire came over and took a sip from Sorla's wine. "Mm, that's nice. Yep. I've done all I can, or at least all I want to do today. And nice distraction, by the way." Claire turned and winked conspiratorially at Riley. "This one is something else. When we get a bit more settled, we'll put on a music night. You'll come, right?"

Riley could see Sorla was blushing. "I'd love to hear you both."

Claire linked arms with Sorla. "Well, that's settled then. Hey, how did you two get on in the barn?"

Riley sipped her wine and watched as the two friends bounced off each other companionably.

"We got through a heap. And we discovered a stowaway."

Claire stopped in her tracks. "A what?"

"Hidden in one of the stalls is a mother cat with two little kittens."

"Get outta town!"

"Serious. I'll show you tomorrow when I take her out some breakfast if you'd like."

"I can't wait. Oh, hey, would you mind if I tried out a new salad dressing for dinner? I found a great new recipe."

"Sounds fun." Sorla turned to Riley with a lopsided grin. "Our Claire loves nothing better than using us as guinea pigs for her food creations, so you've been warned."

Claire put her hands on her hips in mock indignation. "Hey, be fair. I haven't had many failures, and no one's died."

Sorla handed Claire her glass of wine for another sip as a peace offering. "That's true. There has been no official death."

"Oh-ho, that's it! You are *so* not getting your wine back." And with that, laughing, Claire disappeared into the kitchen, complete with Sorla's glass.

Riley smiled. It was easy being around Sorla and Claire. Their friendship was uplifting and their humour infectious. "What can I do?"

Sorla put a friendly hand on her shoulder. "Absolutely nothing, I owe you dinner, remember?"

"I have a confession to make. I'm not very good at doing nothing. I'd feel much happier if I could help."

"Ah, a sister in kind. Fair enough. All right, how about, while I make up a marinade for the meat, you can get the cutlery and dishes out and set the table?"

Riley nodded slightly and offered a gentle smile of gratitude. "Thank you."

Sorla winked at her. "Come on, let's go and see what charming elements Claire has chosen to inflict upon us."

As they walked into the kitchen Riley's mobile phone started to ring to the tune of "The Devil Went Down to Georgia," which made Sorla grin in surprise. Riley unholstered her phone from her belt. "Will you excuse me for a moment?"

Still grinning at Riley's ringtone choice, Sorla said, "Sure."

Riley walked a few steps off to the side. "Hello, Riley speaking."

Sorla got the meat out of the fridge and started to cut some of the pieces up on a big chopping board.

"Hi, Pauly, what's up?"

Sorla saw Riley stand still, listening to whoever was on the line.

"I see." Riley was standing rigidly, shoulders tensed.

Although Sorla had no intention of eavesdropping, she couldn't help but overhear snippets of the conversation. Something in Riley's body language suggested this was not a *Hey, how you doing?* kind of phone call.

Sorla watched as Riley's head dropped.

"Uh-huh." Riley ran her fingers through her hair. "Can you hold him for another"—she looked at the time on her phone—"twenty minutes?"

Sorla stood with an empty bowl in front of her on the bench, all pretence of being busy and getting the meat in the marinade long forgotten.

Sorla heard Riley sigh ever so faintly. Riley hung up and took a moment to gather her thoughts before slowly turning around and walking towards Sorla and Claire at the bench. She held up the phone briefly. "I'm sorry. I'm going to have to offer my apologies for dinner."

Sorla wiped her hands on the tea towel. "Is everything all right?"

Claire backed off to the sink, to wash lettuce.

Riley avoided Sorla's gaze as she put the phone back into her holster. "Yeah. But I'm afraid I'm going to have to go."

Sorla took a step forward, placing her hand gently on Riley's arm and trying to catch her eyes. "You sure you're okay?"

Riley took in a steadying breath, squared her shoulders, and forced a half grin. "Yeah, it's okay. That was a friend of George's to say he needs a bit of a hand, that's all. I'm terribly sorry for running out on you like this." Riley pulled the keys out of her back pocket.

"That's okay. We can do it another time. Come on, I'll walk you to your truck."

"You don't have to do that."

"I know. But I'd like to." Sorla held the door open for Riley before stepping out into the evening. They walked the first few steps in silence before Sorla cleared her throat. "I want to thank you for everything today. We got so much done and the time simply disappeared. I had a great day. Thank you."

"It should be me, thanking you. I really enjoyed today."

They arrived at the truck. Sorla held the door open while Riley stepped up and inside. She shut the door and pulled herself up onto the running boards so she could look into the driver's window. "You have a perverse sense of enjoyment, Ms. Johnson, if you call being worked to the bone fun, but whatever your quirks, I still owe you dinner. What say I call you during the week and we set up another time?"

Riley kicked the engine over. She turned and smiled shyly. "I'd like that."

As Sorla stepped off the boards, she called out. "Hey, maybe we can combine it with a music night."

"Sounds great."

"All right, I'll be in touch. Thanks again for today."

"Thank you too. See you."

Sorla watched the dust kick up in the red glowing spill of the truck's tail lights as Riley drove away. Standing in the dark, she became aware of how the mood of the evening had completely turned, now Riley had gone. She sighed and made her way back to the house. As she stepped into the kitchen, Claire was chopping up some capsicum into fine slivers. "Everything okay?"

Sorla went back around to the bench and finished mixing up the ingredients for the marinade. "I think so. Something about somebody getting in a spot and needing a hand, so she had to go."

"That's a shame."

Sorla stirred the mix. "Yeah."

"She seems really nice."

Sorla nodded.

"She certainly is gorgeous."

"Mm."

"Well, I don't know about you, but I'm hoping we haven't scared her off. She seems like a really interesting person to get to know."

"Uh-huh." Sorla slid the meat into the bowl and folded it into the marinade mix.

Claire went to the fridge and poured them each a fresh glass of wine. "You two seemed to have hit it off pretty well."

"Mm." Sorla put clear plastic over the top to let the flavours settle in. She took a sip of wine and nearly choked as she cottoned on to what Claire was hedging at. "What?"

"I just said, you both hit it off pretty well. Looks like you had a good day."

"I, no…yes, I had a good day, but it was just that, a good day with an interesting person."

"Uh-huh." Claire had a big smile on her face.

Sorla, on the other hand, was frowning. "What?"

"Nothing."

Sorla picked up the tea towel from the bench and threw it at Claire "Get outta here, Hanson!" The tea towel flew in midair before losing altitude and sinking harmlessly to the floor as Claire's giggling back made its way outside to the garden.

Riley pulled up outside The Galloping Grape's front door and she walked in. The familiar yeasty smell of beer assaulted her senses as she spied the pub's owner and strolled over. "Hey, Pauly."

"Hey, kid. Sorry to do this to you."

"It's no worries. Where is he?" Riley grimaced at the sound of smashing glass and swearing coming from the visitors' lounge. "Never mind. I think I've found him. You know where I am. Send me the bill."

Riley found George sitting on the floor next to an upturned chair with broken glass all around him. She walked over and righted the chair, moving it back to its rightful place. She squatted down next to a mumbling and cussing George. "Come on, George, time to go." She put one arm around his shoulder and reached around with the other to grab his trouser belt. Bending her knees, she flexed her thighs, straightened, and hauled him upright.

Pauly came in with a broom and stood beside her. "You gonna be all right?"

"Yep. I got this. Sorry about tonight, Pauly."

"I'm sorry too. You shouldn't have to deal with this."

"Ain't nobody else gonna do it. It's just the way it is. Thanks for calling. I'll catch you later. And don't forget to send me the bill."

Pauly waved dismissively. "Don't worry about it. You sure you're okay?"

"It's all good. G'night, Pauly. Come on, George, time to ride home."

George's head lolled drunkenly on his chest. "Don't wanna fuckin' go home."

Riley manoeuvred him out the door and across the carpark to where the truck was. "I know, but you've outstayed your welcome here tonight, partner. Come on, *hup*, inside you go." Riley lifted and shoved him into the truck before shutting the door and locking it.

She climbed in and wound the window down. The smell coming off George was enough to make her head spin. She turned the engine over and pointed the truck to home.

George had collapsed on the bench seat and was snoring loudly. Riley sighed as she watched the white painted lines tick by under the glare of the truck's headlights. "You have a crappy sense of timing, George." George burped in his sleep. Riley winced at the onslaught of rancid booze. "Thanks." Within minutes, Riley had pulled into their driveway. She cut the engine and got out to unlock the house before coming back to the truck. She opened the door, stood on the running board, and reached in, hauling George upright. She patted him on his face. "Come on, old man. We're home. Open up your eyes and give me a hand here, will you?" George's eyes didn't open, but he grunted in assent.

Riley managed to wrestle him out of the truck and into the house.

"You want to use the bathroom before going to bed?" George grunted. "Okay, this way." She led him down the hall to the toilet. "Do you need a hand, or are you all right?"

"I know how to take a fuckin' piss." George swayed from side to side as he unzipped his pants.

"Righto. Mind you get it in the bowl then and not all over the floor please."

"Piss off."

Riley leaned against the doorway and waited for him to finish. Soon enough she heard the zip, signalling he'd finished. "You want to wash your hands?" George turned and pushed his way past her as he put his hands out against the hall walls to steady his drunken weave. "I guess not then." Riley trailed behind him as he stumbled into his bedroom. Reaching the bed, he half sat, half fell down onto the mattress. Riley bent down and started to unlace his boots.

"Where'd the hell did you get to today?" he slurred.

"I did a delivery round this morning, then I helped out for a while at Cherry Hill."

"Trying to get in good with the rich Reardon, are you? Don't be thinking you're too good for your roots, huh?"

"No. They needed a hand and I was happy to give it."

"Did they pay you for your work?"

"No. I wouldn't take it. I was happy to help."

"Ya got a dumb, soft heart, like your mother."

"My time, my choice, George." Riley put his boots under the end of the bed. "Can I get you anything?"

"Another drink."

"I think you've had enough for one night. There's water by your bed if you want it."

"Don't want your stinking water, I wanna drink!" George picked up the glass and hurled it straight at her head. Riley saw it coming and managed to duck in time, hearing the glass smash against the wall behind her head and fall to the floor.

"Goodnight, George." Riley went out to the kitchen and put the kettle on to make a cup of tea, figuring by the time she'd finished the tea, he'd be snoring his head off and she could go in and clean the glass up. Sitting at the old kitchen table, Riley reflected on the day. It had been a good day. Riley knew a lot of people but didn't really have many friends. There wasn't someone she could drop in to see, or ring up and ask to the movies. Seeing Claire and Sorla together made her wish she did. Seeing the ease that they shared set off a kernel of yearning and hunger that she didn't know was there. She didn't have time for friends, or relationships for that matter. The town was too small, and George, well, George was just George.

But it had been a good day. She hadn't lied earlier when she said to Sorla she'd had an enjoyable day. In fact, it had been one of the nicest days in a long time. Cherry Hill was a beautiful place and it felt good to be able to help out. There was next week to look forward to as well, with another shot at dinner. Hopefully George wouldn't wreck this one. *Maybe I can word Pauly up and see if he can put him up in one of the rooms out back for the night.* The thought of having another evening cut short at Cherry Hill bothered Riley, although she couldn't quite put a finger on it as to why.

❖

Full from dinner, Sorla leaned back into the chair, staring sightlessly off into the dark distance, her fingers twirling the stem of the wine glass back and forth as she thought back to the afternoon spent with Riley. The day had been such an enjoyable one, getting to know Riley and working together. She had no hesitation in admitting to herself that Riley was a most captivating woman. When promise of her company had been severed with the phone call it left a huge ball of disappointment in its wake at dinnertime that she just couldn't seem to shake. Maybe the phone call was an excuse not to stay. Riley was pretty keen to leave after she hung up. Sorla drained the last mouthful from her glass. Stupid how a day could go from great to arse-up in a matter of minutes.

In self-digust, Sorla pushed herself upright and started to gather the dirty dishes together.

Ed appeared brandishing a fresh bottle of wine, Claire in his wake. Ed looked at them both. "Anyone for a top-up?"

Sorla handed her glass over. "Sure. Ta."

"Claire?"

Claire sat down and placed her hand over the top of her glass.

"No, thanks. If I'm going to stay on a horse tomorrow, I'm going to need a clear head. Been a while since I was that far off the ground."

"You'll be all right, love. It's like riding a bike."

Claire chuckled. "Well, we'll soon find out." Claire passed Sorla her empty plate. "What's Riley's story? Does she have a girlfriend? Boyfriend?"

Sorla started stacking the plates and cutlery up. "How the hell should I know? Why don't you ask her yourself, seeing as you're so damn interested?" She pushed the chair out sharply and carried the plates inside.

She stacked the dishes to one side of the sink and leaned on the counter, closing her eyes. She took in a deep breath before blowing it out in a disgusted rush of air. *What the hell was that about? You need to get your sorry arse out there and apologize, Reardon.* With a final sigh, Sorla pushed off the bench and headed back outside. She plonked back down into her chair and grabbed her wine glass, throwing down a quick mouthful. Placing the glass back on the table, she slowly turned the stem with her thumb and first finger and watched as the goblet rotated to the push and pull of her fingers.

Claire reached out and put her hand over Sorla's. "Sorry, babe. Didn't mean to be such a nosy bugger."

Sorla shook her head and looked up to her two best friends. "No. Don't be. It's my fault. I didn't mean to jump down your throat. I'm the one who needs to apologize."

Ed looked at her. "So, why did you?"

Sorla shrugged and focused on the glass. "Just tired, I guess. It's been a big day."

"Stop avoiding the question."

"I'm not."

Ed stared her down. "Yes, you are."

"Oh, for God's sake, I've only just met her. How would I know?"

"Still avoiding."

Sorla looked up at him, furious. "This is crap."

"Waiting…"

"All right! It doesn't matter which team she's on, I'm not interested."

Ed poked a little harder. "Why not?"

"Because I'm just not."

"Bullshit. That woman is hot. Last time I looked, that bomb took your leg off, not your brain, Fender. What's not to be interested in?"

Sorla thumped the table as tears filled her eyes. "Exactly! And once she finds out I'm a one-legged fucked-up gimp, she's not gonna want to have a bar of me. What person would? So do me a favour and let it go, will you?"

Ed handed her a serviette. "Here, wipe your mouth."

Sorla looked him in the eye. There was a growling edge to her voice. "What for?"

"'Cause there's an awful lot of bullshit coming out of it and it's dribbling down your chin."

Claire leaned over and put a warning hand on Ed's thigh. "Honey…"

Ed took no notice. "You're full of shit, Fender. Mostly chickenshit, by the looks."

Claire turned to her husband. "Ed, let it go."

Sorla pushed her chair back and folded her arms. "No, Claire, let him finish, he's obviously worked it all out. Go ahead, Dr. Freud, what's my problem?"

"You're scared."

"Scared? Now who's full of shit? Why the hell would I be scared?"

Ed's voice grew soft. "You tell me."

Sorla closed her eyes. The rage built inside until it hit her midchest, shattered, and melted into pain, forming tears which flooded and escaped, to run freely down her face. A sob broke free of her lips and her head dropped into her hands as her shoulders shook with rivers of released emotion.

Ed quietly stood up and came around the table and knelt in front of her. He put his hands on her shoulders. "Fender, when someone's interested in you, it's for more than just the outside packaging. It's for the whole box and dice. You're a beautiful woman, Sorla, and always will be, even with your scars. Anyone with half a brain in their head can see that as plain as day. Stop hiding behind your scars. Just be you. If someone's interested in you, it's because of who you are. You can't make that decision for them, only they can. They'll either like you, or they won't, but don't use your leg as an excuse not to try." Ed gently pulled Sorla's head down to his shoulder and let her have her tears.

Sorla raised her head, sniffling, and punched Ed lightly in the shoulder. "You're an arsehole."

Ed grinned and kissed her on the forehead. "Yes, but I'm *your* arsehole and you're stuck with me. Here, now dry your face, you're getting my shirt all wet." Claire quietly appeared with some tissues. Ed stood up and winked at Claire before quietly disappearing back to the kitchen with another load of bowls to be washed.

Claire brought a chair over and sat in front of her friend. Gently, she reached out and brushed some hair out of Sorla's eyes, tucking it behind her ear. "You've been hanging on to that for a while." Sorla shrugged. "Well, we knew you'd have to face it one day. That there would come a time when you might meet someone who was interesting."

"Give me a break, I've only just met her. I don't even know her."

"True, but your mind has acknowledged that she could be a good person to be interested in."

"She seems nice."

"And you had a lovely day."

Sorla shrugged one shoulder.

"And you got to thinking…and then you scared the crap out of yourself."

Sorla sniffed.

"What are you scared of, Sor? That she'll take one look and run away?"

Sorla closed her eyes. She'd talked about this with her counsellor months before she moved to Cherry Hill. Actually, he talked a lot and she just listened. She knew no one would want to look at her, so it didn't matter what he'd said, she just went along with his patter and advice, hoping to get out of the office and away from his incessant noise.

When Riley looked at her this afternoon, walked towards her and straightened the part in her hair, she was too petrified to move. She caught a glimmer of shy interest there and she wasn't sure if her fragile ego could withstand the look of disgust on Riley's face if she knew what she looked like underneath. Even now, she still had the odd piece of embedded shrapnel that would work its way to the surface before slicing through her skin to come out. She was, quite simply, hideous. In a voice hoarse and strangled by a constricted throat, Sorla whispered, "I can't ask anyone to love me when I don't even like myself."

Claire pulled her friend into her arms and rocked her. "Oh,

sweetheart. You've come such a long way. I know there's still a journey to go, but you have to take each day as it comes, love. You'll have good days and bad, and sometimes, like today, you might see a window of opportunity. Just take one step at a time. Get to know Riley. If nothing happens, then that's fine. I suspect, if nothing else, she'll be a handy friend to have. Hey, look on the bright side, if you stay in her good books, you might be able to get mates-rates discounts at the store, huh?"

Sorla dried her face and took a cleansing breath. Claire was right. One day at a time. "Yeah, and she has good taste in hats."

Claire chuckled and hugged her friend before standing up. "That she does, my friend, that she does. It's getting a bit cool out. Do you want to move inside?"

Sorla shook her head. "I might stay out here for a bit and finish my glass."

"All right." Claire kissed her friend on the top of the head. "Well, I'll take the last of these things in and see you in the morning. Try and get some sleep, huh?" She headed back inside.

Sorla stared blindly into the night, listening to the last of the magpies' warbling evening song in the peppermint gums behind the house. Her thoughts turned inwards, reflecting on what her friends had said. She tucked her knees up and rested her cheek on them. In her mind, she acknowledged the wisdom of her friends' words, but her heart knew the truth. Things would never be the same again. And she sure as hell didn't want anyone's pity.

CHAPTER SIX

The day dawned bright and hot. Sorla had managed to catch a few hours' sleep on the couch. Now that she was up, she felt worse than she had before she went to bed. She'd finished her glass of wine and retired back to her own wing with a few whisky chasers. She had a shower and made her way out to the kitchen, where Ed and Claire were up and making breakfast. She quietly sat down at the table and poured herself a cup of coffee. She closed her eyes and sipped, willing the jackhammer at the base of her skull to lie down and die and leave her in peace.

Sorla struggled through the haze. It had been a tough year, from the accident to now. It had been a horror stretch for all of them as she'd struggled to recover and get back to some degree of normality. She tried not to dwell on what-ifs too much any more, preferring to just get on with things, doing whatever she was told, almost like a robot. But while her body slowly recovered and adjusted, her spirit was still fragile. She didn't talk much about it. The few times she did, like last night, then and only then did she crack, but it came at a cost—usually in the form of insomnia or a hangover.

Coming back to Cherry Hill had been a bright spot. She was busy, she had purpose, and she worked hard, which helped her to start sleeping again. It was the happiest and most relaxed she'd been since they'd all come home. She took a deep breath and pushed the jackhammer to the back of her awareness. They had a busy day ahead with the first three cattle shipments arriving. All hands would be needed on deck.

Ed put a plate of scrambled eggs, with some of Claire's sliced bread, in front of her. Sorla looked up at him and he patted her on the shoulder. "You've got a big day ahead of you and your body's gonna need the fuel."

Sorla nodded. She knew he was right. "Thanks."

"No probs. I'm gonna clean up, then head out and make sure everything's ready. I'll see you guys out there." He kissed Claire on the cheek before heading off.

Claire sat down next to Sorla and poured herself a coffee. "Did you get much sleep?"

Sorla grimaced. "A little."

"So, have you thought how we're going to do this?"

"Once we offload them, I thought I might start off on the bay mare and see how it goes from there. What about you?"

"Ed thought the grey looked quiet enough. Be the first time on a horse in a long time, for both of us. If I fall off, just walk over the top of me and pick me up on the way back, will you?"

"Ditto for me."

Claire put her hand over Sorla's arm. "You gonna be okay?"

Sorla put her fork down. She'd managed most of the plate but knew if she had any more she'd be pushing to keep it down. "Yeah. All good."

"If you're not going to eat any more of that, your new cat might like some eggs for breakfast."

Sorla's head lifted a little. "She might at that. I'll just clean up and take it over. Wanna come see?"

"Love to."

❖

Half an hour later, on horseback, they joined Ed at the cattle yards. The first delivery was due within the hour. In total, they were expecting roughly one hundred and fifty head to be delivered by the end of the day. The steers and heifers would be kept in the two adjoining fields north of the yards. The last delivery, of cows and calves, would spend the first couple of days in the paddocks next to the yards in order to settle in, then the plan was to move them out midweek to the eastern flank where there was plenty of feed and a running creek feeding into three dams.

Ed was talking to two locals who had come in to help for the day when he saw the girls approach and waved. He dusted his hands on his pants and came over. "Well look at you two. Don't you look like regular cowgirls. How do you both feel?"

Claire leaned forward and stroked the grey's neck. "So far so good, but then we've only walked them a little way. But it feels good."

"Fender?"

"Mm, okay. Feels a bit odd, but okay. It'll be fine."

"Okay, well, if either of you need a break, the quad's over there, under the lean-to, ready to go if you need it."

Claire smiled. "Thanks."

Sorla sat in the saddle with her hands resting on the horn watching the two local men talking and checking over their horses in preparation for the day's work ahead of them. "It's Don and Perry, isn't it?"

Ed followed Sorla's line of sight and nodded. "Yep. Seem like solid fellas. I asked around town midweek and heard good reports about both of them. If they work out okay, I suspect they'd be happy to stay on. Don worked for your dad about ten years ago, so he's got a bit of a handle on the place, and Perry's got a young family and could do with the regular work. I think they'd both appreciate a steady job."

Sorla nodded in thought. "Well, let's see how they go over the next few days, and if you think they'll be okay, then we can sit down and have a chat and work out how we might like to go about it."

"Sounds fair. We can toss some ideas about after dinner tonight if you like."

Their conversation was interrupted by Don's wolf whistle. Turning to see what he was pointing at, Sorla spotted the dust being kicked up from the first truck coming down the road. Ed patted her on the thigh and flashed her an enormous grin. "Show time, mate. Let the fun begin."

❖

"Can you get blisters on your butt?" Claire groaned and gently rubbed her bottom before putting the small of her hands into her back and stretching.

Ed laughed. "I can have a look later if you'd like. Here, let me take that." He gently took the saddle from Claire's arms and carried it into the tack room.

"I'm so pleased I don't have to go to work until later in the week. I don't think I could do it any earlier. I'm gonna go and sit in a bath of ice."

Sorla chuckled as she brushed her mare down. "That sounds a bit dramatic."

Claire stiffly gathered up the rest of the tack. "Not really. If one of you two was a medic, I'd be begging you for a spinal block about now."

Sorla put her arm around her friend's shoulder. "You're right. Ice is a much softer option."

"As soon as I get the energy, I am so gonna smack you, Reardon."

"Uh-huh. And when might that be, Hanson?"

"I figure I might come good by…Tuesday?" Laughing, they joined Ed and walked back to the house. As they approached the kitchen door, they noticed a box on the doorstep.

Ed picked up the box. "Was either of you expecting a delivery?"

Both shook their heads. Ed carried the box inside and laid it on the table. He pulled a pocket knife from his belt, slit the tape holding the box shut, and opened the lid. He reached inside and pulled out a note, handing it to Sorla to read out loud.

> *Thanks again for a great day yesterday, I had a really nice time. Thought you all might like a little something to celebrate the beginning of your dreams coming true. May you all have many happy horse and cattle years ahead of you.*
> *Riley Johnson*
> *PS: And some pet milk for Miss Pusskins.*

Sorla reached into the box and pulled out a small insulated food cooler bag. Unzipping the top, she spied a bottle of champagne, a punnet of strawberries, a round of Camembert cheese, a box of fancy wafers, and two cartons of cat milk. Claire bumped Sorla with her hip and wiggled the bottle of champagne in her hand. "Looks like hats aren't the only thing Riley has good taste in."

Ed freed the bottle from Claire's fingers. "What say I put this in the freezer to chill while we all go off and soak our weary bones in a nice hot bath? By the time we get out, it should be perfect." Ed grabbed Claire's hand. "Come on, honey, let's go and check out those blisters."

Sorla blinked, looking alternatively between the note and the bag containing the goodies, wondering when Riley would have dropped it off. She put one of the milk cartons, along with the cheese and strawberries, into the fridge before making her way back to her wing. She put the note on the counter, grabbed a beer from the fridge, and headed into the bathroom.

Lying in the bath, sipping her cold beer, she reflected on the day. She ached from head to toe and, if she was honest, didn't think Claire's idea of sitting in ice was a bad thing. She chuckled as she took another sip. *But I'm not going to tell her that.* The cattle had all arrived pretty much as planned. The two local men were a great help and they all worked well as a team. Both men had agreed to come back and help out with the next shipment due on Monday and for the two shipments later in the month. By then, Sorla figured she and Ed would have worked out if they would be suitable enough to offer them jobs.

Lying back in the bath she thought about the box of goodies Riley had dropped off. It was a lovely surprise. Surprise being the operative word. She should ring and thank her. Damn. She didn't have her number. *I know, I'll ring the store.* She could leave a message, or maybe she'd get lucky and there'd be an after-hours contact number on the machine.

She reached out of the bath and snagged her jeans, pulling out the phone from the pocket. She dialled the number for the Stock and Station and lay back, resting her head on the edge of the bath. As the phone rang she sipped on the beer, waiting for the machine message to kick in. She closed her eyes, rolling a mouthful of the hops-infused liquid around her mouth, savouring the decadence of both beer and bath.

❖

Closing the orders book, Riley reached for the ringing phone. "Hello, Johnson's Stock and Station. Can I help you?" Riley heard splashing noises in the background of the call. "Hello? Are you okay?"

"Hi." Cough. "Sorry." Cough. "It's Sorla Reardon." Cough.

Riley chuckled softly. "Hello. Are you all right?"

"Ahem." Cough. "Yes, sorry, you caught me by surprise."

"Surprise?"

"Yeah. What are you doing working on a Saturday night?"

"George is out with some friends. I'm just filling in time until he's ready to be picked up. Why did I surprise you? How come you rang if you didn't think I'd be here?"

"I wanted to thank you for the box of goodies you left us today, but I only had the store number—I didn't think to get yours the other night. I expected the answering machine. When you answered the phone, I got a surprise."

Riley smirked "Ah, I see."

"But now I have you, thank you. That was a really lovely and thoughtful gift. It was a beautiful surprise to have at the end of a big day."

Riley couldn't help the smile. Sorla liked the gift box. "You're welcome. How did it all go?"

"Really well. The trucks came pretty much on schedule and we had time in between shipments to put the cattle in their own settling paddocks."

"And the horses? How were they?"

"They were great. Ed's brother was as good as his word. They were all even tempered and steady, solid workers from the get go. Made life a lot easier, let me tell you. I was a bit worried at first, as I didn't know how they'd go, but it ended up all turning out just fine. Claire has gone off to sit in a bath of ice to numb the pain."

Riley's fingers trailed a scarline across the wooden counter's benchtop. "What about you?"

"I am sitting in a nice hot bath, sipping a very cold beer. It feels great, but I'm not sure if I'm going to be able to drag myself out. I seem to have melted, now that I'm in."

Riley could hear the playful note in Sorla's voice. "Perhaps we need to build you a hoist over the bath, so you can lower yourself in and out after a big day in the saddle."

"Hm, that has some merit. I like that idea a lot. What about you, what did you get up to today?"

"Bit of housework in the morning, then after lunch, I went out and worked with some horses over at Laverty's, on the east side of town."

"I heard some good things about you today."

"Oh?" Riley's fingers stopped still.

"Mm. I asked two of the men we've got helping us who they could recommend to help us break in our new horses. They gave us a couple of names, but both said you were the best around."

Riley was having trouble concentrating as she heard the movement of water and was desperately trying to turn off the images of Sorla naked in her head so she could concentrate on what Sorla was saying. "That was very nice of them."

"In fact, they went on to say that while the other people were good, if it was their animal, they would only want you. They reckon you can talk to horses. Is that true?"

She scrunched her nose up. "You make me sound like Dr. Dolittle."

"So. Is it?"

"I think we both know the answer to that. No, I don't talk to them."

"So what's your magic, lady?"

"It's more of a…cooperation."

"Cooperation?"

Her fingers worked the scratched surface lines again. "We work towards an understanding of each other."

"I see. And have you ever had any that you couldn't *cooperate* with?"

"No, not yet. But I guess there will be some, somewhere down the track, who might need someone different than me to work with them."

"That stands to reason."

Riley heard a bit more splashing and the sound of water dripping.

"Hang on a minute, the water's getting a bit cold. I'm just going to hop out…"

A delightful image of Sorla naked, rising from the bath, water streaming down her body, flashed before her eyes, only to be sharply dispelled as the phone slipped from suddenly numb fingers and fell loudly onto the countertop, to skid off the side and crash to the floor. Riley quickly scrambled to pick the handset up, embarrassed to find her voice was quite suddenly gravelly. "Sorry."

"What happened?"

"I, ah, dropped the phone. Sorry." Riley cleared her throat with embarrassment. "You were saying?"

"I was wondering, when you come over later in the week for dinner, if we could have a talk about the horses here. I would love to hear your thoughts on them."

Riley rubbed her hand over her face, grimacing at her teenage reaction to the mental images of Sorla standing up out of the bath. "Thoughts. Ah, yeah, sure, I can do that. No problems."

"What night would suit you for dinner this week?"

Riley took a deep breath for concentration. "Well, the rest of your order should be here by the end of the week. What say we make it Friday? I can deliver the rest of the order and see the horses at the same time."

"What time do you think you can make it?"

"I guess it'll depend a bit on how many deliveries I've got. Sometimes Fridays are busy and other weeks they're light on."

"Maybe, if it's a light day, do you think you could come the same time as before, and we can make a day of it? We can go for a ride, check on the cattle, and I can show off some more of the place if you'd like."

"I'd like that a lot. How about I see how the week is shaping up and get back to you with a more definite time a little closer to the day?"

"That, my friend, sounds like a plan. You're on."

Riley's face burst into a grin and her chest swelled. Her cheeks were flushed and warm from Sorla calling her a friend. "I had better let you go before you catch a cold."

"Not to mention that I have some lovely champagne chilling as we speak. Thank you again. That was a lovely thought."

"You're very welcome. I hope you all enjoy it. You certainly deserve it, after such a big day."

"It'll be the perfect way to wind down. We'll toast a celebration to new beginnings. Have a great week and I'll talk to you in a couple of days."

"You too. 'Night, Sorla."

"'Night, Riley."

It was a bit after eleven when Riley pulled into the parking lot of The Galloping Grape. Strolling inside she spotted George hunched over a glass at the bar, with Pauly on the opposite side, wiping down the bench top.

"Hey, kid."

"Evening, Pauly. How's your night been?"

"Pretty steady. How 'bout you?"

"Much the same. How's our friend here been? Has he been better behaved tonight?"

"Yup. No problems at all. Regular lamb, aren't you, George?"

George grunted. Riley could see he was almost asleep in his glass. "Can I ask a favour?"

"Sure, kid, anything for you. What do you need?"

"Do you think you could put George up in one of the rooms out back next Friday night?"

"Sure. No trouble at all. You goin' away?"

"No. Just out for dinner with some friends."

"I'd be happy to, love. God knows you could do with the break."

"Thanks, I really appreciate it. I'll come by first thing Saturday and pick him up."

"He don't strike me as the early morning type. Why don't you sleep in yourself? I'll stick him in fourteen, out the back. You just collect him when you're ready."

"Thanks again, Pauly. I owe you."

"Honey, you don't owe me a thing. I'm just lookin' after my best customer."

"All the same, put it on the tab."

"No problems, kid."

Riley stood up and uncurled George's hand from the glass. "Hey, George. The bar's closing. Time to head home."

George looked up and smiled. "Is it time already?"

"Uh-huh. Would you like a lift?"

"How could I refuse such a pretty face?"

Riley rolled her eyes. "Come on then."

Pauly took the glass away. "'Night, George."

George grunted as Riley persuaded him to stand and turn towards the door.

"'Night, Pauly. Thanks again."

"'Night, kid. Take it easy."

CHAPTER SEVEN

D o you want me to make you some breakfast before I go?" Riley opened one of the curtains in George's room in order to open up a window. The room held the heavy odour reminiscent of George's night at the bar and would benefit from some fresh air flowing through. She turned around to see his eyes scrunched up and his face turned into the pillow. She decided to leave the rest of the curtains drawn.

"No."

"Okay, well, I've left your meds on the kitchen table. Try and have something to eat with them."

"Go away."

"That's my plan. Coffee's here on the bedside table."

"Go!"

"I'll be at the shop if you need anything. I'll see you later." Riley turned and headed towards the door. A thump on her back followed by a sharp, searing heat ignited the nerve endings along her ribs, spilling down onto her hip. Riley gasped as she stumbled against the door frame. A mug landed on the floor at her feet. The coffee she had made George. She half turned her head to look at him, but his head had hit the pillow and he was fast asleep. She took a moment or two to take some deep breaths to steady herself before stripping off the scalding shirt and pants. She went to the bathroom and turned the shower on and stepped in, still wearing her underwear. The water was cold but was starting to take the worst of the stinging heat out. She leaned forward with her hands against the glass partition, trying valiantly to stop shaking.

He'd been good lately. She'd let her guard down. Nothing like a reminder, served with milk and sugar. After a few more minutes she turned the shower off. Trembling with the cold, she stripped off her underwear and dried herself gingerly. She looked in the mirror and saw that where the coffee had landed was red but not blistered, so no harm done. There was a nice bruise where the mug had caught her ribs which was starting to colour and spread. She sighed and shook her head. After putting her dirty clothes in a bucket to soak in the laundry, she donned fresh clothes and headed out the door.

Her first stop was the library. There were a few things she wanted to look up and learn a bit more about, and the library was only open for a couple of hours on the weekend.

❖

Sorla threw her hat on the rack hanging near the kitchen door. "Well, that's the last of them until the end of the month. Hope there's plenty of beer in the fridge. Damn, did I swallow some dust today!"

Ed chuckled as he walked past her. "That's because you spent most of the day riding around flapping your gums." He held his hand up like a puppet and mimed, talking in a falsetto voice. "Oooo, who's a pretty cow, what a sturdy looking lad you are, come on little one, keep up with Mumma, blah, blah, blah…"

Sorla had pulled out three beers from the fridge. She handed one to Claire and held two in her hand. "Well then, Mr. Strong-and-silent-type, you won't be needing your beer, seeing as you were so quiet today and didn't get any dust in your gob, so I'll have yours for you instead." Sorla grinned cheekily at him.

"Nice try, Fender. Come on, hand it over." Ed held his arm outstretched to receive the beer.

Sorla opened both bottles and took a sip from each. "Nope, all mine."

Ed growled at her. "Fender."

Sorla took another sip from each and dared him to come get her. "Nuh."

Ed barked out a laugh. "That's it, you are so dead, Reardon. Give me that beer!" Laughing, he launched off the edge of the counter and made a grab for the beer, but Sorla dodged his hand and ran into the lounge room, catching her foot on the edge of the couch. She managed to twist midair, holding the bottles aloft, to land sprawled out along its length. "Oof!"

Ed came barrelling after her. "Hey, you okay?"

"Yup, caught my damn foot on the corner. Hey, will you look at that." Sorla grinned. "Didn't spill a drop."

"Just as well." Ed snatched one of the bottles and took a deep swig. "Ah, now that's the perfect way to end the day."

Claire came over and nudged Sorla's thigh. "Shove over, sister, before I fall on top of you. I'm too tired to be graceful."

Sorla swivelled around and sat upright just as Claire flopped, as promised, onto the couch. She threw her feet up onto the coffee table and laid her head back. "How many years do you have to ride before you get callouses on your rear end?"

Sorla and Ed grinned at each other over the top of Claire's head. Ed winked at her. "Oh, lots."

Sorla grinned. "Uh-huh, heaps."

Claire whimpered.

They sat in companionable silence, sipping their beers. Ed broke the peace. "How 'bout you, Fender. How'd you pull up?"

"Okay. Probably feel it more tomorrow."

Claire raised her head. "How's the stump feel?"

Sorla grimaced. "Bit raw. It rubbed a bit more today, in the heat."

"Did you try using that extra cotton sock liner?"

"Yeah, it helped a bit. I guess I just have to keep on experimenting."

"Okay. Give me a yell if you want me to have a look at it."

Sorla sighed quietly. "Thanks."

Claire patted her thigh. "No biggie."

Ed slid in to the seat on the other side of Sorla and added his feet to the table surface. "Today was a good day."

Sorla raised her glass. "I'll drink to that." Ed clinked his bottle with hers. "Hope we get some rain soon though. The feed in the paddocks is starting to burn off in this heat. Maybe we should buy some feed in for the cattle, in case the rain's a way off."

Ed scratched his chin in thought. "Might not be a bad idea. We could store it at the back of the stables until I get the side shed fixed up."

"Too easy," Claire agreed. "Hey, does Riley sell bulk hay?" Claire turned to Sorla, who was peeling the label off the beer bottle.

"I don't know. I s'pose so. I'll ask her when she comes out on Friday."

"Have you thought about what you want for dinner on Friday? I can always pick up anything you want on the way home from work."

"Haven't got that far yet. Maybe have another shot at a barbecue if the weather's nice?"

Ed sat up. "Hey, if we do, can you make your famous chicken wings? You know, the ones with the chilli sauce?"

Sorla laughed. "You are such a sucker for those. We haven't had them in a while. Might be nice. Yeah, okay. Wings coming up."

❖

Sorla sat on the edge of her bed in a T-shirt and underpants. She'd had a bath and had just made her way into the bedroom when she heard a knock on the door. "I'm in the bedroom."

Claire stuck her head around the corner of the door. "Just came to see if you fancied anything in particular for dinner." She walked over and sat on the bed next to Sorla.

Sorla shook her head. "I'm happy with whatever's going."

Claire noticed Sorla had the towel covering her legs. She nodded in their direction. "How are they?"

Her jaw was clenched tightly with the muscles bunching and twitching at the sides of her face. She sighed and shook her head. "Cranky."

"What say you scoot up on the bed and let me take a look, huh?" Sorla used her arms to pull herself up the bed. She lay back and put her arm over her eyes and felt Claire move to the side of the bed and gently pull the towel down. She knew what Claire would find. On the left, her good leg was swollen, making the lines of scars stand out in bright pink contrast against the surrounding tight white skin.

Her right leg ended two inches below her knee. The stump's end was an angry red with raw patches of skin marring its surface in several places. The knee was swollen. There was a place, about two inches above the knee, where shrapnel underneath the skin was stretching the skin's surface and trying to get out. In the shower she'd gingerly run a finger over it and could feel a sharp corner.

Her injuries were not unlike most IED blast victims' who sustained wounds from the explosive devices used in Iraq. Sorla'd survived—two other personnel who were with her on the day of the blast didn't. Her legs had copped the worst of the blast, but she'd also sustained shrapnel wounds up her torso, leaving a legacy of intersecting scars currently hidden by her T-shirt.

Claire rested her hand on Sorla's thigh. "How's the nerves?"

Sorla's jaw was still tightly clenched. Some days the nerve endings felt like lots of bee stings, annoying, but tolerable. Other days it could be sharp darts of stabbing pain. Today was definitely one of the latter. She shook her head.

"Okay. I'll be back in a minute."

Having collected what she needed, Claire returned to the room where she handed Sorla a glass of water and a couple of tablets. "Here. Take these."

Soundlessly Sorla raised herself and propped herself up on an elbow. She accepted the glass and painkillers quietly. "Thanks."

"You're welcome. You should have said something earlier."

Sorla shook her head and handed back the glass before lying back down again. "Didn't bother me too much before. Guess I was too busy. Now I've stopped…" She shrugged.

Claire patted her thigh. "Not to worry. Let's get it cleaned up."

Claire wrapped ice packs in a cotton cloth, placing one on the main part of the swelling on Sorla's good leg and the other across her right knee, over the sharp protrusion. Carefully she cleaned the angry raw marks on the stump and rubbed some cream over them. "You might need to give the leg a rest for a day or two to let some of these heal." Sorla nodded.

Claire added some cream onto Sorla's good leg, spending a few minutes massaging the cream in. She put gloves on and lifted the ice pack on Sorla's right leg. She got the scalpel and gently slit the skin over the protrusion, revealing a small shard of metal. She pulled it out with the tweezers, applied some pressure and a Steri-Strip to close the cut, then placed a dressing over the top. She finished off by oiling her hands and gently massaging Sorla's thigh and knee. By the time she had finished, Sorla was on the verge of sleep, barely registering as Claire gathered her supplies and closed the door behind her.

❖

Riley rolled the window of the truck down to move the hot air in the cabin as she drove out of town. She hummed a happy tune. She could barely contain her excitement at the thought of going out to dinner tomorrow with some new friends. With Sorla.

Sorla was a puzzle. She found herself drawn to her, but at the same time she knew she had to desperately try to resist. Sorla was a customer. Mixing business and pleasure was something she always went to great lengths to avoid. Her private life was off limits. And then there was George. She had to look after George. How could she explain that? Best not to even start. It was too hard. Too complicated. Too messy. Best just to be friends. Riley sighed. Trouble was, friends shouldn't make your heart race or cause your cheeks to flush just thinking about them. Maybe she should pay a visit to one of the girl bars in the city and scratch the itch. It had been a while, maybe that's all this was, a build-up of sexual tension. She'd never been short of fanciers on the rare times she did visit. Maybe she should try and find a weekend spare sometime soon and see if she couldn't quench the feelings that were building. Thinking through the coming weeks, she knew once the rodeo hit town she'd be busy, if previous years were anything to go by. Maybe next weekend she should go for a drive.

Looking down at her list, Riley chewed on her bottom lip. Quite a few orders had come in during the week. She'd decided to do all the week's deliveries, except Cherry Hill, on the Thursday. That way, she could still call in and see Mickey like she'd promised. Sorla's deliveries could be loaded on the Friday morning. That would allow sufficient time for the delivery but not make it too obvious how keen she was to get there.

She made her last delivery and headed down the road to Mickey's. Pulling into the gate, she saw him on Jericho, walking around the yard. She pulled up and walked over to the yard next to the stable. She waved as he came closer. "Hiya."

"Hey, cutie. Wasn't expectin' you 'til tomorrow."

"I was out this way and thought I'd drop in. How's the saddle?"

"Mighty fine, little one, mighty fine. Never had one so nice before. Even Jeri approves. You've done a lovely job, Midget."

"I'm glad. Anything need adjusting?"

"Nope. I think you pegged it spot on."

"Good to know."

"You got time for a cuppa?"

"I've always got time for you, Mick."

"'Kay. How 'bout you put the kettle on while I pack up here?"

"I can do that. See you in a bit then."

"A bit it is."

Riley knew her way around Mickey's kitchen, having spent many an evening meal with him and Pearl. She put the kettle on the stove to boil and gathered the pot and cups from the cupboard. She set them up on the table. She'd baked the night before and placed a couple of pieces on a plate on the table. She put the container in the pantry cupboard, next to the biscuit barrel. Just as she'd poured the tea, Mickey came through the door and over to the sink to wash his hands.

"Hm, chocolate brownies. Did you put nuts in 'em?"

Riley smiled and kissed him on his leathery cheek as she put the teapot on the table. "Uh-huh."

"That's my girl."

"I've put some dinner in the fridge for you. All you have to do is heat it up."

"Thanks, Midget. Don't mind saying, it's nice to have a break from your own cooking every now and then. So, why're you so early?"

Riley put milk in her tea. "Couple of reasons. I've got a big day tomorrow and I was already out this way doing a delivery and thought I'd pop in to say hello."

"Well, always glad of the company for sure. What's happening tomorrow, then?"

"I'll be out at Cherry Hill, looking over some green horses they got in the other week."

"You were at Cherry Hill last week, weren't you?"

"I was."

"How's it going out there?"

Riley took a sip of her tea and thought about the question. "Early days yet, but they seem to be doing okay. Last week they had a shipment of horses in—a mix of shy, green, and some seasoned workers, by the looks. They had some cattle shipments too. Not sure how many."

"And what about the folk runnin' it? They seem decent enough?"

"Uh-huh. There's Ged Reardon's girl, Sorla, and a married couple, Ed Thornton and Claire Hanson. They're all nice. Apparently, at one stage, they were all in some special international defence force group working alongside the Marines overseas. Now they've come back to settle on the farm and want to try to make a go of it."

"Hmph. Well, it'll be interesting to see, that's for sure."

"How about you. How're you doing?" Riley knew this was a big month for Mickey. Apart from the rodeo celebration, the end of the month also marked Pearl's birthday. Traditionally the three of them spent the day together, cooking, eating, and sitting under the shade of the camphor laurels out back, reminiscing. Even with Pearl's passing a few years earlier, Riley still spent most of the day with Mickey, cooking lunch together and talking about good times. If the weather was fine, some years they would spend the afternoon fishing in the creek.

"I'm doing okay. Got my tackle box out the other day and looked over some of the flies an' lures. I reckon I got the perfect fly this year for that old brown fox in the pond. I've got a good feeling this is the year I'll beat him." Every year Mickey said the same thing, and every year the fish got the better of him, but it was always a good day out for both of them.

Riley looked out the window and noticed how low the sun had gotten. "Sorry, Mick, I'm afraid it's only a short visit today. I'm going to have to push off. Still got a fair bit to do when I get back." Riley started to clear the table.

"Leave those, I can clean those up. It'll give me somethin' to do."

"You sure?"

"I'm sure. Now come and give an old man a hug before you go." Riley came round the table. Mickey put his arms around her and gave her a tight squeeze and a quick kiss on her head. Riley flinched as his arm pressed on the bruised ribs on her back. Mickey didn't miss the sign and held her at straight arm's length. "You okay?"

Riley hugged him back, kissing him on the cheek, trying to be casual. "All good. Must have overdone it this morning, with all the deliveries." Mickey narrowed his eyes at her. "Truly." Mickey gently placed his gnarled hand under her chin and looked at her.

Riley patted his hand. "Seriously. Nothing to worry about." Mickey looked at her, unconvinced. "Gotta go, Mick. Love you. See you next week, huh? If you need anything in the meantime, just holler." She quickly kissed him again and headed out the door before he had a chance to say anything.

❖

Friday morning dawned warm and bright. Sorla had been up a couple of hours, finally giving up on sleep, but she hadn't been idle. Her suite was now set up. The kitchen was organized, the bedroom and guest room sorted, and the lounge room completely unpacked, with all trace of packing boxes gone. She sat down on the leather couch and looked around appreciatively at her efforts. Getting stuck in unpacking the boxes and getting everything sorted seemed to have settled her somehow. It wasn't until she had unpacked everything that she realized how much she needed to work through that process in order to feel grounded again.

For the last couple of days she had left her prosthesis off and used her crutches in order to let her stump start to heal. Today, with Riley coming, she had her leg back on, which helped her to get around a lot better with the moving and sorting of things in her suite. It still felt tender, but if she took it steady, she felt confident that she could last the day without doing any further damage.

She had used the last couple of quieter days to work through some paperwork. A letter had arrived midweek from the Department of Defence agreeing to meet with them to discuss a proposal they had made regarding a rehabilitation work program for ex-service men and women, and a contract to supply livestock for meat. The idea of the program was to re-establish the ex-service personnel back into the rural communities, hopefully setting them up with some trade skills in the process.

The meeting would take place Monday week. She made a mental note of the time and the date of the appointment and thought she should probably have a look through her wardrobe to make sure she had something suitable to wear to the meeting. If not, she might have to schedule a trip into town and see if there was something she could pick up that would do the job. She smiled to herself. Maybe her favourite fashion assistant could give her some tips on the best place to shop.

Riley had phoned the night before confirming she would be there a bit after nine. Being the first one up, she had made enough breakfast for everyone and left it warming while she made her way out to the barn.

She sat on the floor and watched as Miss Pusskins devoured her own breakfast, humming in satisfaction with each mouthful. The kittens were crawling all over Sorla's lap, walking up her arms to balance on her shoulders. Their eyes had opened earlier in the week and they were full of adventure, albeit on wobbly, uncoordinated limbs.

She had just rescued one of the kittens, who had scaled the heights of her shoulder and was preparing to leap off. "Now you listen here, Super Kitty, you are gonna hurt yourself jumping off like that. You're not old enough for a flying cape just yet." She gently put the kitten on the ground next to her leg, only to watch it pull itself up and head back up her arm again.

Riley cleared her throat from the doorway. "It's never too early to learn about occupational health and safety." She pushed off from the door frame and wandered over to sit next to Sorla. "Good morning. Sorry, I'm a bit early. Hope that's okay."

Sorla blinked, recovering from Riley's sudden appearance, surprised she hadn't heard the truck pull up. "Hey, there. No problems. As you can see, I am entertaining the children, while Mumma takes a break. They're absolute scallywags."

"Oh look, their eyes are open! Wow, you've grown heaps since I last saw you." Miss Pusskins, having finished breakfast, came up to Riley, sniffed her fingers, then proceeded to crawl into her lap and started cleaning herself. Riley stroked her head and down her silky back. "You look better too, little lady." Within a few minutes, the cat had curled up and was dozing on Riley's legs.

Both watched as the kittens continued to play for a few more minutes until their energy stores ran out and they too curled up into little balls of slumber. Sorla looked at her lap where the sleeping babies lay. "They're real time wasters, aren't they?"

Riley smiled. "I know what you mean. But it's a nice way to start the day. Mother Nature sure is wonderful."

"That she is, my friend, that she is. But this doesn't get the work done. Shall we put these sleeping monsters to bed and unload the truck?"

"Yes, ma'am. Lead on."

In the end it didn't take long to unload the last of the supplies. Although her leg felt better, Sorla knew she was moving stiffly. She tried hard to walk normally, hoping Riley wouldn't notice, but suspected she'd been found out when it became obvious that Riley was unloading the heaviest of the items from the truck.

"How did you get on with your cattle?"

"Good. They look like a solid bunch. I thought maybe we could pack a lunch and head out to check on them later, 'specially the cows and calves, down near the creek line."

"You okay?"

"Me? Yeah. All good." Sorla dusted off her hands, smiling nervously and avoiding looking at Riley. "Just a bit out of the habit of being on horseback all day. Not as young as I used to be."

Riley nodded but said nothing, much to Sorla's relief.

Riley reached into the passenger side of the cabin and lifted out a box. "Oh, before I forget, I brought out some spare gear for you to look over, like I promised. It's a mixed bunch, but it's all in good nick and will get the job done if you're interested."

Sorla ran her hands through the box of goodies ranging from lead ropes to halters, saddle blankets, and blinkers. "These look great. How much do you want for them?"

Riley shook her head. "Nothing. They're yours if you want them. Be nice to see them go to a good home."

Sorla shook her head in protest. "C'mon, let me give you something for them. There's a decent amount of gear in this box."

Riley patted her lightly on the shoulder. "Serious. They're yours if you want them. They're just lying around the shop collecting dust. I'd much rather see them somewhere getting used. If you think you can make use of them, then that's great."

Sorla looked into the box. The equipment looked freshly wiped down and conditioned and the blankets smelt clean and washed. Without delving too deeply into the box, it looked like Riley had remembered pretty accurately the list of things they needed. She was very touched by both the thoughtfulness and generosity of the gift. Without giving it much thought, she leaned over and kissed Riley on the cheek. "Thank you. They're perfect."

Much to Sorla's amusement, Riley blushed and looked down as her feet scuffed the dirt. "You're welcome."

"Wanna help me unpack them in the tack room?"

"Sure. After you." Walking behind Sorla, Riley put her hands to her cheeks, feeling the radiating warmth. Hanging the gear up, they now had another four complete sets. Riley brushed her hands off. "If you want to leave the broken bits with me, I can take them with me to repair so you'll have some spares if you'd like."

"Spares are always handy, so yes, thanks, on the condition you at least let me pay for the repairs."

"I'm sure we can work something out. Now, tell me about these horses of yours. What did you have in mind?" Sorla led them out the back to the two holding yards. They each stood on the lowest fence board and hugged the top railing. Riley keenly observed the horses in the yards. The big blue roan mare stood proudly with her head tossed high. She was returning their examination in kind with one of her own of them. She shared a yard with a light bay mare who pranced nervously backwards and forwards. In a smaller yard, off to the side, was a dark bay mare with two young horses, a chestnut filly and a dun colt. The foals were skittish and in high youthful spirits, with the mare watching on in calm interest.

Sorla rubbed the bridge of her nose. "I want to be able to work with them, but I think there's some breeding potential in there too."

"So you want to do more than just have them as working horses?" Riley's eyes never left the the small mob as they walked the fence perimeters.

"Well, I guess that depends on them, in part."

"How so?"

"My Da taught me that to get the best out of anyone, man or beast, they have to love what they're doing. So if they want to race, or if they like working, or raising babies, then that's where they'll be happiest."

Riley was quiet a good long while as she looked over the horses. Ged Reardon was renowned for his knowledge and understanding of horses. Riley never really knew him, but already she felt a kinship of appreciation for the man. Seeing his reflection in Sorla filled her with a sense of peace and well-being, knowing that these horses had found themselves a good home. "You said you and Ed picked these ones out?" Sorla nodded. "Tell me what you see when you look at them."

"Well, the colt and the filly have lovely lines, strong legs. They're bright and inquisitive. The mare with them, she's a bit soft looking and her best years are behind her, but look how she watches the young ones. That one is a good mother. She's the group's matriarch for sure. We tracked the previous owner down. Said she had a temper and was a biter, but she made great babies. So basically, she's been a baby machine, with minimal handling, who's getting to the end of her prime."

"Uh-huh. So what would you like to see happen for the queen over there with the youngsters?"

"She can keep her throne, but if we can somehow get her to a place where we can work together happily and safely, then I'll be happy with that."

"The babies?"

"Well, ideally, get in and handle them early and then watch them to see how they develop and take it from there."

Riley turned her head away from the horses, giving full attention to Sorla. "And the last two? Tell me about them."

Sorla threw her head back and laughed lightly in the sun. Riley thought she had never seen anyone look quite so lovely. Feeling on unsafe ground she quickly turned back to look at the two horses in question.

"Oh, that's easy. We plain and simple fell in love with these two from the outset. The light bay mare reminded Ed of a horse he had growing up. Said he simply had to have her."

"And the blue roan? Why'd you pick her?"

Sorla had an enormous grin on her face and her eyes danced with excitement. "Because she's Irish through and through. She's got the dark Irish highlights. Look at her—she's feisty, she's stubborn, and she's full of spirit. How could you *not* fall in love with her?"

"Do you know her background?"

Sorla shook her head and frowned slightly. "Not really. She doesn't like to be handled, and when we saw her at the sales, she had what I thought were signs of healing marks on her flanks. Like someone had whipped her, or struck her with something."

Riley looked at the mare closely. Up close she could see some thinning of the hair on the flanks, which supported Sorla's theory. "And what did you have in mind for her?"

Sorla's face lit up. "She would make magnificent babies. But really? I'm not sure. I just knew that, when I saw her, I had to have her." Sorla shook her head and turned to face Riley. "It was like we clicked somehow." Her voice grew husky and she shrugged. "I can't explain it."

Riley had to concentrate on breathing. She knew exactly what Sorla was talking about. She just wondered if they were still talking about the horse.

The blue roan mare threw her head back and whinnied, stamping her feet.

The spell broken, Riley chuckled. "She certainly is a madam."

"What do *you* think?"

Riley scratched behind her ear and looked them over once again. "I think you pegged them nicely. I see a lot of potential in both pens. I think you and Ed made some really nice selections."

"So, do you think you'd be interested in taking them on?"

Riley looked over at the mare and foals. "I'd love to. But you don't know anything about me. You're taking an awfully big gamble on a stranger to work with these spirited creatures."

Sorla smiled. "Not really. I asked about town about you, and rumour has it there is none better. But even if I hadn't asked about, I see the way you look at them. You can see their potential, the same as me. I know in my bones that you'll look after them. I wouldn't have asked if I thought any different."

Riley felt her cheeks warm ever so slightly. "Thank you."

"So will you do it?"

Riley looked at the mob and smiled broadly. "Love to."

"How about we grab a quick cuppa and we can discuss the terms of arrangement?"

Chapter Eight

Over coffee, they agreed that Riley would come out and work the horses two afternoons in the week and a full day on the weekend. Sorla offered a significant fee per horse, but Riley would only accept a worker's per diem fee for the hours she put in.

"Something tells me, Johnson, that you'll never make your fortune. You give away gear and you only charge workman's wage rates for a potentially dangerous and demanding job."

Riley shrugged. "I do all right for what I need."

Sorla picked up the mugs and put them in the sink. "If you say so."

Riley stood up. "So who would you like to start with?"

"I'd love you to work on the blue roan, but I think the most sensible choice would be the matriarch. Hopefully she can help out the youngsters when it's their turn. What do you think?"

Riley's face burst into a conspiratorial grin. "Actually, I was thinking exactly the same thing."

Laughing gently they both headed out the door and back to the yards. Sorla had her new hat on. She'd noticed how hot it was in just the short time they were out looking at the horses the first time and knew she'd be needing the shade before the morning was done. "What can I do?"

"Can you get me a halter and a small lead rope please? Choose one that you can make hers—that way she'll get her smell on it and come to recognize it as hers."

"Okay. Back in a minute." Sorla came back with the requested halter and rope and two cold bottles of water. As she came towards

Riley she noticed she was chewing something. "Are you hungry? Did you want me to get you something to eat?"

Riley smiled. "No, I'm fine, thanks. It's just a peppermint. Horses like the smell of it, better than coffee."

"Oh?"

Riley winked at her and held a hand out for the halter and rope. "Thanks."

"Can I do anything else?"

"Why don't you pull up a chair? There's one in the cabin of the truck, behind the passenger seat. The first session always takes a while. If you could just watch her for me—how she moves, what her reactions are to various things—and then we can compare notes at the end. Oh, have you picked a name out for her yet?"

"Well, as she's the matriarch, why don't we call her Queenie."

Riley grinned. "Okay, Queenie it is."

Sorla grabbed the chair and settled in to watch, noting how Riley breathed in time with the mare. The mare moved to the left. Riley followed. The mare snorted and moved a step to the right. Riley mirrored the move. The synchronized dance went on for fifteen minutes before the horse broke, making a dash halfway around the yard before skidding to a stop. Riley walked to the centre and turned her back on the mare, head lowered.

Sorla sat spellbound, not even sure if she'd remembered to blink. Slowly the mare took a step towards Riley. Then another tentative one. Riley stood still, breathing slowly, head lowered. The mare stood less than four feet away. They stayed frozen in place for what felt like an eternity, before the mare threw her head back and trotted back to the fence line. Slowly, Riley turned and followed her and the dance began anew. For every step the mare took, Riley matched it. With each step, Riley slowly got closer to the mare, until they were sharing a very small space. When the mare stepped, it was like Riley knew she was going to move before even she did, and their steps synchronized perfectly.

At last Riley had stepped so close to the mare that they were only inches apart. Slowly, Riley turned her back on the mare and walked to the centre. She slowed her breaths, lowered her head, her arms down by her sides, and waited. At first the mare just stood and watched. After a few minutes, she stamped a foot, as if to try and get Riley's attention.

When that didn't work, she took a couple of steps forward towards Riley, step by tentative step, with Riley standing motionless. Sorla was on the edge of her chair, not game to move or breathe, as she waited to see what would happen.

Step. Step. Wait. Step.

Riley and the horse were so close, Sorla knew she could feel the horse's breath over her shoulder. She could feel the mare's nervous vibrations.

Step.

Wait.

Still Riley held herself perfectly still. Sorla sat, watching to see what Riley would do next. The horse was right behind her. Sorla watched Riley waiting stock still. The horse took the last step forward, hesitating briefly, before nudging Riley between the shoulder blades with her muzzle. Sorla's hand went to her mouth.

She saw the smile build on Riley's face as the mare nudged her again. Slowly Riley turned and raised a slow hand to rub the horse on the forehead. The horse lowered her head into Riley's hand. Riley slowly bent down until she was next to the horse's nostrils, and Sorla watched, amazed, as she gently breathed into the horse's nose. *Ahhh, the peppermint.* As Riley continued to breathe into the horse, her right hand secured the horse's muzzle, while the left hand slowly reached around to the side of the horse's mouth. Sorla watched, fascinated, as Riley stuck a finger in the mouth and stroked the horse's tongue. The horse responded by dropping her head into Riley's body. Sorla sat transfixed as the horse relaxed into Riley's arms. Still stroking the tongue, Riley straightened and began to rub the head and neck of the mare.

Next she gently took the halter that she'd tucked into her back pocket and rubbed it up and down the mare's neck. In slow movements, she gently and smoothly slipped the nose halter over the head and secured it with one hand. Then she clipped the lead rope on.

Slowly Riley lowered her body until she was almost squatting beside the front legs. Sorla saw her gently pull down on the rope. The horse resisted. Riley put her finger back in the horse's mouth and gently stroked the tongue. Again, she gently pulled downward on the rope. As the horse's head dipped, she released the pressure. A few more pull and release moves and the mare's head was lowered to the ground. Riley stroked and scratched the mare's face. Slowly she stood up to gently and rhythmically stroke the groove running down the horse's muzzle to the tip of the nose.

Finally, Riley led the horse in a gentle circuit of the yard with just a hand under her chin. As she got to the gate that she'd let the youngsters through earlier, she reached up and scratched behind the mare's ears. The horse leaned into Riley, clearly enjoying it. Reaching up, Riley slowly slipped the halter off her head, opened the gate, and let her walk through to join the young foals. Closing the gate, she stood briefly and watched as the mare took a few steps in before turning her head to look back at Riley. The mare gently snorted and nodded her head before walking over to nuzzle the young pair.

Slowly Riley turned and walked over to the fence. She carefully climbed up and over and made her way towards Sorla, who was standing with an enormous grin on her face. "That was the most incredible thing I have ever seen! I don't care what you say, it sure as hell looks to me like you can talk to horses."

Sorla looked at her watch. The whole thing had lasted about eighty minutes. She shook her head. There was sweat running down Riley's face and along the line of her neck. Sorla remembered the bottles of water and quickly handed her one. "Here, looks like you could use it."

Riley smiled gratefully. "Thanks." She sat down on the grass in the shade of a peppercorn tree, next to Sorla's chair, and rolled her shoulders, her movements stiff from holding still for so long. She closed her eyes and drank long swallows from the bottle. "Oh, that's nice. Thanks."

"Okay, Dr. Dolittle. Talk me through what you did just then."

Riley shrugged with one shoulder. "We danced a little."

Sorla flicked Riley's hat playfully. "Seriously, what was that you just did?"

Riley half turned so she could look at her. "Tell me what you saw." She took another, smaller sip from the bottle.

Sorla put her head on the side and narrowed her eyes in thought. "You got each other's measure, then, wherever she went, you went. In the end you were leading the movements, instead of her. Then you backed off and she came to you. And I see now what you meant by the peppermint smelling nicer than coffee. Why did you do that?"

Riley wrapped her arms around her knees. "Have you ever seen how two horses greet? They get face to face and breathe into each other, it's sort of a sign of friendliness, if that makes sense. I find, for some horses, it kind of helps calm them down."

"That's amazing…And that other stuff, when you stuck your fingers in her mouth?"

"Another trick I learned that helps settle them and keep them calm."

"Where'd you learn all this stuff from?"

Riley shrugged. "Growing up on the rodeo circuit, I had a lot of time to watch how horses behave and react to different things. Later on, I found some books which helped, but mostly I just watched a lot."

Sorla shook her head in disbelief. "Wow."

Riley plucked at some grass stalks. "The trick to it all is that you have to be calm within yourself. If you're not, the horse knows and they won't want anything to do with you. You can have all the tricks under the sun, but none of them will work, unless you can let all your troubles go and find a peaceful place to ground yourself."

"Well, you've certainly blown me away. I still can't quite believe it. I was so mesmerized, I'm not sure if I breathed or not."

Riley playfully nudged her with her shoulder. "Well I'm kinda glad you did. Otherwise it could have been a bit embarrassing, having my boss come out and watch, only to pass out on me."

Sorla nudged her back with a grin. "I was going to suggest we ride out and check on the cattle, but it's pretty hot out. How d'you feel about going for a drive, instead of riding?"

"Works for me. Is there somewhere I can wash up first?"

"Sure. Go on through to the house. You remember where my bathroom is? You wash up and I'll put this stuff away and collect lunch. Meet you back here in ten."

❖

As Riley stepped into Sorla's lounge room she noticed that it was vastly different from when she had last visited. Before, it had been a couple of pieces of furniture, some photos on the mantelpiece, and a myriad of taped-up boxes. Now the room was fully unpacked. A large CD collection and stereo unit sat in one corner, along with a flat-screen TV and theatre system set up. Some tasteful art adorned the wall, colourful thick rugs in burgundy and green stretched out on the floor, and more photos now were hung in frames or on the sideboard unit. Putting her bag down, she walked over to the mantelpiece and saw, as well as the photos she'd seen before of Sorla, Ed, and Claire in their fatigues, there was a black-and-white photo of a dark-haired girl on horseback, supported by a smiling couple, which, given the similarity in looks, could only be Sorla's parents. Conscious of invading Sorla's privacy, Riley quickly made her way to the bathroom and cleaned up from the morning's activities.

Retracing her steps, she found Sorla in the kitchen packing a basket.

"You were quick. All done?"

"Uh-huh. Can I do anything?"

"All under control. Ready for the extended tour?"

"You bet. I'll just chuck my bag in the truck."

"Bring it with you—we can swap it over when we get back."

They put Riley's bag and the lunch basket in the back of the Jeep before climbing in and heading off. As they drove out, Sorla talked about her family. "We've had cattle and horses in our veins for a while now. Some generations did a great job, others not so much. Da was the last one left working the land. He passed his love of it all to me."

"What about your mother?"

Riley couldn't see Sorla's eyes as she had sunglasses on, but she picked up on her hands clenching the steering wheel tighter for just a brief moment before she relaxed them. "My mother lasted a bit over seven years here before she left. She took me with her. I only got to come out here in the holidays, but it was too late for me, I already had the dirt under my fingernails. I knew that this would be where I would end up. This is my home."

"Do Claire and Ed come from here too?"

Sorla chuckled and shook her head. "No, Claire's a city girl, but Ed's a hayseed child like me. He grew up on a farm, along with his three brothers. He's the youngest, with his older brothers still at home running the family property, so he was more than happy to come and share in the running and owning of this one. He always jokes that even with two bossy women in charge, there'd still be fewer arguments than with his brothers. Claire loves him to the moon and back and will go wherever Ed goes. But Ed knows she needs some city time, so they go back a couple of times a year to eat fancy, dance 'til late, go to the theatre, and listen to bands."

"You three seem really close."

"Mm, we are. When we left the service we were separated for a while, doing our own thing, but we kept checking in with each other, to the point where we figured it would be easier if we all came back here. I guess, after living and working closely with people for such a long time, we had a hard time adjusting back to suddenly being on our own."

"Like being in a pack. You each have your own roles, but you work better when you're together."

Sorla smiled. "Something like that. Being on our own didn't feel right, like a big part of us was missing. We couldn't settle. This way, we can still each do our own thing, but we're all still altogether."

"That sounds nice."

Sorla nodded thoughtfully. "It is. I don't know what I'd do without them. They're my best friends in the whole world. What about you?"

Riley looked out the window. "What about me?"

"Do you have any brothers or sisters?"

"No. It's just me and George."

"Your mother?"

"She died when I was five. An accident. She got kicked by a horse and ruptured her spleen. She bled out before she got to the hospital."

Sorla reached over and put her hand on Riley's thigh. "Oh, I'm sorry."

Riley smiled sadly and shrugged a shoulder. "It's okay. I don't remember much about her."

"That must have been tough on your father. Being a single parent."

Riley looked out the window again. "It sure was a burden he hadn't banked on. By all accounts, he wasn't real happy when my mother fell pregnant, but he tried to do the right thing by her, and married her."

Sorla could see Riley didn't feel comfortable talking about herself. *Time to lighten up the conversation a little.* "Tell me about your name. Riley's pretty unusual."

Riley coughed a short soft laugh. "Well, I was s'posed to be a boy. He always said his first child was going to be called Riley. He never thought it would be any other way. You can imagine George's joy at finding out he had a girl. It's why he calls me RJ."

Sorla gripped the steering wheel and blew out a sad breath. "That's some story. Can't have been easy."

Riley turned away from the window, half smiling. "It was what it was. Can't say I knew any different. I met some good people along the way. So I reckon I did okay." Sorla turned the Jeep to drive parallel to a creek line. Riley nodded out the window. "You sure are lucky to have this running through your place."

"I know. According to family records, it's only run dry twice in our family's time here. There's an underground spring up further that feeds it and of course there's the feeder streams where water flows off the small ridges to the east."

"Looks like some nice deep pools in spots too."

Sorla turned the Jeep carefully around a cluster of rocks before suddenly putting on the brakes. "Oh, shit." She pointed out the window. Just around the bend in the creek, a cow was standing midhock in water, bellowing across the creek where her calf was caught up on a fallen tree branch half submerged in the water. The flow of the creek was strong, and the water was lapping under the calf's chin. It cried helplessly back at its mother.

Sorla turned the car off and both of them hopped out.

Riley turned to Sorla. "You got any rope?"

"Dunno. Hang on, I'll have a squizz." Sorla opened up the back of the vehicle and looked through a box of tools and equipment. All she could find was a small length of hessian rope about ten metres long. It certainly wasn't enough to reach the calf from where they were. She came around to the front of the car to find Riley stripping down to underpants and a singlet top. She held up the length. "All I've got is this. It's not long enough. What are you doing?"

Pulling off her socks and stuffing them in her boots, Riley pointed her head in the direction of the calf. "He's getting tired. His head's dipping into the water. How long is the rope?"

"'Bout ten metres."

"Okay, I'm gonna go in and try to hold him up. Can you back the Jeep down as far as you think is safe? Hopefully we can tie off the rope and pull him out from there."

Before Sorla had time to think, Riley waded into the water and was soon in up to her chest, heading towards the crying calf.

Sorla jumped in the Jeep. She drove forward a few feet to get a better angle to the creek, then hit reverse. She opened her door, sticking her head out to get a better look as to how far she could go back before she would have to stop the vehicle. As soon as she heard the crunch of tyres on the creek-bed stones she pulled up and got out.

Riley had made it to the calf and had her arms wrapped around him. The water was flowing freely and with the calf wriggling, trying to get free, Riley was soaked and struggling to hold the beast.

Sorla stood on the bank. "Okay, now what?"

"Do you think it'll reach?"

"Hang on, I'll do a test throw." Sorla stood on one end of the rope and threw the other end neatly out towards Riley. It hit her shoulder briefly, before being carried off in the current. "Yeah, I think we'll be okay." She pulled the rope back in and tied the end off on the back of the Jeep. "Okay, now what?"

"You'll have to bring it in."

"What?"

"You'll have to bring it over."

"I can't do that."

"Yes, you can. Just hop in and bring it over."

"What if I throw it to you?"

"I can't let go to catch it. His head will go under."

"But I could toss it onto your shoulder, like before."

Riley shook her head. "Current will only carry it away. I need you to bring it in and tie it around him while I hold him up."

Sorla turned around and faced the Jeep. She couldn't look at Riley. Panic started to fill her lungs and she was finding it hard to breathe.

"Sorla. You can do this." Sorla shook her head. "Yes, you can. You can do this."

"I can't."

"Sorla, turn around. Turn around and look at me." Again, Sorla shook her head.

Riley softened her voice. "Sorla. Please, turn around and look at me. Come on. Please."

Sorla slowly turned around.

"Sorla, I can't do this on my own. I need you."

Sorla shook her head and hugged her arms around her chest as her chin trembled. "You don't understand."

"Sorla, it's okay."

Sorla shook her head. "No, it's not."

"Yes, it is. Take off your shirt and pants, leave your leg and boots on the bank, and wade in." Riley's eyes never left Sorla's. "We can do this. Come on, it'll be okay."

Sorla stood there with her mouth open. "How did...?" She swallowed. "You know?"

Riley nodded. "I guessed, but I wasn't sure. Sorla, please. You can do this. This little one needs you. *I* need you. Please."

Sorla closed her eyes and gritted her teeth. She undid her shirt, nearly ripping it off her shoulders in an attempt to be rid of it. She was furious at herself and she was frightened. She couldn't look Riley in the face any more. She couldn't bear to see Riley's revulsion when she caught sight of her scar-riddled body. She sat down and pulled her boots off, then her pants, before disconnecting her leg and pulling off the silicone sock. Clad only in her sports crop top and underpants, she looped the rope around her shoulder and scooted down the last of the creek bank on her bottom and hands until she got to the water's edge. She sucked in a breath, shocked at how cold it was. She swam over to Riley, scowling, still not looking at her.

Riley watched her approach.The calf was their first priority, and the best way to do that was to just get it done, but the look of self-consciousness and hurt on Sorla's face was as plain as day.

As Sorla swam up and stood in front of her, Riley leaned forward and kissed her on the cheek. "Thank you. Now, let's get this little one out. Do you have enough to tie around his chest and under his arms?"

Sorla nodded and wrapped her arms around the beast. Her hand brushed against Riley's abdomen, then down to her thigh, as the rope went around. Goosebumps jumped out on Riley's arms, and it had nothing to do with the temperature of the water. Sorla, busy, didn't seem to notice.

Sorla took a step back. "Okay, done. How do we do this?"

Riley took a deep breath to gather her thoughts. "Okay, we get either side of his chest here. I'll hold him up, while you pull us back to shore with the rope."

Sorla half bobbed, half swam to the opposite side of the calf. "Okay. Ready?"

Riley nodded. "Ready."

Hand over hand, Sorla pulled them back to the creek bank and the car. The calf's mother was next to the vehicle, anxiously waiting, bellowing encouragement. As they came to the bank, the calf's feet found purchase on the stones. With fast and agile hands, Riley whipped the rope off over the beast's head, and the calf ran out of the water and straight to its mother, where it started to seek comfort in the form of frantic suckling. Riley stood up grinning, midcalf in water with her hands on her hips. "Well, will you look at that. That's a beautiful thing."

Sorla sat with her back to the calf, still in the water, shoulders bowed. Riley stood beside her and gently offered her a hand. Sorla brushed it away. "I don't need your pity."

"Good, 'cause I'm not offering it. I'm simply offering to help you to get your butt out of the water before you catch pneumonia." Sorla still sat there. "You can either take my hand and we walk out of this together as cleanly as possible, or I can go and sit in the sun over there, and you can crawl out, when you've had enough, and get dirt and crap all over yourself in the process." Again Riley gently offered her hand. "So, what'll it be?"

Sorla sat sulkily. Riley stood still, with hand extended, and waited. Sorla slapped the surface of the water in frustration before reaching up and accepting the extended hand of help. Grabbing Riley's forearm, she pushed up with her good leg, hopping briefly for balance. Riley stood beside her and allowed Sorla to put her arm around her. As soon as Sorla balanced herself, she nodded that she was ready. Riley wrapped her arm around Sorla's waist, and together, they walked back up to the Jeep.

As they got to the vehicle, Riley spoke softly. "How about we sit in the sun and warm up a bit first? It'll give us some time to dry off and have some lunch. Then we can get changed and head on back if you like." Sorla nodded. "Okay, how about over there, near the tree?"

Riley settled Sorla down onto the grass before returning to the Jeep. She took her time folding the clothes, figuring Sorla might appreciate a bit of space. She put the clothes in a pile and tucked them under her arm before locating the lunch basket and carrying it over. She laid Sorla's clothes in front of her before turning and setting out the lunch basket contents. Sorla had packed some sandwiches, a thermos of coffee, and a bottle of wine.

While the creek water had been cold, neither of them was in danger of suffering from hypothermia in the heat of the day, so Riley figured the coffee could wait. She wordlessly poured a glass of wine and handed it over to Sorla, who was sitting with her knees pulled up to her chest, her arms wrapped around them. At first she didn't make a move to take the wine glass. After a few minutes, Riley extended her index finger and gently stroked Sorla's shin on her good leg. Sorla's chin quivered and she closed her eyes as tears etched a path down her cheeks. She put her head down on her knees as a sob escaped her lips.

Riley put the glass aside and quietly came and sat next to Sorla. Every instinct in her wanted to wrap her arms around her, but she knew that Sorla was on the edge and to touch her would push her over, so she did what she was good at, she waited. Slowly Sorla's sobs subsided. She lay with her head resting sideways on her knees, gently sniffing. Riley reached into her jeans pocket and withdrew a hanky and handed it to her.

Sorla slowly sat up and took the offered cloth. "Thanks."

Riley rested back against the tree and looked over in the distance to the reunited cow and rapidly drying calf. "You're welcome. The wine'll taste better if you've got a clear nose."

Riley handed her the wine glass. Sorla took it and sipped before straightening up to lean back against the tree and close her eyes. "I suppose Claire told you."

"Nope."

"Then how did you know?"

"I didn't. Not for sure. I put a few things together, but it was your gait mostly, 'specially when you get tired."

Sorla chuckled. "My gait?"

"Uh-huh. Your right leg doesn't move as smooth as the left. When you get tired, you also get stiff in the hips and you walk slightly forward."

"Is that right?" Sorla opened her eyes and turned to look across at Riley, who was looking down, plucking strands of grass from beside her.

"But the giveaway is your footprint."

"Come again?"

"It's quite different from your left. Your foot doesn't have the same rolling motion as the other one when you walk, so your footprints are different. Then I remembered when you bought the shoes, you only tried the left one on. I know you worked with the Marines. I went to the library and did some research and learned about IEDs and Iraq and the high number of injuries they caused, and I put two and two together."

"You did, huh?"

"Then when you wouldn't get in the water, I figured maybe that was why."

"I see."

"How long ago did it happen?"

"A bit over a year ago. I was the lucky one. Two others who were in the truck with me died." Sorla sipped her wine and looked off into the distance. "Some days, it feels like a thousand years ago. But sometimes…when I close my eyes, I'm straight back there." She lifted her chin and shook her head.

"Were you close to the two that died?"

"Not really. I knew them, but they were on a different shift normally. They were filling in because I'd organized a swap as a present, so Ed and Claire could go on an anniversary date together, otherwise it would have been Ed in with me." Tears filled Sorla's eyes and spilled over.

Riley reached out and gently wiped away the tears and rested her hand alongside Sorla's cheek. "But he wasn't with you. He's okay, and you're okay too." Sorla shut her eyes and leaned into Riley's touch. "I have no doubt it was horrible, and to lose those two people must have been heartbreakingly sad. War is sad. But you are here and you have a chance to keep living, and to rebuild the dream of your ancestors. And by doing that, you also honour those two who didn't come home."

Sorla thought about Riley's words. Her simple summation struck a chord inside her. She was right. War *was* sad. No one came out without some sort of scars. But she came out. Others didn't. She had a chance to live her life. For herself, for her friends, for her family, and for John and Annette, who would never get the chance to grow old.

"How come you didn't want to get in the water?"

"My leg doesn't swim very well."

"But the rest of you can. What stopped you?"

Sorla tried to swallow past the lump in her throat. "Because I didn't want you to know. I didn't want you to see me."

"Why?"

"Because I didn't want to see the revulsion in your eyes when you saw what I looked like."

Riley gently took Sorla's glass from her hands, placing it on the grass beside her. She reached and placed a finger under Sorla's chin and turned her face towards her.

"Look at me. What do you see in my eyes?"

Sorla closed her eyes and tried to shake her head from Riley's fingers. "Pity."

Riley softly tapped her on the nose. "You're wrong. Look again."

Sorla opened her eyes and stared at Riley's face, inches from her own. Her lips were slightly parted, her eyes had darkened, and there was a hint of a sheen of moisture on her upper lip.

"I don't see any scars. I see a beautiful woman, with a bruised heart and a limp that makes funny footprints. Someone who, when they smile, lights up a room. Someone that has good friends who love her, and a magnificent place to call home. I see a woman who has travelled the world and seen terrible things but still sees the beauty in life all around her. I see a woman who is brave and strong and one who's as wilful and Irish as a certain horse we both know. That's what I see." Riley gently took her hand away and handed Sorla back her wine glass. "I'll be back in a minute." Riley rose and walked back towards the car.

Sorla took a sip of her wine. As she raised the glass, she noticed her hand was shaking and her heart was going a million miles an hour. She had to concentrate on her breathing. She'd thought Riley was going to kiss her. Wished she had. She put the cool of the glass against a very warm cheek, then smiled. *She called me beautiful.*

Riley returned to the tree with a jar in hand.

Sorla looked up at her. "What have you got there?"

"I noticed some raw patches on your leg. Thought this might help."

She handed the jar to Sorla, who took the lid off and sniffed the golden ointment inside. "Mm. That smells nice. What's that?"

Riley started to unpack the lunch basket. Riley winked at her. "Secret recipe. Great for cuts, bruises, sunburn, sore muscles, and nappy rash."

Sorla laughed. "I think I'm okay on the nappy rash front."

Riley sat back on her heels and chuckled. "You can never be too sure."

"Seriously, who made this? What's in it?"

"I made it. I use it for everything. If nothing else, at least it smells pretty."

"It sure does. I can smell lavender, but there's other things in there too. Honey?"

Riley winked at her. "I told you. Secret recipe. Try a bit on your stump and see if it helps."

Riley noticed Sorla rubbing her arms. She handed over her shirt. "Thanks." Riley put hers on as well, before they both made short work of the sandwiches. She held the thermos up. "Coffee?"

Sorla was frowning. "No thanks."

"What's up?"

"Nothing."

"You're a terrible liar."

Sorla sighed. "It's the nerves in my legs. Sometimes they get cranky. It'll pass. Can you reach into the basket for me? There should be a packet of tablets in the bottom there somewhere. Can you grab them for me please?" Riley found the tablets and handed them over with a bottle of water. "Thanks."

"Does this happen a lot?"

"Not as much anymore, but I've had a busy week, so they're a bit tetchy."

"And the tablets make it go away?"

Sorla shook her head. "Not really. They just take the edge off. I don't normally like to take them, they make me sleepy."

"So does anything else help?"

"Sometimes Claire massages them for me, but mostly I just wait 'til it passes, then keep going."

"Okay. Lie back."

"What?"

Riley handed over the two pairs of folded jeans. "Put that under your head and lie back."

"No, really, I'm okay."

Riley gently clasped Sorla's hands. "Do you remember what I told you I saw?" Sorla nodded. "Lie back for me. Close your eyes. Let my hands tell you what my eyes see."

Sorla looked into the blue depths of Riley's unwavering steady gaze. Suddenly the fear left her. She let herself melt into the safety of what Riley's eyes were offering her. She lay back, lowered her head, and closed her eyes.

The smell of lavender slowly wafted around her as Sorla felt herself giving in and melting under Riley's firm but gentle hands. She could feel the tense muscles relaxing and becoming pliant under Riley's persuasive fingers and palms. She was vaguely aware of Riley massaging her thigh before swapping to her bad leg. She knew she should be tense and nervous, but strangely she wasn't. She vaguely felt herself drifting off to sleep. The last thing that crossed her mind was that Riley was more than just a horse whisperer, she was magic, full stop.

❖

Sorla gradually became aware of a faint citrus smell and a soft buzzing sound. She opened her eyes to see a bee, lazily checking her out. She carefully brushed it away and wondered what she was doing sleeping outside under a big lemon-scented gum tree. Then the memory of the morning kicked in—the calf, the creek, and the massage. She looked down to see that Riley had covered her with the cotton picnic cloth. She raised herself up onto her elbows and looked around, scanning for any sign of where Riley might be. The Jeep was still there. Finally, a movement from the corner of her eye caught her attention. Riley was walking along the creek bed. Sorla smiled. Great legs.

Riley glanced her way and burst into a genuine smile. She waved and walked over, sitting down next to Sorla. "Hey."

"Hey, yourself. Whatcha doing?"

Riley shrugged. "Just enjoying the day and exploring your creek a bit."

"Sorry about crashing out on you."

"That's okay. Your body obviously needed it. Feel better?"

Sorla took stock of herself. Apart from feeling a bit sleep groggy in the head, she did feel better. Her legs felt fine. "I do. Thanks."

"Would you like a coffee?"

"Yes, please."

Riley poured out two coffees. "Milk and sugar?"

"Just milk, please." Riley poured the milk and handed a cup over. "Thanks."

"You're welcome." They sat and sipped in companionable silence, watching as birds came down to drink from the stream and bees floated in the air looking for pollen.

Sorla stared into her mug. "I have an apology to make." Riley looked at her with questioning eyes. "I haven't been a very good hostess, or friend, today. I've sat and watched you do all the work, cried at the thought of getting wet, and now, after lunch, I've fallen asleep on you for"—Sorla looked at her watch; it had just gone past four o'clock—"crap, over three hours."

Riley smiled and looked over to the hillside where the cows were grazing with their calves. "I think it's been a good day. I don't usually get a chance to just stop and appreciate what's around me. Thank you for sharing that with me today."

"I suppose we should put our pants back on and head back."

Riley rolled her eyes. "Oh all right, if you insist." Laughing, Sorla threw her pants at her head. Sorla rolled her prosthetic liner on, then slipped her stump into the leg collar before pulling on her pants and boots.

Riley stood. "All set?"

"Yep." Riley extended her hand, and this time Sorla gratefully accepted the pull-up. She stretched her back as they walked side by side back to the car. Sorla got in and reached for the ignition key. Pausing, she turned her head and looked over. "My gait, huh?"

Riley smiled. "Yep."

Sorla shook her head and smiled too as she started the engine and pulled away from the creek. Riley pointed to her right. "What's that place?"

Sorla brought the car to a stop and glanced at the small cottage on the hillside. "That was built not long after my great-great-grandparents first arrived. There was a measles epidemic that broke out in the town. Two babies died here, and one of the maids. After that, my great-great-grandfather built this, so that for any future epidemics, they could send the sick out here with someone to look after them and lessen the impact on the rest of the family. I think they used it a couple of times for influenza over the years."

"Did someone come out and check on them?"

"The story goes that someone would ride out every few days and drop off some food and to see if anyone was still alive. The cabin has its own water supply and there's always a stack of wood cut for the fire. I used to come out here as a kid when the world got too much, or when I just wanted to camp out for a bit and test my survival skills."

"Well, you survived, so I guess you did all right then."

Sorla chuckled and put the Jeep into gear. "I guess I did."

They arrived home, and while Riley showered, Sorla poured herself a glass of wine. She thought about the day and how easy it had been to share in Riley's company. She thought about what Riley had said to her and how she'd coaxed her until she gave in and relaxed. She thought back to Riley's morning session with the mare and how they *danced* a little. It occurred to her that Riley may have danced a little with her too this afternoon. She twirled the golden liquid in the goblet and smiled. *I think I just got whispered.*

Riley appeared in the doorway. She'd changed into a clean pair of jeans, with a three-quarter-sleeved red shirt that opened with a V-neck. The red suited her as her blue eyes sparkled. Her damp hair was tied back, her feet were bare. Somehow the bare feet looked incredibly sexy to Sorla, who was delighting in taking her time to look Riley up and down as she bent down to put her toiletries back into her carry bag near the couch.

"Can I get you something to drink?" Sorla asked.

"No, I'm fine for the minute, thanks."

"Okay, must be my turn then to get wet. There's a guitar in the corner if you want to play. If you want one of the others, you know where the music room is."

"Thanks."

As she headed down the hall, she could hear the first tentative plucks on the strings, followed by the strings being tuned. She smiled and shut the bathroom door. She was planning on having a shower but decided a bath would take longer and give Riley a chance to enjoy herself.

Half an hour later, Sorla stepped into the hallway. She could hear the strains of Eric Clapton's "Tears In Heaven" being played. Riley was rusty and hesitant in spots, but it was obvious that working with horses wasn't her only talent. The girl could play. Sorla leaned on the door frame and listened as the tune wound itself to its conclusion. "That was beautiful."

Riley jumped. "Oh! Sorry. I didn't hear you." She got up and put the guitar back on its stand.

"Please, keep playing."

"Oh, no. It's fine. Thanks for letting me though."

"You should take it home with you."

"No, I couldn't do that. If anything should happen to it, I'd just feel sick. No, but thank you for the lovely offer though."

"Okay, well, it's there if you want."

Riley nodded.

"I brought the hair dryer out and wondered if you wanted to dry your hair? Seems to me you've spent half the day wet."

"I don't mind. It's okay."

"You sure? Come and sit in front of me. It won't take a minute. When we were stationed overseas we'd take turns drying each other's hair. Come on. It'll be fun. Just sit down here on the floor." Sorla saw the hesitation in Riley's eyes. "Come on."

Riley sat down in front of Sorla's knees. Sorla patted her shoulder and whispered in her ear, "Relax. I won't bite."

The hair on the back of Riley's neck stood up as the soft, warm breath tickled her ear. Her nipples tightened. Oh, this was a bad move.

But before she could get up, Sorla had turned the dryer on and was untying her hair. Sorla's fingers were gentle as they teased out Riley's locks. The soft brush of fingertips across her brow made her eyes close, and the fingers continued up the underside of her neck, separating the lengths for the warm air to dry. A feather-light fingernail brush around the rim of her ear made her shiver. Just when she thought she couldn't stand much more, Sorla turned off the dryer, gently fingering the strands into place. "There you go."

Riley stood up on slightly shaky legs. She knew she was blushing but there wasn't a damn thing she could do about it. "Thanks. That feels nice."

Sorla stood up and reached out and tucked the side lengths behind Riley's ears. "You have lovely hair. I don't think I've seen it out before. It's beautiful."

"Horses think so too, sometimes. They chew on it."

Sorla withdrew her hand, giggling. "Well, if you leave it out over dinner, I'll do my best to remember not to nibble."

Chapter Nine

While Claire and Sorla got dinner started, Ed and Riley talked shop out on the patio. Riley sipped on a tall glass of iced water. "We sell a bit of feed, but if you're looking at bulk supply, then Ted Saunders usually has the best stuff in town, and he delivers. But be warned, he's a bit of a shark and he'll pull one on you if he thinks he can get away with it. He tried to sell me green hay last week, so just be careful." Riley gave him another couple of names and prices so that he would have a choice of feed suppliers.

Ed wrote the names in a small book he kept in his breast pocket. "Thanks for that."

Riley put the knives and forks out. "How're your new farmhands getting on?"

Ed cleaned the top of the barbecue plate. "They're hard workers and nice fellas. We all get on really well. Having Don's history on the place is handy too. We offered them permanent jobs last week. Why? Is there something I should know about them?"

Riley smiled as she folded the napkins. "No. You've got two good men there."

"I'm glad to hear it."

"Ed, can I ask a question?"

"Sure, shoot."

"How come you call Sorla *Fender*?"

Brandishing a pair of salad tongs and a salad bowl, Claire stepped through the doorway to the patio. "I think the answer to that depends on which one of the two you ask." Ed chuckled. Riley looked from one to the other, waiting for an explanation.

Ed said, "When we were in the States, Sorla and I literally ran into each other. We each, naturally, blamed the other one, and Sorla ended up with a big dent in her truck's fender. We got into a spat over it and I said something like *Who the heck do you think you are?* She looked at my name tag and smiled and said, *I'm your new boss, deal with it.* So from then on, I called her Fender."

"Ah. I see."

Sorla joined them, a tea towel draped over her shoulder and a pan with the wings in her hands. "Hope you've got that barbecue fired up, Edward."

He jumped up and mock saluted. "Yes, ma'am."

Having handed the wings off to Ed, Sorla sat next to Riley, grinning. "I've been thinking—Irish would make a great name for the roan mare. What do you think?"

Riley nodded and returned the smile. "Has a nice ring to it."

"Irish it is then."

Claire turned to Riley. "So, what are you plans for tomorrow?"

"I thought I might come back early, if it's all right, for an hour or two and work with Queenie. Then I'll head back and put in a few hours at the store."

Claire sipped her wine. "Why don't you stay the night? That way you can get up and start when you're ready. It'll save you going home and coming back out again."

Riley thought about what Claire offered. It did make perfect sense and she would have plenty of time to work the horses before heading into town to open up for Saturday morning customers. Once trading was done, she could pick up George from The Galloping Grape and take him home. She looked up to see Sorla smiling at her. Riley smiled shyly back. "That's a lovely offer, but I should go home."

Claire looked at her with her head cocked to one side. "We've got plenty of room. It's no trouble. Are you sure?"

Riley shook her head. "I'd love to stay. But I really need to get back. Thanks all the same." To stay would be courting danger.

"Okay. Well, if you change your mind."

"Thanks. Um, if you'll excuse me for a minute? I'm just going to top up my water."

Sorla and Claire watched Riley's back as she stepped into the house.

Claire frowned. "Was I too pushy?"

"No, she probably has to get back to check on George."

"Okay, that makes sense. Shame, though."

Sorla was still looking at the door where Riley had entered the house. "Mm. Be back in a minute." She found Riley at the sink with both hands outstretched, chin lowered to her chest and eyes closed, gripping the edge of the basin. She came up beside her and leaned against the counter's edge.

"You okay?"

Surprised, Riley's head snapped up and she blushed to the tips of her ears. She quickly stood upright. "Hey."

"Sorry. Didn't mean to startle you."

"That's, that's okay. I was just getting some water."

"You sure you're okay? You seem a bit jumpy."

"Yeah, yeah, all good." Riley stepped to walk past, only to be stopped by Sorla putting a hand on her arm.

"You forgot your water."

"Oh. Right, I…"

"What's the matter?"

"Nothing."

"*Riley?*"

Riley averted her gaze from Sorla's and shook her head slightly. "I think I got a bit too much sun today is all."

Sorla stepped closer. She lowered her voice. "Now who's a terrible liar?" She slid her hand up to gently cup Riley's face, her voice softened. "Riley? What's wrong?"

Riley closed her eyes and shook her head. "I'm sorry, I think I'd better go."

"What do you mean *go*? What's the matter?"

Sorla's thumb gently caressed Riley's cheek. For a brief moment, Riley leaned into the intimate contact, before her sad eyes opened. "I thought I could do this, but it's too hard." Riley moved away from Sorla's hand, again trying to step around her. "I'm sorry. I have to go."

"I don't understand. Why do you have to go? What's going on?"

Riley shook her head. "I'm sorry. I made a mistake."

"A mistake? What are you talking about?"

"It doesn't matter."

"The hell it doesn't matter! Did we offend you or do something to upset you?"

"No. No. It's just…"

"Is this about this afternoon?"

"I…"

"It is, isn't it? All that stuff you said to me? It was bullshit, wasn't it? And now you've got a guilty conscience or something, and you want out."

"No, no, that's not it. Oh God."

"Then what the hell is it? I thought we were getting on well. I thought we were friends."

Riley shook her head. Her throat grew tight with bottled up emotion. "I can't."

"Can't what?"

"I, just…"

Sorla's voice rose in exasperation. "Can't *what*? Tell me."

Riley closed her eyes, her voice a strangled whisper. "I can't be *friends*!"

"What?"

"I'm sorry. I'll leave you the name of another good horse trainer, and—"

"No. Wait. What? Why can't we be friends? I don't understand."

"Please. I'm trying to do the right thing. You're a client, you've employed me to work with your horses, but you're going to need someone else."

Sorla paced, waving her arms. "I don't want anyone else training my horses but you."

"I'm trying to keep it professional."

"Professional? What's that got to do with friendship?" Desperation roiled off her.

Riley put her hands over her face, her voice a tortured whisper. "Because I can't be friends, and I can't be professional, when all I want to do is kiss you."

"What?"

Moisture gathered in Riley's eyes. "I thought I could do this. I thought I could just be friends, but I can't. It's my mistake. I was wrong. I'm sorry. I have to go." Riley pushed past Sorla heading for the door. Sorla followed close behind. As Riley stopped to open the door, Sorla caught her arm, spun her around, and kissed her, hard, on the mouth. The kiss was angry, demanding, frustrated, and hungry.

A sob escaped Riley as she met Sorla's lips with a desperate edge of her own. Their lips battled to claim and to mark, in an explosion of need. Finally, Sorla's lips began to gentle and caress, her tongue lightly brushing Riley's upper lip. Her left hand cradled the side of Riley's face, while the other hand slipped to encircle her waist, pulling their bodies tightly together.

Sorla groaned as Riley's tongue darted out and met hers as the kiss deepened. Sorla slid her hand up Riley's side. She could feel the muscles tensing. Her head spinning, she lightened the kiss, until, panting for air, they parted, coming to rest with their foreheads together. Sorla raised her head and kissed Riley's closed eyelids. "I think I've wanted to do that since I first laid eyes on you."

"I thought it was just me."

"No, not by a long shot. So now what?"

"You need to find another trainer."

"I told you, I don't want anyone else."

Riley shook her head. "And I told you, I can't—"

"Why not?" Riley shook her head. "Are you married?"

"No."

"Boyfriend? Girlfriend?"

"No."

"Then what's the problem? Is it me?"

"No. God no. It's me. There are too many complications…things I can't explain. Please."

Sorla read the pain in Riley's eyes. "Okay, okay. How about we just play it cool for a minute?"

"I can't—"

"*Wait.* I still want you to train the horses. How about we just go back to that for a little while? We'll figure the rest out somehow. Let's just do this one step at a time, huh?"

"I don't know."

"Please, stay for dinner. If you want to go, I won't stop you, but I'd really like it if you could stay."

After a minute, Riley shook her head. "I have to go and find another creek."

"A creek? What for?"

"To sit in. That's what I did this afternoon, when you fell asleep. I sat in the creek for nearly an hour."

Sorla burst into giggles. "You're kidding me."

Riley smiled crookedly. "Nope. Damn near froze my butt off."

"Did it help?"

Riley chuckled. "Not much."

"Will you at least stay for dinner?"

Riley closed her eyes briefly and drew in a big breath before blowing it out. She opened her eyes. "I think I need a glass of Claire's wine."

Sorla grinned. "Okay. I can do wine."

Together, they made their way back outside.

❖

"I am so stuffed, I don't think I can move." Ed lay back in his chair, legs out, belly extended, eyes closed.

Sorla ruffled his hair. "Well, you did go back for a fourth helping."

Ed leaned sideways, laying a big wet kiss on Sorla's cheek. "Beaut wings, Fender."

Claire stacked the dishes. "Why don't we adjourn to the music room? Ed, honey, why don't you pour everyone a fresh glass and take Riley on through and set up? We'll just put this lot in the dishwasher and be right there."

Within minutes Claire and Sorla made their way to the music room where Ed was rasping out a soulful version of "House of the Rising Sun," accompanied by Riley on acoustic guitar. In between verses, Ed would tear out a harp riff. Riley sat facing Ed, her back to the door, and Claire and Sorla slipped in quietly and sat on the leather couch. When Ed's song morphed into "God Bless the Child," Sorla watched as Riley listened with her head to the side, eyes closed, until she picked up the melody and picked out the tune to complement Ed's harp.

Sorla couldn't tear her gaze away as Riley became lost in the music. Her head was bent over the guitar in concentration. She was hesitant in parts, but rapidly gained in confidence and fluidity as time went on.

Ed finished his song and it was Riley's turn to take the lead. With eyes still closed, she played Elton John's "Your Song." Ed sat back and listened, smiling when he saw Claire rise from the couch to walk over and pick up the tune on the piano. Together, they made the piece float effortlessly around the room, soothing and sweeping the tune to its conclusion.

The song ended and for a brief moment no one moved as they hung on to the lingering essence of the tune. Eyes slowly opened and breaths deepened. Ed leaned over and patted Riley's shoulder. "That was beautiful."

Riley was suddenly aware of the eyes of the others. She cleared her throat nervously and stood up to place the guitar back on its stand. "Thanks. That was fun."

Claire turned on the piano stool. "Don't you want to play some more?"

Riley shook her head and shyly smiled. "I don't remember too many more tunes. Too rusty, I guess."

"Well, I think we need to make it our mission to help you dust off that rust. You play a sweet guitar, girl."

Claire turned back to the piano and belted out a funky blues tune with Ed joining in. Riley sat over on the couch with Sorla. Sorla had a gentle smile on her face. "That was really lovely. Claire's right, I think we need to build up your playlist. You have a really lovely style."

"Thanks."

Ed interrupted them, a violin and bow in hand. Sorla shook her head, but he smiled and poked her with the end of the bow. "We're not gonna do all the work here. Stretch your fingers, Fender, and take us home." He poked her a couple more times for good measure before she gave in and stood, accepting the extended instrument.

Ed took her place on the couch and patted Riley's knee as he sat down. "Wait till you hear this." Claire started a soft lilting melody. Sorla stood with eyes closed, swaying slightly, before gently gliding in and taking the lead. Back and forth they wove, each one taking turns at holding and telling the melodic storyline.

Riley sat on the couch with her knees pulled up to her chin. Unshed tears welled in her eyes as she listened to them weave their magic. She closed her eyes and rested her forehead on her knees. In the music, Riley could hear gentle drops of rain and see the first early morning rays of sunlight peeking over the horizon to tickle the land. She could feel flower petals opening with the touch of the sun and smell the gentle breeze that heralds summer rain. She opened her eyes and saw that Sorla and Claire swayed and moved to the music they made, gently bringing it all together. She knew in her heart she was right. She and Sorla couldn't just be friends.

Claire tapered off and stilled, as she sat and listened to Sorla branch off into an Irish lullaby, before turning the pace on its head and morphing into a traditional dance tune. Claire grinned at Ed, who jumped up and met her halfway across the room. He took her hand and together they jigged away to Sorla's energetic reel. By the time Sorla brought the tune to its end, everyone was laughing and cheering. It was the perfect way to end the evening of music.

Beaming, with their arms wrapped around each other and breathing heavily, Ed and Claire laughed in delight. Ed stood straight and dragged Sorla into his arms along with Claire and gave them each a squeeze. "God, that feels good. We haven't done that in such a long time. Good food, good company, and great music."

Claire poked him in the ribs. "And a newly discovered band member! What an excellent evening all round. But, as much as I hate to admit it, I'm beat. I am going to thank you all for a wonderful night and bid you all adieu 'til the morning."

Claire hugged Sorla. "'Night, old friend."

Sorla hugged them both. "'Night, you two. Thanks for the tunes."

Claire kissed Riley on the cheek. "Thanks for coming and helping to make it such a nice night. I'm hoping we can do it again, and hoping you'll consider joining our band on music nights."

"Thanks for having me. I had a lovely night. Thanks for letting me share in the fun."

Claire gently squeezed her hand. "Anytime."

Ed followed, offering Riley a peck on the cheek. "'Night, Riley. Thanks for everything today. See you in the morning."

Riley stood and brushed her hands on her trouser legs. "I'd better push off too."

"You sure you won't stay? The guest room is all set up if you want."

Riley shook her head and jammed her hands into her pockets. "No, really, thanks all the same."

"Okay then. Come on, I'll walk you out to the truck."

Outside the air was still warm, but a gentle breeze with a hint of honeysuckle on it was starting to cool things down. They came to a stop at the driver's door of the truck. Riley turned to Sorla and said,

"Thank you for a lovely dinner and a fun night. I'm sorry about earlier and losing the plot, I—"

Sorla put her hand on her arm. "It's okay. I lost the plot myself today. How about we call it even and leave it at that?"

Riley opened and shut her mouth before nodding. "I'll see you in the morning then, about seven, for the horses."

"So you'll train them?"

Riley straightened her shoulders and looked her in the eye. "We made a deal. I'll see it through."

"I appreciate that."

Riley held out her hand to say goodnight. Sorla brushed it gently aside as she pulled her softly in for a hug. "Thank you for today."

Riley closed her eyes and surrendered briefly to the hug, loving the way their bodies fit together, reciprocating with arms wrapped around Sorla's shoulder and waist. Finally Sorla loosened her grip and stepped back from the hug. "I'll see you in the morning then. Drive safely."

"Will do. 'Night."

CHAPTER TEN

As promised, Riley was back at seven sharp the following morning. As she climbed out of an old, beat-up dual-cab Hilux ute, she noticed to her amusement there were three camp chairs set up alongside the yard. Ed and Claire were in two of them, sipping on steaming mugs. She waved. "Morning."

They both waved back. Claire called out, "Hope you don't mind if we sticky beak?"

Riley gave them the thumbs-up sign that it was okay before walking over to greet Sorla. "Morning."

Sorla held out the harness and lead rope. "Good morning. I got these ready. Did you want anything else?"

Riley looked over at Queenie in the yard. She squinted into the morning sun. "We might get the full tack out today, blanket, saddle, the works. If she's up to it, we might see how she goes getting dressed. Have you picked out a set to be hers?"

"Uh-huh. I'll just go and get it."

"I'll come and give you a hand. We can leave it inside the gate."

"Righto."

As they walked into the barn and through to the tack room, Riley thought Sorla moved a little less stiffly this morning. "How'd your leg pull up this morning?"

Sorla smiled. "Pretty good actually. Must be that magic cream of yours."

Riley chuckled. "Either that, or the impromptu ice bath you had in the creek."

Sorla chuckled too. She reached out and pointed at an old softened saddle that was broad across the back skirt. "I thought maybe that one."

Riley walked over and ran her hands over it, nodding. "This will be good. It's got a nice wide base here which will be more comfortable for her hips." Riley hefted the saddle effortlessly, while Sorla gathered the blanket. Riley smiled. Above each saddle and tack box was a blank signboard. Above the saddle she'd picked up was painted *Queenie*.

Riley put the saddle and blanket inside the yard gate while Sorla took her seat next to Ed and Claire. Standing in the yard, Riley waited, watching the mare as she nervously paced backwards and forwards. She had the lead rope tucked into her back pocket. She simply stood until the mare stopped pacing and stood still, eyeing her carefully. Riley stepped forward, the mare stepped sideways, and Riley followed. The dance began. After a few minutes of matching each other, Riley stepped to the middle of the yard and turned her back on the mare, head down, breathing deeply. It took a few minutes, but the mare, one tentative step at a time, stepped forward until eventually she stood behind Riley. She stamped her foot as if to say *I'm waiting*.

Riley slowly turned and rubbed the mare on the forehead. She bent down and breathed into the mare's nostrils. The mare rubbed her face against Riley's shirt. Riley's right hand rubbed the groove on the mare's nose, while the left hand came around underneath to rest under the mare's mouth, where just like the previous day, she stuck one finger in and massaged the horse's tongue. The horse visibly began to drop its head and relax. Riley smoothly applied the halter one-handed.

After eighty minutes Riley took off the saddle and rubbed the mare down, removing the harness and offering her a piece of apple she had in her pocket as a reward. Then she opened the pen and let her back in with the two young horses. She gathered up the tack and carried it out the gate where all three observers greeted her. Ed and Claire had delighted if slightly amazed looks on their faces, while Sorla stood off to one side beaming. She stepped forward and offered Riley a chilled bottle of water.

"Mm, thanks." She closed her eyes and drank deeply before coming up for air and wiping her mouth. "Lovely."

Ed clapped her on the shoulder. "You know what? Thanks to you, I owe Don twenty bucks. And you know what? It's the best bet I've ever lost."

Claire looked at him. "What do you mean?"

"When Don heard you were training the horses, he said I wouldn't believe what you could do. He told me you could work miracles in a really short space of time. I told him I thought he was exaggerating and bet him twenty bucks it would take you close to a week to get a saddle on her. You did it in what? Two sessions?"

Sorla nodded and looked at her watch. "A total of a bit over three hours."

Claire was shaking her head incredulously. "You know, I don't know much about training a horse, but that looked utterly awesome. It was like you hypnotized her. She just followed you, like magic. I couldn't take my eyes off the both of you."

Riley jammed her hands deep into her pockets. "Thanks."

Ed picked up the saddle. "I'll just put this away."

Claire held her hand out for the lead rope and halter. "I'll look after those, if you like." Together she and Ed went to the barn, leaving Sorla and Riley standing there.

Sorla smiled. "They're right, you know. You *are* amazing. I wish my Da could have met you. I think you would've blown him away."

"I wished I could have met him too. From what I hear, he was a nice person who really knew his horses."

"Yeah, he was. Have you got time for a coffee?"

Riley shook her head. "Sorry. I have to clean up and get ready to open up the store."

"Okay."

"Well, I'd better go."

"Thanks again for this morning."

"You're welcome. I guess I'll see you on Wednesday, then?"

"What time?"

"How does two sound?"

Sorla smiled. "Two sounds perfect."

Riley echoed her smile. "Two it is. See you."

"Bye."

Riley headed down the road and drove back to town. As she was parking the ute in front of the store, she caught sight in her rearview mirror of Sorla climbing out of her Jeep, hefting a bag. She jumped out and smiled. "Hello. Didn't expect to see you so soon. What's up?"

"We each forgot something."

"Oh?"

Sorla handed over the bag. "You forgot your bag, from yesterday."

"Oh, thanks. Sorry about that."

"And I forgot to do this." Sorla quickly stepped into Riley's space and took her face in her hands, leaning in and kissing her tenderly on the mouth. The bag fell from Riley's hand onto the ground with a thud as she melted into Sorla's touch, her hands coming up to encircle Sorla's waist and pull them closer. Sorla pulled back gently with a final quick, light kiss. She gently ran her thumb over Riley's bottom lip. "See you Wednesday." Sorla turned and walked back to her car.

Riley stood shell-shocked next to her truck. Her lips were still tingling and the buzz of blood in her ears was dizzying. She closed her eyes and rubbed her face before opening her eyes to bend down and retrieve her bag. She unlocked the front door, turned the sign to *Open*, and stepped inside.

❖

Right on three, Riley walked into the pub. "Hiya, Pauly. Sorry, I'm a bit later getting here than I thought."

"Hey there, kid. That's no worries at all. George is out the back, but be mindful, he's in a bit of a mood."

"Oh?"

"He wasn't too bad early on, but ever since he had lunch with Robbie Peters he's had the filths."

Riley frowned slightly. She stepped outside to see George sitting at a table finishing off a beer. "Hey, George. Sorry I'm late. How was your night?"

"Fine."

"Did the boys come for the poker game last night?"

"Yep."

"How'd you go?"

"Did all right."

"Well, that's good. You ready to come home now?"

"No."

"Is there a reason why?"

"I like it here."

"I'm sure you do. But I think I should get you home and into some fresh clothes. You can always come back down later."

George grunted as he stiffly pushed his way up off the bench seat. Riley gripped his elbow to steady him but he shook her off angrily. "Get off."

Riley raised her hands clear. "Sorry. Just trying to help."

"Don't need your help."

"Righto. The ute's this way."

It was a quiet, tense drive home. Riley pulled into the drive, got out, and opened George's door. It was a well-rehearsed routine for them both. She put her hand under his knees, lifting his bad leg out, gently placing his foot on the ground. As she bent down to lean in and help him out, he shoved her in the middle of the chest, making her stagger backwards. "I said I don't need your help."

Riley stepped back and blew out a slightly confused breath at his mood. "Okay, I'll just go and unlock the door then." On stiff legs George made it into the house. He went straight to the kitchen where he grabbed a glass and made his way back to the lounge room where he poured himself a glass of straight scotch. He threw the contents down in two swallows before loading up another shot.

Riley carried his overnight bag in and put it by the bed. Coming into the lounge room she watched as George threw the second glass down before pouring a third. She came over and put a hand on his arm. "You might wanna slow down a bit."

"Fuck off."

"You're in a mood. Did something happen this morning?"

George narrowed his eyes. "You tell me."

"What do you mean?"

"What did you get up to last night and this morning?"

"I had dinner with friends, came home, went back out this morning to work with a horse, then came back into town to work at the shop. Then I picked you up."

"Uh-huh. Anythin' unusual happen?"

"No. Just some of the regulars coming in for a few bits and pieces."

The third glass disappeared and a fourth was poured, which emptied the bottle. George growled. "Nothin' you wanna tell me?"

"No. What's the matter? Pauly said you were fine until you had lunch with Robbie. Has he done something to upset you?"

Spittle flew from George's mouth as he pointed at her with the now-empty bottle. "Ha! That's a laugh. Coming from you."

"I don't know what you're talking about. What's wound you up? Did Robbie say something?"

"Did you see Robbie this morning, by any chance?"

Riley thought back to the morning's faces. She shook her head. "No, can't say I did, why?"

"Well he saw you. Sucking on that Reardon girl's face, in the centre of bloody town no less! He said you didn't put up a fight. Looked like you enjoyed it."

Riley closed her eyes as she felt the blood drain from her face. "Shit."

George started to pace with the bottle in his hand. "So is it true, then? You're a fucking queer?"

"George…"

"Makes sense, now I look back. Ya never had a boyfriend."

Riley held out her hand for the bottle. "Let me take the bottle."

"What the hell did I do wrong?"

"George, it's not you."

"Damn right it's not me. I'm not fucking queer! Maybe it's from your mother's side? She had a pussy cousin. Man shook hands like a wet fish."

Again she held her hand out and crooked her fingers for the bottle. "George, come on…"

"Get the hell away from me. Like life isn't shit enough, you gotta go and crap on my head by makin' out with your new dyke friend in the centre of town, for all the freakin' world to see. How the hell am I gonna be able to show my face in town? Huh?"

Riley shook her head. "I'm sorry. I never meant—"

George screwed his face up as the rage built inside him. In three large strides he crossed the room and shoved Riley so hard in the chest that she stumbled backwards, catching her heel on the corner of the coffee table. She felt herself falling and cried out as she fell heavily onto the hardwood floor. George staggered towards her until he was standing over the top of her. He took off his belt. His eyes narrowed and his top lip curled into a snarl. "You never meant what exactly?" He slapped her in the head. He spat the words in her face. "To be a *dyke*?" He hit her hard on the chest with the belt. "To get caught?" He hit her again on the backswing. "To be *born*?" His rage was burning bright and out of control. The belt rained down again and again against her flesh.

A whimper escaped her lips as she valiantly tried to cover her head and face with her arms.

"To fuck up my entire life?" Riley curled into a ball. Puffing, George staggered and stopped. Spent, he dropped the belt onto the ground next to her. He kicked her. "Goddamn you. You disgust me." He threw the empty bottle at her back, hard, the glass smashing and splintering around her. He staggered out the front door, slamming it behind him.

She wasn't sure how long she lay there on the floor, but eventually her tears dried and she knew she had to get up. She carefully rolled away from the glass, gingerly pushing herself up to her hands and knees. She took a breath and staggered upward until she was standing on shaky legs, black spots swimming before her eyes momentarily with the effort. Taking in a few careful measured breaths, the moment passed. She wrapped an arm around her ribs and looked around the room. Slowly, she walked over and righted the coffee table before making her way out to the laundry, retrieving a broom and dustpan and brush to clean up the glass.

When she was done she went and lay down on her bed, pulling the cover up over her head. She knew George wouldn't be back tonight. That had been the pattern over the years. She never knew where he went and she never much cared. She closed her eyes and welcomed the blackness of the temporary oblivion.

CHAPTER ELEVEN

There weren't too many hours in the day or night leading up to Wednesday that Riley didn't try to work out an excuse not to turn up at Cherry Hill. She couldn't find one that she felt comfortable enough to deliver convincingly. As she drove out, her heart ached at the thought of not turning up, and her stomach was in knots knowing that she was. As she pulled up next to the barn, she put her sunglasses on and jammed her hat on low and tight. She saw that Ed and Sorla were waiting.

Sorla walked over to greet her. "Hi." She came towards her with a big smile and shaped up as if to hug her.

Riley sidestepped and cleared her throat. "Hi. Sorry, I can't make today for very long, I have another appointment I have to get back for. Shall we get on with it?" She walked past Sorla towards the yards. With her head down, Riley sliced up an apple with a pocketknife, giving her an excuse to not look at anyone. "Which one of you two do you think will be the mare's main rider?"

Ed looked over at Queenie. "Well, given her age and her size, I would think probably Sorla or Claire would be best."

"Okay. Sorla, can you get her saddle ready please?"

"Everything is over there on the railing, ready to go."

"Okay then. Give me a few minutes, and then when I give you a nod, I want you to come in through the gate. Just stand there until I give you further instructions. Understand?"

It didn't take a genius, or Sorla, long to figure out Riley was virtually giving her the cold shoulder. She was being polite enough but didn't look at her and appeared very stiff and distant. What had happened?

As Riley walked into the yard, even Queenie seemed to pick up on Riley's mood and tossed her head about nervously. Sorla watched as Riley turned her back on them. She could see she was wound as tight as a coil spring. She watched as Riley went through the routine, unwinding slowly to finally relax. The horse sensed the change and began to settle as Riley continued to stand perfectly still. Sorla saw Queenie sniff the air, curiosity winning out as the mare cautiously approached Riley until she was close enough to nuzzle her hand. Riley's palm opened to reveal a slice of apple. She turned and offered the slice to the mare as a reward for being brave. Riley smoothly slipped the halter on over her head. Without looking up, she raised her voice slightly. "You can come in now please."

Sorla opened the gate and made her way in. Without turning, Riley asked her to pick up the blanket and bring it over. Sorla approached. "Come over and breathe into the horse's nose. Let her smell you." Sorla did as she was told. "Now take the blanket and rub it down her neck and sides a few times before laying it on. Then go and get the saddle and put it on her slowly."

When Sorla had done as requested, Riley led Queenie around the yard a few times. Then she had the horse stand still and instructed Sorla to lean on the saddle. Eventually she asked Sorla to slowly and carefully pull herself up to sit on the mare's back. Queenie paced nervously at first, but Riley stayed at her head feathering her tongue and stroking her nose to calm her down. Gradually the mare stood still, appearing for all the world to be unconcerned, as if Sorla wasn't there.

"That's it." In a quiet voice Riley reassured her. "Nicely done. Now I'm going to lead you both around a few times. As we turn, gently squeeze your thighs in the direction you want her to turn. Okay?"

Sorla licked her lips in concentration. "'Kay."

They did several circuits of the yard, turning this way and that, until Riley smoothly handed over the reins, allowing Sorla to guide the horse around herself. Riley backed off and stood at the gate with arms folded, watching them.

"Okay. Now, bring her to the middle and make her stand." Sorla steered her in. "Stroke her down her neck a few times. Don't pat. Then when you're ready, slowly dismount, come around to her head, and rub her forehead." Sorla followed the directions to the letter. As she stood beside the horse's head, she grinned in triumph. Riley handed her a slice of apple. "Now reward and thank your horse."

Sorla giggled. "Do I get a piece of apple too?"

"No. You get to come back and do it on your own tomorrow."

Sorla's smile fell away. "On my own? Won't you be here?"

"Yes, I'll be here, but you're going to do all the work tomorrow. You and Queenie."

"But what if we're not ready?"

"You're ready. I wouldn't suggest it if I thought otherwise."

Sorla kept mindlessly stroking Queenie's nose while she watched as Riley walked over to the horse's midsection to let out the saddle's girth cinch strap.

"Riley?"

"Yes?"

"Are you okay?"

"Yes."

"You sure? It's just, you seem a bit…tense."

"No. I'm fine."

"Have I done something wrong?"

"No. Sorry, I'm just very busy. Are you right to finish up here?"

Sorla knew a brush-off when she saw one. "I think I can manage."

"Right, then. I'll see you tomorrow. Same time?"

"Sure. Same time."

"Bye." Riley turned on her heel and walked through the gate. She nodded her hat in Ed's direction before quickly striding to her truck and heading off.

Ed picked up the saddle. "What's up her nose today?"

Sorla frowned as she watched the dust plume get smaller down the road. She shook her head. "Wish I knew."

❖

Riley managed to get as far as the gate joining the main road before the tears came. And she didn't sleep much that night. Apart from finding it hard to find a comfortable position to lie in that wasn't bruised, she was overwhelmed with guilt at how badly she had treated Sorla the previous afternoon. She knew she had been horrible, but she knew it was the only way. She had given her word on the job at hand. She just hoped she could hold it together long enough to finish up with the horses as she had promised.

That day she'd had two appointments cancelled and an order for a saddle withdrawn. It seemed Robbie Peters's news travelled further than just George's ears. The sideways looks, suspicious glances, and averted eyes reminded Riley of when they'd first moved to town. It saddened her to think how all the years of goodwill could be turned on their head by one man's need to gossip. Riley knew she just had to keep her head down and ride it out. It was a small town. There would be another scandal soon enough.

Riley detoured to see Mickey on her way to Sorla's that afternoon. If he was going to hear the gossip from anybody, then it should be her. She'd cooked an extra portion of casserole and it was sitting safely nestled on the front seat of the truck as she made her way out. Pulling up next to the house, she saw that he was in the garden trimming the spent rose heads from the bushes. She made her way over and greeted him with a kiss.

"Was wonderin' when you'd be out."

Riley looked down at her boots and nodded.

"You better go on in and put the kettle on then."

She turned and went into the house while he packed the clippings and secateurs into a bucket on the porch before washing up.

Mickey sat down to the table as Riley poured the tea. "Thanks for the dinner, Midget. Looking forward to it." Riley traced the pattern on the tablecloth with a trembling hand. "But I don't s'pose that's the real reason you came for a visit now is it, young 'un?"

"No."

"If it's about the gossip going about town, I already heard it."

"And you're still talking to me?"

"Well, s'not like I get too many visitors out here. Be a shame to turn away my favourite one, just 'cause of a moment's indiscretion."

Riley, prepared for a fire-and-brimstone lecture, was completely caught off guard by Mickey's kindness. It was too much for her and the pent up despair she had been bottling up deep inside spilled over as she wept. She tried to stifle it with a hand, but the release valve had been opened. She bowed her head with the weight of it all and let the tears fall.

Mickey held the hand that had previously traced the patterned cloth until her tears subsided. He pressed a folded hanky into her palm. Riley wiped her face and blew her nose.

"You know, when Pearlie and I were courtin' in the early days, it was hard for Pearl. See, she came from monied people and it was an enormous an' embarrassing situation for her family, what with her running away to be with me on the rodeo merry-go-round. Then, when we couldn't have kids of our own, well, people treated us like we was diseased. I came to the conclusion that most folk can't see further than the end of their nose, and if something different comes along, it frightens 'em 'cause they don't know what to make of it."

Riley was back to nervously tracing the pattern again.

"You're a lot like that, young 'un, in that people don't know what to make of you. You did a lot of things people said you couldn't do—you looked after George, better than he deserves, you built a business, and you're a good community person. People got used to how you are. Now you've gone and surprised 'em again. It's gonna take a while. Some won't like it, some will be fascinated by the unusual of it, and others won't give a toss, and keep on keepin' on. But you're a smart cookie and y'know that already. You're here to see which camp I'm sittin' in."

Riley took a wobbly breath and smiled weakly. "In part. Mostly, I came out to tell you myself, before you heard the rumour from someone else. Somebody saw me kissing Sorla Reardon."

"Way I heard it, she kissed you."

Riley shrugged. "Doesn't much make any difference. It happened."

"True enough."

Riley sighed. "I've had some appointments and orders cancelled."

Mickey shook his head. "I can imagine. What does George say?"

When she closed her eyes, she could still hear his venomous words in her head. Riley softly snorted. "No different to most days, I guess. I've just given him another reason to be angry."

Mickey shook his head sadly. "He always was a dumb arse."

"So which camp are you in? Do I disgust you too?"

"I am not gonna lie to you and tell you I understand. I don't quite get it myself, but I'm not distressed or disgusted by it either. You see, Pearlie and I, we talked about it several years back."

Riley's head came up in genuine surprise. "What? But how did you know…?"

Mickey smiled. "Not me, Pearl. We often wondered why, for such a pretty thing, you never had any boyfriends. It was Pearl who saw where your eyes went when you thought no one was looking."

Riley felt herself blush.

"We talked it over. We knew what the sting of a small town mind could do. We wanted to make sure if that was the way it was gonna be, that we would be here for you, no matter what. So to answer your question, Midget, I ain't changed camp. I'm still here. I still love ya. It's just we've thinned the crowd out a little for the minute."

Fresh tears coursed down her face at the enormity of the gift that Mickey and Pearl were in her life. She felt quite undeserving of such generosity.

"Now all you have to do is decide what you wanna do from here."

Riley sadly shook her head. "I don't know, Mickey. Sometimes, I feel so much. I don't know what to do with it."

"I can't help you with that. Only you can decide what it is you want and what it is you're prepared to live with."

"I know. It's all just so overwhelming. It seems no matter which way I turn, I'm upsetting someone. Either way, it just makes me feel sick."

"Yup. Sounds familiar."

"I guess I've got a lot of thinking to do."

"Well, you know where I am if you need to chew an ear."

"I do. Thank you."

"Well, I'm looking at the time getting away and we both have jobs to attend to." Mickey walked her to the door. "Thank you for coming out to tell me. That was a mighty brave thing you done."

"I had to, Mick. I'm just sorry someone got to you before I was brave enough to do it."

"Don't mind. You came, and I appreciate it."

Riley threw her arms around his neck and kissed his cheek. "You're my family, Mick."

He kissed her back. "And you're mine, young 'un. Now off you get before you see an old man get all soft and soppy."

"Bye, love you."

"Love you too, girl."

CHAPTER TWELVE

Riley pulled up next to the barn and was greeted by Claire. "Hey, stranger."

"Hi, Claire. Wasn't expecting to see you here today."

"I pulled a late shift. I'll head on in a bit later."

"Whatcha got there?"

Claire held up a padded cotton cat bed. "I found this in town and couldn't resist. Thought I'd pop it in the cat's new digs. Wanna come see?"

"Sure." Riley followed Claire into the feed shed and noticed an old wooden dresser in one corner with the drawers open. The kittens were curled up sound asleep on the blanket from her truck.

"We found this and thought it would make a great little cat cave for the family. Miss Pusskins seems to spend most of her time here in the feed shed now anyway." Claire kneeled down. "Here you go, Missy. Try that on for size." Claire stuffed the bed in one of the half-open drawers, where the cat immediately hopped in and started purring and marching on the spot, kneading the bedding.

Riley smiled. "I think you're on a winner there."

"Hey, do you want a cool drink before you start? I can't believe how hot it is."

Riley looked around the shed and sniffed the air. It seemed heavy and ripe from the hay sitting in the corner. "When did your hay get in?"

"Late Wednesday afternoon. Why?"

"Smells hot. You might need to keep an eye on it."

"Come inside and we can let the others know."

"Thanks, but I think I'll make a start out here."

Claire put her hand on Riley's arm. "Can I ask you a personal question?"

Riley looked away and shrugged. "I guess."

"You and Sorla. You guys okay?"

"Yeah. Why?"

Claire tilted her head on its side and looked closely at Riley's face. "Well, for two people who confess to being okay, you both look like crap and you both look miserable."

A long moment passed before Riley sighed. "I just have a bit going on."

Claire hooked her arm into the crook of Riley's elbow. "Can I suggest something?" Riley shrugged with one shoulder. "How about you come on inside with me and we grab something to drink. Nothing big."

Riley's guts roiled in nervous tension. "I don't know."

"Just for a bit. C'mon. Please?"

Riley blew out a breath. "I should come in and apologize. For yesterday."

"Thatta girl. Come on. I know I could do with a cold iced tea and getting out of this heat for a bit. I feel like I'm going to explode. Aren't you hot?" Claire was in a singlet top, long shorts, and sandals. She looked at Riley who was covered pretty much head to toe in a hat, a long-sleeved shirt done up to the collar, jeans, and boots.

Riley quirked a weak half smile. "I guess it's what I'm used to."

"Well, even after spending all that time over in the Sandbox, hot weather and I still aren't friends. We tolerate each other, but on days like today…only just."

As they approached the kitchen door, Riley hesitated on the doorstep, nerves getting the better of her. Claire offered her an encouraging smile. Riley took her hat off and stepped over the doorway.

Claire raised her arm in the direction of the lounge room. "Why don't you go on through."

Riley took a shaky breath. Sorla was sitting on one of the couches in the lounge room. She had paperwork on the coffee table in front of her and either side on the couch, a pen wedged behind one ear, and was poring over a document, frowning slightly. She grabbed the pen and scribbled a few notes on a notepad before chewing the pen end in deep thought. She'd heard Riley arrive, heard her chatting with Claire, and now she sensed her entering the room. Still looking intently at the notes she'd just made, she broke the silence. "Are you gonna come all the way in or just stand there staring?"

"I was thinking more of another option."

"Which is?"

"Run."

Sorla put her pen down and sat back in the seat, finally looking up at Riley. "And why would you want to run?"

"Because I'm chicken and my stomach's in knots."

Sorla looked at her sideways. "And why is that?"

Riley looked down at her boots and took a deep breath before looking up again. She nervously fingered her hat. "Because I owe you an apology. For yesterday. I was curt and rude, and I'm sorry."

For a brief flash, Sorla could almost picture what a very young and small Riley must have looked like. She gentled her voice. "Will you at least come and sit down? You're making *me* nervous standing there."

Riley walked the long way around and sat on the opposite seat. "You look busy. I should let you get back to it."

Sorla pushed the papers to one side. "I'm just going over some plans and notes for next week's meeting. It can wait."

"You look tired."

"So do you."

Claire arrived with a tray of drinks. She quietly put a glass in front of each of them and left just as discreetly. Sorla crossed her arms. "So, are you going to tell me what's going on, or do I have to play twenty questions?"

Riley licked her lips and had a few false starts, before the words finally came out. "I'm trying to juggle a few things at the minute, and it's getting harder. And when you arrived, I got rattled. I told you, I can't do the relationship thing—but I don't know what I'm supposed to be doing. I seem to be handling it all wrong. And yesterday, I took that out on you, and that wasn't fair, and I'm sorry." Riley got it all out in a rush and sat, trying to catch her breath.

"I suppose I didn't help the situation either, the other day in town, did I?" The corner of Riley's mouth quirked. Sorla's shoulders stiffened. "I see. Well, in that case then, I'm sorry too. Do you think you can still do your job and finish the horses?"

"Yes. But if you would prefer somebody else, I understand."

"No. I said I didn't want anybody else. We'll just go back to making this a business arrangement, pure and simple." Riley nodded her head in acknowledgement. "Thank you for your apology. Is there anything else?" Sorla sat forward on the seat and spread her paperwork back out in front of her in a silent dismissal.

"Just one thing. About the—"

Horns started blaring, cutting the conversation short. Both Sorla and Riley stood bolt upright looking around, and Sorla exclaimed, "What the…?"

Claire came running through the room pulling on jeans with the mobile phone to her ear. "We're coming!"

Sorla demanded, "What's going on?"

Claire was looking up the contacts list for a number on her phone. "The boys just drove in—feed shed's on fire! I'm calling the fire brigade."

Riley was already halfway out the door and streaking across the yard, Sorla not far behind her.

"Riley, the horses are in the barn! Help me get them out." Sorla assumed the boys were at the shed trying to douse the flames, so it would be smart to get the horses out in case the barn became involved. It was an old wooden building. If the flames got to it, there'd be no stopping them.

As they approached the barn's doorway, the inside was already full of smoke, and the horses were dancing and whinnying with fear. The young foals were running from side to side in their shared pen, terrified. Riley turned to Sorla. "You open up the doors and make sure all the yard gates are open. I'll start herding them out to you." Sorla nodded and took off.

Riley stepped into the thick smoke, running through to the tack room, pulling out a handful of halters and saddle blankets. She quickly haltered Queenie and tied head ropes around the two foals. She tore up one of the blankets and wrapped it around the foals' eyes. She got a few grazes from their hooves down her shins, which she barely registered through the adrenaline rush. Positioning the foals either side of the mare, she led them out to the yards where Sorla was still opening and propping open the gates. She met her halfway across one of the yards and handed them over. "Lead them out as far as you can before taking off the blinds. We don't want them running back in."

Sorla grabbed the ropes. "Gotcha!"

Riley turned and ran back in. She was able to herd Ed's horse out easily enough to Sorla, who gave her the thumbs up. Finally she turned and went back in for Irish, who was kicking the horse stall walls in pure terror. Riley was coughing heavily as the smoke thickened, reducing visibility in the barn to just a few feet in front of her face. She couldn't risk opening the gate with the horse's level of fear and the thickness of the smoke; it was likely she would run in the wrong direction. Riley had half a blanket left from the one she originally tore up. She ran over to the sink, and opened the taps full bore, soaking the blanket. She turned off the tap and ran back over to Irish's stable.

She knew she would only get one shot at this. Taking a deep breath she calmed herself and opened the stable door, just as Irish reared. She stepped to one side as the mare came racing at her. As Irish drew level, Riley tossed the wet blanket over her head. The mare stopped and tossed her head to get the foreign material off, giving Riley the few precious seconds she needed to grab a handful of mane and swing up onto the mare's back. Startled, Irish reared again, causing the blanket to slide off her head and down the length of her neck. Riley hung on with both hands to the dark locks of her mane, her fingers woven in tight. With her long legs wrapped around the mare's flanks, she dug her heels into the mare's sides and cried out to get her to run forward.

Just as Irish made it to the far gate, Riley pushed herself up and pulled on the mane to get the horse's attention, enough to marginally slow the mare's breakneck speed now that they were clear of the barn. Just as Irish approached the gate that led out to the open paddocks, Riley slipped off her back, pulling the wet blanket with her. She ran back to Sorla.

Sorla gave her a quick hug. "Come on. Let's go help the boys!"

They ran around the corner to see Ed, Claire, and Perry on buckets with Don setting up the portable water pump. He kicked the diesel engine into gear and opened up the hose nozzle, hitting the face of the flames with the water. Riley and Sorla grabbed two more buckets and joined in the effort.

Ed ran over to Don and screamed over the noise of the engine.

"Try to keep it from crossing to the barn!" Don nodded. Half of the feed shed was freely alight and flames were licking across to gnaw at the ceiling beams, trying to spread its fiery body to encompass the roof line.

Riley threw her bucket of water onto the door frame and saw a small figure just inside. It was a singed Miss Pusskins, crying in distress for the babies. Riley scooped her up in her arms and ran back and handed her to Sorla. She turned and grabbed her torn piece of saddle blanket and shoved it into Ed's fresh bucket of water. She wrapped the wet cloth around her head and ran through the doorway, straight into the burning shed.

She dropped low to the ground and crawled with one hand, holding the cloth to her face, the other helping her to balance and feel her way forward. The smoke and heat were so intense they forced her eyes closed. She couldn't see through the smoke or the tears. She finally bumped into the cupboard. She felt around through all the drawers. In the last drawer on the bottom, right up the back, she felt two lifeless little bodies. Scooping them up, she wrapped them in the blanket and held them to her chest.

The fire crawled overhead as the flames in the roof popped, crackled, and roared with hunger. As Riley turned to head back out, she heard a roof beam give way over her head. She couldn't see where it was coming from and barely had enough time to put her left arm up as a partial shield, when she felt the heavy timber crash onto her arm and continue down to assault the back of her head and left shoulder. She fell to the side with the momentum of the blow, trying to be careful not to land on the kittens, rolling the timber off her shoulder and back.

The blow to her head made her feel dizzy. All she wanted to do was lie down, but she knew if she did that she would die in the shed. Pushing herself up to a crawling position, she forced herself to make her arms and legs move. Her left arm felt numb. She used it to hold the babies to her chest, while her right arm helped pull her forward. Looking ahead, she could just make out the silhouetted doorway. She gritted her teeth and dragged up the last of her energy from deep inside. With a final burst of effort, she made it through to outside where hands grabbed her and pulled her free. Ed dragged her over past Don and the pump. She coughed and spat but gave him the thumbs up, as he quickly assessed that she was okay. In between coughing spasms she pushed him and waved him back to fight the fire with everyone else. Sorla was kneeling beside her. Riley handed over the wet babies to her.

Sorla looked down at their inert little bodies, tears pouring down her face.

Riley grabbed her arm and tried to croak out in between coughs. "You need to…breathe…mouth-to-mouth."

Sorla nodded and leaned over, blowing tiny puffs of air into their noses and mouths. She rubbed their little chests as she breathed. Miss Pusskins was by Sorla's side, crying for her babies. Sorla looked up, distraught. "It's no use."

"Keep…going."

Claire came over. "The fire brigade's here!"

Claire took one of the babies from Sorla and copied what she was doing. "Let's get them in to the infirmary, and we'll try them on some oxygen."

Together they jogged back to the house with the babies in their hands, breathing and rubbing as they went, Miss Pusskins running right behind them.

Riley watched them go as she concentrated on her breathing. Someone from the fire brigade came over and handed her an oxygen mask, which she accepted. Closing her eyes, she gratefully sucked in the fresh cool air, willing the oxygen all the way down to her toes with every deep breath she took.

❖

"They're not breathing!" Sorla cried, as she held an equally distressed Miss Pusskins in her arms.

Head bent over the little bodies on the infirmary bed, Claire gently rubbed their chests. "Give them a minute."

Sorla wiped at the tears on her face with a frustrated swipe of her hand. "They're dead, aren't they?"

"Have a little faith, Sor. Just hang in there with me. Come on, little ones, you can do this."

For long seconds, the only sound to be heard was the gentle hiss of the oxygen. Even Miss Pusskins had stopped crying, watching intently as Claire worked diligently on the little prone bodies. Finally her efforts were rewarded with a squeak from first one, and then the other little kitten. "Look at that!" Claire's looked up and laughed, tears in her own eyes. "Go, you good things. Keep going, you beautiful babies."

Sorla laughed, which quickly turned to sobs. She put Miss Pusskins on the bed, and the cat quickly padded over and began to lick and clean the kittens. With hands over her mouth, Sorla back stepped to the wall, where she slid down onto the floor, crying into her knees. In three strides, Claire crossed the room to join Sorla on the floor, pulling her distraught friend into her lap, where she curled up into a ball, sobs racking her body.

Claire gently held her until the intensity of the tears had been spent leaving Sorla to lie sniffing and trembling. Claire gently leaned down and wiped her face with a tissue from her pocket, stroking Sorla's hair until even the sniffling slowed and became only an occasional sniff. "You okay now?" Sorla nodded into her lap. "Wanna tell me what that was about?" Sorla shook her head. "Come on, honey, try. This was about more than the kittens, wasn't it?"

Sorla closed her eyes and nodded. Her body started to shake again and her eyes flew open in fear. Claire hugged her tight. "Come on love, breathe for me. Remember how we practiced? Breathe in, hold-two-three, out-two-three. Now again, come on, Sor, breathe with me. In, hold-two-three, out-two-three. That's the way. Come on, a couple more, hon. That's it, you got it." Sorla followed Claire's coaching until she evened out. Claire rubbed her back. "Better?" Sorla nodded. "Where did you go, just then? When you closed your eyes?"

Sorla's throat closed over so that her words barely came out. "Fallujah."

"Uh-huh. And what did you see?"

Fresh tears coursed down her face. "I saw the truck explode, screaming…and John and Annette…the flames. I saw their bodies…" Sorla turned her head and burrowed into Claire's lap.

"It's okay, love, I've got you. Come on back for me. Turn your head and look around the room. Feel where you are. Centre yourself. Take your time." Sorla moved slightly. "You wanna try to sit up?"

Sorla nodded, slowly raising herself to sit with her back against the wall. Claire got her a bottle of water.

"Thanks."

"You haven't had one that nasty for a while." Sorla sipped her water wearily. "Guess the build-up of a big couple of days and the fire knocked you for six, huh?"

Sorla shrugged.

"How do you feel now?"

"Tired mostly."

"Wanna stand up and help me check on your babies?" Sorla smiled weakly but nodded. Together they stood and walked over to see the babies suckling on their mother. Sorla ran her finger over each of their heads gently.

Claire turned the oxygen down low. "We should get them checked out by a vet. I don't know much about how cats work I'm afraid."

"You did a great job."

"Well, if it wasn't for Riley, they wouldn't be here at all."

Sorla lifted her head and looked surprised, having temporarily mentally put aside what was happening outside. "We should go and check on everyone."

"How about you go and get some colds drinks ready, while I give Ed a call and see how it's all going?"

Sorla headed to the kitchen and made up two jugs of iced tea and two of iced water and was putting them on trays when she looked up and saw Claire arrive. "I've poured you a glass already."

"Mm, thanks. Ed says the fire's just about out—they're just wetting down the last bits now. Feed shed's gone, but the barn's okay. He and Riley are coming over to get the drinks."

"Everyone okay?"

"Ed said he and the boys are fine."

Sorla narrowed her eyes. "And Riley?"

"Ed said she's got a cut on her head. He said she won't let anyone near it. Says she's fine. He wants me to try to have a look at it when she comes over."

Sorla shook her head to dislodge the feeling of being slightly dissociated. She knew rationally it was just a part of the shock of the day, but it left her feeling slightly out of focus with what was going on. She concentrated on her breathing and willed herself to be better.

Hearing the door open, she turned to see two very smoky-smelling, soot-covered bodies walk in. Ed came straight over and hugged first Claire, then Sorla, before going over and throwing down a tall glass of iced water in three huge gulps. Ed groaned. "Oh, that is beautiful." He poured another, sipping this one more slowly.

Riley stood slightly back from the group with her hat on, still cradling a scrap of the torn blanket over her left arm. Claire pulled a chair out for her and patted it. "Ed tells me you got a bump on the head."

Riley stayed standing. "It's nothing."

"Well, why don't you let me take a look at it, while you're here?"

"I'm fine."

Sorla cleared her throat. "Fine doesn't bleed all over my floor. I want you to go to the hospital and get that cut checked out."

"No, thanks, I'll be right."

Adrenaline and fear lent an edge to Sorla's voice. "I'm not asking, I'm telling. Technically, you're an employee of mine. You've been injured on the worksite. I am legally bound to have you medically checked over, treated, and cleared."

"Sorry, I don't do hospitals. I told you, I'll be fine. Thanks all the same."

"I don't care if you *do* hospitals or not, I am not risking this venture simply because you don't like hospitals."

Claire poured Ed another glass and said, "How about we do a deal?" Both women looked at her like she was mad. "How about, Riley agrees to let me check her out, and if there are any issues and they can be treated here, then that's what we'll do, and she doesn't have to go into town."

Sorla crossed her arms in front of her chest, frowning.

Claire held up a finger. "But, if there *is* something that I think needs more help than I can give it here, then Riley agrees to go to the hospital."

There was a huge pregnant silence before Sorla unfolded her arms and poured a drink for herself. "I can live with that." She tapped her fingers on the table and asked Riley, "Do we have a deal?" She watched as Riley's body tensed under the pressure of the offer.

"Fine." Head down, frowning, without looking at anyone, Riley stomped off towards the infirmary, with Claire trailing behind.

CHAPTER THIRTEEN

Once in the infirmary, Riley spotted the little feline family unit in the basket, all curled around each other. "They okay?"

Claire squatted beside the basket. Reaching in, she rubbed the back of Miss Pusskins's neck and smiled as the cat closed her eyes and purred under her touch. "I think so. But we're going to run them into town to see a vet shortly. Speaking of getting checked over, how about you hop up onto the bed for me?"

"Really, Claire, I'm fine. There's no need to bother."

Claire gently touched Riley's elbow and guided her to the bed. "It's no bother. Come on, up you get."

Riley carefully sat on the edge of the bed. "I'm gonna get it all dirty."

"That's okay. It's easy enough to clean up." Claire got a tray ready with some saline, gauze, scissors, and pads. She washed her hands and pulled some gloves on. "Can you take your hat off for me please?"

Riley did as asked, squinting marginally with the increase in light. Claire shone a pen torch in her eyes and asked her to follow her finger. "How did you cut your head?"

"A piece of timber fell from the roof."

"One of the big beams?"

"I guess. Felt heavy."

"Did it just hit your head?"

"Yes."

"Did you black out at all?"

"No."

"Do you feel dizzy, or sick on the stomach?"

"I did when it first hit me, but it's okay now. Just got a bit of a headache is all. A couple of Panadol and a wrap should fix it."

"I'm just going to feel around your head, then go around the back and take a look."

Claire gently walked her fingers all across Riley's head, being especially careful where the cut was. Then she walked around to examine Riley's back. "Did the beam hit you anywhere else?"

"No."

"Uh-huh. I'm going to try and clean it up, so this might sting a bit." Claire gently proceeded to clean the wound using the saline-soaked gauze. "Hm, you've got yourself a nice cut here, my friend. This is going to need stitches."

"You can do that here though, right?"

"I could. I'm just going to wrap it up for the minute first. I want to see if there's anything else we need to deal with." Claire's hands efficiently padded and wrapped Riley's head.

"No, it's just my head."

"Still, I wouldn't be doing my job if I didn't give you the full going over."

"Claire, really, I'm fine."

Claire walked to the front and smiled at her, patting her thigh. "Good, because if you're fine, then this won't take long. Can you take your shirt off for me?"

"There's no need…"

Claire took a hold of Riley's hand. She bent her knees slightly to meet Riley's gaze and hold her attention. "Riley. You and I made a deal out there in the kitchen. We can either do this here, or we go into town to the hospital. Okay?"

For long moments Riley just looked at her before finally nodding sadly. She closed her eyes to the inevitable but couldn't hide her bottom lip from quivering.

Claire brushed Riley's cheek gently with her thumb. "It'll be okay." Riley's right hand came up and started to undo the press buttons on her shirt. "Thank you. I'm just going to listen to your chest." Claire put the stethoscope to her ears, and Riley turned her head away from what she knew Claire was about to see—a variety of bruises crisscrossing Riley's chest and abdomen, in various stages of pink, purple, blue, and black, with a particularly eye-catching nasty, large bruise on her ribs.

"I need to check out your back too, honey. I'm just going to slip your shirt off, okay?"

Riley offered no objection and gave in.

With slow, gentle hands, Claire undid the shirtsleeve cuffs before softly pushing the shirt off her shoulders and down her back. "Looks like the beam hit your shoulder too, as well as your head. It's got a pretty decent bruise on it and a small burn. Does it hurt?" Riley opened her eyes and shrugged her right shoulder. "Can you move your arm?" Riley moved her upper arm marginally to the left and right, up and down. "I'm just going to slide the rest of the shirt off your left arm."

Riley watched as Claire lifted the scrap blanket away and pulled the sleeve down over her arm and hand. As she lifted the arm, Riley flinched ever so slightly. There was a burn right over the middle of a significantly sized distended lump in the middle of her forearm. The arm was clearly broken.

Claire cradled Riley's arm with her own and tested for a pulse and the capillary reflex in the fingernail beds, explaining as she worked. "Can you move your fingers?"

Riley shook her head. She was afraid to form words.

"Are there any other surprises I should know about?"

Riley shook her head.

"Okay, how about we put your shirt back on?" Claire helped her and finished by buttoning it up. She pulled a stool on wheels over to sit facing Riley. She put a hand on her knee. "Your head, I could stitch here, although being a head injury, it warrants an X-ray to be on the safe side. The burns don't look too bad and we could probably do them here too. I don't think your shoulder's busted, but again, it really needs to be X-rayed to know for sure. But your arm is broken, honey, and we both know, I can't fix that here. The fact that you can't move your fingers and your blood flow looks to be compromised says to me you definitely need an X-ray to see what's going on inside."

Riley picked at a loose thread on the seam of her jeans. Claire slipped her hand over Riley's restless one.

"The bruises…is that why you didn't want to go to the hospital?"

Riley held back tears as she nodded.

"Does anybody else know about this?" Riley shook her head. "I see."

Riley looked up into Claire's face. "What if I iced my arm and strapped it? We could do that here."

"How do your fingers feel, honestly?"

Riley sighed softly. "Numb."

"You might have some nerve or muscle damage. If that's the case, you need to get it assessed and fixed. If you don't, you run the risk of losing the ability to use your fingers or hand. You need both of those to do your work. Besides, we made that deal, remember?"

Riley's shoulders slumped. She knew she'd been clutching at straws, but that was all she had left.

"Who did this to you, Riley?" Claire's voice was soft, as if she knew how much the questions hurt. "Was it George?"

The tears that she had been holding back finally spilled over. Her chin quivered and she bowed her head in shame as the weight of being revealed came crashing down on her. Claire held Riley to her chest. Riley shook her head and mumbled into Claire's shirt. "I can't go to hospital. It'll just make things worse."

Claire pulled away from Riley and sat back down on the stool facing her. "Honey, that arm needs help. Sweetheart, *you* need help. Those bruises? That's not right. That needs to be stopped. There are people who can help. You don't have to live this way."

Riley shook her head. "You don't understand."

"You're right, I don't understand, but someone beating you up isn't right, Riley. Either way, you have to go to hospital and get that arm looked at, and they're going find out, just like I did."

Riley wiped her face with her good hand. She'd given it her best shot, but the day was fast becoming a train wreck. She couldn't stop the wheels in motion and had no choice but to ride it out and deal with whatever happened on the other side.

"There are people who can help. I'll come in with you if you'd like."

Resigned, Riley shook her head. "I'll be okay."

"Well, I have to go into work soon anyway, so what say I come with you and keep you company for a while?"

Riley was tired. Tired of holding in secrets, tired of always having to be strong, forgiving, patient, or understanding. Claire was offering her support and friendship. It would be nice to have a friend in her corner before the shit hit the fan. "That would be nice. Thank you."

"Okay then, how about we get you tidied up a bit before we head into town?"

"Claire?"

"Yes?"

"Is there a bathroom in here?"

"Do you feel sick?" Riley nodded. "Hang on." Claire spun around and pulled off a bag from the bottom of the trolley, quickly handing it over just as Riley's stomach made its statement. She held Riley's hair back until she'd finished, handing her a tissue to wipe her mouth. "Done?" Riley nodded. "Want some water to rinse your mouth out?"

"Yes, please."

"Only a few small sips, in case you have to have surgery on that arm. Feel better now?"

"Yes, thank you. I'm sorry."

"Don't be. Comes with the job. Just relax for a bit, while I clean up."

Riley nodded.

Claire was efficient and finished in no time. "How about you wait here, while I go and get my gear ready for work, and then we'll head in?"

"I need to get my purse from the truck. It's got my cards and things in there. Can I do that and meet you at your car?"

"How's your head? You dizzy?"

"I'm fine. I promise. You won't find me kissing the dirt outside." Riley set her jaw stubbornly. If she were to go in with Claire, she wanted it to be on her terms.

"Okay. I'll meet you at the car then. Just be careful."

"Thank you." Riley carefully got off the bed and put her hat back on. She didn't feel great, but she felt confident enough that she could do what she needed to do. She slowly walked out the door and down the corridor, passing through the lounge room and into the kitchen.

Sorla was still sitting at the table with Ed. They both looked up as Riley walked through. "Everything okay?"

"Yes. Thank you." With her head down, Riley didn't slow or stop, but continued through and out the door. She made it to her truck without incident, retrieved her purse and went and sat in the back seat of Claire's car to wait.

❖

Claire followed a few minutes later. Sorla sat up straight anxiously. "Is everything all right? You were both gone such a long time."

Claire pulled up a chair and sat down at the table. "For the most part, yes."

Sorla frowned. "What does that mean exactly?"

"Riley has a few injuries and she has agreed to come with me to the hospital when I go into work in a little while."

"What's wrong with her that she has to go to the hospital? Is she okay?"

Claire reached over and patted her hand. "Yes, she'll be fine. She has a nasty cut on the back of her head, what looks like a badly bruised shoulder, a couple of burns, and a busted arm."

"What? And she didn't want to go to the hospital? Is she mad?"

Claire shook her head. "No, she's not mad. Far from it."

"Then why the hell did she say she was fine when her arm's broken? That doesn't make sense."

"She has her reasons."

"What sort of reasons?"

Claire shook her head. "I can't tell you that, but I can tell you this, Riley agreeing to come with me to the hospital is a big deal, bigger than you can imagine, and before you ask, no, I'm not going to tell you. But I will say this—Riley is going to need a friend over the next little while."

"I don't understand."

Claire said, "I know, and I'm sorry. All I can tell you is that things are about to get even more complicated for her than they are now."

Sorla trusted Claire with her life, no questions, no doubt. She didn't understand one bit. She was hurt at the secrecy, but she would trust Claire and do her best. Sorla nodded once.

Claire stood up and kissed her cheek. "Thank you. Now if you'll excuse me, I need to get my bag and head on in before my patient changes her mind. Are you able to take the cats to the vet's?"

Sorla nodded. "I'll give them a call and head on in. Perhaps I could drop in and see how Riley's doing after that."

Claire squeezed her shoulder. "That sounds like a great idea."

❖

Sorla dropped the cats off to the vets where it was agreed they would be kept overnight for observation. As Sorla drove, making her way towards the hospital, she realized that a small load of tension had been removed, knowing that the cats would be okay. In just a short amount of time, they had become a part of her Cherry Hill family and Sorla felt a great deal of love and responsibility towards them. Claire gave her directions over the phone as to where to find Riley. Walking up to the corridor that Riley was in, she spied Claire coming towards her and waved her down.

"How did you get on with the cats? What did the vet say?"

"The vet says we're heroes. We saved their lives. I said, naturally, we're soldiers, that's our job."

Claire stood with a quirky grin on her face and hands on her hips. "Seriously."

"Seriously? Well, he said because of what we did, he thinks they'll be okay. Miss Pusskins has a few small burns that he's put some cream on. He wants to keep them in overnight, but basically, he seems quite confident they'll all be fine."

"That's great news."

"I know. How's Riley? Can I see her?"

"Soon. She's got some people in with her at the minute."

"The doctor?"

Before Claire had a chance to respond, two police officers and a doctor walked out of one of the rooms. They stood in the hallway in discussion, with one of the officers taking notes, before the two parties shook hands and went in opposite directions. A nurse went into the room with a tray, coming back out a short time later.

Claire touched Sorla on the elbow. "Be back in a sec." Sorla saw that Claire caught up with the doctor and had a brief conversation, before turning back to join her. "Okay, we can go in now. She's just been given a pre-med, so she might get a bit sleepy soon. They're going to take her up to theatre shortly to fix her arm."

Sorla realized they were heading in the direction of the room that the police officers had just come out of. She stopped still in the middle of the hall and grabbed Claire's arm. "Is that Riley's room? The one the police came out of?"

"Uh-huh."

"Claire, what's going on?"

Claire shook her head. "I can't tell you, I'm sorry."

"Has this got anything to do with the fire?"

"No, not in the slightest."

Sorla looked at her, puzzled, but she trusted her friend and so put aside her reservations for the moment and went into the room. The first thing that struck her in the softly lit room was how small Riley looked in the bed. Someone had cleaned her up, and now that the soot and dirt had been removed from her face, Sorla could see clearly how pale Riley was and how dark the circles were under her eyes. Her eyes were closed and her bad arm was lying underneath the covers which were pulled up to her chest. She came and stood beside the bed.

At her approach, Riley's eyes cracked open. She coughed. "What are you doing here?"

Sorla reached over, smiling, and smoothed a stray lock of hair out of Riley's eyes. "Hello. Nice to see you too. I just dropped the cats off to the vet's and thought I'd pop in and see how you're doing."

"How are they?"

Sorla sat on the side of the bed. "They're going to keep them in overnight, to keep an eye on them, but the vet seems to think they'll be fine."

"That's good news. You and Claire did a great job with them."

"Well, that's only because you were incredibly crazy and brave, running into a burning building to get them out. You didn't have to do that, you know."

Riley licked her lips as her eyes grew heavy. "Yes, I did. They're Cherry Hill's first babies."

Sorla noticed that Riley's speech was slowing and becoming a little more pronounced in its drawl. "Well thank you, that was an incredibly brave thing that you did."

"S'okay."

"How are you feeling?"

"Bit foggy. They gave me a needle and it's made my head all weird."

"That's the pre-med. Claire said they're going to take you in to surgery to fix your arm."

"Sorry for being a pain. I didn't mean to."

"Why were the police here?"

Riley closed her eyes and shook her head slightly. "They know."

"Know what?"

"Doctors told 'em. Can't take it back."

"What?"

"Tried to hide from Claire. Couldn't. If it wasn't for my arm... doesn't matter now. Too late."

"I don't understand. Too late for what?"

"Such a mess."

"What's a mess?"

"That's why I can't fall for you—too hard."

"What's too hard?"

"Don't wanna hurt you."

"Riley? Riley?" Sorla rubbed Riley's good arm, but it was too late. The pre-med had kicked in and she had fallen asleep.

Chapter Fourteen

The room was dark when Riley opened her eyes. There was a slight glow from the corridor and lights shining from the machine behind her head somewhere. Her nose itched. She reached up clumsily and felt a plastic tube across her cheeks and into her nose via some prongs. She licked her lips. She felt very thirsty. Looking around, the day's events began to come back to her. She remembered going to Cherry Hill, the fire, and coming to the hospital. She remembered the police and going off to theatre. She must be back, then.

She lifted the sheet and saw that her left arm was strapped to a fibreglass mould that went from her elbow to her fingers. It was held on with Velcro straps. In the middle of her arm was a sizeable nonstick dressing.

She turned her head as she heard squeaking shoes, to see Claire walk in the room.

"Ah, you're awake. How do you feel?"

"Head's a bit woolly, but okay."

"You thirsty? Would you like some ice chips?"

"Yes, please."

Claire poured some out of a jug sitting on a table next to her bed. "Hang on and I'll sit you up a bit." She raised the head of the bed and repositioned the cushions behind Riley's head. "Better?"

"Thanks."

Claire handed her the cup and Riley's eyes closed in delight at the first mouthful.

"You just missed Sorla—she sat here with you after they brought you back from theatre."

Riley frowned. "What time is it?"

Claire sat down on the edge of the bed. "Nearly midnight."

"She shouldn't have done that. She looked so tired."

"She thought you might like a friendly face when you woke up. Seems you were pretty tired yourself. You've been asleep awhile. I sent her home about an hour ago. Now you're stuck with me."

"How long do I have to stay in here?"

"If all goes well, you can probably go home tomorrow."

"I left my truck out at your place."

"That's okay, we can sort something out."

"Do you know where my clothes are?"

"Why, did you want to make a run for it in the night?"

"No, my phone's in my jeans pocket. I need to ring Pauly, to get him to find a room for George for the night."

"I think he'll be fine."

Riley began to get agitated. "No. He'll be waiting for me to pick him up and take him home. I have to ring Pauly." She threw the blanket off her bed and tried to get up.

Claire stood up, gently putting her back into bed and tucking the covers around her. "It's all under control. The police that were here earlier? They went to pick him up and have a chat with him. They were going to look after him tonight and make sure he got dinner and had somewhere to sleep."

Riley lay back and closed her eyes as tears coursed down her cheeks. She held her good hand up, trying to hide her face. Claire softly pulled her hand away to hold it in her own. "It's okay, honey."

Riley shook her head. "I've made such a mess..."

"You didn't make this mess, Riley. It's not your fault, love."

"Yes, yes, it is. I made some bad decisions and it's all gone to hell in a handbasket. I've hurt people with my decisions."

"Like who?"

"Like George and Sorla, to start with, and you. You shouldn't be here babysitting me. Your shift's finished. You should be home with Ed."

Claire chuckled. "I'll go shortly, so you can get some more sleep. How have you hurt Sorla?"

Riley smoothed imaginary creases from the bed coverings. "I haven't been completely honest with her. When things got hard, I took my frustration out on her and that's not fair." Riley shook her head. "I shouldn't have taken on the job, then she wouldn't be stuck in the middle. Oh God, Claire. I'm in over my head. I should have walked away."

"Well, for what it's worth, I'm glad you didn't. We wouldn't have gotten to know you, and Miss Pusskins and her babies would probably be dead if it weren't for you. Sorla's a big girl and I think you have more in common than you think." Riley shook her head. Claire filled her glass with some more water and ice chips, leaving it on the bedside table. "I think you're both putting in too much effort trying to swim away from each other. And even though you're both trying so hard, you still look like you're drowning. Maybe you should try swimming towards each other and see how that goes. You both deserve a break and someone to lean on for a while. Maybe you can help do that for each other." Claire stood and straightened Riley's blanket. "I'm gonna leave that thought with you and go home and cuddle up to my gorgeous husband. I'll see you in the morning. Sleep well." Claire leaned over and kissed Riley's cheek. "Goodnight, Riley."

"G'night."

❖

Riley spent a good part of the night thinking about what Claire had said. She also thought about Sorla—how she looked, how she laughed, how wonderful she felt when she kissed her. She had tried so hard to deny her feelings and the attraction, but it seemed the harder she tried to push it away, the stronger the pull between them became. Claire said she had sat with her after surgery. That was a surprising thing in itself, considering she hadn't been much of a friend in return this last week.

Riley watched as the sun rose outside her window, wondering how long until the doctor did his rounds and she could be cleared to go home. She was stiff and sore, but none of those sensations were new. She still had a cough, which was annoying, especially given her bruised ribs, but nothing that she thought would warrant her staying any longer.

Claire stuck her head around the corner of her room a bit after seven. "Hey, there. Good morning."

Riley sat up and smiled. "Morning. You're back early."

Claire came and sat on the side of the bed. "I managed to pull a seven 'til two. How'd you sleep?"

"Okay."

Claire put her fingers under Riley's chin and tilted her face to the light. "Uh-huh. And those bags under your eyes tell me a slightly different story. Care to have another go?"

Riley shrugged. "I got a few hours in. You look like you didn't get much either. Why's that?"

Claire frowned. "It seems that after Sorla got home last night, she grabbed a few things and took off again. We haven't seen her since, and she's not answering her phone."

"You look worried."

"I am, a bit."

"Why's that?"

Claire paused thoughtfully. "I don't think I would be compromising Sorla's privacy by telling you this, as I think you have enough background information after the cow-and-calf episode that what I'm about to say won't be telling tales out of school. When Sorla and I brought the kittens back to the infirmary, after we'd got them breathing again, Sorla had a bit of a flashback to when she got hurt."

"Does she have those often?"

"No, not as much any more, but it's been a stressful week and I think all of those things, along with the fire, sort of set her off."

Riley frowned. "I certainly wouldn't have helped in that regard. And you're worried that she's not home because…?"

Claire frowned. "She hasn't done it in a while now, but when it gets too much, she either locks herself away or she disappears and goes walkabout. Getting her back on track is hard work. Ed says she's taken the car keys and a couple of bottles have gone from the liquor cabinet. We don't know where she is. If something happens, we don't even know where to start looking for her." Riley sat deep in thought. "Ed's been out looking since dawn."

"How soon do you think it'll take the doctor to clear me to leave?"

"I don't know. If he doesn't have any surgery scheduled, I'm guessing he'll be around to do his rounds about nine."

"Do you think we can make it happen sooner?"

"I don't know, why?"

"I have an idea I might know where she is. I could be wrong, but

I'd like to try. Do you think you can organize a doctor to release me early? Then I'll call a taxi and get a ride out to pick up my truck from your place."

"You should be resting."

"Well, if I'm wrong, I'll come back and wait it out with you guys."

"Okay, leave it with me and let me see what I can do. In the meantime, I'll get someone in here to give you a hand having a shower and getting dressed."

"Thanks."

"No worries. Talk to you in a bit."

True to her word, Claire had a nurse come in to help her. Riley sat on the bed dressed, finishing off breakfast, when Claire came back with a doctor.

"Well, Miss Johnson. I've been told you're in a hurry to leave us."

"No offence, but places to go, people to see."

The doctor reviewed her chart. "You'll need to take it easy over the next few days, but I see no reason to keep you here any longer. My main concern is what you are going home *to*. I believe that the police will want to see you again in the next couple of days to ask a few more questions." He reached into his coat pocket and pulled out some cards. "Here are some numbers I want you to look at and think about. There's the number of a local support group, a shelter, and a counsellor. I've also given you my card with my work and mobile phone number, if ever you want help, or need to talk to someone."

Riley looked down silently at the cards he had given her.

"Normally, I wouldn't be happy about releasing someone in your situation quite so soon, but your friend here assures me that she and her husband will be keeping a close eye on you, should you need help."

Riley looked incredulously over at Claire. No one had ever offered to have her back before now. It felt good to have a friend in her corner. Claire threw her a wink as Riley's eyes started to mist over.

The doctor outlined her discharge instructions, then asked, "Where are you staying tonight?"

Riley frowned at the question. "At home."

The doctor gently patted her on the knee. "You might like to consider staying at a friend's place for a while, given the circumstances."

Riley looked down and fiddled with the straps on her wrist. "I can manage."

"The police report and pictures say otherwise. I doubt your father will be happy to see you home in the next couple of days."

Riley smiled sadly. "It'll be okay."

The doctor reached into his coat pocket a second time and pulled out a piece of paper. "I thought you might say as much. I have taken the liberty of making you an appointment to see a friend of mine. She comes up and holds clinics twice a week at my practice. Next week is booked out, but I have made you a time for the following week. I'll let you go early today if you'll promise me you'll keep that appointment."

Riley didn't know what to think, other than she thought the doctor was pushy and presumptuous.

"Just one appointment, Riley, that's all I'm asking. You've got nothing to lose by going."

Riley really wanted to leave the hospital. An appointment wasn't such a big thing to agree to. She could always make up an excuse and cancel it later. She'd just tell him what he wanted to hear so she could leave. "All right." She extended her hand and took the note, folding it one-handed and sticking it in her jeans pocket.

"Thank you. Here's your script—you can get it filled by the pharmacy downstairs before you go. Look after yourself, Riley. See you in a week."

"Thanks, Doctor. See you next week."

After watching the doctor leave, Claire turned back to Riley. "He's right you know, you shouldn't go home. Come and stay at Cherry Hill. There's plenty of room."

Riley carefully got off the bed. "Thanks. That's very kind of you, but I really am okay."

"From what I've heard, George wasn't very happy about being visited by the police."

Riley snorted softly. "Situation normal. Really, thank you though. If things get bad, I can always go over and stay at Uncle Mickey's house."

"Who's Mickey?"

"Mickey and his wife Pearl…they sort of took me under their wing, during the rodeo days, when I was little. They're my family. Pearl's gone now, but I still have Mickey. So you see, I've got somewhere else to go if I need to. But thank you all the same for the kind offer."

It didn't take long for Riley's scripts to be filled. While she waited, she called a cab and arranged to have it meet her outside. Its honking horn announced it had arrived.

Claire gave Riley a gentle hug. "Just be careful and try to go steady today. Please?"

"I will. Thank you for everything, Claire. I'm sorry you got caught in the middle of my mess. I didn't mean to put you in that position. I—"

Claire held her hand up. "Don't be. I'm just glad I was there. Promise me you'll call if you find her."

"I promise. I'll talk to you later, regardless."

"That's a deal. I'll tell Ed you're on your way."

CHAPTER FIFTEEN

Half an hour later the taxi dropped Riley at the front door of the main house at Cherry Hill. Ed stepped out and walked over, wrapping his bear-like arms around her, hugging her close. "Come inside and share a coffee with me and I'll bring you up to speed." Over coffee Ed explained that all Sorla had taken with her were her car keys and some scotch. "I don't know if she took any of her medications with her. Claire said you might have a hunch on where she is."

"It's a bit of a wild guess really. She made a passing comment about a place she used to go to as a child. I figured if I retraced some of our steps from the other day when we checked the cattle, maybe I could get lucky."

"Okay. Sounds as good a plan as any. I was going to go and check out the creek on the eastern side. Sorla said she used to like fishing and camping there when she came home for holidays. Are you okay to drive? I could get one of the boys to drive you if you needed."

"I'll be right. I might need your help packing a bag with some food though, just in case. She wouldn't have had anything to eat in a good while."

"That's a good idea. I'll pack one too." With the bags packed, they each headed off after trading mobile phone numbers.

Riley found she could drive one-handed and change the gears, provided she took it slow. It took close to an hour and a few wrong turns and backtracking before she found the creek where the calf had been stranded. From there she headed up the hill and pointed the truck due north. Before long she spotted the small hut. Driving closer, she saw that Sorla's Jeep was parked off to the side. Riley sat in the truck for a few minutes, trying to quell the butterflies in her stomach, wondering just what she was going to say. In the end she had no idea. Better just to dive in and see where the current took them.

She knocked on the door. There was no response. She knocked again and waited. She heard the sound of a bottle falling over inside. Gingerly testing the door handle, it turned easily in her hand. She saw Sorla sitting on the floor with an empty bottle prostrate beside her, her back resting against an old overstuffed couch. Sorla looked dishevelled and exhausted, her head cradled on her arms, perched on her bent knees. Her eyes were closed. Without looking up or opening her eyes, Sorla said, "I'd offer you a drink, but there isn't any."

Riley sat down beside her, quietly moving the bottle out of reach. "That's okay, it's a bit early for me anyway."

Sorla grunted. "What are you doing here?"

"Thought you might like a friendly face when you woke up."

Sorla snorted. "A friendly face. Not a *business* face?"

Riley closed her eyes and breathed briefly through the stab of hurt. After the way she'd behaved, she deserved that. "And to return the favour. Apparently someone came and sat with me when I was in hospital. Trouble is, I wasn't a very appreciative recipient of the friend's thoughtfulness."

"You were unconscious at the time."

"Well, the thing is, when I found out about what they had done, it made me feel pretty good to know that person was watching out for me. So I thought I would try and extend the same favour, seeing as, rumour has it, they've had a crappy couple of days too."

"How did you know where to find me?"

"I had a talk with Claire. She told me about what happened after the fire, when you got upset. Then she told me later this morning that she and Ed were worried about you because you took off and hadn't come home. It triggered a memory from the other day, when you said you sometimes came out here when you were younger and needed time out from the world for a bit. So I took a chance, hoping you'd be here."

"You have a good memory."

Riley laughed softly. "Not really. You should've see how many wrong turns I took getting here. Amazing how easily you can get lost in a big wide open paddock." Sorla smiled briefly at the comment. "Have you slept any?" Sorla shook her head. Riley reached behind her and pulled off an old pillow from the couch, placing it on her outstretched thighs. "How about you put your head down for a few minutes, while I keep watch?" Riley could see Sorla's body swaying with fatigue.

"I'm okay."

"I know you are. Just for a minute. You can hop up anytime. But here's an offer, if you'd like, to just rest a little." Riley put her hand on Sorla's shoulder, adding a little pressure in an attempt to persuade her to lie down.

"Just a minute then." Sorla gave in and slowly sank down.

"Uh-huh, just a minute." Riley gently stroked Sorla's forehead and watched as her eyes closed and her breathing evened out. Even long after she knew Sorla was asleep, Riley couldn't stop stroking her face and forehead. She had craved to touch her ever since they had met. Even if it never happened again, Riley enjoyed the few stolen moments she had, as she tucked a lock of hair behind Sorla's ear. Before too long, the pull of sleep lured Riley's own eyes to close. She rested her head back onto the arm of the couch, letting herself drift away to the sound of Sorla's deep breathing and the rhythmic rise and fall of the body in her lap.

Riley managed to doze for an hour. Looking down, she saw that Sorla was still deeply asleep. She shifted Sorla's head to a cushion and stiffly stood up, shaking her legs to get the blood flowing back again. She stumbled outside and down to her truck, where she coughed until her eyes watered and her head ached, then pulled out her phone and dialled Ed's number.

"Riley—how'd you go?"

"Hi, Ed. All good. I've found her."

"Hang on and I'll put you on speakerphone. I've just got in and Claire's here."

"Hi, Claire."

"Is she all right?"

"Yeah, she's sleeping. We're at a small hut, northeast of the creek where all the cows and calves are. She looks like she's had a hard night, but she seems okay." Riley could hear Ed and Claire murmuring in the background before Claire came back on the line.

"How are you doing?"

"I'm okay."

"Uh-huh. How are you really?"

Riley smiled. Claire was no fool. "Got a bit of a headache, but I just took something for that from my party bag from this morning. I'm still coughing up bits of the feed shed, but apart from that, I'm okay."

Ed's baritone chimed in to the conversation. "So, what are your plans?"

Riley looked at the sky, which had in a few short minutes grown ominously dark and heavy, with flashes of lightning skittering around in the belly of the clouds. "Looks like we're gonna get a storm pretty soon. As Sorla's still asleep, I suspect we'll be here awhile yet. I guess how long depends on the storm and how Sorla feels when she wakes up."

They said their goodbyes, and Riley hung up and made sure the windows in her truck were up. Next she checked on Sorla's truck, before collecting the bags and heading inside. After dropping the bags onto the table she went back outside and gathered some sticks and kindling near the side of the hut. The wind had begun to pick up and the air temperature was dropping rapidly, the smell of the oncoming promise of moisture heavy in the air. Riley closed the door quietly behind her and knelt by the fire. She set the kindling alight and gradually fed the flames until a healthy blaze had taken hold in the fireplace. When she was happy, she unfurled the fire guard to protect the room from any stray sparks flying out.

She found a kettle, filled it with water, and placed it near the fire in readiness to heat. It had been a long day and a cup of tea was most definitely warranted. Looking around the kitchen she located a supply of tea, coffee, powdered milk, and dried packet soup inside one of the cupboards. In the bag that Ed had packed were small tins of fruit, a couple of sandwiches, some muffins, a chocolate bar, some ibuprofen tablets, and a couple of bottles of water.

Riley smiled at Ed's thoughtfulness. She was once again amazed at Ed's and Claire's friendship and generosity. They were all very hands-on, touchy-feely, affectionate people. Riley wasn't used to that. She remembered Ed giving her a big hug when she pulled up at the house. It felt a little foreign and shocking, but at the same time it felt genuine and nice. She felt envious of Sorla's relationship with them. But they'd been away to war together. They were more than friends. They had a bond like no other. *They're family.*

Riley placed the food items on the bench top before walking back to squat by the fire, feeding it some more wood, the smell of burning eucalypt softly enveloping her. Overhead the first big fat drops of rain began to fall on the tin roof. She hung the kettle onto a hook which was attached to an iron arm suspended over the fire. It would take a while before it boiled. She took the light cotton blanket from the couch and draped it over Sorla before opening the door to stand in the doorway to watch the play of the clouds and flashes of lightning dance across the ever-darkening sky.

Standing in the doorway, with the breeze softly whispering past her, Riley felt peaceful. It had been a stressful few days, but now Sorla was asleep, safe behind her, the crack and pop of the fire emanated a soothing essence of woodsmoke to linger in the hut, and the air outside was being brushed clean with the fingers of wind and rain across the surface of the earth.

None of her problems had gone away and there was still much to be sorted through and resolved, but here, at this point in time, Riley's soul felt content and at peace. The hiss of boiling water broke the spell, grabbing her attention. Pushing off the doorway and squatting down by the fire to rescue to kettle, she swung the iron arm off the heat of the flames. Turning around to see if Sorla had been disturbed by the noise, she found warm dark eyes watching her. She smiled. "Hey."

"You're still here?"

Riley shrugged. "Didn't have anywhere better to be."

"What are you doing?"

"Thought you might like a hot drink when you woke up."

"No, I meant…"

"I know what you meant. I told you before, you looked after me before, now it's my turn. Would you like something to drink?"

Sorla looked at her. "I'm too tired to fight or argue. I'd love a cup of coffee if you have one."

"One coffee coming up. Do you feel up to eating something? Ed packed some muffins, sandwiches, or there's chocolate?"

At the mention of food, Sorla's stomach rumbled audibly. "Maybe some chocolate?"

Riley nodded and set about making the drinks.

Sorla pushed herself up to a sitting position. "How are you feeling? How's the arm?"

"Okay, thanks. Makes me drive a bit slower, but that's probably not a bad thing."

Sorla smiled. "Somehow I can't picture you as a hoon."

She grinned. "Would you like to have your coffee down there, or do you want to have it at the table?"

"Table's good." Sorla stood up stiffly and stretched her back before wandering over to sit down at the table. "Thanks. How long was I asleep?"

"Not long. Couple of hours."

The rain began to come down in earnest. Riley sipped her coffee. "We might be here awhile. I've set the water to heat if you want to have a wash to freshen up."

Sorla grimaced. "Am I that bad?"

Riley chuckled. "No. I was thinking more that it might make you feel a bit better. I know it helps me after a long night. I've got some fresh clothes if you wanted to change."

"That sounds nice." Sorla broke the chocolate in half and shared it with Riley. "Seeing as it looks like we'll be stuck here awhile, are we going to talk about this?"

Riley looked down into her coffee and shrugged with her good shoulder. "What's to talk about?"

Sorla held her hands out. "This. Us. You said you couldn't be friends, now here you are. I said let's stick to business, and I fall asleep on your lap after your drive all the way out here to come looking for me. What's going on?"

Riley chuckled nervously and ran her hand across her face. "I don't honestly know. Each time I think I've got a handle on it, something happens and my balance is gone. I barely feel in control."

Sorla put her mug down and looked deep into Riley's eyes. "What is it you want?"

Riley shook her head. "Want? It doesn't matter what I want."

"Sure it does."

Riley met Sorla's gaze with a sadness that seemed etched deep into her soul. Her voice was quiet but controlled, as she smiled softly. She stood up and gathered both of their now empty cups and walked them over to the sink. "Life's not that simple."

Sorla followed her. "It can be, if you let it." Riley stood facing the sink, her back to Sorla, shaking her head. Sorla came up behind Riley, her voice a bare whisper. She reached out and gently touched Riley's forearm. "Riley...what do you want?"

Riley didn't move.

"Forget everybody else—what is it *you* want?"

Slowly Riley turned around and faced Sorla with tear-filled eyes. With her good arm she reached behind Sorla's neck and pulled her forward until their bodies meshed. She kissed Sorla with a hunger and a need that was breathtaking. Sorla's arms twined themselves around her hips, pulling their bodies together tighter. She met Riley's kiss with a demanding, hungry answer of her own. She broke off to trail hot kisses down Riley's arching neck and felt as much as heard the groan from her own mouth wrap around their exploding passion. She came back up to Riley's lips, claiming them hotly, tearing a whimper from Riley. Sorla gentled her kisses. She kissed Riley's mouth, closed eyes, cheeks, and finally back down to her parted lips. They stood there breathing heavily, looking at each other.

Riley patted Sorla's chest before lightly pushing her away. "I can't..." She turned away and started to wash the mugs in the sink. "The water should be hot enough for a wash now. I've left you the bag in the bathroom."

Sorla came out twenty minutes later dressed only in one of Riley's long-sleeved shirts. Riley looked up, swallowed before blinking slowly, and turned her head to look away, back to the fire. Sorla padded over to kneel beside her. She gently reached out, putting a finger under Riley's chin, turning her head until it faced her. "I know what I want, and I want *you*. I have ever since I first saw you. I know you feel it too. I see how hard you're fighting it. Why are you fighting it?"

Riley closed her eyes, shaking her head. Sorla leaned forward and kissed her closed eyelids briefly before capturing Riley's lips with a gentle reverence that couldn't be denied. Sorla's hands embraced Riley's face as their lips joined, tasted, and explored. Her hands slid down to gently release Riley's arm from its sling before opening the fastenings on Riley's shirt.

Riley broke the kiss with a sob and turned away. "Don't."

"Trust me," Sorla whispered before reclaiming Riley's lips, soothing them with her compassion and gentle strength, pouring her love into Riley to give her courage.

Riley broke from the kiss and looked at Sorla, lips trembling. Sorla gently opened Riley's shirt and pushed it from her shoulders. She gasped as she saw the bruises. Her shoulder was vivid from where the beam had hit her the day before, but the other older bruises told Sorla a different tale that made her heart hurt.

Riley turned away from Sorla's gaze and, with her good hand, tried to close her shirt.

Sorla reached out to still her movements, gently bringing her back to face her. "Let me love you. Please."

Sorla kissed her with a depth of meaning and love that made the rest of the world disappear. She lowered Riley to the floor and lay beside her. Her hand stroked Riley's stomach. She could feel the muscles contract under her fingertips. Her hand rose and captured a breast whose nipple was taut and straining at the material of the bra. She released it from its prison, soothing it with her lips, nipping, licking, sucking until it stood proud and begging for more.

She gently pulled Riley to sit up and tugged at the shirt. "Off." Without waiting, Sorla slid Riley's shirt carefully off her shoulders and down her arms, quickly followed by the bra. She knelt and looked at Riley. She had a washboard abdomen, rippling under the scrutiny, rising up to ribs that supported two full, firm, beautiful breasts with lightly tanned areolae and nipples that called to her, topped off by wide, proud shoulders and an elegant neck. Even all covered up, Sorla knew Riley was beautiful, but naked, she simply took her breath away.

Riley wrapped her hand in Sorla's shirt and dragged her down to her lips, her mouth ravenous, curious, her tongue exploring and teasing. Her hand slid down Sorla's chest to knead her breast until the nipple pebbled in her palm. She opened Sorla's shirtfront, taking the breast in her mouth, tugging and scraping her teeth over the sensitive point. Sorla moved closer and straddled her thigh as she threw her head back, arching to meet Riley's mouth.

Riley's hand slid down the length of Sorla's body until she found the core of her heat. Her fingers slipped inside the wet folds, and Sorla groaned. Sorla's pelvis started to rock, complementing the attentions Riley was giving her breast. "Oh God. You're gonna make me come. Too soon, too soon."

Riley stroked with determined fingers, striving deep, to match Sorla's rhythm, her thumb brushing across the hardened clit. Sorla tightened around her fingers briefly, and Riley stroked deeper and faster as Sorla's thighs trembled.

"Oh Jesus, there. Yeah. Oh God!" With a final thrust, Sorla burst with an energy and light that was anchored around Riley's fingers. Riley gentled her touch as the pulsing slowed and finally stilled, before withdrawing. Sorla shivered. Leaning down, she captured Riley's lips before kissing her way across Riley's chest, loving her breasts, and making her way down her torso. Breaking the kiss, she sat up, undoing Riley's jeans, sliding them down her long, tapered legs and off onto the floor. Her hands appreciated where her eyes had travelled, running along the length of thigh, gently parting them to nestle between her legs. Riley groaned as Sorla's mouth began to explore and worship her centre, teasing and stroking until she could barely breathe. When Sorla slipped her fingers inside, Riley's head snapped up, a cry tearing from her lips, her hand coming down to the top of Sorla's head, holding her in close, trying to stay connected, as the blood buzzed in her ears. Sorla briefly raised her mouth to gaze at how beautiful Riley looked in the throes of passion.

"Please." A desperate whisper from Riley.

"What is it you want?"

"I want you, I *need* you. Please!"

"You've had me since day one, sweetheart." Sorla kissed her, and while deep inside, brought Riley home with an arching cry.

Sorla pushed herself up, intending to roll off to the side, but Riley reached down and pulled her up until they were level. Sorla kissed her lips, her neck, she couldn't get enough. Riley created a hunger in her like she had never experienced before. Riley pulled her down until she was lying on her.

Sorla tried to raise herself. "I don't want to hurt you, love."

Riley giggled. "You won't hurt me. After what you just did, I can't feel a thing. Please, I want to feel your body on mine." Gently Sorla complied. They both sighed at the pleasure the contact of their bodies created. Riley kissed her gently, a smile breaking out across her face.

Sorla kissed her nose. "What are you smiling about?"

Riley stroked Sorla's calf with her foot. "Perfect fit."

"Mm."

Riley nuzzled her neck as her hand snaked down Sorla's side, down to grab her arse cheeks, pulling her in tight. She lifted her own hips and began the rhythm anew, stroking with her whole body. Sorla slid up, allowing Riley to capture a breast with her mouth. Riley's mouth teased, creating the most astounding sensations that Sorla had ever felt, sparking nerve endings to shoot currents of sensation all the way to her toes. Riley's leg held her in place while her hand slipped between their bodies, finding Sorla's slickness to slide deep inside. Sorla leaned forward, feasting on Riley's mouth as their energy and passion climbed to greater insatiable heights.

Sorla rocked faster as Riley responded, until Sorla threw her head back, arching her back, holding tight to Riley's fingers, exploding with a cry, before falling onto Riley's chest, panting and trembling with aftershocks of pleasure. Riley loosened her hold, relaxing, softly intertwining their limbs.

Sorla lay very still and sniffed lightly. Riley lifted her head. "Hey, what's wrong? I didn't hurt you, did I?"

Sorla sniffed some more. "No."

"What's the matter, then?"

"I never thought I would ever be with anyone again, let alone have someone love me like you just did."

"Why?"

"In case you haven't noticed, I'm damaged goods. I didn't think anyone would want to look at me, let alone love me."

Riley raised her hand and knocked on Sorla's head.

"Ow! What was that for?"

"I was just seeing if your head was hollow."

"What?"

"That's the silliest, most empty-headed thing I think I have ever heard. I thought maybe your brains fell out on the drive over here."

Sorla lifted her head and frowned. "I'm serious."

Riley smiled. "So am I. From the moment you walked into the store, I couldn't stop thinking about you. My brain goes to mush. I've tried for distance, to stay away—but I can't. I think you are the most beautiful person I have ever seen."

Sorla shook her head slightly in bemusement. "You're crazy."

"Well if I am, it's your fault. I feel like…my chest hurts with the ache of you."

A look of horror passed Sorla's face. She threw herself off Riley. "Oh, shit, your chest and shoulder! I'm so sorry. Why didn't you tell me to get off?"

Riley giggled. "I'm fine. What I mean is, you make my whole body ache with a need that I can't describe. Nothing to do with what happened in your feed shed. But I could do with sitting up for a while, if that's okay."

Sorla blushed. She leaned over and kissed her deeply before helping her to sit up. "I know what you mean. When I'm with you, it feels like the sun's come out."

Sorla pulled the cushions and cotton throw off the couch and onto the floor. Coming to sit behind Riley, she put a cushion between her and the couch and another one under Riley's arm. "Scoot on back." Riley did as asked until she was sitting nestled in the vee of Sorla's legs. Sorla covered her with the cotton covering before wrapping her arms around her waist, easing Riley's body back to rest against her length. Her fingers stroked Riley's hair. "I love your hair out. It's beautiful."

Riley held up her encased broken arm. "Can't tie it back."

Sorla kissed the back of her head. "Well, it works for me, but if you want it tied back, let me know."

"Thanks, maybe in a day or two. Head's still a bit sore."

They sat gazing into the fire for a good long while. Sorla's fingers traced a bruise on Riley's upper arm. "What happened?"

For long minutes, Riley stared into the fire. She debated what she was going to answer, in the end deciding that Sorla deserved the truth. "Someone saw us kissing in the main street, and word got back to George."

"He hit you because I kissed you?"

Riley sighed. "No. Because of what it represents. He didn't know I was gay, and now that he does, he's horrified and disgusted. He feels even more of a failure. It represents another thing that has gone horribly wrong with his life. Another thing that I have ruined for him."

Sorla stiffened with anger. "That's bullshit!"

Riley rubbed Sorla's hand soothingly. "No. It's his take on his reality. He comes from a small town and the few opportunities he's had have been taken away from him, or ruined somehow. He's a broken man who's angry at life."

"That's no excuse to hit you."

"He has to hit out at something. Sometimes I'm just the closest thing."

"Why do you stay? Why don't you leave?"

Riley half shrugged. "Because I'm all he has. He can't manage alone. And…he's right. If it wasn't for me, his life would have been quite different."

"But that's not your fault."

"Maybe not, but it's how it is."

Sorla shook her head. "How did George not know you were gay?"

"I never dated or brought anyone home."

"Then how did you…? I mean, what you just did. It obviously wasn't your first time."

Riley laughed. "I never said I was a saint."

"Then how?"

"I go away for a weekend, once or twice a year."

"There must be more gay people in town, surely?"

"Well, if there are, I don't know any of them. It's a small town, Sorla. They don't do out of the ordinary very well."

"You're being a bit dramatic aren't you? In this day and age?"

Riley pondered whether or not she would tell Sorla but figured she should know what sort of town she was living in. "That one person, who saw us kissing?"

"The one who told George?"

"Uh-huh. George wasn't the only one he told. I've had orders cancelled and I've been refused service in a couple of the shops in town. People either don't talk to me any more, or cross to the other side of the street. I'm hoping it'll settle down soon, otherwise I might have to take on a few out-of-town jobs for a while."

"You're kidding."

"Nope. Some people are okay, but a handful are struggling with it. You, Claire, and Ed, you're all new in town. I didn't want you to be hurt, or for people to treat you badly, simply because I couldn't control my feelings—that's not fair."

"That's very noble of you, but we can take care of ourselves."

"I don't doubt that for a minute, but it's been one of the things that has been worrying me. I felt like, no matter what decision I made, someone was going to be hurt, and that's why I've been all over the place. But it doesn't excuse my bad behaviour, and I am so sorry for everything. I'm afraid I've made quite a mess of it." Riley's head bowed under the shame.

Sorla gently hugged her, kissing the side of her head. "You have nothing to apologize for, although I understand now a bit better why you've been the way you have and some of the pressure you've been under."

Riley took a deep breath. "Enough about me, what about you? Why'd you take off?"

Sorla laid her cheek against the back of Riley's good shoulder. "Lots of little things."

"Like?"

"Like us arguing. Not sleeping. The pressure of trying to get everything up and running. The shed fire kind of brought it all to a head."

"Why's that?"

Sorla closed her eyes. "The smoke, flames, and yelling. The fear." Her voice grew hoarse with the memories. "When you brought the kittens out and they weren't breathing, I don't think I was really seeing the kittens."

Riley unhooked herself from Sorla's arms and turned around to face her, her legs wrapping around Sorla's thighs and hips. "What did you see?" Riley leaned back slightly, watching as Sorla's eyes grew unfocused, looking distantly off into the past where the images were all still too recent, too raw.

"I saw John and Annette, after the IED went off. They weren't breathing."

Riley pulled Sorla in, holding her to her chest with her one good arm, wrapping her legs tighter around her waist.

"The smoke and the flames...people yelling...I couldn't do anything. It felt the same." Sorla's arms wrapped around her as she held on for dear life, as her body trembled at the wave of emotion. Riley held her tight, rocking her softly, until time gentled Sorla's tears. With a voice so soft, Riley strained to hear, Sorla said, "When I came home from seeing you at the hospital, all I wanted to do was to escape the shadow of the fear and pain."

"And getting smashed worked?"

Sorla shrugged. "For a bit."

"And how do you feel now?"

"Sad, tired—but when I look at you, it sounds silly, but I somehow feel peaceful, clean, refreshed."

Riley stroked her fingers through Sorla's hair. "Mm, I know what you mean."

Sorla bumped her forehead despairingly on Riley's shoulder. "God. We're a right screwed-up pair."

"Looks like it."

"Now what?"

"I don't honestly know. Neither of us can undo what's been done, whether it be war or people's attitudes. I guess we just have to keep going, as best we can."

Sorla pulled back to look into Riley's eyes. "Do you think we could do it together?"

Riley thought about Sorla's offer. She'd already been outed, thanks to Robbie Peters's big mouth. George was upset, people in town now knew, the business was affected. There didn't seem much point in hiding now. Riley smiled. "We could at that." They came together in a tender, affirming kiss. Riley broke off, raising her head to listen. "Rain's eased off. Do you want to go home? I know Ed and Claire would love to see that you're okay. They've been pretty worried about you."

Sorla sighed. "I'd rather stay here with you, but you're right, I need to apologize to them for running out like I did."

"Why don't you ring them and tell them we're coming while I put the fire out and pack up."

"Will you stay? Please?"

Riley ran her fingertips across Sorla's cheek. "There's nowhere else I'd rather be." With a small moment of surprise, Riley realized that an enormous weight felt suddenly lifted from her shoulders with the truth of those few simple words.

CHAPTER SIXTEEN

Riley woke with first light. At first, she wasn't sure where she was, but then she felt the arm around her waist and the body snugged in behind her, and she smiled. She desperately wanted to roll over and run her hands over Sorla's body but knew that after the last few strained days, sleep was a precious commodity for her new lover and decided that to leave her sleep was a wiser investment for the day ahead. Carefully untangling herself, she got up, retrieving her clothes on her way to the bathroom.

After discovering there wasn't much in the way of food in the kitchenette, Riley crept out of the suite, making her way barefoot to the main kitchen where she found Ed flipping pancakes at the stove and Claire at the coffee pot. Ed greeted her with a bright morning smile. "Well, good morning! Sleep well?"

"Morning. Yes, thank you. I don't think I moved."

Claire held up a mug. "Want one?"

"Yes, please."

Claire brought a steaming mug over as they both sat at the table. She looked Riley over. "You look a bit better this morning. You've got more colour in your face. How's the arm?"

Riley fingered the sling. "Not too bad."

"If you like, after breakfast, I'll take a look at your dressings."

Riley opened her mouth to protest but caught the look Claire was throwing her over the top of her coffee mug. She swallowed. "That would be lovely, thank you."

Claire winked at her. "Good answer."

Riley busied herself sipping her coffee.

Ed looked up. "Fender up?"

Riley shook her head. "No, she's still asleep."

Claire sipped her coffee thoughtfully. "You two look like you sorted some stuff out while you were away."

Riley felt herself blush as she studied the depths of her mug's contents. "A bit."

Claire patted her hand. "Well, I'm glad. I was ready to shake the pair of you."

Riley's head snapped up in surprise. "Sorry?"

Claire laughed. "You two have been throwing sparks for ages. I'm just pleased you got it sorted out before I had to tie you both down and bang your heads together."

Riley was shocked speechless.

Ed took pity as he delivered a stack of pancakes over to the table. "What my darling wife is trying to say is we're both glad. We think you two are good for each other."

"Oh."

"And I'd have to agree with that." They all turned their heads to see Sorla standing in the doorway, grinning her head off. She came over and kissed Riley's cheek before sitting down next to her. "Good morning."

Riley smiled shyly. "Hello."

"I rolled over and you were gone."

"Sun came up and I was awake. Old habit. Besides, I thought you needed the sleep, so I got up."

Sorla leaned over and kissed her tenderly on the lips. "Thank you."

Claire laughed. "Sor, would you stop? You're embarrassing poor Riley. Do you want a coffee?"

Sorla grinned. "Yes, please."

Ed chuckled as he handed out the pancakes. "Come on, tuck in before they get cold."

Around a mouthful of food, Claire groaned. "Great pancakes, sweetheart, thank you."

Sorla drained her coffee cup. "What's everyone's plans for the day?"

Claire brought the coffee pot over and topped up everyone's mugs. "I've got some paperwork to do for a couple of hours, then I thought I might call in to the vet's and see if we can't bring the babies home."

Sorla nodded. "It'll be nice to have them back home again."

Ed sat back in his chair. "I guess Fender and I need to talk about the insurance for the feed shed."

Riley put down her fork. "Can I ask who you got the hay from?"

Ed's eyebrows went up. "Sure. One of the men you recommended. Saunders? He sent a young fellow around to deliver it that afternoon. He unloaded it and stacked it himself, said it was all part of the service."

"Uh-huh."

Ed cocked an interested eyebrow at her. "What are you thinking?"

"I'm thinking you might have been given some green hay in the mix. I remember when I was in the shed, earlier in the day, that it smelt hot." Riley looked around at the group. "Would you mind if I made a phone call after breakfast, to check some things out?"

Ed looked at Claire and Sorla. "No, be our guest."

"Thanks."

Ed looked at her. "Any other plans?"

"Well, I still owe you a day with the horses. Figured, seeing as I'm here, I might as well do that, if that's okay. Then I'll need to head off to collect George."

There was a heavy pause around the table at Riley's statement.

Ed cleared his throat. "My wife is the consummate professional. She holds people's confidence every day, but the night of the fire, she came home upset. At first she didn't tell me what it was about, until finally, I badgered it out of her. I don't know all the details, but I got enough to know that the injuries you sustained in the fire weren't the only ones you carried on your body, and that those other injuries were inflicted by a person."

Riley's head dropped. She couldn't look at anyone. She stared into her coffee. For years she had been able to hide the dirty darkness of it all. Now they all knew. The doctors, the police, Claire, Ed, and Sorla. She felt exposed and ashamed. "I'm fine, thank you."

"I know you are a remarkable, independent, strong woman." Ed's voice was gentle, as if he was walking on eggshells. "But I would feel a whole lot better if you would allow me to accompany you when you do go to pick him up. You see, we've all become quite fond of you, and I would feel much happier if I knew that you got home safely."

Riley squirmed in her seat. The close scrutiny and the sincerity were overwhelming. "I'm sorry. I'm not used to people knowing my business…or making a fuss." Riley tried to clear the lump in her throat. "This is all a bit new for me. Thank you for the offer, Ed. Can I think on it a bit?"

"Sorry, I didn't mean to upset you."

"That's okay. I'm just on a learning curve here, if you'll all just bear with me a bit, 'til I get my head around a few things."

Ed nodded. "No problems. You just let me know when you're ready."

"Thanks." Riley turned to Sorla. "Is it okay if I grab a shower?"

"Sure. Hang on and I'll get you a towel."

Standing naked in the bathroom, Riley realized she couldn't get her shoulder or arm dressings wet, so a shower wouldn't work. She looked to the big ornate bath and grinned. She walked out naked to the lounge room where Sorla was waiting, sitting in one of the lounge chairs, reading over some insurance letters. She looked up to see Riley standing in the doorway. The letters fell unnoticed to the floor.

Riley smiled. "I realized I can't get my dressings wet in the shower. I thought maybe a bath would be okay, but that's a lot of water for one person, don't you think?" She walked over to Sorla, whose mouth was open. Kneeling down next to her she leaned in, claiming Sorla's mouth tenderly, and Sorla responded, drinking thirstily in response. Breathless, Riley pulled back and stood up, holding out her hand in invitation. "Want to share a bath?"

Wordlessly, Sorla stood up, accepting the outstretched hand, and followed her into the bathroom. Riley turned the taps on before turning around and meeting Sorla, stepping into her space, slowly taking her face, caressing the smooth cheeks with her fingertips, and then leaning in to kiss her lips, tenderly at first, but with a growing insatiable need. Riley stepped back to look at her fully clothed new love. "Undress for me."

Sorla went red. "I don't think…"

She stepped once again into Sorla's space. "I would love nothing more than to do it, but one-handed, I'm a little clumsy. Show me. Show me the woman I'm falling for."

Sorla dropped her jeans, closely followed by her underwear.

Riley stepped forward and kissed her again. "Do you know you have a gorgeous arse?"

Sorla closed her eyes and seemed acutely self-conscious.

Riley commandeered her chin with a gentle but firm finger. "Look at me, so you'll know what I say is true. I love your body. I see your arse, your legs, your torso, your face, and all I want to do is run my hands and mouth over them. I love every part of you."

As Sorla opened her shirt, Riley spirited her hand inside the cloth folds, and she ran her palm upside Sorla's stomach and ribs, rising to finally capture a breast, teasing the nipple between her fingertips. "You make my heart ache just looking at you. I hardly know what I want to taste first when I look at you. I want you so bad, I can barely think straight."

Sorla kissed her deeply. "And I want you. Please…take me."

Riley turned off the water, turning back to slide the shirt from Sorla's shoulders. Coaxing Sorla to sit, resting against the top lip of the bath's edge, Riley bent forward to kiss her, branding her, taking her with all the love she had. Wrapping her fingers in Sorla's hair, she gently tipped her head back, kissing and tasting the long lines of her neck, the hollow between her collarbones, rising to nibble on the rise of her chin before coming back up to rejoice in the love of her mouth.

Riley massaged and teased her breast, and Sorla sighed as she arched into her hand. "Yes." Replacing her hand with her mouth, Riley's lips enveloped the sensitive rise of Sorla's breast, sucking on the engorged nipple, sending ripples of pleasure straight to Sorla's groin. "Oh fuck, yes."

Kneeling carefully, not moving her mouth from its worship of Sorla's breast, Riley came to nestle between her legs where she could feel the heat coming off Sorla's centre. Sorla whimpered as Riley's fingers whispered a touch over the seam of her energies. Sorla was wet and hypersensitive, jerking at Riley's first contact, mewling in unconscious response.

Sorla gripped the edge of the bath as Riley's mouth navigated her desire, lifting her, soothing her, stirring her blood to boiling point. When Riley's fingers slid deep inside her, she threw her head back, her hips bucking violently beyond her control as the climax exploded outward, igniting all in its path. She cried out Riley's name as she fell forward, to lean heavily against Riley's head and shoulders, bonelessly trembling with the aftershocks, as Riley's mouth and fingers gently eased her down. Riley rested her cheek against Sorla's stomach as Sorla ran her fingers through Riley's hair. Sorla sighed.

Riley kissed her scarred abdomen lovingly.

Sorla looked at the bathwater. "Join me?"

"Love to."

Riley waited until Sorla had taken her leg off and slipped into the water, before coming in to rest in front of her, keeping her shoulder and bad arm above the waterline. Lying with her head resting on Sorla's shoulder, she hummed in pleasure. "Tell me more about your plans for Cherry Hill."

Sorla gently soaped a cloth, carefully wiping it over Riley's back and shoulders. "Our main aim is to have this up and running as a cattle and horse place."

"But there's more, isn't there? Claire's infirmary's a little over the top for your run-of-the-mill property."

"Mm. The second part of our plan is to have the farm act as a halfway place for servicemen and women looking to get back into the community."

"What do you mean?"

"When we first got back, we found it hard to readjust to normal life. Our normal was to eat and sleep with large bunches of people, working day and night, schedules, shifts, chaos, seeing people die or come back injured. We were constantly on the alert, looking out for each other, working as a well-oiled unit. To come back home and to be on your own with all these feelings still inside…And sometimes, like me, you have to start again, because you can't come back and do the things you used to do any more. It's like you've lost your centre, your core. It's hard to explain. Part of you is really happy to be home again, but part of you just can't settle—you feel like an alien in your own country."

Riley sat still, listening intently to what Sorla was describing and sharing.

"Ed, Claire, and I, we're lucky, we've got each other and we have Cherry Hill. When we got home, we got to thinking how maybe other people could benefit from something like what we have. So we put forward a business proposal to the Department of Defence, where we establish a sustainable cattle farm, supporting servicemen and women interested in working on the land or learning a trade in town, and in return, the Department of Defence supports the Cherry Hill program with a contract to supply meat to the service. If it all comes up roses, there's talk the department might look at other small rural towns to do a similar thing. We're kind of the guinea pigs, if you like."

"Phew. That's some vision."

Sighing quietly, Sorla rested her head back on the edge of the bath, feeling the enormity of the weight of their plan. "We have a meeting on Monday to sort out some of the finer initial set-up details. First steps first though, we have to show that we can establish a successful business."

Riley caressed Sorla's thigh. Sorla rested her chin on Riley's good shoulder. "So, what do you think of our plan?"

"I think…I think it sounds like the best thing this town has seen in a very long time. You obviously have your father's gift for seeing the potential in a situation."

"Do I hear an unspoken *but* in there?"

Riley sighed. "Our relationship might complicate things for you all. You're going to need the support of the community. You're not going to get that if they find out we're an item."

"I think you're being a little dramatic, aren't you?"

"I've been here since I was fifteen. People know me, people trust me. But now they've found out I'm different, some of them have made no secret in turning their backs on me. They don't yet know how wonderful the three of you are. I don't want to see them shut you down before you've had a chance to get started." Riley stepped out of the bath and started to dry herself.

Sorla pushed herself up and swung out, to sit on the edge. "Now hang on a minute, are you suggesting what I think you're suggesting?"

Riley couldn't look at her. "You know it's the most sensible thing to do."

Sorla grasped Riley's hips, slowly turning her around to face her. "No, I don't. And I'll tell you why. You've discounted the most important thing."

Riley stood up straight. "And what's that?"

Sorla grinned. "Money." Riley looked puzzled. "Money talks, Riley, and has the power to overcome prejudice, if it's steered in the right direction. You get the right people on board, at the right time, it creates its own current, until eventually, pretty much everyone wants to dip their toes into the water of its success. If it all works out, they won't care if you run down the street buck naked." Sorla hungrily eyed

Riley's naked torso before her, grinning evilly, waggling her eyebrows up and down. "Hm, then again, my love…"

Riley threw her towel, covering Sorla's head.

Sorla laughed. "Hey! No fair!" She pulled the towel off, still grinning.

Riley leaned over and kissed her. "I'm going to see if Claire can change these dressings, so I can get to work outside."

"What about me?"

"If you're so intent on making this happen, then you, my gorgeous cattle baroness, have plans to devise and stuff to sort, ready for your meeting."

CHAPTER SEVENTEEN

Riley's phone rang just as Claire finished changing her dressings. She recognized Mickey's number. "G'day, Mick."

"Morning, Midget. How you doin'?"

"Fine, thanks. What's up?"

"Heard me some more of them rumours. Says you got yourself into a bit of trouble."

"I'm fine."

"You gonna stop tellin' me tales and spit out the truth, please?"

Riley sighed. "I broke my arm."

"And how did you do that?"

"There was a fire in the feed shed at Cherry Hill, and I got hit by a piece of wood."

"That's not what I heard."

Riley's heart skipped a beat. "And what did you hear?"

"I heard someone's been beating up on you."

Her eyes narrowed. "And where'd you hear that from?"

"From the police that came round to visit yesterday."

"The police? What did they want?"

"They wanted to know what the story is. So do I."

Riley closed her eyes as a pain in her chest grabbed at her, stealing her words.

"Where are you now?"

She tried to swallow past the lump in her throat. "I'm at Cherry Hill. I have some horses to work with today."

"I'll be there in half an hour to give you a hand."

"Mickey, I'm okay, really."

"Well then, you'll have to forgive an old man his folly, 'cause I need to come over and see for myself."

Riley began to protest, but Mickey had already hung up. She looked at the phone in her hand, then at her boots. There was no way out. No way of escaping or winding back the clock. She just had to suck it up as best she could, and keep moving forward.

She had just finished separating out Queenie and the young filly when Mickey pulled up. He sauntered over and climbed the fence to sit on the top rail, watching her work.

She haltered Queenie and led her around the yard, with the young filly trailing behind. Several times the filly got between Riley and the mare, both initially ignoring the skittish young horse. By the time an hour had passed and both were released back with the rest of the herd, Riley had managed to run her hand over the filly several times without her reacting nervously.

Riley walked through the yard gate and over towards Mickey. She stood in front of him, her hat pulled low, eyes to the ground. "You didn't have to come out all this way. I told you, I'm fine."

Not one to be ignored, Mickey put a gnarled old hand under her chin, lifting her face until their gazes met. "I will be the judge of that with my own mind's eye if you don't mind."

Riley's chin trembled as she pulled away from his close scrutiny. "It's just a broken arm, Mick."

Mickey grabbed ahold of her good hand. "Come on, let's go and take a load off over there, on that there bench under the tree." As they sat, Mickey handed her his hanky. She took it and blew her nose. Mickey looked off into the distance. "You know, we talked about it, on and off over the years, me and Pearl, wondering was it our imagination, or if it could be real. You never said anything, and we never asked. Didn't wanna rock the boat if we was wrong. Turns out, not asking was wrong. We shoulda and I'm real sorry. We let you down, young 'un."

"You never let me down, Mick. You have nothing to be sorry about."

"The police showed me the photos, Riley." Mickey's voice became choked. "How long? How long has this been going on?" Riley shuffled her feet, eyes downcast. The old man crumpled into tears, his head folding down into his hands. Riley drew Mickey to her, comforting him and holding him tight briefly. He sat up to wipe his face.

Chuckling, Riley handed him back his hanky. "Wanna share?"

He chuckled in kind and accepted. "Why didn't you say anything? Why didn't you come to us?"

Riley shrugged and looked off into the distance. "I figured it was my lot, and I just had to learn how to deal with it. I learned the signs and knew when to leave well enough alone, for the most part."

Mickey shook his head and curled his fist in anger against his thigh. "We let you down. We were the grown-ups. We shoulda stepped in. You shouldn't have had to put up with that."

Riley's hand encircled Mickey's, soothing its pent-up tension with the soft calm resolve of her fingers. "You and Pearl, you were the best things in my life. You taught me, you loved me, you took care of me."

Mickey shook his head. "Not good enough. I was a coward. I should've seen it. Should've stopped it."

"You did all you could, and I love you both for it. We choose our own roads. You taught me that. You can't go carrying my baggage for me. Please don't be angry or sorry. What's done is done."

"Well I ain't done. I am going to pay me a visit."

"Mickey, there's no need."

"My left eye there's no need! This stops here."

For long moments Riley looked off into the distance, watching as the blue-green eucalyptus-covered hillsides shimmered with the heat haze. "Most of the time, he doesn't even know what he's doing. His brain is pickled, and his liver's not far behind. According to his doctor, he doesn't have much longer to go, the rate he's going."

"Don't matter."

Riley chuckled softly and shook her head.

"What the hell's so funny?"

"I was just thinking the other day, that when George finally does go, we'll have to bury him, 'cause if we cremate him, it'll take a week to put the fire out."

Mickey snorted. "More like a month."

"True enough."

They sat in companionable peace watching the young horses play, with the patient older horses looking on. Mickey cleared his throat. "I have a favour to ask."

"Mm?"

"You know how there's the big fancy dance at the end of the rodeo, where they present the awards?"

"Yeah."

"I wasn't going to go. Haven't been to one since Pearl left us. But, well, I've changed my mind and I was wondering if you would do me the honour of being on my arm?"

Riley knew that the evening would see Mickey's Hall of Fame award presented to him at the ball, and she also knew how hard it would be for him to attend without Pearl. It was always their thing to dance the night away at the end-of-season affair. They were a sight to behold on the dance floor and the envy of every couple for miles.

Riley leaned over and kissed his cheek. "I wouldn't miss it for the world. I would love nothing better than to be your escort for the night. Just don't ask me to dance, okay?"

"And why not?"

"I don't know how."

"Then how 'bout you ask your friends over yonder in the house to teach you, so's you can surprise me?" Riley opened her mouth to protest but was cut off. "Please. You'd be doin' it for me, and for Pearl."

"That's not fair—how can I refuse?"

Mickey grinned. "My thoughts exactly. Now are you gonna introduce me to your new friends, or we gonna leave em' standing over there, gawkin' through the window?"

Riley stood up. "You don't play fair, old man."

Mickey hooked his arm into hers as they made their way over to make introductions.

❖

After introductions, Sorla left Ed and Claire to entertain Mickey in the lounge room while she commandeered Riley to help make the tea. Riley was at the sink filling the jug when Sorla came up behind her, wrapping her arms around her waist. "You okay?"

Riley wrapped her fingers around the safety net of Sorla's arms, leaning back into her embrace. "Yeah."

"You sure?"

Riley sighed. "The police turned up at his house asking questions. He's blaming himself for what's happened with George."

"Did he know about George?"

"No."

Sorla gently turned her around until they were facing each other. "You never told them?"

Riley looked at the floor. "No."

Sorla's heart hurt at the enormous burden Riley had carried around all by herself her whole young life. She couldn't even begin to fathom how Riley had handled it. She didn't know what to say, so she just wrapped her arms around tighter, holding Riley close, as Riley nestled her head into Sorla's neck.

Riley relaxed into the safe embrace Sorla offered her. "Do you know how to dance?"

"Some, why?"

"Mickey wants me to go with him to the rodeo ball, where they present the winners and kick their heels up to mark the end of the season. He's getting a Hall of Fame award and he wants me to go as his partner for the evening."

Sorla pulled her head back smiling, to look at Riley. "That sounds fabulous!"

Riley shook her head. "Tradition has it that the winners take to the floor for the first dance of the night with their partners. Mickey and Pearl were champion dancers. I can't dance. I need someone to teach me how to dance before the ball."

Sorla laughed softly. "I think we can manage that. What sort of dancing do they do?"

Riley looked mortified. "I have no idea."

Sorla smiled as she kissed her warmly on the mouth. "Leave it with me and I'll see what I can find out."

"Hey, I've just had an idea."

Sorla raised her head from kissing Riley's neck. "Mm?"

"You guys should come to the ball and wear your dress-up bits— you know, your fancy uniforms."

Sorla looked a little confused. "Why would we do that?"

Riley grinned. "Free advertising for the cause. You can mingle and chat. There will be all the major sponsors, the big players from in town, as well as other official people from all around the state at the ball. It's a captured audience. You couldn't pay to get them all in one place at the same time any other time of the year."

Riley could see the cogs ticking over in Sorla's mind as she thought the idea through. She grinned and rewarded Riley with a breath-stealing kiss.

Riley came up for air. "Holy smokes."

"Looks like we'd better book a table."

❖

Mickey left soon after the morning tea break, with Ed not far behind him, saying he had an errand to run in town before lunch. Claire caught a lift with Ed and was going to see if she could bring the cats home.

Riley was outside taking the young colt through a similar process that she had run earlier in the morning with the filly, while Sorla finished up some paperwork inside. By the time she came out, Riley had just put the colt back to play with the filly, leaving Queenie with her in the pen. Riley was brushing her down when she heard Sorla approach. "Get done what you wanted with the paperwork?"

"Pretty much, but it's too nice a day to stay inside too long."

"Feel like getting up on Queenie here and taking her through her paces?" Sorla looked excited but Riley could sense her nervousness. "We're just going to do pretty much what we did the other day. I'll be right here. You up for it?"

Sorla grinned. "You bet."

"Righto. The gear's over there, ready when you are."

"How did you carry the saddle out with your arm?"

Riley smiled innocently at her. "Slowly."

In mock exasperation, Sorla shook her head. "What do I do first?"

"Just stand in the middle and breathe. Relax your shoulders. Concentrate on your breathing. Settle yourself. First is the halter. So when you're ready, you need to walk up to her, breathe into her nose, and rub her forehead."

"Will I always have to breathe into her nose first thing?"

"No. It's just in the beginning, while you get to know each other. Once she comes to know you by your smell, voice, and touch, you can just walk up to her like you would any horse you've known for a time."

"Makes sense."

"When you're ready, turn and walk towards her." As Sorla approached the mare, the horse moved away from her. Sorla turned and looked questioningly at Riley.

Riley smiled at her. "Now, you get to dance with her. If she moves left, you move left. If she moves right, then so do you. Match her moves." Sorla took a deep breath and began to mirror the horse's movements. "Okay, now walk to the centre and turn your back on her. That's it. Lower your head and breathe slowly and deeply. Rest your arms by your side, that's it. Just stay like that."

The mare took a few tentative steps towards her. Sorla lifted her head. "Is she coming?" The spell broken, the mare turned and walked away.

Riley smiled. "Look up. See? She's moved away from you. You need to start again. Walk over towards her and start the dance—then, when you're moving together, come back to the centre, and wait patiently."

Sorla frowned in concentration but nodded and set to the task before her. She moved with the mare step for step, until they were in sync, before turning her back and walking to the centre to wait. To Sorla it felt like an eternity as she stood, head bowed, waiting. She breathed deeply and tried to relax her arms. Her nose started to itch and was driving her crazy, but she continued to breathe deeply and ignored it. She was concentrating so hard on being still that she almost missed hearing the mare approach, until she felt the hot breath on the back of her neck. She smiled.

"Now, very slowly, turn and reach out to rub her forehead, like I showed you." Riley's voice was a smooth, lilting, smoky caress. "Tell her she's a good girl." Sorla followed Riley's instructions. "Slowly, slip the halter on over her head. That's it, slowly does it. Good. Stroke her tongue. See how her head drops? She's relaxing. That's the way. Now lead her around to the blanket and put it on like you did before, followed by the saddle. When you put the saddle on, gently rub her belly—she likes that."

When she was all saddled up, Riley said, "Walk her around a bit, then get her to stand. Lean your weight on the saddle a few times, and when you think you're both ready, ease yourself up onto her back and walk her around."

In under ten minutes Sorla was up and circumnavigating the yard.

"Okay, get her into a controlled trot and canter gently around the yard." Sorla followed through. "Now slow her back to a walk. She's about done for the day. Take her to the main gate, get the gear off, reward her, and rub her down before setting her loose with the others. I'll wait for you over by the tree."

Sorla took her time, surprised and thrilled at the sense of peace that enveloped her. She was truly happy for the first time in...? *Years*. She was back at the place she'd always dreamed of returning to. She had her best friends, and they were building a dream together. Sorla stole a quick look over her shoulder to see Riley watching her and grinned. *And the prettiest girl in town is with me.*

❖

"Mickey seems like a good man to know." Ed attempted casual conversation while he cut up a variety of the salad items for the wrap.

"He is. There's not too many people he doesn't know. He's been around the traps a fair while, so not much he hasn't seen. But most important, he's a good man. He's fair, loyal, always happy to learn new things, and is solid in the things he does know. He's patient. Heck, he and Pearl helped raise me, so he definitely has a sense of humour."

"Seems he's got a huge soft spot where you're concerned."

"And I've got one for him. Although George is my father, Mickey and Pearl are my family."

"Pearl his wife?"

She nodded. "She passed a couple of years back now."

"I'm sorry."

"Yeah, me too. I really miss her. Must be 'specially hard for Mick though."

Ed stopped chopping and tilted his head slightly to the side in thought. "I can't imagine life without Claire. It was one of the reasons I was happy not to renew when my time was up in the service. Each day I love her more and more. The thought of living without her scares me more than anything else in this life. I was more than happy to come home when I did. The fact that we *all* got home together is something that I will be forever grateful for."

"You guys seem pretty tight."

"For me...they're *my* family."

Riley nodded, understanding where Ed was coming from. Family didn't have to be blood-based to exemplify the true meaning.

Ed put down the knife. "Sorla's the happiest I've seen her since we all came home. She seems at peace somehow. No, it's more than that—it's like, you've brought the sun back into her eyes."

Riley shook her head. "I think she did that on her own."

Ed shrugged. "Maybe. Let's just say then, you helped her find it again." He leaned over and kissed her on top of her head. "That makes you family too, in my eyes."

Riley pulled up a chair at the table and sat down. "I'm not sure I deserve that sort of credit, but thank you. That means a lot."

"Fender said you wanted some dancing lessons."

Riley explained about the rodeo.

Ed chuckled. "I think if we all pitch in, we can get you the basics."

Claire walked in and wrapped her arms around Ed's waist. "What are we pitching in for?"

"Dancing lessons," Ed said.

"Ooh, count me in. I'm there."

"Okay, how about we make a first attempt after lunch?"

Sorla wandered in and kissed Riley on the cheek as she sat down next to her. "What are we doing after lunch?"

Grinning, Claire pulled an ice-water pitcher from the fridge. "Dancing!"

Riley ran her fingers through her hair. "Oh, brother."

Sorla laughed and patted her thigh. "It'll be okay. Come on, let's eat so we can start swingin' those hips of yours, girl."

Riley felt her face flush and knew if the heat in her cheeks was anything to go by that she must be as red as a beetroot, much to everyone's delight, as laughter lit up the room.

CHAPTER EIGHTEEN

Sorla took charge of the music and the choreographic instructions, while Ed and Claire demonstrated the two-step. "Ed will lead and his hand will guide Claire into which moves he's going to do, but the whole dance is based on two steps...see? Quick-quick, slow, slow. Quick-quick, slow, slow."

Riley watched as Ed and Claire moved though the room.

Sorla held out her hand. "Okay, now try it with Ed." Claire shadowed and gave Riley some tips on where to put her hands as Ed turned her for a promenade, then back again. It was tricky, as she was still one-armed and in the sling, but they were managing admirably. They twisted and turned, spinning backwards and forwards.

Next came the waltz. Riley stepped on Ed's toes a few times, murmuring apologies as she looked down at her feet. Ed tipped her chin up. "Look at me. Feel the movement through the three steps. I know it's tricky with one arm and shoulder, but try and feel it through your hips and waist." They tried a few more steps. "That's it. Nice." Ed steered her around the room in a circle and then back again. "Okay, you try it with Fender, while I take a little-boys' break."

Sorla stepped up and into Riley's arms and chuckled. Riley was frowning and looking down at her feet, with her tongue poking out in concentration between soft lips.

At the sound of Sorla's chuckle Riley looked up, frowning. "What's so funny?"

Sorla kissed her on the top of the nose. "You're adorable. You know that?"

"You say that now, before I step all over your toes. Hope you got a spare foot in the cupboard, in case I wreck this one."

Sorla threw her head back and laughed till tears poured down her face. "It's made of strong stuff. I think we'll be okay." She tilted Riley's chin up. "Don't look down at your feet."

"I can't help it. How else am I supposed to steer them?"

"You feel where your partner is going to take you and you follow them."

"How am I supposed to do that?"

"Kiss me."

"What?"

"Kiss me." Sorla leaned in and claimed Riley's mouth in a commanding, yet gentle way. Riley closed her eyes as she let Sorla take the lead in both the kiss and the dance. By the time she came up for air, they had travelled around the room.

Sorla smiled. "See? Your body just followed without thinking."

"There is no way I can concentrate, let alone think, when you kiss me like that. Is that a legal dance move?"

Sorla chuckled. "Does it matter? It worked, didn't it?"

"Yeah, but…"

"The trick is *not* to think so much. Just let your body go with the flow."

Riley blushed and whispered in her ear. "Might not be such a good idea. Right now my body is in need of a cold shower."

Sorla laughed. She was enjoying seeing Riley become distracted, knowing she was the cause. "How about we take a break and have another go later on?"

Having bid farewell to Claire and Ed, Riley and Sorla quietly made their way back to Sorla's suite where Riley had left her bag of medicines from the hospital. Sorla watched her throw her head back and swallow a couple of tablets, grimacing slightly at the aftertaste. She walked over behind Riley to rest her chin on her shoulder. "You okay?"

Riley turned in her embrace. "Mm. Just a bit achy."

Sorla gripped her hand and led her to the couch, picking up Riley's tub of salve on the way over. "Come on. Time for some of your own medicine, Dr. Dolittle." Sorla sat on the couch and pointed down to the floor. "Sit." She placed a cushion behind the small of Riley's back as she lowered herself to the ground to sit in front of her outstretched legs.

Sorla opened Riley's tub of salve and set it on the arm of the couch, reached over and gently freed Riley's arm from the sling, then undid her shirt and bra, sliding them off.

Even marked and bruised, Riley's body took Sorla's breath away. She watched as her chest gently rose and fell with each breath. Her eyes travelled the planes of her broad shoulders and softly sculpted arms, coming back to her perfect breasts. She dipped her fingers in the salve, rubbing it together between her fingers to warm the mixture. "Tell me if this hurts."

Gently she smeared the salve over Riley's shoulder, softly massaging the surrounding muscles to loosen them up. Her hands made their way over to knead her neck, fingers teasing up into the base of her hairline, before weaving their way down either side of her spine, easing out to her ribs. She made her way back up Riley's body, pausing briefly to slip a pillow in behind her neck. Sorla bent forward until she was level with Riley's ear. "Lean your head back, gorgeous."

She dipped her fingers into the salve once again. The heady scents rose throughout the room as the mix warmed in her hands. She continued to work the salve carefully around the injured shoulder, across to the trapezius, near her neck and shoulder blades, and down to the deltoids at the end of the shoulders, before sweeping back up to work across the chest wall. Sorla watched, fascinated, as Riley's nipples puckered, hardened, and rose to peaks. Her eyes and hands were magically drawn to them, her salve-coated fingers gliding across in a massage.

Riley's lips parted slightly and the tip of her tongue darted out to moisten suddenly dry lips. Both Sorla's and Riley's breathing began to quicken. Sorla gently nudged her. "Move forward." She slipped behind her onto the floor, never once losing hold of her new focus. As Sorla fitted in behind her, Riley leaned back, melting into her with a soft sigh. Sorla captured her lips, her tongue teasing the wanting mouth.

Sorla slid her hand ever so slowly down to cup Riley firmly between the legs, alternating the pressure in a steady rhythm, the pressure building until Riley moaned in anticipation. Sorla deftly undid Riley's jeans, sliding inside, eliciting a soft rewarding whimper. She knew Riley was close to the edge after the dancing and the massage. Sorla felt her tighten around her fingers as the first tremors began. Riley threw her head back, arching her neck, pressing herself into Sorla's hand as Sorla found her centre and brought her home.

Riley kissed Sorla's forearm and groaned as she lay back against Sorla's shoulder. "What have you done? I can't move."

Sorla chuckled. She whispered in Riley's ear. "Just loving you, babe."

"Love your work."

Sorla kissed the side of her head. "How do you feel?"

"Mm, like I've died and gone to heaven."

"Good to know." She traced lazy patterns against Riley's stomach. After a few minutes, she smiled as she felt Riley's body relax and her breathing even out. She pulled the cover off the couch, covering them both, before putting a cushion behind her own head and closing her eyes. She couldn't remember ever feeling so complete as she did right at that moment, with her lover asleep in her arms.

❖

The surface below her moved. Riley sat up with a start, looking around the room, trying to work out where she was just as two warm hands snaked up her sides and around her front.

"Sorry, didn't mean to wake you. You okay?"

Half panicked, Riley tried to pull away. "Shit, I must be squashing you."

Sorla chuckled, pulling her back to rest against her body, rubbing her stomach with soft circular strokes. "No, you're not squashing me. I moved because I think my bum's going numb, but you are definitely not squashing me."

"I'm sorry I fell asleep on you."

"Don't be. You needed it."

Riley felt acutely embarrassed. "I've never done that before...you know, after sex, without reciprocating."

Sorla smiled and kissed the top of her head. "It's okay, love. Besides, there's plenty of time later on, if you feel so inspired."

Riley grabbed Sorla's arm and looked at her watch. "Not really. I have to head off soon."

Sorla trailed her fingers up and down Riley's arm, watching, fascinated, as goosebumps followed in their wake. "Do you remember this morning, when Mickey left, and Ed and Claire went into town?"

Riley shivered under Sorla's fingers. "Mm."

"Ed and Mickey paid George a visit." Sorla's fingers travelled up Riley's arm, across and down to her chest to circle a nipple.

Riley's hand came up as quick as lightning and stilled Sorla's fingers. She half turned around to look at her, frowning. "What for?"

"Mickey wanted to have a talk with George, and Ed went as backup." Riley turned away to lean forward, pulling her legs up to hug her knees. "While they were there, Pauly offered to look after George tonight, so you can get some rest." Riley pulled away and put her forehead down onto her knees at the news. Sorla reached out and rubbed her back soothingly. "What's the matter, love?" Riley shook her head. "Come on. Talk to me. What are you thinking?"

"That I feel completely naked and exposed."

"How do you mean?"

"In less than forty-eight hours, I've gone from being an incredibly private person, minding my own life, to having what feels like everybody knowing my business."

"You've had a hell of a coming-out week, love."

Riley huffed out a dry laugh. "Is that what's it been?"

"Kind of, in an oversimplified way."

"I don't know if I like it." Riley's voice was so tiny, so defeated, that Sorla had to strain to hear.

Wrestling from her position on the floor, Sorla stood up stiffly and held out her hand. "Come with me." She led Riley to the bedroom, undressed, then turned the covers down on the bed and lay down. She patted the mattress beside her.

Riley looked at her. "What are you doing?"

"We're both getting naked. Come on." Riley looked at her. Sorla patted the bed again. "Humour me. Come on."

Riley slid her jeans and underwear off and carefully lay on the bed beside Sorla. "Okay. Now what?"

Sorla rolled over until she lay on top of Riley. "Now we're both naked."

"It's not the same."

"Yeah, it is. Think about it. If someone walked into the room right now, what would they see?"

"That you're mooning them."

Sorla laughed. "Apart from my glowing glutes."

"Two naked people in bed."

"But how much of our actual nakedness would they see?"

Riley thought of the image they offered from the doorway. "Not much, I suppose."

"Exactly. Sometimes, when life strips you bare, it's your friends, and people who care about you, who can support and shield you. There will always be rubberneckers who want to gawp and sticky beak, but those who care have got you covered. That's what Mickey and Ed did, and Pauly too. They did it out of love and care for you. They just offered you support and some breathing space, until you get your feet back again."

Sorla lay her head on Riley's chest, her fingertips gently outlining Riley's muscles, while Riley mulled over what Sorla had said. There was some truth in it. She still felt uncomfortable and didn't like how people were now looking at her, but she also knew that Sorla was right. She had people who had her back and wanted to support her. Perhaps part of her lesson in all of this was to learn to let them help. It wouldn't be an easy lesson, but then, most of life's lessons weren't.

Riley grinned. "I suppose this means I don't have to rush off, then."

Sorla grinned back. "I suppose so."

Riley kissed her. "I'm not feeling tired anymore. In fact, you could say I'm feeling a little inspired."

"Is that right?" Sorla nipped her bottom lip playfully.

Riley wrapped her leg around Sorla and turned her with her good arm, so she now lay on top. "Most definitely."

Sorla woke close to five a.m. At some point in the night Riley had turned onto her back and she had followed, rolling over onto her side with her arm and leg wrapped around Riley's torso, her head resting on Riley's right shoulder. She lay quietly looking at her lover's profile. Her fingers craved to trace her eyebrow line and to stroke her cheekbones, but she tempered them to stillness so as not to wake her.

Her thumb absentmindedly caressed back and forth on Riley's chest. *I don't remember the last time I slept so well.*

"What are you thinking?"

Sorla lifted her head, startled. "I thought you were asleep."

"Can't sleep with all the racket going on."

"What racket?"

Riley tapped a finger on Sorla's forehead. "The cogs turning over double time in here. What are you thinking?"

Sorla lay her head back down, listening to the soothing pattern of Riley's heartbeat as her fingers traced freely in ever widening circles now that she knew Riley was awake. "I was thinking that on the nights you've been here, how I've slept like a baby. I haven't slept very well since Iraq. But with you, it's like…it's like you soothe my soul."

Riley's hand came up to stroke Sorla's head. "I think I sort of know what you mean. Here with you? I feel settled. Complete, somehow."

Sorla rolled until she was lying on top of Riley and staring into her eyes. She traced her eyebrows, and nose, and finally her lips, which parted to kiss her fingertips.

Sorla's throat closed over with the emotional realization. "I don't want you to go."

Riley closed her eyes and shook her head slightly. "And I don't want to leave." Her voice was husky with the shared emotion. "But we each have things we need to do. You have a big meeting to prepare for tomorrow, and I need to head back home to get ready for the week, do some laundry, and pick up George."

Never before had Sorla felt such impending loneliness as she did at the thought of Riley leaving. Her chest ached with the realization that she was not only falling in love with Riley, but that she was coming to need her in her life.

Eyes closed, Riley could feel the tension growing in Sorla's body. Her hand glided to Sorla's hip, fingers slowly massaging in ever widening circles, expanding to move up the side of her ribs. "I'm still here." One leg insinuated itself around Sorla's thigh, wrapping itself tightly to snag Sorla in closer, her hand slipping further upward to massage and caress Sorla's breast. Her mouth found its way along her jawline and down her soft throat. She heard a moan but couldn't be sure whether it came from her mouth or Sorla's. She nipped the point of Sorla's shoulder, then slid back up to claim her lover's mouth insistently.

While her mouth took command, her fingers came down and spread around Sorla's hips, to start up a rocking rhythm. Sorla knelt astride Riley's waist. She closed her eyes as Riley's hand stroked her stomach, then once again claimed her breasts. Sorla's hands embraced Riley's, shadowing Riley's explorations. Her head lolled back, eyes closed, lips moist and open as her breathing picked up a notch when Riley took a nipple between her fingertips and teased it until she thought it would burst. She responded by grinding her hips harder into Riley's core.

Riley growled and thrust up with her hips to meet Sorla's urgent rhythm. Sorla bent forward, capturing Riley's mouth, kissing her hard, until both their lips were full and swollen. Sorla leaned forward until her elbows were beside Riley's shoulders and she was breathing hotly and rapidly into Riley's ear. "Come…with me." She dipped her head to take one of Riley's nipples in her mouth.

Riley cried out at the pleasurable assault as she felt her core heat and expand, the impending energy building, climbing from her toes, and rising ever upward. She responded by gripping Sorla's hips tighter, increasing the shared pressure. She could feel the tension building in Sorla's thighs as their breath quickened to match the pace set and shared. Their thighs were tight with the strain, their bodies shining with moisture. Riley offered a final upward thrust of her hips, only to be met with a low, deep grind from Sorla, adding the final pressure to the pot that caused them both to catch and boil over the edge with matching cries of release, before collapsing into each other's arms.

For long moments, neither said a word as they lay, panting. Not wanting to ruin the moment with words, Riley kissed the top of Sorla's head and was well met by Sorla with a gentle kiss to her chest. Wrapped in each other's arms, they slept through dawn.

Breakfast was a quiet affair after a shared shower. Claire had gone into town, and Ed had left early to move some of the grazing cattle in preparation for the new shipments due later in the week, but only after Riley assured him she would be okay to pick up George. Now, standing wrapped in each other's arms outside, leaning on Riley's truck, neither could find the will to break apart. Sorla had her head tucked against Riley's neck with her eyes closed. Riley's cheek rested against the side of Sorla's head as she gazed off into the distance.

"I wish you'd let Ed go with you."

"I'll be okay."

"I worry about you."

Riley gently squeezed her in appreciation of the concern. "I know, but it'll be all right."

"What if I come with you?"

A wry half grin stole over Riley's mouth. "That would be nice for me, but I'm not so sure that it would be so good for George."

Sorla sighed. "I don't like it."

"I know." Riley wrapped her arm around Sorla tighter with what little reassurance she could offer.

"Can we just stay like this?"

Riley chuckled. "It's a nice thought, but it won't get the day done."

"Can I call you?"

"Only if I don't call you first."

"You'll be out Wednesday?"

"Yes. When do the cattle arrive?"

"First shipment's this Tuesday, last one's Friday week."

"Do you think we can squeeze in another dance lesson on Wednesday?"

"You bet."

Riley gave Sorla a final hug, sighed, and straightened, bracing herself for the inevitable. "I better go."

Sorla patted her on the chest before looking up into her eyes. "I know. I don't want to let you go, but I know that I have to. I think you've gone and stolen my heart, Johnson. You know that, don't you?"

"Good."

"Good?"

Riley chuckled. "Uh-huh, 'cause you've got mine. Seems only fair to have yours."

Sorla laughed, playfully slapping her lightly on her good arm before pushing her away. "Get outta here before I change my mind and lock you in the house."

Riley stole another quick kiss before stepping into the truck and starting the engine. She leaned out the window and threw her a wink. "Good luck with the meeting tomorrow. You'll knock 'em dead, gorgeous, I know it."

"Hope so, babe. I'll call you tonight?"

"Looking forward to it. See ya."

"Bye, sweetheart."

Riley smiled as she made her way down the driveway, past the wooden gate and main fence adjoining the road. *Sweetheart. I like how that sounds.*

Chapter Nineteen

Riley walked into the front bar and spotted Pauly setting up the chairs in the dining room. She waved and headed in his direction. "Hiya—he out back in his usual spot?"

Pauly looked her up and down, noting the sling. "Hey, kid. How you doing?"

"I'm doing fine, thanks. And thanks for putting George up for me. I really appreciate it."

"You're welcome. Do you have to go straight away? Or can you spare me five minutes?"

Smiling, Riley patted him on his shoulder. "Sure."

"Good, good. Come, sit over here. Can I get you a coffee, or something to drink?" Pauly led her to a sunny table, offset from the window.

"No, I've not long had one, thanks all the same. What's on your mind?"

"Me and some of the lads have been talking, and we were thinking we could set up a roster, to take your old man home at night, save you coming to pick him up all the time."

Riley stiffened slightly. She knew in her heart the offer was one made with good intentions, but as she'd explained to Sorla, she didn't like the feeling that came with people knowing about her personal life. "That's a really nice offer, Pauly, and I am touched, but I'm okay, really."

Pauly patted her hand resting on the tabletop. "I figured you'd say something like that. Will you at least give it some thought? Please?"

"I can think about it, but my answer won't change."

"Oh, and one more thing, the boys have started a kitty."

Riley's eyes narrowed in suspicion. "What for?"

"So that George can have a sleepover once a week to give you a break. We were thinking a Friday or Saturday night, maybe?"

"No, thank you."

"It's already been decided by the boys. All you have to do is pick which night you want."

Riley began to stand up. "It's a generous offer, but I don't need anyone's charity."

Pauly grabbed her hand and tugged her back down to sit in the chair. "It ain't charity. We all agreed, it's simply returning the favour."

"What favour?"

"All the things you've done for folks 'round here over the years. The bridles and saddles you either made or fixed up for free for the kids' Pony Club, the prizes donated every year for the town's big Christmas raffle, the horses you've trained and fixed for nothing for the families who couldn't afford to pay you, and the time you give over every year to help the disabled kiddies on their summer camp, and the special saddles you made them so they can go riding like everyone else. You've been helping folks out for years. Now some of those folks'd like to do something for you, in return."

"It's not necessary."

"Well, we think it is."

"No, thank you, Pauly."

Pauly sighed, shaking his head. "I told the lads you were too proud and independent to take the offer. So I have another one. How about we put George up each year, for the week of the rodeo? He spends most of his time here anyway. And the boys can keep an eye on him and make sure he gets to bed safe and gets up, showered, and shaved. That way, you can do what you need to do during the week, and you can pick him up on the Monday afterwards. Whaddya say?"

Riley shook her head.

"Come on kid, this is a good deal. And it can keep everyone happy. George'll be safe, you can have the week to concentrate on things, George gets to stay here and relive his glory days for a whole week, and the boys feel like they can give something back for you and for George." Pauly reached out and held her hand in both of his big ones, eyes pleading. "Please?"

"Damn you, Pauly! Stop looking at me with your big puppy-dog eyes. Okay, already. I'll think about it."

Pauly broke out into a gold-toothed grin. "Thatta girl."

"How's he been?"

"Cantankerous. Moody. Sometimes quiet. He's had a bit to think about."

Riley sighed, running her fingers through her hair wearily. "I never planned for any of this to happen."

"I know. But life has a way of creeping up on you and surprising you when you least expect it, huh?"

Riley smiled wryly. "You can say that again."

"Does she take your breath away?"

"Wha…?"

"Does your heart race when you see her? When you're with her, do you lose track of time?" Riley nodded. "When she walks out of the room, do you miss her?"

Riley closed her eyes and felt her chest swell and ache for Sorla. "Yes."

"As my Nona used to say, these are the signs that you have been given a gift. Use it wisely." Pauly stood up and patted her cheek affectionately. "Love is love, *cara*. It is a rare and special thing. For what it's worth? My advice is to hang on tight and see where it takes you. Be happy, kid."

Riley's chest and throat ached at Pauly's tenderness.

"Come on. He's out back."

George was sitting in the sun, eyes closed. Riley couldn't help but notice how he was shrinking and his skin seemed to appear just that little bit more yellow in the daylight. Riley squatted down next to George's chair, gently rubbing his arm until an eye cracked open. "Hey, George. Time to go home."

George opened both eyes to squint at her, his eyes watering with the effort. As Riley stood, he looked her up and down, grumbling a disapproval at having been woken up. He saw her sling, grunted, and turned away. As he stiffly straightened and began to prise himself out of his chair, Riley hooked her good arm under his and around his waist, gently easing him upright. He pushed her away, stumbling slightly with the effort. "I can manage my own damn self."

"Right you are, then. Truck's just around the corner when you're ready." Pauly and Riley escorted George as he shuffled to the truck. Pauly helped him get into the passenger seat, strapping him in while Riley stowed his overnight bag in the back. As Pauly clipped his belt up he got in George's face. "Play nice, George, or there will be a queue of us coming round to kick your arse."

In response George simply grunted, before leaning his head back and closing his eyes, effectively shutting everyone out.

Pauly shut the door. "You right, kid?"

"Yes, thanks. And thanks again for all your help. I owe you."

"The only thing you owe me, kid, is a promise to think about that offer."

Riley waved as she started the engine. "I will. See you."

Sorla milled around the house, desperately trying to stay busy so she didn't have to think about how empty the house now felt. She ran the vacuum cleaner over the lounge room, mopped the kitchen, and did a load of laundry. She smiled to herself when she noticed one of Riley's shirts had made it into the laundry basket. It was the one she had worn home from the cottage after Riley had driven out and found her. *So much has happened in such a short space of time. God, I miss her.* A car pulled up outside. Gazing out the window, she saw Claire struggling with grocery bags. "Hang on and I'll give you a hand."

It didn't take long to unload and unpack Claire's morning efforts. Claire put the last item away and brushed a stray strand of hair out of her eyes. "Feel like a coffee?"

Sorla patted her on the shoulder. "I'll make it. You sit down and put your feet up for five."

"Don't mind if I do. Glad I went in early, it's starting to warm up outside. Riley get off okay?"

"Yeah." Sorla carried over the steaming mugs, placing them on the table before sitting down to mindlessly stir in some sugar.

"You okay?"

Sorla was quiet for a brief moment until she half shrugged. "House feels quiet and empty."

Claire waited for more.

Sorla looked up, put her elbow on the table, and rested her chin in her hand. "How is it, one minute, I am an independent person, with clear goals and a direction to follow, and the next, I'm trying to stay busy doing the laundry so I don't think about the fact that I feel like something is missing? I have the meeting tomorrow, which I haven't finished writing up the report for yet, but I just can't seem to concentrate. My head's all over the shop." Sorla shook her head. "I don't know what's going on." Sorla looked up to see Claire with an enormous smile on her face and scowled at her. "What?"

Claire reached over and patted her friend's hand. "It's called love, Sor."

Sorla's eyebrows rose and a soft smile crept over her face. "Is that what this is?"

"Mm. Looks like it's gone and snuck up on you and bitten you big-time, honey."

Sorla blinked a few times as Claire's words sank in. "Now what do I do?"

Claire stood up and kissed the top of her head. "Enjoy it. Nurture it. And never take it for granted."

❖

"Hey, sorry to call so early. Is this a good time?" Sorla asked.

Riley smiled into the phone. "Now that I'm talking to you, it is."

"Are you okay?"

Riley chuckled. "I'm fine. How're you doing?"

"Technically, okay."

"Technically?"

"I miss you."

Riley sat on the back doorstep watching the sun go down, as it painted the sky with outstretched fingers of gold and amber. "I miss you too. Tell me about your day."

They exchanged the details of their day and plans for tomorrow.

Sorla sighed. "And I have an appointment with my shrink."

"You don't sound like you're looking forward to it."

"Ha. No. Not always my favourite thing to do."

"Why's that?"

"I guess because I try so hard just to get on with life, and appointments with Susie...she has a way of peeling back the layers and looking at all the microscopic details, details I try to ignore, so to have them brought up is a bit like shoving them in my face. She doesn't let me hide or get away with anything. She's good, but it's not always comfortable."

"What sort of things do you talk about?" Riley was intrigued.

"Well, I'll have to give her a rundown on how I've been since I last saw her, flashbacks, nightmares, not sleeping."

"Uh-huh."

"And I'll tell her about you," Sorla added.

"Me?"

"Yep, you."

"What about me?"

"How I sleep better when you're around. I don't have any nightmares. How you make me smile and laugh. How wonderful it feels to fall in love."

Riley closed her eyes and let the wave of emotion that Sorla's statement made wash over her. It lifted her and filled her with a warmth she didn't know was possible. A lump formed in her throat.

"You still there?"

Choked up, Riley couldn't get her voice to work. She nodded silently.

"Riley?"

Riley could hear the trepidation in Sorla's voice and knew she had to get her act together. She cleared her throat as her voiced rasped with feeling. "Yeah. I am. You tell her, I feel the same way."

"You do?" She could hear the tears in Sorla's voice.

Riley laughed softly, feeling light and free at having said out loud what she had been holding tightly inside. "I do. I love every bit about you, Sorla Reardon." A crash of glass sounded from the other end of the house.

"What was that?"

"Sounds like George is awake. I better go." Riley stood up and stretched. "Good luck with your meeting tomorrow and the appointments."

"Thanks, babe. You gonna be all right?"

"Yeah, it's all fine. He probably just knocked the glass over beside his bed."

"Okay then. You know where I am?"

"I do. Thank you." Riley meant it with all her heart.

"Sleep tight. I love you."

"Love you too. Sweet dreams."

"'Night."

"Bye."

As Riley had predicted, George had knocked the glass over, the shattered fragments glittering on the floor in the hallway light's reflection. Fortunately George had rolled over and gone back to sleep, seemingly none the wiser. Sighing, Riley retrieved a dustpan and brush to clean up the mess. She smiled to herself ruefully. Falling in love with Sorla had turned her whole world upside down, but here, with George, it was still realistically Groundhog Day.

CHAPTER TWENTY

Riley spent most of the day stacking all the things she would need at the rodeo stall, in a corner of the main shed out the back. She had made arrangements for her stall tent to go up in its usual spot the following day, which meant she could start carting the gear over on Thursday and be unpacked and ready to start repairs and orders for the early comers on the Friday. It had been slow going, with her shoulder still being sore, but she was careful, leaving some of the heavier things aside for later in the week. Her shoulder was stiff and sore, but felt better for the movement. Her forearm was a challenge, but with patience and creativity, she was managing to find ways to work around it.

"Hey, RJ!"

Riley looked up from her list and waved as she watched Eric Gardner approach. Riley hired Eric and his wife Gloria every year to help out at rodeo time. In truth, they were the closest things to friends that she had. "G'day Eric. How's things?"

"Fine, fine. And you?"

"Good, thanks. Whatcha up to?"

"Gloria and I thought we'd grab some lunch next door and wondered if you'd join us."

Riley looked at her phone, and suddenly realized it had gone past one. Her stomach seemed determined to get in with an answer first and growled at the invitation. Riley smiled and patted her stomach. "I'd love to. Give me five minutes to wash up and tell George where I am, and I'll meet you over there."

"Super. See you in five."

After being effectively dismissed with a grunt from George, she found Eric and Gloria in the back of the café and sat in the booth bench opposite them. "Hey, guys, good to see you again. What's news?"

Eric and Gloria shared a shy smile. Gloria took hold of Eric's hand and silently nodded at him before he turned to Riley. "The good news is that we're both ready and rearing to go come rodeo week at the store and the stall. The not so good news is that next year, we might need to get another person in to help with the stall."

Riley looked back and forth at them both, slightly puzzled. "Oh?"

"Unless you don't mind having a high chair and playpen out the back of the tent."

"A high chair? Why would I…?" Riley saw the high colour in Gloria's cheeks. She also saw the pride fairly radiating off Eric as he looked over at his wife. It became obvious that they were expecting their first child. "Oh-ho. For real? When? Oh, that's wonderful! Congratulations. I'm so happy for you both." Riley stood up and hugged them both. "When's the baby due?"

Gloria held out her hand, grasping Riley's in hers. "I'm just gone five and a half months. We didn't say anything earlier because we wanted to wait and be sure before saying anything."

Riley nodded, appreciating the enormity of the news, given their past miscarriages. "Should you be resting? You know, taking it easy?"

Gloria laughed. "No, the doctor said I can work, but not to lift anything too heavy, just to err on the side of caution."

Riley nodded seriously. "No problems. Eric and I have that covered."

"We wanted you to be amongst the first to know. You've always been good to us. We also wanted to know if you would consider being the baby's godmother."

"Me? Are you sure? I mean, I'd be honoured, but are you sure you want *me*?"

Gloria nodded. "We've talked it over a lot, thinking who we wanted as role models for our kids. We couldn't think of anyone better than you. From the first day we came into town you have been nothing but kind and supportive, helping us settle in, helping us set up with the family, getting Eric here a job at Lawson's, and giving us casual work at the store when we needed the money. You're the sort of person that we want our baby to grow up knowing."

Riley frowned and played with a serviette she plucked from the holder. "I am truly touched and honoured, but this is a small town. You might be better off choosing someone else who could be slightly less… controversial as a role model than me."

Eric shook his head emphatically. "Nope. We've heard the scuttlebutt, same as other folk around abouts. It doesn't make any difference to us. We just hope that you're happy. In fact, made us even more proud, knowing that, no matter what, our baby will have people in their life who are broad-minded and will be able to understand and support them in whatever their life choices might be."

"Wow. That's…" Riley pulled at her ear, taken back by the request. "Thank you, both. I would be honoured."

Eric rubbed his hands together gleefully. "Great, then that's settled. Speaking of commitments, when would you like us to start in the store and the stall?"

Riley held up her splinted forearm. "I might need you to start a bit earlier this year, if that's okay? Moving some of the stock about is a bit tricky at the minute."

Gloria gasped. "Oh, dear. What have you done to yourself?"

Riley shrugged with one shoulder. "Had a bit of an accident and broke my arm."

They both turned and looked at each other before nodding. "No problems at all."

❖

Riley heard her name being called as she walked back to the shop. She turned and scanned the street, finally spying Claire on the opposite side of the road waving at her. She changed course, crossing to meet her. "Hi."

Claire kissed her on the cheek. "Hello there. You're just the person I wanted to catch up with." Obviously noticing that Riley wasn't wearing her sling, she added, "How's the arm?"

"Not too bad. It feels a bit better having it out and moving it around, but I've got the sling back at the shop if it gets too much."

Claire nodded. "Can you spare me an hour?"

The morning had been quiet and she knew that George could catch her on the phone if he needed her. "Sure, why not."

Claire grinned like the Cheshire cat. "Great. I was just having a look around town for dresses for the ball, and you won't believe it, but I think I've found your gown, Cinderella."

"Serious?"

"I know. Couldn't quite believe it myself. I only came in to get some ideas and I found this little number up the back, tucked away. Something tells me it will be perfect. Come on, let's try it on."

Claire dragged her into the dress store, where Elsie Butcher stood behind the counter eyeing the pair over the top of her wire-rimmed glasses. Her glass-bead chain shimmered in the light as she took her glasses off, leaving them hanging on her generous bosom. She smiled at Claire. "Hello again, I wasn't expecting to see you quite so soon."

Riley shot Claire a questioning look.

"I was in here earlier asking about the styles of dresses that are worn to the ball. Elsie, here, has been a wealth of knowledge."

Elsie looked Riley up and down in her heavy cotton drill work shirt, jeans, and boots. "So this is our Cinderella? Hm, turn around, dear."

Riley looked over at Claire, not sure that she liked being viewed and assessed with such scrutiny. Claire laughed. "Relax, we're just getting an idea of what we have to work with so we can find the perfect outfit for you."

Reluctantly Riley let Claire turn her, as both women looked her over carefully. Elsie came from around the counter to stand at Riley's side. "Nice shoulder line, tiny waist…what dress size are you, dear?"

Riley was horrified. "Um, I don't know."

Putting her spectacles back on, Elsie looked at her over her glasses and tutted. "Never mind." She drew a tape measure from around her neck and took some of Riley's measurements, all the while murmuring to herself. Finally, Elsie turned to Claire. "I think you're right. Let me go get it and your friend here can try it on." Elsie bustled out the back behind a curtain only to return a short while later with a white dress draped over her arm. It was the softest silk, broken only by a diamanté laddered row that ran from under one arm to where it tapered off at the waist. It was a single shoulder, straight, ankle-length gown that flared out ever so slightly at the base. A thigh-high split ran to three inches below the diamanté line. A large part of Riley's back and left side would be bare, save for the ladder of sparkles stretching and joining the front and rear panels together. It would show off Riley's sculptured body in a subtle and stylish way. Elsie handed the dress to Claire. "You go and help your friend try it on while I find some shoes. Do you know what size feet you have?"

Riley looked down at her boots. "Either a seven or a five, depending on where the shoes come from."

"Uh-huh, and I'm guessing we don't want anything too high in the heel."

Claire looked at Riley's boots and chuckled. "Possibly not."

Riley looked back and forth between the pair as they talked over her head, seemingly oblivious to her presence. Claire grabbed her hand. "Come on, I'll give you a hand." Claire showed her how to put the outfit on and then left her the privacy to get changed, returning to Elsie to discuss shoes. A few minutes later Claire spoke from outside the curtain. "How are you going?"

"I feel half-naked."

"Show me."

Riley opened the curtain and stepped out to see Claire's mouth fall open and Elsie beam like a proud parent. Riley stood self-consciously in front of them, smoothing down the material, trying to hold the split closed.

Claire smiled, stepping up to straighten the shoulder strap. "Turn around for me."

Riley dutifully turned the full circle until she was back facing Claire. She whispered, "I had to take my bra off—I couldn't work out how to hide the strap."

Claire patted her waist. "That's okay. We'll fix you up with something in a minute. What do you think?"

"It's a bit breezy."

Claire threw her head back and laughed. "Honey, you are gonna be the talk of the town in that gown. You two were made for each other. Sorla is gonna melt when she sees you."

Riley knew she was blushing. "You think?"

Claire turned Riley around so she could see herself in the full-length mirror. She undid the clasp tying Riley's hair back, fingering it out so it hung softly over her shoulders.

Riley looked down. "It's lovely, but there's a bit too much showing. People are going to see."

Claire patted her good shoulder and spoke quietly. "I've got some make-up concealer that will hide whatever marks haven't faded by then. The shoulder strap should hide your burn dressing and we'll figure out something for your arm. Come and try some shoes on so you can see the whole outfit."

Elsie had found a small-heeled pair of silver open-toed strappy sandals that set off perfectly the silver diamanté strip on the dress. She nodded at Riley. "You might like to practice walking in those shoes for a little while each night, so you get used to the feel of them."

Riley nodded solemnly. "Okay."

"I also took the liberty of selecting some undergarments that will suit the outfit. You could get away without them, but I am guessing you might feel a bit more comfortable if you wore something underneath."

Today was apparently her day to blush. "Yes, please."

Elsie smiled. "I thought as much." She handed Claire the garments. "When I first saw that dress, I knew it was special. I was right. You look simply stunning, my dear. I'm glad to see it's going to live up to its promise and give the perfect person an opportunity to shine."

Riley kept looking in the mirror in disbelief. The image looking back at her was not the image she held in her mind of who she was. "It's my first ever grown-up dress."

Elsie came up behind her and straightened the neckline. "Then that proves it was meant to be. It's quite simply perfect. If you'd like to get changed, I'll wrap it up for you."

Riley nodded and returned to the dressing room while Elsie and Claire went to the counter. Riley came out a few minutes later with the dress carefully draped over her arm and the shoes resting on top. Elsie boxed the dress up and put the underwear and shoes in a separate bag. Riley pulled out her wallet, only to have Claire put her hand on it. Riley looked up questioningly.

Claire smiled. "Put that away. I've got this."

Riley shook her head. "I can pay."

Claire patted her hand. "I know you can, but this is a thank-you present from the Pusskin family."

Riley opened her mouth to protest but Claire stalled her. "It would mean a great deal if you would let me do this. Please, Riley?"

Riley looked from Claire to Elsie, who gently nodded, agreeing with Claire. "Can I at least pay for the shoes and underwear?"

Claire laughed. "All right, if that will make you feel better."

"It would."

"Then consider it a deal."

Riley turned to Claire and hugged her. "Thank you."

"You are most welcome. I'll come over and help you get dressed on the night too. I can't wait to see Sorla's face!"

❖

By the time Wednesday afternoon came around, Riley was positively jumping out of her skin to see Sorla again. Pulling up to the house yard, her face split into an enormous grin as she saw Sorla waiting for her. She stepped out of the truck only to be enveloped in Sorla's arms and devoured by a hungry mouth.

Coming up for air, Sorla sighed and lay her head in the crook of Riley's neck. "Too long."

Riley's eyes were closed and she was breathing in the essence of Sorla as she rested her chin on the top of her head. "What's that, love?"

"Had to wait too long to do this." Sorla gently reclaimed Riley's mouth in a kiss of warmth and longing.

"Mm. I couldn't get here fast enough."

"Good thing your arm slows you down. Hey! You're not wearing your sling."

"It's in the truck if I need it. I just find it more comfortable now without it. It feels better to keep it moving."

"Okay. You're taking it easy though, aren't you?"

Riley chuckled and kissed her forehead. "I am. I've arranged someone to help me out tomorrow with a lot of the carting and lifting of things between the shop and the stall."

"I suppose tomorrow will be a pretty big day, huh?"

"Eh, hopefully not too bad. If I get stuck in early, we should have it set up, ready to start trading on the Friday, probably by midafternoon."

"What about your gear when you're not there? Aren't you worried someone will take off with it?"

Riley shook her head. "I've organized a lockable shipping container for all the sewing equipment and more expensive stuff. Once I've set up, I mostly camp over and stay with the gear anyway, but there's also a security firm that looks after the stall holders during the week."

"Sounds like you've got it all organized."

"It took a few years of making mistakes and watching others, but I've got it down to a system that I'm pretty happy with now. How did you get on with the cattle yesterday?"

"Terrific. Nice batch of young steers. We're really happy with them. They unloaded really well and have started to settle in nicely over on the northern side. Only one batch to go."

"How did Claire pull up?"

Sorla chuckled. "Not too bad, all things considered."

"And you?"

"I'm tired and a bit stiff, but nothing to complain about."

"Maybe when we finish up with the horses, I could give you a massage."

Sorla leaned the full length of her body along Riley's and smiled. "That sounds divine."

Riley grinned. "Righto, then, how about we hook in and get started?"

"After you." Sorla linked arms with Riley as they walked over to the pens where Sorla had earlier organized for Queenie and the two youngsters to be put.

They worked with all three at first, getting the two youngsters used to their presence and touch before drafting Queenie off and working with the colt and filly. At the end of the session both youngsters were given a treat and reunited with Queenie, who had been enjoying some quality alone time with a bag of oats.

Sorla shut the gate behind them as they headed back to the house. "I don't know about you, but I can hear a cold drink calling my name." Hand in hand they walked back inside the house. Sorla poured the tea into two glasses. Riley sipped hers thoughtfully.

"Penny for them," Sorla said.

"Pardon?"

"For your thoughts."

"Oh, sorry. I was thinking I can come out early on Friday morning to get some time in with the horses, but that after that, I won't get to see much of you over the next week, until the ball on Saturday night."

"Oh."

"I know."

"You've got to eat though. How about on a couple of nights I bring you dinner? That way, I know you'll eat properly and we can spend some time together."

Riley felt a wash of warmth spread over her. Apart from Pearl, she'd never really had anyone make an effort to look after her. It felt nice. "That sounds lovely."

Sorla grinned mischievously. "I have to confess, it's an act of pure selfishness on my behalf, because I'm not sure I can go that long without seeing you. Besides, it might give us a chance to sneak some more dance lessons in too."

"I could use all the help I can get. But I'll be happy, no matter what, as long as you're there."

CHAPTER TWENTY-ONE

Riley never made it back to Cherry Hill on the Friday. The madness of rodeo week ruled her schedule and kept her hard at work around the clock.

For some people, rodeo week was a part of their annual holiday, the regulars coming back year after year, soaking in all the events, the carnival atmosphere, and the music, and meeting up with old friends. There were families, old-timers, stall holders, professionals, amateurs, and rookie kids desperately trying to break in to the big time. The town's numbers continued to swell as more and more people flocked for the event. Traditionally, the end of the week would see the numbers and the level of action peak, with the town completely booked out and all camping spots taken.

The professional riding rounds would be thinned out on the Thursday and Friday, followed by the Grand Parade, which would make its way through town on the Saturday morning before ending back at the big arena, where the finals of all events would be held. The weekend would come to a climax with the ball, where the season's champions would be announced and crowned, the Hall of Fame recipients inducted, and the closing celebration party unleashed, signalling the end of another year.

True to her word, Sorla dropped in twice with dinner, with Claire and Ed dropping by to share a takeaway lunch with her midweek. With each visit, Riley managed to squeeze in a couple of dances, but for the most part, she just worked hard. Repairs took longer than most years, simply because she didn't have the strength and dexterity in her splinted wrist, which also hampered her speed and required a number of workarounds to get the jobs at hand completed. Riley was so busy that for much of the week, she was only managing to grab between three and four hours' sleep each night. Luckily, in the middle of the night, no one was around to hear her occasional weary, colourful, frustrated verbal soliloquys.

Riley rubbed her eyes tiredly before looking down at her phone to see what the time was. It had not long gone ten o'clock at night and she'd been going since four that morning. She was putting the last of the mending touches on a tear in a customer's favourite pair of riding chaps. She was trying to maintain the tension and turn the garment slowly and evenly with her casted hand, while feeding the leather material through with her good hand, when the needle snapped. "Sonofabitch! You couldn't wait 'til I was finished? You had to wait until now to break, you mongrel thing."

A rustle at the canvas door opening interrupted her frustrated rant, her head snapping up to see what the noise was.

There, standing in the doorway, leaning on the pole smiling, was Sorla. "You know, if you kick something, it might make you feel better."

Seeing her lover's beautiful face drained all the tension away. "What are you doing here?"

"I thought you might like some company."

Riley grinned. "I'd love some company, but it's late. You should be at home, tucked up in bed."

Sorla walked straight over and wrapped her arms around Riley's neck. "So should you. You look exhausted."

Riley gently held Sorla's chin, tipping her face to the light. "So do you. Not sleeping?"

Sorla shook her head ruefully. "Not really. I figured we'd probably both be in the same sleep-deprived boat, so…" Sorla stepped out of her arms and walked back out to the tent's entrance, where she picked up a rolled-up swag. "I figured the best way to make sure both of us get some shut-eye is to come out and camp with you. I can make sure you actually get to bed, and you can keep my nightmares away." Sorla dumped her gear at Riley's feet, looking up hopefully.

In answer, Riley wrapped her arms around Sorla's waist, pulling her in tight for a long, slow, sensual kiss. "That sounds like a perfect plan."

❖

Sorla woke to an empty bed, a hint of honey in the air. Walking through a partition to the main body of the tent, she saw Riley hunched over a saddle, rhythmically rubbing it with a cloth, stopping occasionally to dip the cloth into a tin pot beside her, before returning to massage the saddle with the cloth once again. On bare feet, Sorla padded up behind her and wrapped her arms around her neck. Riley stilled and closed her eyes, smiling, leaning back into the offered embrace, as Sorla nuzzled the soft neck that revealed itself to her waiting lips. Riley sighed with pleasure. "Mm, good morning, love."

"Good morning, yourself. Been up long?"

"Not too long."

Sorla saw that another two saddles had joined the ranks of the nine from the night before, while a third lay in her lap being conditioned and polished. Sorla kissed Riley's lips around a smile as she stroked her jawline. "Liar. How long have you been up?"

"Since four."

Sorla shook her head. "What am I going to do with you?"

Riley grinned. "Anything you want."

Sorla slapped her on the arm playfully. "Well, for starters, how about a shower, followed by some breakfast?"

"Good plan." Riley put down the saddle and cloth and stood, stretching, before wrapping Sorla in her arms for a hug. "Thank you for coming out last night. Sorry I fell asleep on you."

"Well, I'm not. You needed it. So did I. I slept like a baby."

They showered and dressed, but Sorla couldn't bear to let Riley bury herself in work again, not just yet. "How about you finish doing what you were working on while I pack up the bedding and then go rustle us up some breakfast and bring it back? And when Gloria gets here, you can still take a break, but maybe we can go for a walk around, just to stretch our legs a bit."

"That sounds nice. Haven't had much of a chance to stick my head out this past week."

"Then it's high time you did, my little turtle love. Go on, off you go and finish your masterpiece while I go and play at domestic goddess."

Riley kissed her on the forehead. "Have I told you you're gorgeous lately?"

Sorla hugged her back. "You have, but you're welcome to keep repeating yourself."

Riley grinned mischievously, squeezing her affectionately before releasing her. "You're gorgeous."

Sorla swatted her with her towel before heading out the back. She made good on her offer, coming back with a feast of eggs, toast, and bacon.

Riley finished up polishing the last of the conditioner off the saddle she was working on before tagging it and stacking it with the rest under the trestle tables near the door. Wiping her hands clean, she gratefully accepted the plate she was handed. "Mm, much nicer than cereal, thank you."

"You're welcome, my love. Enjoy."

Gloria and Eric arrived, and Riley introduced them to Sorla.

"Nice to meet the person who has put the colour back in the boss's cheeks," Gloria said.

Riley squirmed self-consciously behind them, much to the group's pleasure as they laughed good-naturedly. Sorla sat back, fascinated, as she watched the three of them plan out the day's tasks.

Sorla stepped forward. "Before you all take off on your morning's chores, can I ask a favour of Eric and Gloria?"

The couple looked at each other and shrugged. Eric smiled. "I guess. Go ahead."

"Would you be able to mind the stall for, say, three-quarters of an hour, while I take Riley here out for a walk and some fresh air?"

Gloria had an enormously pleased grin on her face and clapped her hands together. "We'd love to. Go on, get out of here, you two."

Riley looked back and forth like a deer trapped in headlights until Eric physically herded her up, shooing her out of the tent. "You heard them, go on, get! Enjoy the sun. Take your time. We've got things covered here."

Riley held her hand out for Sorla to grab as they headed off to investigate the other stalls and rigs set up around the showgrounds. Lots of people waved and called their greetings to Riley as they circumnavigated the grounds. At one point, they stopped to help out a family with a fractious horse who was threatening to kick its stall door down.

Sorla smiled.

Riley asked, "What are you smiling about?"

"You, mostly."

"Pardon?"

"Apart from the fact that I love you, you are great with people. I have really enjoyed watching you in your element. Not only are you good at what you do, you're generous, kind, thoughtful, and irresistible. You're quite amazing."

Riley paused and appeared to be stunned by the compliment, which only made Sorla love her more. "That's really lovely, thank you. That's probably the nicest thing anyone has ever said to me. I'm not sure it's true, but thank you all the same. I just try to treat people decent. I think everyone deserves that."

Sorla squeezed her hand. "Like I said, you're amazing."

Riley chuckled softly. "I think maybe you're biased and you need more sleep, but thank you. For what it's worth, you're the dynamo, my love. I just count myself lucky to have met you and am blown away that you share your love with me."

Sorla playfully tweaked Riley's butt. "You know, with all this mutual admiration going on, neither of us might get our heads into the tent."

Riley laughed. "True enough. Speaking of tents, here we are. After you."

They stepped from the bright sunshine to the dimmer light in the tent. Several of the items had been picked up from the rack and trestle table, and both Gloria and Eric were serving customers.

Eric looked up from the display stand of saddles. "Ah, here she is. Riley, I'd like you to meet Ryan Harrison. Mr. Harrison would like to meet the saddler he has heard so much about, with regards to inquiring about a saddle for next year."

Riley shook his hand. "A pleasure to meet you, sir. How may I help?"

As Riley talked business, Sorla made her way back behind the counter. Gloria caught her eye, beckoning her over, and whispered conspiratorially. "Holy smokes! Wait 'til people find out that Harrison has been here!"

Sorla frowned. "Is he a somebody in the business?"

Gloria looked at her with raised eyebrows. "Honey, he's *the* man in the business. Not only is he the president of the association, but he is also a multimillionaire with huge clout, if you know what I mean."

Sorla nodded thoughtfully. "I see."

Twenty minutes later, Harrison left. Riley was the picture of cool as she thumbed down a list. "Mm."

"Mm? Is that a good *mm* or a bad *mm*?" Sorla teased from across the room.

"I'm not sure—I'll have to wait on the formal offer—but I think I've just been offered a very nice commission to produce some commemorative saddles and equipment for next year's centenary celebrations."

Gloria grabbed Riley by the arms and jumped up and down as they laughed in pure joy. "Holy cow!"

Grinning, Riley nodded. "I know."

Eric gave her a big bear hug. "That's awesome, RJ, and so well deserved. Congratulations."

Riley hugged him back. "Thanks, Eric."

Sorla walked over to cuddle up to Riley's side and kissed her cheek. "Well done, sweetheart. I'm very proud of you."

Riley had a huge grin on her face. "That's not all. He and the association's board have agreed to meet with you, Ed, and Claire to talk about your proposal. He sounded very interested and wants to know more. I said that you'd all be at the ball on Saturday, and that you'd be happy to talk to them. I hope that's okay."

Sorla looked at Riley in amazement. She had managed to turn a significant deal for herself into a telling potential opportunity for her and her best friends. "That's more than okay, it's wonderful. Thank you, darling."

Riley winked at her. "You're welcome."

Eric cleared his throat. "I thought I'd go and grab some coffee before I head off. You guys want one?"

Riley smiled. "Yes, please. In our wanderings, we plain forgot to pick one up."

"Okay. Coffees coming up."

Gloria said, "Hang on love, and I'll give you a hand."

Riley and Sorla barely noticed them leave. They were too busy getting lost in each other's eyes. Sorla's thumb came up to caress

Riley's jawline. "That was very thoughtful of you. Thank you. It means a lot."

"It's the least I can do."

"I hate to leave, but I'd better think about making tracks shortly so that I can go and tell Ed and Claire the news and talk about how we can get prepared. What about you? I saw you looking at a list. You got a busy day ahead of you?"

Riley showed her the list and Sorla whistled at the length. Riley put the list down on the bench. "Mm. Big day. Still, we're on the downhill run now. Not long to go before it's over for another year."

Both of their heads came up as they heard the stall entrance rustle. Sorla watched, captivated, as she saw Riley's expression close down to become a solid, almost hard, plane of neutral.

"Hey, baby cakes. Gonna shout an early morning customer a kiss?" A wiry young blond man swaggered into the stall, winking at Riley, before flashing her a million-dollar smile. He was certainly handsome in a fine-boned way, carrying himself like he knew he was a gift to the world. His enormous belt buckle shone brilliantly as he lightly ran his fingers across his groin. "Thought about you last night. Did you dream of me?"

The hair went up on the back of Sorla's neck, her fists curling tight up by her sides.

Riley calmly walked over to pull off a shirt and leather chaps from the repair rack, placing them on the counter. "No, Jake, on all accounts."

Jake obviously didn't get the fact that Riley wasn't interested. He leaned over the counter to grip her forearm, stroking it with his thumb. "Sure you did. Come on, how about a quick kiss, for good luck in today's finals?"

Riley smoothly disengaged her arm and tallied up his bill. "That'll be forty dollars please."

Jake pulled his wallet out and opened it up. He scanned the contents before offering her up a confident but sleazy smile. "I don't seem to have that much on me." He vaulted the counter to wrap his arms around Riley's waist, pulling their hips in tight. "How about twenty now, and I make it up to you later?"

Riley smiled and patted him on the chest, pushing him away. "How about fifteen now, and you can take your shirt with you, and when you have the remaining money, you can come back and pick up your chaps?"

"Come on now, sweet thing, you know I'm good for it."

"No."

Jake laughed and squeezed their hips tighter. "Come on, baby."

Sorla couldn't take any more. Striding forward, she grabbed Jake's uppermost wandering hand and whipped it behind his back, pulling his hand up hard and tight between his shoulder blades. His knees bent with the shock and pain from the attack from behind.

Sorla murmered in his ear, "When a lady says *no*, she means it." Sorla reached into his pocket, retrieved the wallet, and tossed it on the bench. She pulled out fifteen dollars before stuffing it down his shirt. "Now, you are going to apologize, and then you are going to leave. If you're smart, you'll give a friend the remaining money you owe this fine lady, and ask them to come and pick up your fancy pants. Because if I see your face in here again, I am going to rip your arms off and beat you over the head with them. Got it?" For emphasis, Sorla gave Jake's arm a hard, cruel twist.

"Yes!"

"Yes, what?"

Jake growled, which only earned him another hard twist on his arm, making him whimper.

"Yes, *what*?"

"Yes! I got it."

"Very good. Now apologize for being a rude, overbearing sleazebag."

Jake hesitated.

Sorla increased her grip on his hand in readiness for another cruel pull upward.

"All right. I'm sorry."

"Good. Now pick up your shirt."

Jake did as he was told. As soon as he picked up his shirt, Sorla escorted him to the door. "And remember what I said. Play smart and get someone else to pick up the rest of your stuff. I don't want to see your face in here again. Do I make myself clear?"

Jake grunted.

"Good." Sorla let go of his arm, brushed imaginary dirt off his shoulder, and waved in his face. "Now run away and don't come back."

Jake turned on her like a wild cat, snarling, which only earned him a bigger grin and a wink from Sorla as she dusted off her hands. Turning on his heel, he stormed off, straight into Eric, who had to swerve in order to narrowly avoid being run over and spilling all the coffees.

"Whoa! Who put the burr in his shorts?"

Sorla barely heard him. As soon as she'd seen Jake clear the area she turned to see if Riley was okay.

Gloria took the tray of coffees from Eric and set it on the counter. "What the hell just happened?" Eric asked.

Sorla half snarled. "A sleazebag named Jake just happened."

Gloria's eyes grew wide. "Jake, as in…?"

Riley sat on the stool behind the counter and nodded. "Yes. Jake Turley."

Eric stood up tall and rigid, his face darkening. "If y'all will excuse me, I think I might go and find this lad and have a man-to-man talk with him."

Riley shook her head. "No. Please. Thanks, Eric, there's no need. Sorla here saw him off."

Eric patted Sorla on the shoulder. "Good for you. He might be a talented bull rider, but he's still an arsehole who needs to be taught a lesson or two."

Riley took another deep breath and straightened up. "I'm fine, really. But thank you everyone. How about we hand out the coffees and get on with our day, hey?"

Sorla respected her need to gain back control of the situation, patting her on the thigh before standing up to give her some space. "That sounds like a great idea."

Eric handed the coffees around. "Did you want me to stick around for a while?"

Riley shook her head. "No. We'll be good here. The sooner you can get the deliveries done and back to the store to help out George, the better."

"Okay, but if you need anything, you just holler and I'll come straight back."

Riley patted Eric's forearm. "Thanks." Gloria went off with Eric to say their goodbyes out the front.

Sorla gently moved a stray lock of hair from Riley's eyes. "You sure you're okay?"

Riley smiled weakly. "Yes, I am. Thanks for rescuing me."

"I take it you know each other, then."

Riley blew out an exasperated breath. "He's notorious on the circuit. He *is* a good bull rider and is rising up the professional ranks really fast. He fancies himself as a bit of a modern love god."

Sorla snorted. "One who doesn't know the meaning of no, obviously."

"Mm."

"What a creep."

"Yes. It's a shame he's both good at what he does and good-looking. Trouble seems to follow him like a bad smell."

"I'm not surprised. What a pig."

"That's not fair on the pig."

Sorla smiled, offering her a hug and kiss. "Well, it'll have to do until I can think of something more appropriate." She looked at her watch and grimaced. "You gonna be okay here?"

Riley smiled and kissed her on the nose. "I am. I've dealt with him before. He just took me a bit by surprise this morning is all. Gloria is here too. Go on. You need to be on your way and get on with your day. He won't be back anytime soon."

"You'll call me?"

Riley kissed her again. "I will. And thank you for last night."

"It was my pleasure. See you tonight?"

"You don't have to come back, you know."

"I know. But I want to, if that's okay."

Riley smiled. "It's more than okay."

Sorla kissed her slowly, tasting every inch of Riley's mouth and lips, before easing back. "It's a date."

"Looking forward to it. Have a great day."

"You too, babe. Remember, anything at all. Call me."

"Yes, ma'am."

❖

Knowing that Sorla would be back for the night, Riley worked like the devil was on her tail, only stopping to quickly eat some fruit and consume a couple of coffees throughout the day. She shooed Gloria off home with Eric, close to six. Gloria was reluctant to go as Jake still hadn't sent anyone to retrieve his chaps and she didn't want Riley to be in the stall alone, but Riley reassured her that Sorla was coming back and so managed to convince Eric to take her home. Although Riley had been careful to make sure Gloria took lots of breaks throughout the day, she couldn't help but notice how tired she looked and was secretly pleased when Eric turned up to take her on home for the night.

She was working on repairing the skirt around a saddle when she heard a throat being cleared. Looking up, she spied a young man, perhaps not long turned twenty, standing uncertainly in the doorway. Putting her tools down to one side, she stood, wiped her hands on a rag, smiled, and walked towards him. "Hello. How can I can help you?"

"I've come to pick up Jake Turley's chaps, for tonight." As he spoke he held out the cash.

Riley's face sobered. She nodded and pulled the chaps off the rack, folding them and placing them in a bag in exchange for the cash. "What's your name?"

"Paul. Paul Butler."

"Thank you, Paul. Jake your friend?"

"Yes, ma'am."

"Then do yourself a favour, and be careful."

Paul blushed fiercely, jamming his hat onto his blond head. He nodded in her direction before tucking the bag under his arm and leaving. Riley shook her head and put the money in the till.

"Hmm, such a serious face. What are you shaking your gorgeous head about?"

Riley smiled, feeling a rush of warmth steal over her, flooding her senses, as she recognized Sorla's honeyed tones. Her gaze swept up and down Sorla's length, taking in the Western-style shirt, open to reveal just enough cleavage to make Riley's mouth water, the snug-fitting low-hipped jeans, and the boots she bought off Riley when she first moved into town. "My, my, my. Don't you look the part of the town's newest cattle baroness?"

Sorla put down the basket she was carrying and slowly turned. "Just trying to fit in. Do I pass muster?"

Riley walked over and wrapped her arms around Sorla's waist. "Oh, you are definitely a ten out of ten, my love."

"Why, thank you. Who was that I just passed?"

"One of Jake Turley's mates, come to retrieve the last of his repairs. He said he needed them for tonight, so he must've made the semifinals."

Sorla ran her fingers across the curve of Riley's cheekbones, around her jawline, and down her throat, stopping at the base of the vee in her shirtfront. "Did you have any more trouble today?"

Riley's voice grew husky as she closed her eyes against the trail of fire Sorla's fingers wrought. "No."

"Did you get through your list?"

"Mostly."

Sorla grabbed Riley's waist, pulling her in tight against her body as she nuzzled her neck. Riley tipped her head back, her lips parting with the escape of a satisfied sigh. Sorla nipped her earlobe. "Guess I'd better stop this then, so you can get back to work."

"Yes." Riley's voice came out as barely a whisper.

Sorla chuckled. She eased off her attentions and patted Riley on the chest. "Come on. Show me your list and how much you have left to do."

Riley kissed her and retrieved the list. "So this is all you've got left?"

"Uh-huh."

"And how long will that take you?"

"They're not big jobs, so two hours maybe, if no more orders come in."

"You must have worked double time today."

Riley grinned. "I did. I wanted to try to get as much done as I could, so we could spend some time together, catch some of the events outside if you wanted, maybe even an early night."

Sorla held up her basket. "I brought dinner. What say I go and scout some of the tents for something special to go with it, while you finish up on some of those items on your list?"

"Sounds great."

Sorla kissed her on the lips briefly. "Okay, back soon."

"I'll be here."

❖

After dinner, Riley and Sorla made their way over to the sponsors' stand, finding some seats near the front. There they watched barrel racing, saddle broncs, and finally the bull ride. Before the bull riding event started, the semifinalists stood in a line in the middle of the arena, facing the crowd, where they were each introduced with a brief account of their progress throughout the season. Cheers went up for each of the contestants. As Jake Turley's name was announced, female squeals from the audience could be heard above the cheers. He played his audience like a true showman, his eyes working the crowd as he smiled and waved. At the last minute, he caught sight of Riley. He winked at her and grabbed his crotch, thrusting his hips suggestively in her direction before throwing his head back, laughing, and walking back to prepare for the round to begin.

Sorla growled and she balled her fists on her thighs. Riley took Sorla's hands into hers and soothingly stroked until her fingers began to relax. Still growling, Sorla managed to mumble a few decent curses. "Hope he falls off the bull and gets kicked in the nuts."

Riley held Sorla's hand tenderly in her lap. "Don't let him get to you."

"If he comes anywhere near you again, I swear I'll…"

Riley stood up and held out her hand for Sorla to join her. "Come on, love. I think we've seen enough."

"Hrmph."

Riley tipped her head back during the walk back to the stall, appreciating the cooler evening air. Working in the tent was hot and airless, particularly in the middle of the day. Now that she had stopped, combined with the wine she'd had with dinner, a wall of weariness descended upon her.

CHAPTER TWENTY-TWO

Riley sent Eric and Gloria off home with gift vouchers for a restaurant in town, a baby boutique store, and a handy week's pay for them both in their pocket. All in all, it had been another successful year for all of them. Now she was headed to Mickey's. Her phone rang, and she pulled off to the side of the road to answer, grinning, having recognized the number on screen. "Hello there."

"Hey, gorgeous. All done for the day?"

"Yep, another year down."

"So where are you now?"

"On my way to Mickey's. Claire's going to meet me there and help me get dressed."

"What will you be wearing?" Riley could hear the smile in her voice.

"Can't tell you."

"Do I get a hint?"

"Nope."

Sorla chuckled. "Fair enough. I suppose I'd better let you get on your way then, so you two can work your magic, huh?"

"Uh-huh."

"I'll see you soon then."

"You bet."

"Save some space on your dance card for me, hey?"

"Always."

Pulling up into Mickey's driveway, Riley spotted Claire sitting on the front porch step with Mickey, chatting and laughing away like two old friends.

Mick stood up to hug her. "Here she is. Hey, Midget. You got away okay, then?"

"Yep, all done and dusted for another year. Hi, Claire, how was your day?"

"Good, good. I got off a bit earlier so that we could have plenty of time to spruce ourselves up."

"Did you bring your outfit too?"

"Most certainly did. How about you throw yourself in the shower and we get this party started."

Riley could feel the butterflies begin to flutter in the pit of her stomach. She put a nervous hand to them and blew out a shaky breath. "Okay. Let's do this."

Three-quarters of an hour later, Riley stood facing Claire, smiling as she openly ogled her dress blue uniform. "Oh my. You are simply stunning. You are so made for that uniform. You're breathtaking. Turn around for me?" Claire turned. "Phew. You are sharp. Ed is one lucky man."

"Well, thank you. You look simply breathtaking yourself. Shall we go out and show Mick?"

With one final look at her reflection in the mirror, Riley took in a nervous breath, straightened her shoulders, and stepped out to join Claire and Mickey, who handed her a champagne flute. She was taken back by the tears running down the old man's weathered cheeks and went straight into panic mode, looking down at the split in the dress, and her near-bare side. "Oh God. It's too much, isn't it? I'm sorry, I could change, there's still time. I'm sorry."

Shaking his head the old man stepped forward and enveloped her in a hug. "My darlin' girl, you are beautiful." He straightened up and held her at arm's length to get a good look at her. "We knew you'd grow into a beauty. Pearl would be so proud. *I'm* so proud." He fished around in his pocket to liberate a velvet box. "Pearlie always said that you could have this when you were grown up. I gave it to her when we got engaged. I would love it if you'd do us both the honour of wearing this. Nothing would make me prouder than knowing that both my girls were with me tonight."

From the velvet box Mickey pulled a fine silver chain with a sapphire teardrop pendent suspended from its length. He handed it to Claire. "Would you do us the favour of putting it on please, Claire? My old hands don't do the fine fancy little clasp thingies no more."

Claire deftly put the necklace on, stepping back so that all could see. Riley closed her eyes and placed her hand on her chest to hold the pendent tenderly, before opening her eyes, to see two smiling, tear-streaked faces looking back at her. "This is not a night for tears." Riley bravely smiled through her own. Holding her glass aloft, she offered a toast. "Congratulations, Mick, on being recognized for all your years of hard work and sacrifice, for a sport you love and have played such a big part in developing. We are all so proud of you. To Claire, for everything. You are quite simply magic. I couldn't have done this without you."

Mickey let out a whooping holler of joy, making the girls jump just a little, before he threw his head back and laughed. "I am the luckiest man alive with the two most gorgeous girls comin' in with me. Ha!" They all shared a good laugh at Mickey's joy.

Riley put her glass down. "Oh, I almost forgot." She went to the bedroom and came back out with a small covered box. She opened it to reveal a small decorative spray of lily of the valley and pinned it on Mickey's lapel. She nodded and stepped back, smoothing down his coat front.

Mickey's hand shook as he raised it and placed it lovingly on Riley's cheek. "Thank you. It always was Pearlie's favourite."

Claire sniffed quietly in the background, dabbing her face with a tissue. "Dammit. You two are hell on my make-up. Let me go check, and then we should look at getting a move on. We don't want to be late."

Mickey's face softened as he looked at Riley and held her hand. "Our girl's all grown up. I would love nothing better than to have Pearl here, but there's no one else I'd rather have in her place than you. I mean it, Midget. You're an absolute beauty to behold."

"Thank you. I just want to make you proud. I love you."

"You've always done that, girlie, an' I love you too. Now let's collect this other young, gorgeous girl and get ourselves off to the ball."

❖

"Fender! Will you stop pacing for Christ's sakes? Claire just texted, they're on their way and will be here in a few minutes. Jeez."

"Sorry. How do I look?"

Ed smiled and kissed her cheek, whispering in her ear, "For the thousandth time, you look fine. She is gonna love it, so just take a deep breath and pretend like you've got your shit together."

Sorla took a big breath, and then another for good luck, smoothing slightly damp, nervous palms down her blue dress uniform. They'd arrived on time and had found the bar, and each now nursed a beer, waiting for their girls to turn up. They'd managed to find their table which was at the front, slightly off to the side. Sorla was kind of hoping to be towards the back but accepted that, as they were on Mickey's table, they were up the front, along with the other honoured guests, dignitaries, and award winners of the night.

People were starting to arrive. Some had already taken their seats, while others stood around having a drink, waiting for the official part of the evening to begin, starting with the award winners being announced as they walked into the room.

"Hey—there's Claire." Ed waved to catch Claire's eye and direct her over to them. He wrapped her in his arms and gave her a kiss. "Mm, no matter how many times I see you in your dress blues, you still make my heart race, Slick."

Claire brushed his lapel and smoothed his tie. "You too, gorgeous."

"Would you like a drink?" Claire nodded and Ed went off in search of the bar.

Sorla looked at Claire, then nervously at the open doorway and finally back again. Her fingers were blindly peeling the label off the bottle. Claire laughed at her friend. "Will you calm down—they'll be here in a little while. The officials have got them all out the back, lining them up in order."

"How is she? Does she look tired? I wish she'd had more sleep. What is she wearing? Do I look okay?"

Claire stilled Sorla's shaking fingers on the bottle. "Anyone would think this was your first date. She's fine, I'm not telling, and you look fabulous. Oh, good, here comes my drink. Thanks, babe."

Before Sorla could ask any more questions, the PA system came to life, with the master of ceremonies announcing the agenda of the evening and requesting that the crowd take their seats. The first entrants introduced were the association's board members, followed by the event's major sponsors, then the winners of the day's finals, closely followed by the season's event champions. As each entrant was announced, the ball crowd cheered and clapped enthusiastically. All awardees were seated and the crowd hushed in expectation. Someone had found a spotlight and aimed it at the doorway. Mickey's name was called to rapturous cheers, applause, and a standing ovation.

Sorla's heart was hammering as she waited for Mickey and Riley to appear. She stood up, along with most people in the room, ready for their entrance, and when the light caught hold of Riley as she stepped from out of the doorway, she felt her knees give way. It was only Claire's and Ed's quick thinking that kept her upright until she could hold herself stable again. Claire took the bottle from her fingers and put it down on the table. She hooked her arm through Sorla's elbow and whispered in her ear, "Breathe, Sor."

"She's beautiful."

Claire laughed in delight at her best friend's reaction. "Yes, she is. You might like to close your mouth honey, before you start drooling."

Sorla couldn't take her eyes off her. Ed was wolf-whistling, laughing his head off, clapping like a madman. As the shock passed and Sorla realized the most stunning woman in the room belonged to her, she beamed until her cheeks hurt. She clapped her hands so hard her hands were tingling, her fingers just a blur of movement.

Ed nudged her with his shoulder. "Woo-hoo, Riley! You were right to be nervous, Fender." He reached over and gave Claire the biggest hug and kissed her on the mouth. "You did an awesome job, babe."

Cameras flashed like a lightning storm on fast forward. Riley could barely see for the blinding spots dancing in front of her eyes. She heard her name being called and simply turned her head in its direction, smiling at wherever she thought the voice was coming from, as she let Mickey lead her to their table at the front of the room. He pulled the chair out for her, seating her between him and Sorla.

As soon as Mickey seated Riley, and then himself, the rest of the table followed suit, the general chatter in the room starting up as others resumed their seats. Several people walked past Mickey, slapping him on the back or shaking his hand. One of the sponsors delivered a bottle of champagne and an ice bucket to the table, along with half-a-dozen glasses, and captured Mickey in a conversation.

Riley looked down at her hands nervously clenched on her lap. She felt a warm hand slide over hers and hold them safely.

"You are an absolute vision of beauty, which I have no words to describe."

Riley felt herself blush and shyly looked over at Sorla whose eyes were misted with emotion. "Thank you. You take my breath away. You look stunning—you all do. I can't believe I am sitting here with you all looking like you do. I can't keep my eyes off you."

"Would you like something to drink?"

Riley nodded. "In a minute. Can I grab some water first please?"

Sorla poured her a glass and handed it over. "You okay, babe?"

Riley nodded. "Not used to people looking at me and being in a room with this many people."

"Wanna take a walk outside and grab some air for a minute?" Riley looked over to see what Mickey was doing. Sorla patted her hand. "I think Mr. Chairman has him tied up, so he won't miss us for a minute or two."

Riley nodded. "Yes, please."

Sorla stood up and took Riley's hand. She guided her through the crowd with a gentle but supportive hand low on her back until they were outside. They kept walking until they were around the back of the hall, clear from the noise and the worst of the lights. Sorla put her hands on Riley's waist to steady her. "Take some nice deep breaths for me. That's it. A couple more. There you go. That better?"

Riley closed her eyes, her body magnetically drawn to Sorla's seeking comfort and stability as she leaned in close, her arms entwining around her neck, holding her close. The very nearness of Sorla, body to body, instantly soothed her frazzled nerves and her rapid skittish heartbeat. "Sorry. It was all a bit much for a minute."

Sorla's hand caressed Riley's lower back in small soothing circles. "That makes sense. It can't be easy when you're the focus of everyone's attention, and believe me, you stole the room, honey."

A self-deprecating half grin twisted Riley's mouth. "I think being partially naked helps."

Sorla burst out laughing. "Oh yeah. It definitely helps. My

hormones can't decide what they want to do most, but either way, I can't stop looking at you. I can see I am going to have to keep an eye on you tonight."

Riley ran her finger down Sorla's cheek, her voice deepening. "You don't need to worry about me. I only have eyes for you."

"Good thing too, cause it's reciprocal." Sorla sealed the moment, pulling her in gently to claim her with her mouth in a slow, sensual, appreciative kiss. "Feel better now?"

"Mm, I do. Thank you."

"Shall we head back in before they come looking for us?"

Riley nodded and they made their way back in to join their friends at the table as dinner got under way, followed by the first of the speeches.

Riley leaned over and whispered in Sorla's ear. "Have you worked out what you're going to say to the association and any potential investors?"

"Uh-huh. We sort of nutted out a spiel to sell the overall general concept. Anyone wanting more detail, we thought we could catch up with them during the night and have a more detailed conversation later on, one on one."

Riley grinned. "Excellent."

"Why's that?"

Riley just winked at her. Before Sorla could ask what was going on, they paused to listen to Mickey's presentation and acceptance speech. By the time the old man finished, there wasn't a dry eye in the house, with the crowd once again on their feet applauding the man who had been instrumental in making the modern-day rodeo clowning skills and professional standards into what they were today. As the room took their seats once again, the master of ceremonies caught Riley's eye and nodded. She took a last sip of water before standing.

Sorla looked up with questioning eyes. "Where are you going?"

Riley placed a hand on her shoulder. "I want you to show the room your passion. It's time to share your dream." With that, Riley stepped up onto the stage to wait beside the master of ceremonies, who offered her an encouraging smile and nod.

"Before we break for the official photographs, we have a very exciting potential development happening in our community. Here to introduce the driving party in the new program is a long-time friend and supporter of our rodeo, Miss Riley Johnson, of Johnson's Stock and Station."

Riley mouthed her thanks to the compère as she was handed the microphone. She waited until the cheers and whistles abated before beginning. "Thank you. I have the distinct pleasure of introducing a group of people who have recently moved here to begin to build a dream. This dream has several core concepts anchored within its heart. It involves a personal dream of fulfilment, a dream to rebuild a local legacy, the desire to share this dream with others who need to find a place to call home, and a town, who by embracing and sharing in this dream, has the potential to benefit, expand, and develop itself as a community, and to be seen as a place that wants to invest in its future. I would like to invite the team who are building this dream, Captain Thornton and Majors Hanson and Reardon, to share with you their vision. Please join me in making them welcome."

The three stood as one and made their way to the stage. Ed took the microphone first and outlined their plans for the farm, its stock, and the community involvement they hoped to achieve over time, with workers, families, and exchange programs to further boost the industry. He handed off to Claire, who talked about the expanded opportunities to bring visiting medical specialists, who were participating in the program, to the town, who would also be available for the community to access. Finally, the mic was passed to Sorla, who talked about the dream of being able to rehabilitate, retrain, and reintroduce ex-servicemen and women back into civilian life.

"When I was overseas, all I dreamed of was coming home. Coming back to the place I grew up, the place that held my heart and soul. Stonesend…this place is special. The people, the land, the lifestyle. This is the place we would like to share with the outstanding people that we have lived and breathed and fought with, side by side. This is a place that we hope they will want to call home, where they will build new family legacies, learning and sharing from the wonderful ones you all represent. If anybody would like to hear more about the program, the three of us will be available throughout the evening, or feel free to get in contact with us after tonight. Thank you all for listening." Sorla handed the microphone off to Riley as the crowd applauded with great enthusiasm.

Looking out at the sea of faces before her, Riley smiled until they quietened. "Johnson's are proud to announce that we will support this endeavour by offering to sponsor an apprentice in either the retail or saddlery industry, depending on the candidate's area of interest." The crowd clapped as excited voices buzzed with the idea. "Just this last week, I have been speaking to an influential local about the Cherry Hill program. Ted Saunders, would you mind joining us up here, please?"

Ted Saunders, who looked positively shocked and required a few good-natured jabs from people at his table to get him to come up to the stage, made his way to stand next to the group, looking mildly embarrassed and uncomfortable.

"Ted here, as most of you know, is a major supplier of feed across the area. Recently, there was a fire at Cherry Hill where this team operate from. In the process, they not only lost a fresh shipment of feed, they also lost the shed. Thanks to the efforts of the local fire brigade and the staff at Cherry Hill, they managed to stop the fire before it could become much worse. Ted was shocked at the news of the loss to people who are not only new in the area, but who are trying to create this wonderful new community opportunity. Those of you who know Ted know he is a humble man and not one to blow his own horn. So at the risk of embarrassing him, I would like to tell you what he has done. Just this week, Ted has very generously offered to not only replace the feed they lost, but he has offered to join the program, offering a traineeship to a participating member of the pilot program. And as a good-will gesture, on behalf of the town, he has generously offered to pay for the materials to help with the rebuilding costs of a new feed shed." Sorla's, Ed's, and Claire's expressions of surprise were priceless, and almost as enjoyable as the look on Ted Saunders's face at Riley's announcement. Again, the crowd was enthusiastic with their cheers and whistles. Riley offered them a shy wave in conclusion. "And on that note, I would ask you please, if you wouldn't mind once again, put your hands together for Captain Thornton and Majors Hanson and Reardon, and for Ted Saunders for his leadership in community spirit and generosity."

As the crowd cheered for the trio, official photographers scrambled to request group shots to go into the local paper and various magazines. Ed, Claire, and Sorla were in hot demand, pulled away for a variety of conversations with several of the major sponsors and the association members.

Riley brought refreshments all-round for her friends, subtly handing them each a drink, as they talked to the various interested parties. Finally nabbing a drink for herself, she went and resumed her seat at their table, to be joined by Mickey shortly afterwards.

"That was a mighty impressive thing you just did then, Midget." He looked over at the flock of people surrounding Sorla, Ed, and Claire. "Looks like you been planning that for a while now."

Riley threw a conspiratorial wink at him, smiling as she sipped her drink. "Just a bit. All they needed was a nudge. It's up to them now where it goes."

"How'd you get Saunders to open up his wallet like that?"

"I explained how wonderful an opportunity for publicity it would be."

"Horse hockey!"

Riley grinned cheekily. "That, and how if he didn't get on board, I would tell everyone it was because of his shonky deal that the shed burnt down in the first place, and that bad word travels faster than good publicity."

Mickey threw his head back and laughed until tears coursed down his cheeks. "I love it! For such a sweet-faced creature, you sure do have a cunning and devious mind."

Riley shrugged, smiling. "All's fair in love and party games, Mick. You taught me that."

"And right you are, Midget. Well done, lass."

CHAPTER TWENTY-THREE

The house lights dimmed and spotlights hit the vacant dance floor as the band got itself in position to begin the musical part of the evening. From the shadows of the stage the MC took hold of the mic. "Ladies and gentleman, we now begin the last part of the evening's formalities, the dance of this year's celebrated and recognized winners. Mickey Donovan, would you and your partner kindly take to the floor?"

Mickey stood and held his hand out to Riley. She placed her hand into his gnarled and weathered palm, to elegantly rise, following him to the dance floor, his hand protective in the small of her back. They walked to the middle of the floor and turned to face each other, the band waiting for Mickey's signal to begin.

Mickey bent his head and kissed the lily of the valley spray on his lapel, before kissing Riley on the cheek. He signalled to the band, who began to play a gentle, lilting waltz.

Sorla stared, mesmerized, as Mickey guided Riley effortlessly around the floor, their limbs in unison, Riley's dress softly moulding around her body. Every now and then the thigh split opened on a turn to give a hint of long shapely limbs gliding in time to the music. The room was so quiet that it seemed for all the world that there was no one else in the room, bar the two dancers.

With a gesture and nod from the MC, the other evening's winners slowly stood and took to the dance floor, joining Mickey and Riley in waltzing around the circuit. By the time the band changed tunes and the dancers had shifted into a two-step, people had begun to flood the dance floor, signalling that it was time to bring the party to life.

The run of two-step tunes took a break and the bandleader

announced a jive tune. Claire leaned over to Sorla. "Looks like your girl needs rescuing. My turn." Claire tapped Riley on the shoulder to take a turn with Mickey, who looked as pleased as punch to have another gorgeous woman lining up to come and ask him to dance. Smiling in relief, Riley gratefully handed Mickey over to Claire and sat back down at the table next to Sorla.

Sorla kissed her cheek, smiling with pride, and holding her hand. "You were sensational."

"Was it okay? My legs were shaking so much I thought I was going to fall over."

Sorla laughed. "Well, no one would have known. You looked like a natural. I see what you mean about Mickey. He sure can dance." They both turned to watch as Mickey and Claire jived and laughed, turning the tune on its head with their light, fancy footwork.

At the end of the tune they hugged, then turned to applaud the band in appreciation before coming to sit back down. Within a few minutes one of the ladies from the sponsors' table came and asked Mickey if he would dance with her, and he was quickly whisked off to begin a full and promising evening of new dance partners.

Ed and Claire followed Mickey out to join the crowd of revellers. Sorla sat at the table, hugging a glass in her hands. She wanted desperately to dance with Riley, but didn't want to embarrass her, or place her in a situation that would make things uncomfortable for her with the conservative townsfolk. The longer the evening dragged on, the darker her mood became.

❖

Riley was asked to dance by several of the association members and sponsors. While she listened attentively to their small talk, she watched Sorla's tension grow and knew that to resolve her partner's unease, the next move had to be hers. As the song ended and she was escorted back to her table, she took a sip of water, then held Sorla's hand. Most of the couples who had been dancing, including Ed and Claire, had taken a break as the band eased into a slow and tender song. A song for lovers. Riley took a deep breath. She might have had the closet kicked in around her when she was outed by Robbie Peters's gossip, but here, now, tonight, she had the opportunity to take back a little control. She knew some people would talk, but at least she would be the one determining what they would be talking about. She copied Mickey's move from earlier in the evening, by standing and holding out her hand in invitation. "Major Reardon, would you do me the great honour of sharing this dance, please?"

Sorla looked up, a question in her eyes. "You sure you want to do this, love?"

Riley smiled and nodded. "Never surer."

Sorla slowly rose and accepted Riley's hand as they made their way out to the dance floor. As they took to the floor, the room fell silent for the hint of a heartbeat.

There were a couple of audible gasps, some chatter, and soon Ed and Claire were dancing beside them.

The foursome held the floor and were joined by Mickey and his partner, and several of the sponsors and association dignitaries and their wives. The crowd, having seen the acceptance, either went back to their conversations or joined in on the dance floor as the brief awkward moment passed, slipping off into the dark recesses of past tense.

Riley's arms were wrapped around Sorla's neck. Her eyes closed as she smiled in complete contentment, feeling the warmth of Sorla's body up and down her length where their breasts, hips, and thighs touched. She shivered as a thrill ran through her body.

She could hear Sorla humming to the tune softly in her ear.

"You cold, love?" Sorla asked.

Riley stared into Sorla's eyes. Riley's throat was so tight, she could barely get the words out. "Just the opposite."

Sorla nodded and licked her lips.

Riley followed the movement of Sorla's tongue, groaning slightly as she grew warm with desire.

Sorla leaned in close and whispered, "How long do you think it's polite to stay for?"

Riley shook her head. "I don't know, but I'm hoping not too much longer, because I think I might just combust."

Sorla laughed and twirled her around the floor. Lost in Sorla's eyes, the room receded from Riley's awareness, until she felt a tap on her shoulder. She started when she saw how dark and stormy Sorla's face had become. In confusion, she turned to see what had upset Sorla.

Jake Turley stood behind her in a cheap tan satin suit, his hair slicked back, a shoestring tie dangling midline against his puce-coloured shirt, a sleazy cocksure grin on his face, his arms wide open in optimistic invitation. "Wanna dance with a real man, sweet cheeks?"

Riley looked him up and down, barely containing the disgust from her face. "No, thank you." She turned back and continued to dance with Sorla.

Shocked, Jake stood mutely in the middle of the dance floor. He stepped up to Riley and tapped her more forcefully on the shoulder. "I said, do ya wanna dance?"

Riley didn't even bother to turn around to look at him. "No." Sorla began to steer her away.

Jake's cheeks turned scarlet as people began to look at him, stranded in the middle of the dance floor being rebuffed. His face grew dark with anger. He strode over to Riley, tearing her arms away from Sorla, pulling them apart forcefully. With a snarl on his face, he shook her arm. "I said, *dance* with me!"

Just as Sorla stepped up, ready to take him on, Ed stepped between them, towering over them all. He silently grabbed Jake's arm in an iron grip, squeezing his wrist so Jake had no choice but to release his hold on Riley's arms, leaving marks behind as a legacy as to how hard he had gripped her. As soon as Jake's fingers opened and released Riley, Ed whipped Jake's arm around behind his back and quietly, but swiftly, escorted him bodily from the room.

During the altercation the band had stopped playing. It seemed that almost everyone had frozen into place, watching the scene play out. With Jake now out of the room, and sensing that the moment had passed, the band struck back up again, encouraging the dancing to resume.

Sorla stepped up and put her hands under Riley's elbows, cupping them softly. "You okay?" Riley was pale, but she nodded. "You want to keep dancing or sit down for a while?"

"Can we keep dancing for a bit, please?"

"Sure." Sorla carefully took her in her arms as they swayed back and forth to the music. Claire came over to murmur something about going outside to see if Ed had ripped the boy's head off or not, receiving a vague acknowledgement from Sorla, who was riveted to Riley's side, intensely conscious of how her lover was trembling in her arms after the rather public display.

As Mickey danced past them both he caught Sorla's eyes with his own questioning ones. She nodded at him and he mirrored back in acknowledgement, reassured that Sorla was looking after his girl. Sorla held her tight, rubbing her thumb in soft, soothing circles at the base of her neck. Gradually she felt Riley's trembling subside and the tension begin to ease as she relaxed into her body to the pulse and sway of the music.

When the song ended they made their way back to the table just as Ed and Claire came back inside. Claire diverted to the bar, bringing back a cloth and a glass of ice. Ed came over and squatted between them, putting his arms around their shoulders. "You two okay?"

Riley nodded and Sorla patted his hand. "Yes, thanks. Did you sort it?"

Ed brought one of his hands around in front and flexed it open and close, offering up a dark smile of satisfaction. "I believe so."

He sat next to Claire who quietly put the ice cloth on his hand. She winked at him and kissed him on the mouth. "My hero."

Sorla hadn't let go of Riley's hand. "I had it, you know."

Ed nodded. "I know you did. I just didn't want to see you get blood all over Riley's dress when you ripped his balls off."

Sorla looked at him and then at Riley, who was still too quiet, and realized Ed was right to try and lighten the mood. "Hm, you're probably right, you've saved us a big dry-cleaning bill."

"Uh-huh. And he looked like a screamer. I hate boys that scream. And I know you woulda made him call for his Mumma."

Sorla laughed and saw Riley's mouth lift in a slight smirk. Sorla nodded dramatically. "Oh yeah. I woulda had him crying like a baby."

❖

Mickey had such a line-up of ladies wanting to dance with him that he was more than happy to stay and drive himself home when he was ready, leaving the foursome free to make their way home. Riley cuddled up to Sorla in the back seat, Sorla's arms wrapped around her, warm and tight. Although Jake Turley had put a blemish on the evening, it didn't take away from the overall thrill and enjoyment of the night. She had been Mickey's proud partner, had helped open the door for her new friends to talk about Cherry Hill and their dream, experienced her first ever ball, and most importantly, danced with the love of her life, with freedom, dignity, and open honesty. She cleared her throat. "Tonight has been one of the best nights of my life. Claire, you are my Fairy Godmother—you made me feel special, pretty…and, if I'm honest, half-naked." The car occupants all laughed.

Claire smiled at her in the rear-view mirror. "It was truly my pleasure. I have to confess, I had a ball. Sorla's not huge on letting me pick her outfits." Sorla snorted and rolled her eyes, which only made Claire laugh more.

Riley caught Ed's eye in the rear-view mirror. "Ed, thank you for stepping in and being Sorla's back-up buddy."

"Truly my honour."

Riley half turned so she could look right into Sorla's face. "And you made me feel safe, special, and very loved. Thank you." Sorla hugged her gently in recognition of her words and kissed her cheek. "And I decided tonight, there is no way that I could ever have signed up for any of the defence forces."

Sorla stiffened and pulled her chin back in question, looking at her. "Why's that?"

Riley chuckled. "'Cause you all look far too hot in your fancy-pants uniforms. If I joined up, I would probably get arrested."

They all laughed as Ed turned into the big wooden gateway that signalled home.

Ed and Claire bid them good night as each couple made their way back to their own wings.

Shutting the door behind her, Sorla looked at Riley. "You look tired, love. You wanna head off to bed?"

Riley shook her head. "Can we maybe grab a wine or something and dance a little more?"

Sorla's eyebrows rose. "Sure, love. How about you find some music, while I pour us a drink." A moment later, she joined Riley on the couch, handing her the wine glass. Sorla was smiling.

"What are you smiling about?"

"I was just thinking about Mickey and how there was a flock of women almost chasing after him, trying to get him to dance with them. Boy, he sure can move."

Riley chuckled. "It was nice to see him let his hair down. I know he misses Pearl terribly, but it was good to see him have some fun tonight."

"When he started the first dance with you…I thought he was going to burst with pride. Hell—I thought *I* was gonna burst, and not just with pride."

Riley put her glass down and reached over to liberate Sorla's glass before turning back to run her finger up and down Sorla's dress-coat lapel. Wordlessly she stood and reached for Sorla to join her. They moved together, swaying to the music, enjoying the pureness of the tactile experience. Overwhelmed, Riley could stay silent no longer. "I can't stop looking at you. I can't decide if I want to undress you slowly or simply just look at you in your uniform all night long."

Sorla said, "You know, when you and Mickey first walked in the room?" Riley nodded. "When I first saw you? I thought I was going to pass out. You're so beautiful"—she shook her head—"I don't have the words. All I know is the most beautiful girl in the room was mine."

"Thank you for looking after me this week, and with Jake. I've never had anyone do that for me before."

"Then might I suggest you haven't been hanging around the right people, my love."

"When I danced with you and everyone in the room looked at us? I have never felt happier. I want them all to see that I love you."

"And I love you too, baby, with all my heart."

"Good. Now take me to bed, before I explode."

Sorla's chuckle morphed into a sensual growl. Still dancing, she steered Riley towards the bedroom. "With pleasure."

CHAPTER TWENTY-FOUR

Sunday was declared a day of rest, with Monday back to normal with Riley heading off early to open up the shop and tidy up the gear that had been packed up from the week's stall. She wouldn't have to pick George up until after work, which gave her plenty of time to get things squared away. She listed the orders that had come in during rodeo week into sequences of degrees of urgency and the length of time required to get the jobs done. She had a good couple of months' orders ahead of her with some new design requests whose uniqueness and complexity would challenge her. She found herself looking forward to working through the concepts to produce a product she would be proud to put her name to. Smiling, she noted that one of the new saddle orders was for a young woman whose saddle she had repaired in a rush overnight job, in time for the finals.

It turned out that Monday was indicative of the whole week. Riley barely saw Sorla at all, apart from a quick couple of drop-ins to the store when Sorla was in town for meetings, with the only quality catch-up time during exchanged phone calls in the evening.

Since coming home, George had been quiet. Riley noticed how much older he was looking. He fell asleep in the chair more frequently and seemed to tire faster. He'd even asked to come home a bit earlier on a couple of nights during the week. She wondered if she should change his end-of-the-month doctor's appointment for something a bit earlier. At breakfast that morning, Riley thought his eyes looked a bit yellow. "You look tired. You feel okay?"

"Yep."

"Do you want to stay home today instead of coming in to work?"

"No."

She noticed he was only pushing his breakfast around on his plate. "Not hungry?" He pushed the plate away and sipped his coffee with shaking hands. "You're sure you're okay?"

"Yes. Now piss off an' let me finish my breakfast in peace."

"Sorry. I just worry about you."

"Well, don't."

Riley sighed and pushed away from the table, clearing the dishes as she went. She'd not long finished drying the dishes when she heard a crash, coming from the other end of the house. "You all right?" She listened, but got no response. "George?" She threw the towel down on the sink and strode swiftly up the hall in the direction of the noise. "George? You okay?"

Rounding the corner of the room she found him lying on the floor, curled up in a ball, clutching his stomach and groaning. She knelt beside him to see blood trickling from the corner of his mouth, a pool of red vomit beside him. "Shit. Hang on." She ran to her room and picked up her mobile, calling the emergency services as she ran back into the room. While she talked on the phone to the operator she rolled him onto his side and sat behind him, her hand stroking his head. "It's okay, it's okay. The ambulance is on its way. Won't be long."

Sorla found her in the waiting room, sitting on a chair, knees pulled up to her chin, her head resting on them, eyes closed. Sitting down beside her, she put her hand on her back. "Hey, gorgeous."

Blue eyes slowly opened and smiled wearily back at her. "Hey, what are you doing here?"

"Claire called and told me they'd brought George in. Thought maybe you could do with some company."

"Didn't you have a big meeting today?"

"I rang and cancelled."

"Why'd you do that?"

"Because you, my love, are far more important than any meeting. How's he doing?"

"I don't know. They've taken him into surgery. Something about putting a band on a bleeding vein." Riley told her what had happened over breakfast. "How did Claire know?"

"She's on theatre rotation this week and read his name on the charts when they took him up. Why didn't you call me?"

"I thought you'd be getting ready for the meeting and I didn't want to make you late for the appointment."

Sorla put her arm around her and pulled her in for a hug. They were still sitting like that when the surgeon came out to talk to them. "George has lost a bit of blood. We're just giving him a transfusion now, but he's stable and holding his own for the minute. The bleeding is as a result of scarring on his liver. The scarring reduces the blood flowing through his liver and, as a result, more blood flows through the veins of the esophagus. This extra blood flow has caused the veins in his esophagus to balloon outward, like a varicose vein. This morning, one of these veins broke open and started to bleed. We've put a band around it and we've got him on some medication, but we'd like to keep him in for a day or two, to make sure his meds are okay, run some tests, and have a look at his treatment options."

Riley nodded. "Can I see him?"

"He's in recovery now and will be for a couple of hours." The doctor looked at his watch. "You can probably see him about lunchtime." Any further conversation was cut off when the doctor's pager went off. He bent his head to look at the message before standing up. "I'll be in to check on him later this afternoon. We can have a better talk then about what happened today and where he can go from here. I'm sorry, I have to run."

"Thank you."

He waved, striding off down the corridor to disappear behind swinging doors.

Riley sighed in relief.

Sorla rubbed her back. "What do you want to do now?"

"I suppose I'd better put a sign on the shop door, then go home and clean up the mess. I'll come back later with some pyjamas and toiletries. What about you? Can you still make the meeting?"

Sorla shook her head. "I've made arrangements for them to come out tomorrow, after lunch. We were hoping you'd be able to come out and show them some work on the horses."

Riley's brow furrowed in thought. "I can probably do that. With George here, I'll have to rearrange a few things, and I'll have to do some deliveries tomorrow, but I could swing by after that, say, in the afternoon."

"Perfect. Want some company while you clean up?"

"That'd be nice. Thanks."

❖

Sorla looked around Riley's house with interest. It was a simple weatherboard home. The furnishings in it were sparse and old, but well maintained and functional, reminiscent of the seventies. Everything was as neat as a pin, which made her smile. As a Virgo, she appreciated order and saw a kindred spirit in Riley's neatness.

The only photos evident in the house were in the lounge room, one of George holding aloft a trophy and two of him in action on the back of a bucking bronc in the ring. As Sorla continued to look about, she couldn't help but notice there weren't any photos of Riley, or of her mother.

Sorla followed Riley into the laundry where she was putting away the cleaning liquid and sponges after cleaning the floor. "You need a clean shirt, love. How about you go and throw yourself in the shower while I get you some clean clothes? Where's your bedroom?"

Riley pointed behind her to a door that led out to an enclosed porch. "Through there."

Sorla found the room, housing a single bed against the porch wall with a stack of books stacked underneath it and a steamer trunk butted up at the end. Wooden floorboards stretched across the room, leading off to a door that opened out onto the backyard. An old-fashioned walnut veneer two-door cupboard stood as sentry against the house wall, with hanging space on one side, four drawers, and a couple of open shelves on the other side. She opened up the cupboard and pulled out a pressed shirt and jeans. She opened up the door to look for underwear, revealing a faded black-and-white photograph pinned to the inside of a little girl laughing, as she swung off the hands of two adults. Looking closely at the photo, she recognized a young Mickey and assumed the woman holding Sorla's other hand must have been Pearl. For a brief moment Sorla's heart cramped at the love in the photograph evident in the eyes of the adults looking down to the laughing child. Scanning the room, this was the only personal item she could see.

Hearing a noise behind her, she turned to find Riley standing in the doorway, a towel wrapped around her torso. Blushing, she looked down at the floor. "Not exactly the Taj Mahal."

Sorla shrugged and smiled. "Sure as heck's better than some of the digs I've lived in over the years. You must be able to see some nice sunsets from your room."

Riley smiled, tilting her head slightly. "On hot summer nights, sometimes I sit on the doorstep over there and watch as the storms roll in and light up the night sky."

As Riley got dressed Sorla sat on the bed and looked through the pile of books under her bed. She held aloft a particular book with a strained look on her face. "Algebra? Really? Why would you do that to yourself?"

Riley shrugged. "I read something about it in the paper a couple of weeks ago about some high school competition or other and wondered what it was all about."

"And what do you think?"

"At first, it didn't make a lot of sense, but then I got another book, which explained it better, and it kind of makes sense now, for the most part, although some things I still haven't worked out yet."

"And did you like it?"

"It's not really my thing, but it feels good to know about what people were talking about in the article."

"Do you ever miss not going to school?"

Riley shrugged. "Can't miss what you never had. I can pick up a book and learn about whatever I want, whenever I want, from the library. I don't need to go to school for that."

"No, I don't suppose you do."

"What's the time?"

"It's nearly midday."

"I better get back to the hospital."

"Okay. Want me to come with you?"

Riley shook her head. "No, I want you to go home and get ready for the meeting tomorrow."

Sorla winced at the unexpected brush-off. "We'll manage."

Riley stepped forward, taking Sorla in her arms. "I love every minute I spend with you, but I would feel happier knowing that you were at home and getting everything ready."

Sorla kissed Riley's eyelids, cheeks, and finally her lips. "I'll do you a deal. How about I go home and get my stuff together for tomorrow, if you pack a bag and come and stay tonight?"

Riley claimed her lips. "Deal."

❖

Lying in bed, Sorla lay sprawled out on top of Riley, tracing patterns on her chest. "So how did George take the news that he'd have to stop drinking?"

"Let's just say that I'm surprised you couldn't hear him from here."

"Ah, so he's open to the idea, then?"

Riley chuckled. "Not in a million years. By what the doctors say, this is just the beginning. They talked about putting a shunt in, but I'm not convinced it's going to be worth their efforts. George has no intention of stopping drinking. He knows the score."

"How do you feel about that?"

"Doesn't much matter what I think. It's his life, his body, his choice."

"But it affects you."

"So does the weather. You just learn to work with it."

"Have you considered a nursing home, or a hospice?" Sorla felt Riley's body tense underneath her.

"No."

"Why not?"

"Money, for starters. Those places are expensive and the nearest one is a long way away. He doesn't know anyone there."

"He'd get to know people, and I could help you out with the money side."

"No."

"Would you consider it?"

"No."

"Why not?"

"If this is George's sunset, then he deserves to sit and watch it out where and how he chooses. That won't include being sober and going to a place where they treat him like an invalid and where he doesn't know anybody. And thank you for the offer of help, but I have always managed, and I will continue to manage, on my own. I don't do handouts, not even from you."

"It's not a handout, love, it's—"

"No. Thank you."

"Will you at least think about it?"

"No."

"Oh, come on. You're being ridiculously stubborn."

Riley gently pushed Sorla off and sat up, reaching for her clothes. With her back turned she pulled her shirt on, stood, and pulled on her jeans and socks.

Sorla sat up. "Where are you going?"

"Home."

"What? Come back to bed."

"No, I need to go."

"Why? Because I called you stubborn?" Riley said nothing, continuing to pull on her boots. "Will you say something? Is it the money? What? It's no big deal."

"It is to me." Riley stood up and left, quietly shutting the door behind her. Sorla sat up, stunned, and listened as Riley's truck started up and drove off, eventually fading into the distance. Sorla threw the pillow in frustration at the door. "Goddammit! And you think *I'm* stubborn?"

❖

Claire was already at the breakfast table when Sorla walked in. She grabbed a coffee and sat down grumpily. She didn't sleep much after Riley had left and was not in a good place now that the sun had risen. Claire buttered her toast, looking sideways at Sorla. "Was that Riley's truck I heard leaving last night?"

"Yes."

"Is George all right?"

"As far as I know."

"Can you pass the jam please? Did you two have a fight?"

"We were talking about George, and I asked if she'd thought about a nursing home for him. She got her nose out of joint and left."

"Because you mentioned a nursing home?"

"Yes. She said she wouldn't consider it because he wouldn't know anyone and it was too expensive. I said he'd make new friends and offered to help with the money. That was when she got upset."

"And that's it?"

"Pretty much. I asked her to think about it, and she flat-out said no. I told her I didn't care about the money, it's no big deal, she said it was to her, and then she left. So there you have it."

"I see." Claire put the lid back on the jam and took the first bite of her toast, chewing thoughtfully.

Sorla rolled her eyes and looked over at her friend. "What?"

Claire took a sip of her coffee before carefully placing the mug down on the table. "Seems to me, you made a sensible suggestion, along with a generous offer."

"That's right."

"And she explained why she didn't think it was a good choice."

"She was just being pig-headed and stubborn."

"I see. And you think her reaction was over the top?"

Sorla put her mug down loudly. "Absolutely!"

"Riley's worked her heart and soul out keeping her, George, and the business afloat."

Sorla frowned at her, annoyed. "I know that."

"You suggested a problem that makes George go away, effectively disappear, and offered to throw money at her because you have the money to spare and it's no big deal to you."

"That's right."

"And then you insinuated that by her not taking up both those options, she was stupid."

"You make *me* sound like the bad guy. All I did was offer to help."

"I know you did, honey, but in the process, you discounted and insulted everything that Riley has fought so hard to achieve in her life."

"Bullshit."

"Think about it, Sor."

"I offered to help."

"Yes, honey, you did. You made a suggestion to make George go away, the one thing Riley gave up her childhood for, to nurse him back to health, to establish a career so that they could stay in town and be self-sufficient. She has given up just about everything in her life to help that man. She works all the hours God made to keep them afloat. You said you could give her money, because it doesn't mean anything to you. Problem solved." Sorla glared at her. "You don't get it, do you?"

"What's to get?"

"You made Riley feel like her whole life was worthless and pointless. For what it's worth, I'd have walked out on you too, babe." With that, Claire picked up her breakfast dishes and put them in the sink.

As Sorla watched her friend quietly leave she put her head in her hands. "Fuck."

❖

Riley didn't get any sleep. Her guts were in turmoil after last night. She visited George briefly before opening up the store. He was in a foul mood as well. It was the longest he'd gone without a drink and he was not in a good place physically, or mentally. As soon as Riley walked into his room he lashed out at her, hurling verbal abuse and insults as well as his glass of drinking water.

The nurses heard the commotion and came running, calling for backup to help sedate him. Riley sat with him, holding his hand until he fell asleep. She left a request to speak to the doctor on his rounds later that day to find out how they could keep George more comfortable while he was in hospital, along with her phone number, before leaving to go to work.

Morning business was steady, which was just as well, as it kept her mind off replaying last night's conversation over and over in her head. Fortunately, there weren't too many deliveries on her list and she felt confident that they could be done in time to honour her promise to be at Cherry Hill by midafternoon to perform the requested demonstration with the horses.

She'd also made time to duck out and pick up the present she'd ordered for Mickey. It was Pearl's birthday the following day. She never missed it. She had planned to ask if Sorla would come with her, but after last night, she decided it was probably best if she went on her own. She had framed a series of photographs—the black and white from her bedroom, Mickey and Pearl's wedding, a photo of him riding in the parade on Jericho with his new saddle, and one of her and Mickey dancing together at the ball. In the centre of the photographs was a lily of the valley spray identical to the one Mickey had worn on his lapel to the ball. She carefully wrapped the frame up, placing it under the bench seat of her truck in readiness.

By two o'clock she only had one delivery left to go on her list. The day was hot, the clouds building up, hinting at a promised storm later on. She decided to cut across the back road to save some time. Halfway to her destination she felt the shudder and jar of the tyre wobble before the telltale slide. Her rear tyre had blown. Up ahead, off to the side, was a popular camping reserve. She pulled the truck off the road in under the shade of an old willow. Stepping out of the truck, she surveyed the damage. There was a sizable tear in the tread. She shook her head. *Crap. Well, don't suppose the damn thing will change itself. Might as well get on with it.*

Retrieving the jack and tool wrap from behind the seat, she unwound the spare from up under the rear tray of the truck, laying it on the ground beside the flat in readiness for the change. As she lay on the ground under the truck body looking for the best place to position her jack, she heard a vehicle pull up. She'd just got the jack into place and was about to slide out when a pair of boots walked up to stand next to the spare tyre. She slid out from under the truck, momentarily blinded by the sun, unable to recognize the person standing there. It wasn't until he squatted down and spoke that the hair rose on the back of her neck.

"Reckon you owe me a dance, sweet cheeks." Jake Turley towered directly over the top of her, showering her with an evil, lecherous grin.

CHAPTER TWENTY-FIVE

Sorla was in the horse yard with Queenie and the two young horses, explaining to the three men leaning over the fence railing the work that had been put in to the three horses in the space of a few training sessions, and the results of that training. She isolated Queenie, taking her through the steps that Riley had taught her, until she was haltered, saddled, and ridden around the yard.

She handed the visitors over to Ed to take them on a drive around the property and an inspection of the herd so she could finish off with the horses. After handing out treats to her equine charges she quickly put the equipment away and headed back to the house to clean up. Claire was sitting at the kitchen table with the phone in her hand, frowning and tapping the phone book in front of her in thought.

Letting the screen door slam behind her, she pulled the fridge open forcefully, pulling out the jug of iced tea. "Wanna glass?"

Claire was deep in thought and missed Sorla's question. "Sorry?"

"I asked if you wanted a glass?"

"Sure, thanks."

Sorla filled two tall glasses and plonked them noisily onto the table before throwing herself down in the chair. Her voice and her body language clearly showed her bad mood. "Nice of Riley to turn up."

"Mm." Claire worried her bottom lip as she flicked through her address book.

"What are you doing?"

"Has Riley called you today?"

"No. Least she could have done was text to say she wasn't coming. Or rung one of you if she didn't want to speak to me. Why?"

"I just rang the hospital and she hasn't been there since this morning. She's missed an appointment she had to see George's doctor, and she's not answering at either the store or her mobile phone."

"Well, you know me, when I do a job, I like to do it properly. Looks like I've pissed her off so much she's not talking to anyone. Cheers to me!" Sorla held her drink aloft in a sarcastic salute to herself before draining her glass and storming out to get changed.

❖

Her eyes darted left and right, but with Jake squatting over the top of her, she realized with a sinking heart, there was nowhere to go. Still grinning, he stood up and offered her his hand to get up. Riley brushed it away and stood, dusting her hands off on her jeans. Without looking at him, she turned on her heel to walk away, but Jake walked backwards and grabbed her elbow, turning her back to face him.

"Hey, hey, now is that any way to be nice? I was being polite."

Riley once again tried to step sideways away from him. Jake quickly stepped around her until he was once again in her face. "Hey. Don't be walking away, I'm talking to you."

Riley took a steadying breath and tried to appear calm, even though her stomach was lurching and her legs were shaking. "Jake, I don't have time for this. I'm late with deliveries, and I have people waiting on me. Now if you'll excuse me, I have to be going." Riley tried once again to step around him. He made no move to stop her. A small bit of tension in her gut began to ease as she walked past him.

Turley sauntered to the front of the truck and leaned on the driver's door. Riley stopped dead in her tracks, her heart starting to race, sweat breaking out on her brow. With one long quick stride, he pushed off from the door, his hands grabbed her waist, and he whipped her around to face him. As he pushed her back against the truck, his hands slid up and grabbed her arms, pulling them behind her back. He pressed himself along Riley's length and looked her up and down hungrily, pinning her with his weight against the truck, before slowly reaching up and ripping open her shirt, tearing it off her shoulders. He licked his lips, smiling. "Your friends aren't here to save you this time, so you an' me are gonna have us that dance." As he spat the word *dance* in her face, he thrust his groin, making no secret of his intentions.

Riley felt panic begin to rise. She knew the odds were against her. Jake was strong and used to wrestling beasts much larger than her—she was strong, but she didn't know if she could fight him off. She still hadn't finished changing the tyre on the truck. With options limited, her only thought was to try and catch him off guard and to run.

Jake ran one hand through Riley's hair before grabbing a fistful and pulling her head back sharply. He leaned in and sniffed. "You smell good." He licked her up the side of the neck, groaning. His other hand slid up to cruelly grab and squeeze her breast. "Oh, yeah…" Riley bit her lip to stifle the onslaught of pain. There was no way she was going to give him the satisfaction of making any sounds. He leaned into Riley's ear, whispering lewdy about an offer of being a real man for her, snickering, as she felt him shuffling his feet, restless with sexual energy.

Her phone rang and for a brief second both froze, before Jake spun her around, pushing her face against the truck window so that he could reach into her back pocket and liberate the phone. He waggled it in her face. "Nuh-uh. We are not getting disturbed by your friends again." He dropped it to the ground and crushed the screen with the heel of his boot, before kicking it away into the grass. As Riley saw her last hope of help disappear, she made up her mind. It was now or never. Riley lowered her head, letting her knees go soft, bending slightly, cutting off Jake's access to her throat and making him lean forward, slightly off balance, to accommodate her slumping form.

Jake took half a step back, confused at Riley's reaction. "What the…?"

Before Turley had time to think, Riley tensed her thighs, thrusting lightning fast upward, throwing her head back. She heard the satisfying crunch as the back of her head smashed into his nose. Yowling with the pain, he let her go to clutch at his nose, which streamed twin torrents of blood.

Jake looked at her with an open mouth. Turning, Riley transferred her weight to one leg before striking out with her boot. She miscued her kick, and instead of hitting him dead on in the groin like she had hoped, she hit him high of the mark, knocking him off his feet and winding him. He lay on the ground, clutching his stomach, trying to breathe. Riley knew she'd missed but there was nothing that could be done about it now, so she grabbed the small opportunity she had and took off running.

Riley's lungs were burning, but she had to keep going. She could hear Jake's footsteps and curses getting closer. She looked left and right, desperately looking for options, *any* options, when she felt the pain hit her between the shoulder blades. A rock. She stumbled and went down, dazed as to what had happened. Scrabbling in the dirt, she tried to get up, only to be stopped as Jake arrived, pinning her down with his knees in the small of her back.

They were both breathing heavily. Jake slapped her in the back of the head. "Why'd you run for, huh? Now I just gotta drag ya back." Riley struggled, earning her another slap, much harder than the first. "Sit still a minute." Riley tried in vain to arch her hips and lift him off.

"I said, sit still." He grabbed her head and banged it into the dirt, causing dark spots to swim in front of her eyes. She quietened, waiting for the ground to stop tilting on her.

She felt him reaching for something, before feeling the scratch of hemp rope being wound tightly around a wrist. He roughly grabbed her other hand and tied it to the first. He snarled when the fibreglass splint wouldn't allow him to get a tight enough knot. Grunting, he undid the rope, took the splint off, throwing it away to the side, before grabbing her wrist back and tying it off tightly with the other one. He got off her. "Get up."

Riley didn't move. She was struggling to get her breath back now that he was no longer sitting on her, and trying hard not to vomit. He nudged her with his boot. "Get *up*." When she didn't move, he kicked her, causing her to roll sideways and curl up on her side. Sighing, he picked her up off the ground by her trouser belt, swung her up and over his shoulder, and proceeded to carry her back to camp, before tossing her onto the ground and sitting miserably beside her, holding a cloth to his bloody face.

"You broke my *nose*." With a grunt, he straightened it.

Jake rose and disappeared briefly before coming back with a bottle of bourbon. He sat on the ground next to her and bit the lid off the top of the bottle, spitting it off to one side. He took several large mouthfuls before lowering the bottle, grimacing and coughing. "You know, all you had to do was dance with me at the ball, but no, you played at being a right royal stuck-up mole in your fancy outfit with your new friends. But your new friends aren't here now, sweet cheeks—it's just you an' me. So not only are we gonna dance, but the way I figure it is, you owe me for making so much trouble, and I aim to collect." Jake crawled up into a crouch until he was level with Riley's ear. His breath was hot and heavy with the sweet sickly smell of bourbon, almost making her gag. "So we're gonna make our very own little party. What do you say to that?" Laughing, he stood up and started to set up camp, leaving Riley to lie in the dirt.

In between rolling out bedding and picking up wood for a fire, Jake swigged down large mouthfuls of the bourbon. Riley watched him, trying to figure out what to do next. Sooner or later the booze would affect his ability to think and to react. Working through her possibilities, Riley figured she could try and make a break for it now, or wait until he'd had a skinful of drink and hope that something came up then. She closed her eyes and shivered as she remembered how Turley had pawed her earlier, and she decided she wanted to go sooner rather than wait.

Jake had his back to her, setting the fire, when she worked out that if she could roll under the truck, she could get up and make a run for it, hopefully unseen, from the other side. Biting her lip and concentrating on being as quiet as she could manage, she started to roll under the chassis. Riley silently grimaced as she rolled over the truck's keys she'd taken out of the ignition and put in her back pocket earlier, when she had pulled over and gotten out to inspect the tyre. It was a long-ingrained habit of hers to always pull the keys out of the ignition when she wasn't in the truck. They stuck painfully into her hip but helped remind her of how careful she now had to be.

She had just cleared the undercarriage and was attempting to get up when she heard Turley shout. "Hey! Come back here." He rushed over and grabbed her arms, pulling her upright and dragging her backwards, around to the side of the truck. "You can't leave yet, gorgeous, the party's only just beginning."

Riley kicked out, flailing wildly, but Jake just picked her up and held her off the ground. He shook her roughly, laughing at her. "Feisty little thing, aren't you."

Riley tried to kick him, which he easily dodged, which only made him laugh harder. "You need to chill out a bit and wait 'til I get everything set up all nice." He dragged her over to the rear of the truck and tied her up to the tailgate.

Turley retrieved his bourbon, walked back over to where Riley was, and knelt down, holding the bottle to her lips. "Wanna drink?" Riley shook her head. "Come on, it's a party after all."

Riley again shook her head. Jake tried to prise her mouth open to pour some liquor down but stopped short when Riley bit his hand. "Ow!" He backhanded her across the jaw, standing up sharply, shaking his hand in pain. He looked down and spied a perfect row of teeth marks bleeding sluggishly. Riley smiled sweetly up at him as she spat out a mouthful of blood onto the dirt. He kicked her in the thigh, stomping off. Turley sat by the fire, throwing sticks on intermittently and watched her, drinking steadily, his eyes never leaving her, hers never leaving him.

He returned to her with a bandana wrapped around his hand. Jake stood over her, leering, and threw down the last mouthful of booze, before putting the bottle up onto the tailgate of the truck. He wiped his mouth and rubbed his hands together. "Time to dance."

As he reached for her, Riley kicked out and tried to get as far away from his hands as the rope would allow. Laughing, Turley picked her up, slamming her against the back of the truck. He pressed himself against her body, grinding his hips into her as he loosened the rope from the tailgate. He grabbed her by the belt and held her tight against him. With her hands behind her back, Riley was powerless to do anything but go wherever he pulled her.

Together they swayed unsteadily back and forth, Turley taking opportunities to kiss and lick her neck. His hands roamed from her hips, up and down her back, across her breasts, and back to snag her pelvis in tight as he rubbed himself against her. Riley could smell his sweat and heard his breathing quicken. He grabbed a fistful of her hair, pulling her in close, to claim her lips in a cruel, bruising encounter. She struggled to pull back. He laughed. "Stop fighting it, sweet cheeks. You know you're gonna love it."

Riley pulled her head back and head-butted him. He saw her coming, managing to move his head back a little so she only caught his lip. He licked the blood from his split lip and grinned at her. "Oh, this is gonna be fun."

He picked her up and threw her on the ground. Riley landed

awkwardly on her bad shoulder and grunted with the pain. Turley dropped to the ground and straddled her waist. From his pocket he pulled out a folding knife. Riley froze as she saw the light glint off the sharp blade. *Oh, dear God.*

Turley saw the fear in her eyes and laughed. "Now you're gonna behave yourself, aren't you? I don't wanna have to get rough. I want this to be good for you too, baby. After all, I have a reputation to maintain." Laughing, he hooked fingers under her bra, lifting it slightly away from her body, sliding the knife underneath and slicing it neatly in half. He licked his lips as Riley's breasts were exposed. Quickly he sliced the shoulder straps, pulling the broken remains of the garment away from her body and throwing it into the undergrowth.

"Oho, you're better than I imagined." He ran his hands over her chest, pinching her nipples, leaning down to suck and bite her. He laughed when he felt her flinch as he bit down hard on the top part of her left breast, drawing blood. He snarled in her face. "Now we're even." He sat up and moved down her legs to undo the top button of her jeans. "Heard me a nasty rumour you don't like meat. Heard you prefer to hang out with bean flickers. Is that true?"

Underneath her hands, partly embedded in the dirt, her fingers found the outline of a rock. One chance.

"Wait!" Riley's plea shocked Turley into stillness. "You want to dance? Then untie me." Turley's eyes narrowed in suspicion. "How good do you think your reputation's going to be when people hear you had to tie me down, huh?"

Turley thought, then nodded at her. He half rolled her sideways, to loosen the rope bindings, giggling drunkenly as Riley rolled back, exposed and facing him.

Jake leaned down to violently stab the knife into the dirt, up to its hilt, by Riley's head. He reached down to undo his belt.

Riley clenched her stomach muscles and sat bolt upright. This time, her head-butt didn't miss, her forehead catching him square across his already damaged nose and top teeth. She felt the skin split on her eyebrow on contact but didn't care. Dazed, he recoiled backwards, clutching his face. Riley pushed and twisted with her hips, bucking him off her body, and twisting, she hefted the rock and threw it as hard as she could, smack-bang between his eyebrows, dropping him like a sack of stones. Swiftly, she rolled and rose. Riley pulled the knife from the ground, just as Turley tried to get up. She waved the knife at him. "Don't move, or I swear, I'll gut you like a fish."

Turley struggled to his knees, breathing heavy.

Riley looked around and saw a dead tree limb within reach. She picked it up and pointed it at him. "Don't. Move."

He tottered to his feet and had just enough time to look up at her before she swung the tree branch, catching him under the jaw. He spun, eyes rolled back in his head, and fell into a crumpled heap.

In a blind panic Riley tossed the branch aside and started to run. She knew she was too far away from help on foot. She needed to create some distance between them and to find a safe place to hide while she still had the chance.

❖

Two hours later, Sorla's anger had burned itself out, and now she paced the room, biting her nails. Riley hadn't called, or texted, or answered any of Claire's messages—that, Sorla could understand. Sorla had been an arse to her. But the nurses said she hadn't been in to see George all day. Something wasn't right.

Claire put three fresh cups of coffee onto the kitchen table. "When was the last time you tried ringing her?"

She stood still and looked at her watch. "About half an hour ago."

"All right, I'm ringing Mickey again."

Sorla nodded. Her guts had been in knots all day. No one she talked to knew where Riley was, and the store's truck was gone. Ed had driven around and asked a few of the locals if they'd seen her but had come up empty-handed. When she spoke to Mickey earlier, he was confident that she'd turn up for their traditional birthday lunch for Pearl and told her not to worry. He felt confident that she'd soon cool down and come on back.

Claire came back into the room with a worried look on her face.

Sorla stopped pacing. "What did he say?"

Claire sat down and ran her fingers through her hair. "He said she never showed. He's worried now too. She's never done that before. He's coming over so we can all have a pow-wow on what to do next." Ed looked to Claire and held out his hand for the phone. Claire handed it over. "Who are you ringing?"

"The police."

Sorla nodded. They'd done all they could do on their own. They needed help. Between Mickey and the local police, Sorla figured there wouldn't be too many people, or places, that they didn't know. Sorla knew deep in her heart something was horribly wrong, and right now, they needed all the help they could get.

❖

"Where the *fuck* are you?" Turley stormed around the campsite. The sun was high and hot as it approached midday.

"C'mon sweet cheeks, I just wanna talk to you." Turley looked in and around the truck. "I just wanna say I'm sorry. I was drunk. Okay?"

Hidden, she listened, guessing his movements from the sound of his voice.

"Let me make it up to you. C'mon babe. I just wanna say I'm sorry and to make sure you're okay, and then you can piss off an' do whatever the hell you like."

Dead silence.

Turley paced backwards and forwards before jumping into his ute, revving it loudly, tearing off down the dirt road, driving like the devil himself was chasing his tail.

From inside her log, Riley heard him leave, but she wasn't taking any chances. She'd waited this long, she planned to wait a little longer to make sure he wasn't coming back. She lay there for several more hours, dozing on and off until the light began to soften and fade.

She'd run until her lungs nearly burst, only stopping when she ran headlong into a low-hanging branch in the dark, turning her world black. She woke briefly to find and crawl into the belly of an old hollowed-out tree. Her still-healing forearm was swollen and sore and her head felt like it could explode into a million pieces at any moment. She strained to listen for any traffic sounds, any noise, waiting, paranoid, trying to ascertain if Turley and his ute had truly gone. Riley shivered with cold and shock. She knew she needed to get out and get help soon.

She crawled out from the log and stumbled along the creekside track until she made her way back to her truck. She sank to her knees to finish changing the tyre as best as she could manage in the growing dark. Her fingers and hands seemed to move in slow motion. To make matters worse, her brain was having trouble linking logical thoughts together to work through the processes involved in changing the flat. Slowly, using gravity and the tyre weight, she managed to maneuver the old tyre off relatively easily. When it came to putting the new one onto the threads, it took several frustrating, tear-filled goes before it happened. The pain at having to maneuver the weight and lift the tyre almost defeated her. With one final effort, she jimmied the tyre up using the tyre lever, snagging and catching the threads onto the precious holes in the rim of the tyre, where they balanced precariously.

She felt around the dirt, located the nuts one by one, and screwed them on. She couldn't do them up tight, her left arm and shoulder weren't working properly, and she had no idea where the cross bar had gotten to, so she used the socket end on the jack to do her best by hand, hoping to God they would hold long enough to get her out of there and back to Cherry Hill and Sorla.

Riley crawled to the front of the truck, clawed her way upright to the running boards and inside, and fell into the cabin. Each movement now required long moments of resting in between. Riley lay across the seat, panting. The one eye that wasn't swollen shut began to close, until in panic, realizing what was happening, she made herself forcefully open it. She knew she was deteriorating fast and that if she fell asleep now, there was no telling when, or if, she would wake up.

A jumper lay folded on the seat from the morning. Moving slowly, Riley leaned over and pulled it across the seat towards her. With clumsy fingers, she pulled it on and zipped it up. Shivering, she fingered the truck's keys into the ignition. She turned the key, the truck's engine sputted and caught, purring to life, and Riley sobbed briefly in relief. *Thank you.*

She put the truck in gear and turned the wheel to take her home, to Sorla.

Chapter Twenty-six

A map was spread across the kitchen table. Sorla and Claire sat on chairs, while Ed and the policeman, Sergeant Purkiss, looked over their shoulders to the route that Mickey was pointing at, with Don and Perry hovering on the edges of the group listening in. "Eric said that, according to the orders on the books, she had five deliveries to do. Assuming she started at the farthest one away, she'd be comin' home on most likely one of two roads, either that one there, or this one here. My money's on this one. It's shorter and brings her more or less back onto your front road here."

Ed straightened up and leaned over the group pointing at the map. "Okay, how about Don and Perry take this east edge, the Sarge and I will grab this road, and Mickey, you and the girls take this one. We set the radios to channel forty-one and call in every quarter of the hour. Agreed?" There was a chorus of agreement. Ed turned to Don and Perry. "You two right to go?"

Don nodded. "Yep."

Ed slapped him on the back. "Okay. Let's go and find our girl, people."

As they filed out the door, heading towards their vehicles, they all paused, turning their heads, as twin lights caught their attention at the top of the drive into the property. Something wasn't right, as they watched the lights swerve erratically. As if in slow motion, they saw the lights take the turn too wide, coming to a sudden loud crashing halt as the vehicle collided with the front gate post. For a brief moment, everyone stood motionless, staring in shock, the night's silence shattered by the long unending sound of a truck horn.

Claire was the first to react. "Let me get my kit." She ran inside to the infirmary, emerging seconds later with a backpack and a blanket. Don and Perry were already in the truck and waiting for her to join the others in the truck's tray bed. Jumping in with the others, Claire slapped the sides to let them know she was in. Don put his foot down on the accelerator, making the wheels spin briefly in the dirt before gaining a grip and rocketing them off in the direction of the gate.

As they got closer Sorla's eyes opened wide in recognition, her hand shooting out to reflexively grab Claire's, squeezing tight in fear. "That's Riley's truck!"

Before Claire had a chance to answer, Don screeched to a halt next to the truck. Although the rear wheel was slightly askew, the damage was centred around the front part of the truck which was wedged into the gate's main wooden post, steam spewing out from under the bonnet. Sorla's heart skipped a beat as she saw Riley's blond head slumped over the wheel, her head resting on the horn.

Sorla gripped Claire in panic. Claire patted her face. "Give me a minute to see what's going on. You get the blanket ready and pass me my bag when I call for it. Okay? Sor? Can you do that?" Sorla nodded numbly. "Good girl. I need you to hold it together for me, honey. Riley needs you, okay?"

Sorla shook her head, trying to dispel the images of Fallujah flashing before her eyes. She took a deep breath and nodded. "I'm all right. You go."

Claire nodded, finally vaulting out to run to the truck. Ed was already up on the running boards, reaching in to turn the ignition off. Don and Perry were at the front of the truck disengaging the battery, seeing if anything was leaking and how badly it was wedged into the gate in case they needed to tow it off. Claire ran around to the passenger side and crawled into the cabin. Kneeling on the bench seat, she took hold of Riley's chin and neck and eased her head backwards, to rest, braced against the seat's headrest.

"Oh, sweetheart."

Riley stirred at the sound. "Sor?"

"No, honey. It's Claire. I got you love."

"I'm sorry…Tell Sor…sorry…"

"It's okay, honey. She's right here, you can tell her yourself in a minute." Riley's chin slumped in Claire's fingertips as she lost consciousness.

"Claire? Claire, is she okay? What's going on?" Sorla was behind her, standing in the open doorway.

"Just give me a minute, Sor."

Ed's jaw was clenched in anger, but his voice was gentle. "What can I do, love?"

"Can you hold her chin and neck for me? I just want to see if her legs are stuck." A minute later, she added, "No problems there. Okay, Sor? Can you open up the pack and hand me the neck brace please." Claire stuck her hand behind her back to accept the brace. She looked over at Ed. "Can you see if the door will open on your side?" Ed nodded and stepped off the boards. With a couple of tugs, the door came free. "Sor, I need the blanket spread out on the ground around on Ed's side. Don, I need you to come in here behind me and hold Riley for me."

Once Don was next to her, Claire scrambled out and ran around to the other side where she took the lead in instructing everyone as to how they were going to get her out. On the count of three, they smoothly worked as a unit under Claire's instructions, easing Riley out, Claire taking charge of her head and neck, lowering her gently down onto the blanket. Once on the blanket, they gathered around either side of Riley's inert form, and on Claire's count, using the blanket as a stretcher, lifted her ever so gently up and into the back of the truck. They all piled in around her, Don carefully driving them all back, parking outside the infirmary's side door.

In reverse order, they all worked together to lift Riley from the truck, transporting her inside. Sorla stayed with Claire, while Ed took the boys outside to where Sergeant Purkiss could be heard giving the ambulance instructions on how to reach them. Claire pulled a trolley over and pushed Riley's sleeve up, smoothly inserting an IV line and running a bag of saline, before slipping a pulse-ox meter onto her index finger. Unzipping Riley's jumper, Claire listened to her chest with a stethoscope and gently palpated Riley's ribs and abdomen. Quietly zipping the jumper back up, Claire looked at Sorla. Neither said a word.

Sorla stood at Riley's head and kissed her forehead. Tears streamed down her face. "Oh fuck, sweetheart. Oh, baby, where have you been? Who did this to you?"

A knock sounded on the door as Ed stuck his head inside. "Ambulance is here."

Claire nodded. "Send them on through. Sor, can you ask one of the boys if they can go back to the truck and see if they can find Riley's wallet? It'll have her cards and details in it. I'll go with Riley in the ambulance and meet you at the hospital."

Sergeant Purkiss, who was outside the doorway with Ed, put a reassuring hand on Sorla's shoulder. "You can come with me if you'd like and we'll give them an escort into town."

Sorla nodded. "Thanks."

Within minutes Riley was transferred to the stretcher bed, loaded into the back of the waiting ambulance, and was on her way into town, following in the wake of Sergeant Purkiss's lights and sirens.

At the hospital a team was waiting for them in the trauma bay entrance. Stepping out of the police car, Sorla watched helplessly as the team swarmed around Riley, obscuring her from Sorla's vision as they wheeled her inside, only to be swallowed up behind automatic sliding doors.

Ed came up behind her, putting his arm around her shoulders. "Come on, Fender. Let's go and find us a coffee while Claire Bear and her friends look after her." Gently he herded her towards the waiting area where Mickey sat, pale and shocked, with a clipboard resting on his knees with the admission papers attached.

Sorla stared at the clipboard with Riley's name on it.

"You right to help Mick here with the paperwork while I go and rustle us up a brew?"

Sorla blinked. "No." Sorla strode over to the nurses' counter and was soon in deep conversation with the admissions officer.

❖

Riley stirred to wakefulness. Opening one eye, she had trouble focusing. She didn't recognize the buzz of voices around her. Hands were pulling at her jumper and something cold was sliding up one of her trouser legs.

A man leaned into her line of vision and smiled. "Hey, Riley. My name is Dan—"

She started to tremble. The medical team's heads turned to look at the screens as her heart rate picked up, the monitors beginning to beep alarmingly.

Riley felt someone tug on her other trouser leg. Her head turned from side to side trying to see what was happening.

Dan patted her arm. "It's okay, sweetie…"

His voice was deep. Panic flared in her chest. *No! Not again!* She threw herself off the bed and over the side, stumbling and knocking over the monitors. She remembered the knife. Feeling around to her back pocket she found it, drawing it out and waving it blindly, in an attempt to keep the voices and the hands away from her. She tried to focus on where the threat was coming from, her heart hammering inside her chest.

"It's okay, Riley, come on now, drop the knife for me."

A sob tore from Riley's throat as she hurriedly waved the knife in the direction of the man's voice. Fuzzy figures moved before her blurry vision as she frantically swept the knife back and forth to keep the threat away. She vaguely registered someone curse as the knife connected with flesh.

With her remaining strength, Riley backed herself further away from the voices until she hit a wall, only to slide down it, to land, crouched, on the floor. Making herself small, Riley clutched her knees to her bare chest with her bad arm, swinging the knife with her good hand vainly trying to keep the voices at bay.

Claire stepped forward only to be met with the doctor's restraining arm, halting her move forward. "Just wait. Security's on their way."

Claire shook her head, pulling her arm free. "She doesn't need Security. Right now, she just needs a friend and to know she's safe."

"Claire, I don't think this is a good idea. She's clearly irrational and she has a knife. She's hurt one nurse already, I don't want a repeat performance."

Sorla spoke softly from across the room. "She won't hurt me, will you, honey? Riley, it's me, Sorla." Riley sat, motionless, as Sorla moved forward. "Claire's here too, and Ed and Mickey. You're safe now, love." Claire soundlessly handed Sorla a blanket as she stepped past.

Riley turned her bruised and swollen face towards Sorla's voice. Her teeth were chattering and her hand was shaking so hard she was having trouble maintaining her grip on the knife. "Sorla?"

"Yes, honey, it's me. I've got a blanket with me. I'm going to come over and wrap it around you. Is that okay?"

"Yes. Cold."

"I know, sweetheart. Here you go." Sorla knelt down and gently wrapped the blanket around her shoulders and across her front, then extracted the knife from her fingers and slid it across the floor. "There you go, love." She wrapped her arms around Riley's shoulders and pulled her into her chest to hold her safely.

With the last of her defenses gone, Riley crumpled, collapsing into a ball in Sorla's lap, tears of exhaustion rolling down her face, her voice a strangled whisper. "Oh, Sor…"

"I know, baby, I know. You're safe now. You're safe."

Within the safe harbor of Sorla's body shielding her, her gentle voice and words wrapping themselves around her tortured mind, Riley began to relax, trusting her lover to keep her safe. She let her exhausted body and mind succumb, giving in to the struggle, allowing the darkness to steal her away.

❖

Sorla paced the floor of the private waiting room Claire had arranged for them, as they waited for news of Riley's condition. Finally Claire came through the door and motioned for them all to take a seat.

Sorla remained standing. "Tell me."

"You've seen her. I don't need to tell you, she's had a rough time of it. She's not long come back from having some scans and they've just now taken her up to go to theatre. She has a hairline fracture of the skull, a fractured eye socket and cheek bone. Her jaw looks okay but is terribly bruised. Bruised ribs, she's cracked the head of her humerus, but it looks stable, and they'll do a check of the pins and plate in her arm."

"Was…" Sorla could hardly bear to ask the next question. "Was she raped?"

Claire shook her head and held her friend's hands tightly between her own. "No. No she wasn't. She fought hard, our girl. She's physically injured and clearly traumatized—you saw her reaction to a strange man's voice—but the arsehole didn't rape her."

Sorla sat heavily into a chair.

Mickey was slumped back in the chair and looked to have aged overnight as his eyes stared off in shock. Claire reached over to put a hand on his thigh. "She's strong, Mick. You raised her strong. She's lasted this long and found her way back to Cherry Hill with all those injuries. Our job now is to stay positive and to lend her our strength."

Mickey nodded, offering up a weak half smile. "Always was pig-headed in her own quiet way when she made her mind up 'bout somethin' or other."

Claire looked around the group. "That's right, she fought her way to come back to us. It's our turn now to be strong for her and to make sure she knows we're here for her."

Sorla's head dropped as tears coursed down her cheeks. Claire gently lifted her chin with her hand. "Honey, she came back for you. She needs you most of all right now. Can you handle this?"

Sorla closed her eyes as images of Riley flashed before them, her hair shining in the sun, the kittens on her lap, smiling as they tumbled and played together, her beautiful face as she watched the horses play in the yard, her gentle hands, and her warm, expressive eyes that stole her heart every time they looked at her. Sorla nodded. There was no question, no hesitation. She would be here for Riley, no matter what. "Yes."

Claire patted her hand. "Good girl."

CHAPTER TWENTY-SEVEN

Sitting in a chair, Sorla dozed with her head resting on the bed, her hand wrapped around Riley's. The surgery, although long, had gone well. The doctor was confident that everything would function normally when all was healed. She tried to stay awake as long as she could, but too many nights' lack of sleep, combined with the steady rhythm of the monitors attached to Riley, pulled her under as she closed her eyes.

Riley whimpered in her sleep, startling Sorla to wakefulness. She rubbed her tired eyes and yawned, looking at the monitors and back at Riley. She looked small. Sorla barely recognized her. Her face was deathly pale, the bruises standing out in stark, contrasting dramatic shades. The swelling significantly distorted Riley's face to the point that it was almost like she was looking at a different person. There was a bright new white cast on her forearm and stark white patches dotted across her features in the form of wound dressings, with the biggest, most visible one on her forehead, standing out starkly like an alien on the landscape of Riley's face.

She had drips, monitors, and oxygen all attached and a bag hanging off the side of the bed that Sorla didn't want to know about. Carefully, Sorla raised Riley's good hand to her lips and tenderly kissed it. Riley stirred, opening her one good eye, looking around the room, trying to focus. Sorla stood up, smiled, and leaned into Riley's path of vision, brushing her hair away from her face. "Hey, sweetheart."

"Sor?" Riley's eye was distant and glassy. Beads of sweat shone on her face.

"Yeah, honey. I'm right here."

"I'm sorry."

"Sorry for what, love?"

"Didn't mean…to walk out."

"It's okay, honey."

Riley shook her head and tried to use her good hand to throw the covers off.

"Where are you going love?"

"Pearl's birthday…have to get ready."

Chewing the inside of her lip briefly, Sorla wondered where Riley's fevered mind was going, at the same time knowing that she needed to come up with and offer a plausible answer if she was to keep Riley in bed. "It's okay, I told Mickey you'd be late."

Riley seemed to accept this and settled. "Oh. Okay. His present's in the truck. Can you get it?"

"Sure."

"Sor?"

"Yes, love?"

"Can we go home now?"

Sorla put a hand to her mouth to stifle her sob. Quickly wiping the tears away, she forced a smile on her face. "Soon, love. Soon."

Riley's lids started to flicker and lower. "Okay." She licked her lips and closed her eyes. Sorla leaned over and kissed her softly on the lips. Riley smiled lopsidedly. "Love you…"

"I love you too, my darling." But Sorla wasn't sure if she heard her or not, as she had fallen back to sleep.

❖

For the next few days, Sorla spent day and night by Riley's bedside as she drifted in and out of a narcotic-fueled healing sleep. Claire, Ed, and Mickey came by regularly too. A slight grunt from the doorway told Sorla that one more visitor had arrived. In the silhouette of the doorway Sorla could make out a nurse standing behind someone in a wheelchair. It was George. Sorla waved him in. He shook his head and said something to the nurse, waving his hand as if requesting her to take him away.

Sorla's stood up and met them in the doorway and told the nurse, "It's all right, I've got him. I'll take him back when we're done."

George tried to grab the wheels and steer away. "I'm goin' back to my room."

Sorla lifted his hands off the wheels, putting them back into his lap. She leaned down close to his ear, ensuring that he heard what she had to say. "You either come in with me in the chair, or I will drag you in by your ears—either way, you *will* get your miserable arse over there. Only choice you have is how you wanna get there."

George muttered a string of profanities under his breath. Sorla smiled sweetly and waved at the nurse. "Thanks. I won't keep him long." She proceeded to wheel him into the room, parking him by Riley's bedside. He sat hunched over, refusing to look up.

Sorla rinsed a washcloth out and gently sponged Riley's sleeping face, before sitting back down into her chair to stare hard across the bed at George. "Took you long enough to come."

"Who the hell do you think you are?"

"I'm her girlfriend, her lover, her partner. I'm the one who's been here by her side day and night. Where the hell have you been?"

"She don't need me here."

"You're her father for Christ's sakes, George."

"Ain't none of your damn business."

"Riley means the world to me, she *is* my world, whether you like it or not, so I'm making it my business."

"Well, you need to butt out and mind yourself, girlie. You don't know nothin' 'bout me, or my life."

"You're right. I don't know you, but I do know this—Riley gave up her childhood and damn near most of her adulthood to look after you, so that you can live out your life with your drunken mates in the bottom of a bottle, reminiscing about a thousand years ago. I know that, no matter what she does for you, you're a selfish, mean bastard who throws everything right back in her face. She works hard. She's a good person, with a big heart."

"So?"

Sorla stood up and walked around to where George was sitting. She knelt, getting in his face. Her voice was quiet but laced with the steel of the undercurrents of her emotions. "This beautiful woman, your daughter, has been traumatized and beaten half to death. So the least you can do, you selfish piece of shit, is be a man, be a father, and pull your head out of your decaying arse and sit with her awhile." Sorla fiercely locked off his chair's wheels and stormed out of the room, leaving George to sit alone with Riley.

She paced the corridor for a while, then took a seat in the waiting room.

Mickey found her there, elbows on her knees, her head in her hands, and sat beside her. "Didn't expect to see you out here. Everythin' all right in there?"

Sorla ran her fingers through her hair, leaned her head back against the wall, and closed her eyes. "Riley's fine. She's sleeping."

"Okay. So whatcha doing out here on your lonesome?"

"'Cause it's the safest option right now. George is in with her." Sorla opened her tired eyes. "I caught him looking in from the doorway, so I more or less dragged him into the room, told him to pull his head out of his arse and to sit with his daughter. Then I left."

Mickey patted her on the knee. "Ha! Well good for you, kid. Damn sorry I missed it. How long's he been in there for?"

"'Bout half an hour."

"What say you go and grab us both a cuppa, while I collect him and take him back to his room."

❖

Sorla returned with the coffees in time to see Mickey pushing George back to his room. Mickey threw her a wink as they passed. George avoided her gaze.

Sorla took up her usual seat at the bedside just as Riley woke. Putting her coffee down, she stood up and kissed her. "Hey, beautiful. How you doing?"

"'Kay. Bit thirsty."

Sorla smiled at Riley's returned awareness. "Hang on and I'll get you some water."

After a few sips Riley closed her eyes. "Nice. Thanks."

"How do you feel?"

"Like I've been in the bottom of one of your cattle truck deliveries."

Sorla put her hand to Riley's forehead and cheek. "You're not quite as warm as you have been. Looks like your temperature's coming down."

"Was there someone else here before? I thought I heard voices."

"George was here for a while. Mickey's just taken him back to his room."

"George was here?"

"Uh-huh." Sorla sat and watched as Riley processed the information.

"How long have I been here?"

"Four days. What's the last thing you remember?"

"Um...changing the tyre."

Long pause.

"Sor?"

"Yes, love?"

"Can you come up on the bed, and hold me...please?"

Sorla knew of Riley's strength and pride, and she also recognized the enormity of the request. She lowered the railing on the side of the bed, and Riley held up the sheet for her to climb in with her. Carefully, she wrapped her arm around Riley's middle, resting her chin on top of Riley's head. Closing her eyes, she willed every bit of strength and comfort that she possessed to pass to Riley wherever they touched.

They curled up together and slept.

❖

After they woke, Riley showered with a nurse's assistance, then slept for several hours, with Sorla dozing lightly stretched out beside her. A knock on the door stirred Sorla to instant awareness. Two people in dress pants and shirts stood waiting expectantly in the doorway. The man was the epitome of Joe Average. Mid-to-late forties, six foot, he had the body of someone who had probably been reasonably athletic in his younger years but was now growing a little soft around the edges. The woman was statuesque and slim hipped, with brown hair tied severely back into a ponytail. Her face was softened by a tentative smile as she held a badge up, introducing them as detectives come to ask Riley some questions.

Sorla nodded. "Can you come back later when she's awake? I could call you and let you know." Riley's eyes cracked open. "Hey, honey. There's some police officers here who want to talk to you. Are you up for a chat?"

Riley blinked and frowned slightly. "Can I have a minute? Not awake yet."

The male detective smiled and nodded. "We need to have a chat with Riley's doctor too. What say we do that and come back in a bit?"

Sorla smiled at them. "Thanks." Sorla rolled over onto her side to face Riley, propping her head up with one hand. Her other hand came out to softly stroke Riley's jawline.

Riley closed her eyes and leaned into Sorla's fingers. Her chin quivered as moisture glistened at the edges of her lashes. Her voice came out as a pained whisper. "I don't want to do this." When she opened her eyes and found Sorla's, the depth of pain in them tore at the very centre of Sorla's heart. Riley slowly shook her head. "I don't want to remember."

Sorla pushed herself up and wrapped Riley in her arms. "I know, honey, trust me, I know. But it has to be done. The police need to find him and stop him, and to make sure it doesn't happen again. I know you don't want to talk about it, but you need to, babe, it's a part of the healing." Riley sniffed into her shoulder. Sorla rubbed her back. "When I was in the hospital, I didn't talk to anyone. I didn't want to bring back to life what I'd seen, what I'd felt. I wanted to hang on to the numbness. It was the only way I thought I could cope. But someone told me that in order to let your wounds heal, you've first got to bring them out and expose them to the air. It hurts, but it helps to see what you're dealing with, so you can find out how best to treat them and get on with the healing. Only then can you start to find your way onto the road back home. You'll still have crappy days, God knows, you've seen some of me at my sparkling best, but you've got people who love you, honey, and we'll help you get through this."

Riley closed her eyes. "Can you stay? When they come back?"

"Always. I'm not going anywhere."

"I love you."

Sorla kissed her. "I love you too, sweetheart. You wanna try and sit up, ready for when they come back?"

❖

Riley told them all she could remember. There were a few gaps in her memory, but the detectives were reassuring and supportive of all that she could recall. Detective Lisle finished making notes in her notebook before putting her pen down to afford Riley a look of great seriousness. "I'm sorry to have to ask you this, but you're sure it was Jake Turley who did this to you?"

Riley closed her eyes briefly and shivered. "Yes."

Detective Fitzpatrick frowned. "As part of the investigation, we will be looking at the clothes you were wearing when you arrived in hospital, and we will go and look over the area that you identified as the place the assault took place, but is there anything else that you can add to your story that would help us identify Turley?"

"I'm pretty sure I gave him a broken nose…and I bit his hand. He had to wrap it up."

Lisle folded her notebook closed and stood up, patting Riley's hand as she rose. "You've done a great job. We're going to go out and have a look at the campsite now, but we might need to come back and ask a few follow-up questions later on, if that's okay?" Riley nodded slowly. "Thanks, Riley. We know this isn't easy, but you've been great. We'll let you rest now and see you a bit later on. Thanks."

After they'd gone, the room was suddenly very quiet.

Sorla rubbed her hand. "I'm really proud of you, love. You did a great job." Riley stared ahead at a spot on the wall. "You okay?"

Riley closed her eyes. She opened them to find Sorla looking at her, concerned. "Can you help me have a shower?"

Sorla, better than anyone, knew the desire to wash the pain away. If Riley wanted fifty showers a day, then that's what she'd do, anything to try and ease some of her lover's suffering. "Sure, honey."

Chapter Twenty-eight

L ater that day, Detective Lisle turned up again. "How're you doing?"
"Okay."

"Good, good. Look, I won't stay long. I was wondering, if I showed you a few things, if you could identify them for me and tell me if you've seen them before?"

"I'll try."

"We found the campsite you talked about and had a good look around. Your flat tyre is still there, along with your tools, and we found a few other things I was wondering if you could take a look at for me."

She burrowed in a bag to retrieve several sealed plastic bags with writing on them, placing the topmost bag onto Riley's lap. "Do you recognize this?"

Riley nodded. Her mobile. "Jake took it."

Detective Lisle lightly tapped the shattered glass screen. "How did this happen?"

A muscle twitched in Riley's eyelid.

"Riley?"

Riley stared at the phone.

"What happened, Riley?"

"He…he broke it, so no one could ring…"

Sweat broke out across Riley's face, her hands started to shake. An enormous lump filled her throat making it suddenly hard to swallow. Her throat started to constrict, her pulse began to race. Seeing the destroyed phone took her straight back to the nightmare. She was no longer in the hospital, she was trapped, beseiged by Jake Turley. She could smell him, hear his laughter, feel his hands all over her body…

Lisle was persistent. "I'm sorry, Riley, I have to ask. Is this yours?" Riley nodded distantly. In a steady but quiet voice, Lisle pressed for details while Riley was still in the moment. Her voice was quiet, hypnotic, penetrating Riley's visions. "Why is it smashed? What happened?"

Riley's eyes were unfocused. Rivulets of sweat ran down the side of her face to fall, unheeded, to soak and stain her T-shirt.

Sorla urged, "She *told* you. Can't you leave it alone?"

But Lisle leaned in. "What happened, Riley?" Her voice was soft, yet commanding.

In a strangled whisper, Riley's voice rasped out her vision. "He said I needed a proper man." Riley shook her head. "He tried to rape me."

Sorla growled at Detective Lisle as Riley began to sway. "That's enough, Detective. You've got your answer, now back off."

Sorla stroked Riley's face. "Riley, I want you to breathe for me. Come on, deep breath. Listen to my voice. Thatta girl...nice deep breaths. You're in the hospital. Can you smell it? Listen to the sounds... keep breathing for me. Can you feel me beside you? Come on back for me, love. That's the way."

Riley's eyes slowly began to refocus, her body shaking with the aftereffects of having gone back in her mind to the campsite.

"You okay, love?"

Riley shook her head. "I think...I'm gonna be sick." Sorla swiftly grabbed a sick bag that had been left on the bedside table for such occasions, holding it as Riley retched painfully.

The doctor ordered Riley be given something for the nausea and a sedative to help her sleep. She was still soundly asleep when Mickey and Claire arrived. Sorla filled them in on the visit from the detective and the evidence they had found at the campsite. "And she was able to give a positive ID on her attacker. It was Jake Turley."

Mickey's gnarled old fist slammed into his open palm. "Sonofabitch. Sorry, ladies."

Claire patted Mickey on the arm. "Don't apologize on my account.

I can think of a few colourful phrases I'd like to add to that myself. At least they know who they're looking for. Bastard."

Sorla paced the room. "I should have known that he wouldn't have gone away easy. I should have been more—"

Claire grabbed her friend by the shoulders. "Sorla, stop. No one could have known or predicted that he would do this."

Sorla shook her head and cried out in frustration. "But I should have seen it!"

Mickey sat holding Riley's hand while she slept. "You a fortune teller then, are you?"

Taken aback at Mickey's question, Sorla frowned. "No, but I—"

"Then your friend's right. We all feel guilty, like we shoulda done something, but the fact is, none of us saw this coming. You can't stop what you can't see. Has anyone told George?"

Sorla shook her head. "No."

Mickey kissed Riley's hand and stood up stiffly. "It's a small town. I better go an' tell him before he hears it from someone else."

With arms wrapped tightly around herself, Sorla turned and looked out the window, feeling shattered by the overwhelming helplessness that settled around her heart. Claire walked up behind her. Turning her friend from the window to face her, she held out her arms and Sorla stepped into her friend's embrace.

Stroking Sorla's hair, Claire sighed deeply. "It's almost like déjà vu."

Sorla sniffled on her friend's shoulder. "What do you mean?"

"Ed and I used to take turns doing the same thing you're doing right now, after you copped the IED."

Straightening, Sorla shook her head. "The IED wasn't your fault. You couldn't have stopped that from happening."

"Exactly, but it took us a while to convince ourselves that we weren't partially responsible for what happened to you. Every time we looked at you, our hearts bled with guilt, with pain, with a feeling of being completely helpless to take away your pain and suffering. A lot like what you're feeling now."

Accepting a tissue that Claire pulled from her pocket, Sorla dried her eyes. "How did you survive?"

"We loved you, and we loved each other. That's what you have to do for Riley. We can't change what has happened, but we can be here for her and help her to live in the now, supporting her, until she gets stronger and can begin to move past this."

"You make it sound so simple."

Claire snorted. "Did I mention you'll also need a truckload of patience?"

"Only a truckload? I must have been going easy on you."

❖

Sorla and Riley walked outside, and Sorla helped manoeuvre the drip stand and ease Riley down onto a bench seat before joining her. Riley closed her eyes and pointed her face to the sun. "Mm."

"It's a beautiful day, isn't it? Doesn't look like it'll get to be as hot as they predicted." Sorla squinted slightly as she looked up into the bright light.

"It's lovely. Thank you."

Sorla nodded. "That's okay. It's nice to get out." Sorla's fingers idly worried a loose splinter on the bench arm. She wanted to talk about what would happen when Riley was released but was unsure how she'd react, given the last time they were together, when Riley walked out. "Riley—"

"No. Sor. There's something I want to say." Riley opened her eyes but didn't meet Sorla's gaze. "I owe you an apology."

"You don't owe me anything."

"No. Wait. Please. Just hear me out. This has haunted me for the last couple of days and I need to say this."

"Okay."

Riley took a breath and looked off into the distance. "I was angry at you." She snorted softly. "I was angry at me too. And George. What you said, about George…" She shook her head.

"Oh, babe, I'm so sorry, I was a dickhead. I just—"

Riley held up her hand. Sorla fell silent. "You weren't wrong to suggest other ways to look after George, but it's not something I wanted to hear. It's just that the idea of putting him away, because it was easier, or more convenient than looking after him…it really got to me. I know now that's not what you meant, but at the time, in my head, that's how I heard it."

"I'm so sorry, babe. I handled it all wrong. I just wanted to find a way of helping, of making your life easier. But it came out all wrong. You have no idea how sorry I am."

Riley nodded and smiled weakly, affording Sorla a quick glance. "I know." Riley reached out to hold Sorla's hand. "Out there, all I could think about…was coming home to you. I didn't want our last words to be angry ones." Riley's chin quivered as her voice wavered. "I needed to come home, to say I'm sorry. To tell you I love you."

Sorla put her arm around Riley's shoulders and drew her head down. "Oh, my love, you have nothing to be sorry for. I'm the one who should apologize. I was bombastic, pushy, selfish, and a downright tool. And for the record, I love you too."

Riley squeezed her hand in acknowledgement. "I can't just abandon George because it's too hard."

Sorla nodded. "I know."

"I know he's a pain, and I know that he's going to drink himself into his grave, I just…" She shrugged.

"It's okay. I understand." Sorla wasn't sure how Riley would take this next piece of news. She took a breath and chanced it, now or never. "These last couple of days, we've all put our heads together and have come up with a few ideas we'd like to run past you." Sorla felt Riley tense beside her. "Just hear me out first and see what you think." Although Riley's jaw was set, she nodded for Sorla to continue.

"I understand better now about George. And I was wrong to suggest he be sent away, to be cared for by somebody else. But the fact of the matter is, love, you can't, for the minute, look after him and you when you get out of here." Riley's shoulders slumped slightly, but she held her peace, waiting to hear what Sorla said next.

Recognizing she had been given the go ahead to continue, Sorla pushed forward. "We could get him home care, where someone would visit and stay during the day, but that'd mean he'd be alone at nights, and we didn't think you'd like that." Riley shook her head. "Mickey has offerred to take George in, but we'd need George's okay for this, and although it would be a good solution, we weren't too sure that George'd be entirely happy with the plan." Riley relinquished a half smile in agreement. "In the end, Pauly came up with a great idea. One of George's mates, from the pub, was widowed earlier in the year. He hates living alone in his big house. He's offerred to come and live in with George, if you're okay with it. They're already mates, they could keep each other company, and he'd look after George, in his own home, and make sure he eats well. And he can take him to The Grape, like always, and make sure he goes to his doctor's appointments. They'd be helping each other out. It's kind of the perfect solution, for both of them. What do you think?"

Riley was silent for a good few minutes. Sorla was nervous, wondering if she had pushed too far.

"And what about me?"

"I was kind of hoping that you'd come out and stay with me for a while, let me look after you for a change, until you feel better. We can work out where to go after that, whenever you'd like, however you'd like."

Riley looked down at their hands. "I'd have to talk to George."

Sorla desperately tried to rein in her smile. "Of course."

Riley nodded. A silent pause sat between them, but it was a comfortable silence now that a much needed peace had been made.

Riley intercepted Sorla's hand, raising it to her lips, kissing it softly, before lowering it to hold against her chest. Beneath her fingertips, Sorla could feel Riley's heart pounding. "Thank you."

Sorla softly squeezed Riley's fingers in acknowledgement. "For what, sweetheart?"

Riley stroked Sorla's hand. "For loving me. For holding me together."

Sorla stayed very still, letting Riley drive the moment. "I'd do anything for you."

Riley's brows furrowed as she played absently with Sorla's fingers. "It can't be easy for you. I'd understand if…if you wanted out."

"Never crossed my mind." Sorla threaded her fingers through Riley's, letting her know with the simple touch of her body that she genuinely and unmistakably meant what she said. She wasn't going anywhere.

"Why?"

"I feel like I've waited for you all my life. Now that I've found you, I've no intention of losing you." Sorla laughed softly. "You know, it wasn't all that long ago that I felt ugly, damaged, broken. But then I met a most remarkable woman. You know what she said to me? She said, *I don't see any scars. I see a beautiful woman, with a bruised heart and a limp that makes funny footprints. Someone who, when they smile, lights up a room. I see a woman who is brave and strong and one who's as wilful and Irish as a certain horse we both know.* When I look at you, that's what I see. A beautiful, brave, incredible woman, who I am proud to love and call my partner."

Riley turned and looked into Sorla's eyes. What greeted her was love, compassion, tenderness, and honesty. A dam burst within Riley, and for the first time since the attack, her shields crumbled under the wave of love that Sorla was offering her, as she clung to her, weeping the tears of a deeply wounded soul. She wept for the woman who held her, who loved her, who had been beside her all the way, never asking, never pushing, just loving her.

CHAPTER TWENTY-NINE

Riley went back home with Sorla, Claire, and Ed. The first few weeks were hard as she tired so easily, but gradually her stamina started to increase and she found herself able to do more each day. In the evening she and Sorla strolled around the house yard, each night walking a little longer and further than the night before. Sorla, Claire, and Ed were keeping busy, as their pilot program had been given the green light to go ahead. They had finished the interviews and chosen four people to start, two at the farm and two undertaking sponsored apprenticeships with businesses in town.

Eric stayed on to help out in the store. With the baby coming, he was keen to get as much work as he could to help set his family up. He and Gloria were currently living with her parents but hoped to save up enough soon to move into their own place, and the extra income was a welcome boost to their confidence as well as to their finances.

Riley set to working with the light bay mare, progressing to the point where Ed had begun to ride her around the yard. Of the original batch of green horses, the only horse left to work on was the magnificent blue roan mare, Irish. As she leaned on the fence railing and observed the proud creature in the house yard, for the first time in a good many weeks Riley felt a kernel of excitement take seed and begin to grow at the prospect of working with the magnificent creature. Over breakfast that morning, she and Sorla had talked about how best to start.

They made good progress with Irish over several days. The mare, although wilful, was a natural show off who was keen to please. Riley talked Sorla through the process, letting her take the lead with her chosen brood mare. Their connection was evident right from the start.

Several times Riley laughed as she watched the two strong wills battle it out, each one desperately trying to hold out until the other one gave in.

Irish enjoyed nothing more than sneaking up behind Sorla and nudging her unexpectedly from behind if she thought she was being ignored. Riley was leaning on the fence wiping tears from her eyes as Sorla was dusting herself off. She had bent over to pick up the dropped apple treat she had in her hand when Irish nudged her from behind, making her overbalance and land face first in the dirt.

Standing up, Sorla slapped her hat on her thigh grumpily, causing a puff of dust to cloud off it, before slamming it on the top of her head. She turned and glared at Riley with her hands on her hips. "It's not funny."

Riley gently lifted the hat, turned it around, and placed it back on her head, then kissed her on the lips with a big grin on her face. "Yes, it is, babe. Especially when you put your hat on backwards, cutie." Riley wrapped her arms around Sorla's hips and hugged her.

Sorla smirked as she gave in to Riley's obvious delight. It was so nice to see her smiling and laughing again that Sorla would gladly have hit the dirt several more times if it meant seeing the light shining back in her partner's eyes.

"But it looks like we might have to teach your girl some manners."

Sorla was acutely aware of Riley's body melding with hers, and the fact that Riley had initiated the intimate embrace. It was a significant step forward. Sorla playfully rubbed noses with Riley. "Oh? And how do you propose to do that, Dr. Dolittle?"

Riley's eyes darkened a shade as her arms moved up to wrap around Sorla's neck, pulling her down to offer a tentative, tender kiss. "Well, working with a beautiful lady is always tricky."

Sorla was careful to let Riley set the pace, even though her body was pulsing with excitement. "Is that so?"

"Uh-huh, 'specially if they're skitty." Riley playfully nibbled her chin.

"Skitty?"

"Uh-huh. It's all about the dance. You have to take it slow." Riley tipped Sorla's head back and kissed the length of her throat.

The blood was rushing loudly between Sorla's ears and rapidly heading south. "Slow is good."

"You have to let them know how special they are." Riley came back to Sorla's mouth, nibbling on her lower lip.

"Special." Sorla was having trouble putting her thoughts together.

"Mm, *really* special." Riley claimed Sorla's mouth, gaining in confidence as her tongue darted out to trace Sorla's top lip. Sorla accepted Riley's gift of bravery by pouring all her love back into her gentle receptive response, until they pulled away, panting slightly, their foreheads pressed together.

Sorla could feel Riley trembling along the length of her body and wrapped her arms around her protectively, holding her close as Riley clung tightly. It was the first time they had been intimate since the assault and as much as she wanted to take it further, any next step would need to be determined by Riley. Her trembling body spoke volumes. "What say we call it a day and head back inside."

Riley nodded. Sorla kissed the top of Riley's head with Riley's words echoing in her mind. She smiled into the warmth of the sun. *Slow is good.* With arms wrapped around each other they headed back to the house.

EPILOGUE

"Oh, Mickey, that is perfect. Thank you. I love it." Sorla held up an emerald-green saddlecloth with a four-leaf clover and the name *Irish* embroidered on it, with a matching baseball cap for her. She kissed him soundly on the cheek, much to the delight of the gathered small crowd as he blushed furiously at the attention.

He chuckled at her delight. "You're most welcome. At least it'll make the two of you easy to find in a crowd."

Ed retrieved two parcels from beside the couch, handing over one small and one large present. Sorla opened the smaller one first. It was an inch-and-a-half wide leather bracelet with what looked like a chunky mobile phone attached to it. Sorla looked to Ed for an explanation. He was sitting with his arm around Claire, an enormously cheeky grin plastered across on his face.

Sorla held the gift up, waggling it in the air. "Do I get a hint?"

"It's a tracking device and a GPS unit, for next time you wander off."

Sorla rolled her eyes. "Oh, har-har-har, Thornton."

Ed was laughing his head off, earning him a sharp dig in the ribs from Claire with her elbow. "Ignore the clown, open the other one."

Sorla looked up to see Claire and Ed smiling at her. She carefully unwrapped the beautifully wrapped flat package. As the paper came away the present was revealed—a framed photograph of them all at the ball, Claire and Ed, and Sorla and Riley with their arms around each other with Mickey in the middle of the two couples, all smiling and radiating pure happiness. "We got it off one of the photographers who was there. Even he commented on how well it came out."

"Oh, guys, this is beautiful. Thank you. I know the perfect place to hang it too—on the wall in the music room." She got up to hug and kiss them both. "Thank you so much."

As she sat back down, Riley shyly handed over a small flat package. "This is the first part of your gift."

Sorla looked up and met Riley's eyes, lost for a moment in them, before Riley shyly smiled at her. Sorla turned her attention back to the present in her lap and meticulously unwrapped her gift. It was a gilt-edge framed photograph of the two of them dancing at the ball. The photographer had captured them perfectly as they danced, bodies moulded together, gazing into each other's eyes, smiles on their faces. It was the perfect portrait of two people in love.

Sorla stared at the photograph, feeling love surge up and fill her chest. Riley reached for her hand, holding it softly in her palm. With her other hand, she reached into her pocket and pulled out a black velvet box. With one hand, she deftly lifted its lid, pulling out a diamond encrusted rose-gold band, holding it reverently in her fingertips. "You are my world, Sorla Reardon. You have shown me joy that I never imagined was possible, and love I could never have dreamed of knowing. If it wasn't for you"—Riley took a shaky breath—"I don't know that I could have survived these past few months. I love every bit about you, I have ever since the moment I first saw you, and if you'll let me, I'd like to keep loving you with everything I have, for all the years to come."

Riley held up the ring in silent question. Sorla could only nod, looking on as Riley gently slid the sparkling band over Sorla's ring finger, to fit perfectly, snugly, into place. Sorla looked at the ring and their joined hands through misting eyes. She raised her hands to Riley's face, cupping her cheeks to whisper, "I love you," sealing her acceptance with a kiss that tenderly echoed a reciprocating promise of love.

The room was silent, save a few quiet sniffles. Finally Ed stood up, took a deep breath, and cried, "Yeehar! This calls for a celebration." Dashing out of the room, he returned minutes later with a chilled bottle of champagne and five champagne flutes. He poured them all a glass and raised his in a toast. "Riley, even though you trumped my tracking bracelet, I would like to say *about bloody time* you two. Seriously, to two of the nicest people I know—may your love be long, strong, and unbreakable. To the lovebirds!"

"Cheers!"

After much mirth and admiration of the ring, eventually the champagne and the evening came to an end, with Mickey, Ed, and Claire offering their final congratulations and goodnights before retiring. Sorla carried the group picture into the music room, ready to hang in the morning, while Riley went on ahead of her to their suite. Chuckling to herself, Sorla put the tracking device up onto the sideboard. She'd have to think long and hard how she was going to best the effort and get Ed back when it was time for his birthday. Turning off the lights behind her, she made her way down the corridor to their suite.

As she stepped in, she frowned. The room seemed unusually dim. Perhaps Riley had already gone to bed. As she made her way into the lounge room, it all became clearer. The only light that could be seen was coming from the candles lit and spread around the room. Music played ever so softly in the background. Looking around, Sorla wondered where Riley was, until a movement from the doorway caught her eye.

There standing in the doorway was Riley in her ballgown. Her feet were bare. She quietly padded over and relieved Sorla's hands of the photo frame, laying it on the coffee table, before turning and stepping into Sorla's arms. She fit her body perfectly along the length of Sorla's, wrapping her arms around her neck. A finger lightly traced Sorla's eyebrow and jawline, trailing softly downward to trace her lips. "I said earlier that your present came in parts."

Sorla swayed with Riley to the music. "Mm?"

"I love you with more than just my heart. I love you with everything I have. We can't undo the past, the pain, but I want a future together with you." Riley captured Sorla's lips as they swayed to the music. Their mouths danced and teased, growing in enthusiasm and excitement until Riley stepped away. Sorla stopped, hoping she hadn't gone too far. Riley smiled nervously at her. Holding out her hand, she led Sorla around the room, extinguishing the candles, before leading her to the bedroom.

With trembling hands, Riley slowly undressed Sorla, her fingers brushing across shoulders, hips, the curve of a breast. Sorla stood still, allowing Riley to set the pace. When Sorla stood before her naked,

Riley kissed her briefly, before stepping back. Slowly, she reached for the clasp and zipper that held her dress together and undid them. The dress floated to the floor to form a chiffon pool around her feet. She stepped up to meet Sorla, her hands caressing up Sorla's arms. Riley's eyes were dark and stormy, her voice husky. "Make love to me."

With great reverence, Sorla lowered Riley to the bed and proceeded to worship every inch of her body, slowly, sweetly, gently. Skin tingled and blood rushed so fast throughout their bodies that it left them both gasping as hands explored, unhindered, smooth body planes and sensuous curves. Riley turned Sorla, until she lay on top, her thigh in tight against Sorla's centre. Her neck arched backwards as a moan escaped her lips. Sorla pulled their hips in tighter as she arched up to claim Riley's mouth. "I love you."

With tears coursing down her cheeks, Riley grabbed Sorla's hands and held them to her breasts. "I love you too, with all my heart." Together they found the age-old rhythm, hips, thighs, and breath melding, rising ever higher, until together, hands, fingers, and bodies entwined, they leapt off into the burning light of release.

Riley collapsed onto Sorla's chest and lay there, waiting for her breathing to slow and her pulse to settle, shivering with the delight of aftershocks. Sorla's arms wrapped around her, caressed her, soothing her body down from its heady climax. Riley lay with her head against Sorla's shoulder, tracing fingers feather soft across the muscles in Sorla's chest. Reaching up, she kissed Sorla softly on the lips. "Happy birthday, darling."

Sorla kissed her back. "The best ever. You okay, babe?"

Riley knew she had a long way to go, but snuggling down with her head on Sorla's chest, her eyes growing drowsy, her body and her heart in this moment were very much at peace. There was no better feeling. She felt like she had come home. "Never better."

Closing her eyes she let herself go, knowing that whatever happened, whatever the future held, she would never walk alone again. Together they would keep each other strong and safe. Together they would dance.

About the Author

Mardi grew up on the Mid North Coast of Australia, with big rivers, sun, surf, and sand all within reach. Among Mardi's greatest loves are watching storms out to sea and sitting on a rock wall, fishing and watching the world go by.

She moved inland to study, where the mountains called to her and eventually stole her heart. It's where she now calls home, along with her partner, two dogs, and two cats, on a beautiful New England farm.

When she's not working full-time, Mardi is also a volunteer firefighter, firefighting instructor, and a member of a local wildlife rescue service looking after orphaned, sick, and injured native animals.

Her love of storms has transferred from the ocean, to the rolling fields and hillsides high in New England.

Books Available From Bold Strokes Books

Cold to the Touch by Cari Hunter. A drug addict's murder is the start of a dangerous investigation for Detective Sanne Jensen and Dr. Meg Fielding, as they try to stop a killer with no conscience. (978-1-62639-526-8)

Forsaken by Laydin Michaels. The hunt for a killer teaches one woman that she must overcome her fear in order to love, and another that success is meaningless without happiness. (978-1-62639-481-0)

Infiltration by Jackie D. When a CIA breach is imminent, a Marine instructor must stop the attack while protecting her heart from being disarmed by a recruit. (978-1-62639-521-3)

Midnight at the Orpheus by Alyssa Linn Palmer. Two women desperate to make their way in the world, a man hell-bent on revenge, and a cop risking his career: all in a day's work in Capone's Chicago. (978-1-62639-607-4)

Spirit of the Dance by Mardi Alexander. Major Sorla Reardon's return to her family farm to heal threatens Riley Johnson's safe life when small-town secrets are revealed, and love may not conquer all. (978-1-62639-583-1)

Sweet Hearts by Melissa Brayden, Rachel Spangler, and Karis Walsh. Do you ever wonder *Whatever happened to...*? Find out when you reconnect with your favorite characters from Melissa Brayden's *Heart Block*, Rachel Spangler's *LoveLife*, and Karis Walsh's *Worth the Risk*. (978-1-62639-475-9)

Totally Worth It by Maggie Cummings. Who knew there's an all-lesbian condo community in the NYC suburbs? Join twentysomething BFFs Meg and Lexi at Bay West as they navigate friendships, love, and everything in between. (978-1-62639-512-1)

Illicit Artifacts by Stevie Mikayne. Her foster mother's death cracked open a secret world Jil never wanted to see...and now she has to pick up the stolen pieces. (978-1-62639-472-8)

Pathfinder by Gun Brooke. Heading for their new homeworld, Exodus's chief engineer Adina Vantressa and nurse Briar Lindemay carry game-changing secrets that may well cause them to lose everything when disaster strikes. (978-1-62639-444-5)

Prescription for Love by Radclyffe. Dr. Flannery Rivers finds herself attracted to the new ER chief, city girl Abigail Remy, and the incendiary mix of city and country, fire and ice, tradition and change is combustible. (978-1-62639-570-1)

Ready or Not by Melissa Brayden. Uptight Mallory Spencer finds relinquishing control to bartender Hope Sanders too tall an order in fast-paced New York City. (978-1-62639-443-8)

Summer Passion by MJ Williamz. Women loving women is forbidden in 1946 Hollywood, yet Jean and Maggie strive to keep their love alive and away from prying eyes. (978-1-62639-540-4)

The Princess and the Prix by Nell Stark. "Ugly duckling" Princess Alix of Monaco was resigned to loneliness until she met racecar driver Thalia d'Angelis. (978-1-62639-474-2)

Winter's Harbor by Aurora Rey. Lia Brooks isn't looking for love in Provincetown, but when she discovers chocolate croissants and pastry chef Alex McKinnon, her winter retreat quickly starts heating up. (978-1-62639-498-8)

The Time Before Now by Missouri Vaun. Vivian flees a disastrous affair, embarking on an epic, transformative journey to escape her past, until destiny introduces her to Ida, who helps her rediscover trust, love, and hope. (978-1-62639-446-9)

Twisted Whispers by Sheri Lewis Wohl. Betrayal, lies, and secrets—whispers of a friend lost to darkness. Can a reluctant psychic set things right or will an evil soul destroy those she loves? (978-1-62639-439-1)

The Courage to Try by C.A. Popovich. Finding love is worth getting past the fear of trying. (978-1-62639-528-2)

Break Point by Yolanda Wallace. In a world readying for war, can love find a way? (978-1-62639-568-8)

Countdown by Julie Cannon. Can two strong-willed, powerful women overcome their differences to save the lives of seven others and begin a life they never imagined together? (978-1-62639-471-1)

Keep Hold by Michelle Grubb. Claire knew some things should be left alone and some rules should never be broken, but the most forbidden, well, they are the most tempting. (978-1-62639-502-2)

Deadly Medicine by Jaime Maddox. Dr. Ward Thrasher's life is in turmoil. Her partner Jess left her, and her job puts her in the path of a murderous physician who has Jess in his sights. (978-1-62639-424-7)

New Beginnings by KC Richardson. Can the connection and attraction between Jordan Roberts and Kirsten Murphy be enough for Jordan to trust Kirsten with her heart? (978-1-62639-450-6)

Officer Down by Erin Dutton. Can two women who've made careers out of being there for others in crisis find the strength to need each other? (978-1-62639-423-0)

Reasonable Doubt by Carsen Taite. Just when Sarah and Ellery think they've left dangerous careers behind, a new case sets them—and their hearts—on a collision course. (978-1-62639-442-1)

Tarnished Gold by Ann Aptaker. Cantor Gold must outsmart the Law, outrun New York's dockside gangsters, outplay a shady art dealer, his lover, and a beautiful curator, and stay out of a killer's gun sights. (978-1-62639-426-1)

White Horse in Winter by Franci McMahon. Love between two women collides with the inner poison of a closeted horse trainer in the green hills of Vermont. (978-1-62639-429-2)

Autumn Spring by Shelley Thrasher. Can Bree and Linda, two women in the autumn of their lives, put their hearts first and find the love they've never dared seize? (978-1-62639-365-3)

The Renegade by Amy Dunne. Post-apocalyptic survivors Alex and Evelyn secretly find love while held captive by a deranged cult, but when their relationship is discovered, they must fight for their freedom—or die trying. (978-1-62639-427-8)

Thrall by Barbara Ann Wright. Four women in a warrior society must work together to lift an insidious curse while caught between their own desires, the will of their peoples, and an ancient evil. (978-1-62639-437-7)

The Chameleon's Tale by Andrea Bramhall. Two old friends must work through a web of lies and deceit to find themselves again, but in the search they discover far more than they ever went looking for. (978-1-62639-363-9)

Side Effects by VK Powell. Detective Jordan Bishop and Dr. Neela Sahjani must decide if it's easier to trust someone with your heart or your life as they face threatening protestors, corrupt politicians, and their increasing attraction. (978-1-62639-364-6)

Warm November by Kathleen Knowles. What do you do if the one woman you want is the only one you can't have? (978-1-62639-366-0)

In Every Cloud by Tina Michele. When Bree finally leaves her shattered life behind, is she strong enough to salvage the remaining pieces of her heart and find the place where it truly fits? (978-1-62639-413-1)

Rise of the Gorgon by Tanai Walker. When independent Internet journalist Elle Pharell goes to Kuwait to investigate a veteran's mysterious suicide, she hires Cassandra Hunt, an interpreter with a covert agenda. (978-1-62639-367-7)

Crossed by Meredith Doench. Agent Luce Hansen returns home to catch a killer and risks everything to revisit the unsolved murder of her first girlfriend and confront the demons of her youth. (978-1-62639-361-5)

Making a Comeback by Julie Blair. Music and love take center stage when jazz pianist Liz Randall tries to make a comeback with the help of her reclusive, blind neighbor, Jac Winters. (978-1-62639-357-8)

Soul Unique by Gun Brooke. Self-proclaimed cynic Greer Landon falls for Hayden Rowe's paintings and the young woman shortly after, but will Hayden, who lives with Asperger syndrome, trust her and reciprocate her feelings? (978-1-62639-358-5)